# ANATOMY
# OF A SCANDAL

## SARAH VAUGHAN

**EMILY BESTLER BOOKS**

—

**ATRIA**

New York  London  Toronto  Sydney  New Delhi

# To my father, Chris,
## with love.

EMILY
BESTLER
BOOKS

ATRIA

An Imprint of Simon & Schuster, Inc.
1230 Avenue of the Americas
New York, NY 10020

First Emily Bestler Books/Atria Paperback edition October 2018

**EMILY BESTLER BOOKS/ATRIA** PAPERBACK and colophon are trademarks of Simon & Schuster, Inc.

For information about special discounts for bulk purchases, please contact Simon & Schuster Special Sales at 1-866-506-1949 or business@simonandschuster.com.

The Simon & Schuster Speakers Bureau can bring authors to your live event. For more information or to book an event, contact the Simon & Schuster Speakers Bureau at 1-866-248-3049 or visit our website at www.simonspeakers.com.

Interior design by Laura Levatino

Manufactured in the United States of America

20   19   18   17   16   15

The Library of Congress has cataloged the hardcover edition as follows:

Names: Vaughan, Sarah, 1972- author. Title: Anatomy of a scandal : a novel / Sarah Vaughan. Description: First edition. | New York : Atria/Emily Bestler Books, 2017. | Description based on print version record and CIP data provided by publisher; resource not viewed. Identifiers: LCCN 2017010834 (print) | LCCN 2017015464 (ebook) | ISBN 9781501172182 (Ebook) | ISBN 9781501172168 (hardcover) | ISBN 9781501172175 (softcover) Subjects: LCSH: Upper class—England—Fiction. | Women lawyers—Fiction. | BISAC: FICTION / General. | FICTION / Literary. | FICTION / Contemporary Women. | GSAFD: Suspense fiction. | Mystery fiction. Classification: LCC PR6122.A85 (ebook) | LCC PR6122.A85 A85 2017 (print) | DDC 823/.92—dc23LC record available at https://lccn.loc.gov/2017010834

ISBN 978-1-5011-7216-8
ISBN 978-1-5011-7217-5 (pbk)
ISBN 978-1-5011-7218-2 (eBook)

"He needs guilty men. So he has found men who are guilty. Though perhaps not guilty as charged."

—Hilary Mantel, *Bring Up the Bodies*

# One

## Kate

My wig slumps on my desk where I have tossed it like flattened roadkill. Out of court, I am careless with this crucial part of my wardrobe, showing it the opposite of what it should command: respect. It's handmade from horsehair and worth nearly six hundred pounds, but I want it to accrue the gravitas I sometimes fear I lack. I want the hairline to yellow with years of perspiration, the tight, cream curls to relax or to grey with dust. It's been nineteen years since I was called to the Bar, but my wig is still that of a conscientious new girl—not a barrister who has inherited it from her, or more usually his, father. That's the sort of wig I want: one dulled with the patina of tradition, entitlement, and age.

I kick off my shoes—black patent courts with gold braid on the front, shoes for a Regency fop; a parliamentary official; or a female barrister who delights in the history, rigmarole, and sheer ridiculousness of it all. Expensive shoes are important. Chatting with fellow counsel, or clients, with ushers, with police, we all look down from time to time, so as not to appear confrontational.

Anyone who glances at my shoes sees someone who understands this quirk of human psychology and who takes herself seriously. They see a woman who dresses as if she believes she will win.

I like to look the part, you see. To do things properly. Female barristers can wear a collarette—a scrap of cotton and lace that acts like a bib, a false front that goes just around the neck and costs about thirty pounds. Or they can dress as I do—white, collarless tunic with a collar attached by studs to the front and back, cuff links, a black wool jacket and skirt or trousers, and depending on their success and seniority, a black wool or wool-and-silk gown.

I'm not wearing all of that now. I shed part of my disguise in the robing room of the Old Bailey—robes off; collar and cuffs undone; my medium-length, blonde hair, tied back in a ponytail for court, released from its band and just a little mussed.

I am more feminine out of my garb. With my wig on and my heavy-rimmed glasses, I know I look asexual. Certainly not attractive, though you may note my cheekbones—two sharp blades that emerged in my twenties and have hardened and sharpened just as I have hardened and sharpened.

I am more myself without the wig. More me. The person I am at heart, not the person I present to the court or any previous incarnations of my personality. This is me: Kate Woodcroft, QC; criminal barrister; member of the Inner Temple; a highly experienced specialist in prosecuting sexual crimes; forty-one years old; divorced; single; and childless. I rest my head in my hands for a moment and let a breath ease out of me in one long flow, willing myself just to give up for a minute. It's no good. I can't relax. I have a small patch of eczema on my wrist so I smear E45 Cream there, resisting the desire to scratch it. To scratch at my dissatisfaction with life.

Instead, I look up at the high ceilings of my chambers—a set of rooms in an oasis of calm in the very heart of London. Eighteenth century, with ornate cornicing, gold leaf around the ceiling rose, and a view, through the towering sash windows, of Inner Temple's courtyard and the round, twelfth-century Temple Church.

This is my world—archaic, anachronistic, privileged, exclusive. Everything I should, and normally would, profess to hate. And yet I love it. I love it because all this—the nest of buildings at the edge of the City, tucked off the Strand and flowing down towards the river; the pomp and the hierarchy; the status, history, and tradition—is something I once never knew existed, and to which I never thought I could aspire. All of this shows how far I have come.

It's the reason that whenever I grab a cappuccino, I always slip a hot chocolate with extra sachets of sugar to the girl hunched in her sleeping bag in a doorway on the Strand. Most people don't notice her. The homeless are good at being invisible or we are good at making them so—averting our eyes from their khaki sleeping bags; their grey faces and matted hair; their bodies bundled in oversize jumpers; and their equally skinny wolfhounds, as we scurry past on our way to the seductive glitz of Covent Garden or the cultural thrills of the South Bank.

But hang around any court for a while and you will see just

how precarious life can be. How your world can come tumbling down all too rapidly if you make the wrong call. If, just for one, fatal split second, you behave unlawfully. Or rather, if you are poor and you break the law. Courts, like hospitals, are magnets for those dealt a wrong hand from the start of life, who choose the wrong men or the wrong mates and become so mired in bad fortune they lose their moral compass. The rich aren't quite as affected. Look at tax avoidance, or fraud, as it might be called if perpetrated by someone without the benefit of a skilled accountant. Bad luck or lack of acumen doesn't seem to dog the rich quite as assiduously as the poor.

Oh, I'm in a bad mood. You can tell I'm in a bad mood when I start thinking like a student politician. Most of the time I keep my *Guardian*-reading tendencies to myself. They can sit oddly with the more traditional members of my chambers; make for heated discussions at formal dinners, as we eat the sort of mass-catered food you might get at weddings—chicken, or salmon en croute—and drink our equally mediocre wine. Far more diplomatic to limit oneself to legal gossip such as which QC is receiving so little work they're applying to be a Crown Court judge, who will next be made silk, or who lost their cool with an usher in court. I can rattle through such conversations while thinking of my workload, fretting about my personal life, or even planning what to buy the next day for dinner. After nineteen years, I am adept at fitting in. I am skilled at that.

But in the sanctity of my room I can occasionally let myself go, just a little, and so for a minute, I put my head in my hands on my mahogany partner's desk, squeeze my eyes tight shut, and press my knuckles in hard. I see stars—white pinpricks that break the darkness and shine as bright as the diamonds in the ring I bought for myself because no one else was going to buy it for me. Better to see these than to succumb to tears.

I've just lost a case. And though I know I will get over the sense of failure by Monday—will move on because there are other cases to pursue, other clients to represent—it still rankles. It's not something that often happens or that I like to admit to because I like to win. Well, we all do. It's only natural. We need it to ensure our careers continue to sparkle. And it's the way our adversarial judicial system works.

I remember it came as a huge shock when I had this spelled out to me early in my Bar training. I went into the law with high ideals, and I have retained some. I haven't become overly jaded, but I hadn't expected the need to win to be so brutally expressed.

"The truth is a tricky issue. Rightly or wrongly, adversarial advocacy is not really an inquiry into the truth," Justin Carew, QC, told us callow twentysomethings, fresh from Oxford, Cambridge, Durham, and Bristol. "Advocacy is about being more persuasive than your opponent," he continued. "You can win, even if the evidence is stacked against you, provided that you argue better. And it's all about winning, of course."

But sometimes, despite all your skills of persuasion, you lose, and with me, that invariably happens if a witness turns out to be flaky, if they didn't come up to proof with their evidence, if, under cross-examination, their story unravels like a skein of wool tapped by a kitten—a mass of contradictions that becomes ever more knotted when pulled.

That happened today in the Butler trial. It was a rape case clouded by domestic violence. Ted Butler and Stacey Gibbons, who had lived together for four years, for most of which he had knocked her about.

I knew the odds were stacked against us from the start. Juries are keen to convict the predatory rapist, the archetypal bogeyman down a dark alley, yet when it comes to relationship rape, they'd really rather not know, thank you very much.

Though, in general, I think jurors get it right; in this case they didn't. I sometimes think they are stuck in the Victorian era. She is your wife, or common-law wife, and it's completely private, what goes on behind closed doors. And, to be fair, there is something rather mucky about delving so intimately into a couple's lives: about hearing what she wears in bed—an oversized T-shirt from a leading supermarket chain—or how he always likes a cigarette after sex, even though she is an asthmatic and he knows it makes her chest tight. I wonder at those who sit in the public gallery. Why do they come to watch this sad, sorry drama? More gripping than a soap opera because these are real people acting it out and real sobs coming from the witness, who, thankfully, those in the public gallery can no longer see. Her identity is shielded by a screen so that she doesn't have to watch her alleged assailant, fat-necked and piggy-eyed, in a cheap suit and black shirt and tie—his menacing take on respectability—glowering behind the reinforced glass in the dock.

So it feels smutty and prurient. Invasive. But still I asked the questions—questions that pry into the most exposing, frightening moments Stacey has ever experienced—because deep down, despite what that eminent QC told me all those years ago, I still want to get at the truth.

And then the defense lawyer brought up the issue of porn. An issue that could only be raised because my opponent had made a successful application in which he argued that there was a parallel between a scene in a DVD on their bedside table and what happened in this case.

"Is it not possible," my learned friend, Rupert Fletcher, asked in his deep, coercive baritone, "that this was a sex game she now finds a little embarrassing? A fantasy indulged in that she felt went a little too far? The DVD shows a woman being tied up, just as Ms. Gibbons was. You may feel that at the point of penetration, Ted Butler believed that Stacey Gibbons was going along with a fantasy they had discussed at some point beforehand. That she was just acting a part to which she had, in all willingness, already agreed."

He relayed further details of the DVD, and then referred to a text message in which Stacey admitted, "It made me hot." I saw the shudder of distaste on a couple of juror's faces—the women in late middle-age, dressed smartly for court, who perhaps anticipated sitting in on a trial for a burglary, or a murder and whose eyes have been well and truly opened by this case—and I knew that their sympathy for Stacey was disappearing faster than a tide slithering from the beach.

"You fantasized about being tied up, didn't you?" Rupert asked. "You texted your lover to let him know you'd like to try such things."

He waited a beat, allowing Stacey's sobs to ring around the windowless courtroom. And then, "Yes," came her muffled admission. From then on it did not matter that Ted half-choked her as he carried out the rape, or that there were welts on her wrists from where she struggled to free herself—rope burns she had the foresight to record on her iPhone. From then on, it was all downhill.

I pour myself a shot of whisky from the decanter on the sideboard. It's not something I often do, drink at work, but it's been a long day and it's past five now. Dusk has settled—soft peach and gold illuminating the clouds, making the courtyard excessively pretty—and I always think alcohol is permissible once it's dark. The single malt hits the back of my throat, warms my gullet. I wonder if Rupert will be celebrating in the wine bar opposite the High Court. He must have known, from the welts, from the choke, from the smirk on his client's face as he heard the verdict, that his client was as guilty as hell. But a win's a win. Still, if I were defending a case like that, I would have the decency not to gloat, far less to buy a bottle of Veuve to share with my junior. But then again, I try not to defend such cases. Though you're deemed a better barrister if you do both, I don't want to sully my conscience by representing those I suspect to be guilty. That's why I prefer to prosecute.

For I am on the side of the truth, you see, not just the side of the winners, and my thinking is that, if I believe a witness, then there is sufficient evidence to bring a case. And that's why I want to win. Not just for winning's sake but because I am on the side of the Stacey Gibbonses of this world, and of those whose cases are less muddied and even more brutal: the six-year-old raped by her grandfather; the eleven-year-old repeatedly buggered by his scoutmaster; the student forced to perform oral sex when she makes the mistake, late at night, of walking home alone. Yes, particularly for her. The standard of proof is high in the criminal court: beyond a reasonable doubt, not on the balance of probabilities—the burden of proof applied in the civil court. And that's why Ted Butler walked free today. There was that seed of doubt. That hypothetical possibility conjured up by Rupert, in his caramel voice, that Stacey, a woman whom the jurors might assume was a bit low-class, had consented to rough sex, and it was only two weeks later, when she discovered that Ted had a bit on the side, that she thought to go to the police. The possibility that she might be traumatized and shamed, that she might fear she would be mauled by the court and disbelieved, as she has been, does not appear to have occurred to them.

I refill my heavy crystal glass and add a splash of water. Two shots is my limit and I keep to it. I am disciplined. I have to be, for I know my intellect is blunted if I drink any more. Perhaps it is time to go home, but the thought of returning to my ordered, two-bedroom flat doesn't appeal. Normally I enjoy living alone. I am too contrary to be in a relationship, I know that—too possessive of my space, too selfish, too argumentative. I luxuriate in my solitude, or rather the fact that I don't need to accommodate anyone else's needs when my brain is churning as I prepare a case, or when I am dog-weary at the end of one. But when I lose, I resent the close, understanding silence. I don't want to be alone to dwell on my professional and personal inadequacies anymore. And so I tend to stay late at work, my lamp burning when my colleagues with families have long gone home; searching for the truth in my bundles of papers and working out a way in which to win.

Tonight, I listen as the heels of my colleagues clatter down the eighteenth-century wooden stairs and the burble of laughter drifts up toward me. Early December, the start of the run-up to Christmas, a Friday night, and I can sense their relief at reaching the end of a long week. I won't be joining my colleagues in the pub. I have a face on me, as my mother would say, and I've done enough acting for one day. I don't want my workmates to feel they have to console me—to tell me there are other cases to fight, that if you are dealing with a domestic, you're on to a losing streak from the start. I don't want to have to smile thinly while inside I rail. I don't want my anger to curdle the atmosphere. Richard will be there, my one-time pupil master, my occasional lover— very occasional these days for his wife, Felicity, has learned of us and I don't want to rock, still less to wrench apart, his marriage. I don't want him to feel pity for me.

A crisp knock on the door: the rat-a-tat-tat that belongs to the one person I could bear to see at the moment—Brian Taylor, my clerk for the entire nineteen years I have been in One Swift Court. Forty years in the profession, and with more nous and a better insight into human psychology than many of the counsel for whom he works. Behind the slick salt-and-pepper hair, the neatly buttoned suit, the perky "Miss"—for he insists on sticking to hierarchy, in the office at least—there is a sharp understanding of human nature and a deep sense of morality. He's also intensely private. It took me four years to realize that his wife had left him, four more before I realized it was for another woman.

"Thought you'd still be at it." He pops his head round the door. "Heard about the Butler case." His eyes flit from my empty whisky glass to the bottle and back again. Saying nothing. Just noting.

I make a noncommittal murmur that comes out as a growl in the back of my throat.

He stands in front of my desk, hands behind his back, relaxed in his own skin, just waiting to offer some pearl of wisdom. I find myself playing along with it and lean back in my chair, unfurling just a little from my bleak mood, despite myself.

"What you need now is something meaty. Something high-profile."

"Tell me about it." I feel the breath rush from my body: the relief of someone else knowing me so clearly and stating my ambition as a fact.

"What you need," he continues, and he looks at me slyly, his dark eyes alight with the thrill of a juicy case, "is something that will take you to the next level. That will completely make your career."

He is holding something in his hand, as I knew he would. Since October 2015, all cases have been delivered electronically:

no longer wrapped in dark pink ribbon like a fat billet-doux. But Brian knows that I prefer to read physical documents, to pore over a sheaf of papers that I can scrawl on, underline, cover with fluorescent Post-its until I create a map with which to navigate a trial.

He always prints my papers out and they are the sweetest of letters, presented now with a magician's flourish.

"I've got just the sort of case you need."

# TWO

## SOPHIE

Sophie has never thought of her husband as a liar.

She knows he dissembles, yes. That's part of his job—a willingness to be economical with the truth. A prerequisite, even for a government minister.

But she has never imagined he would lie to her. Or rather, that he might have a life she knows nothing about: a secret that could detonate beneath her lovingly maintained world and blow it apart forever.

Watching him that Friday, as he leaves to take the children to school, she feels a stab of love so fierce she pauses on the stairs just to drink in the tableau of the three of them together. They are framed in the doorway, James turning to call goodbye, left arm raised in that politician's wave she used to mock but which now seems second nature, right hand cradling Finn's head. Their son—fringe falling in his eyes, socks bagging round his ankles—scuffs at the tiles, reluctant, as ever, to go. His elder sister, Emily, ducks through the doorway: age nine, determined not to be late.

"Well, bye, then," her husband calls, and the autumn sun catches the top of his still-boyish crop, illuminating him with a halo, highlighting his six-foot-three frame.

"Bye, Mum," her daughter shouts, as she runs down the steps.

"Bye, Mummy." Finn, thrown by the change to his routine—his father taking them to school for once—juts out his bottom lip and flushes red.

"Come on, little man." James steers him through the door: competent, authoritative even, and she almost resents the fact that she still finds this attractive, commanding. Then he smiles down at his boy and his entire face softens. Finn is his weak spot. "You know you'll enjoy it when you get there."

He slips his arm over his son's shoulders and guides him down their neat, West London garden, with its sculpted bay trees standing like sentinels and its path fringed with lavender, away from her and out down the street.

*My family*, she thinks, watching the perfect-looking trio go—her girl racing ahead to embrace the day, all skinny legs and swishing ponytail, her boy slipping his hand into his father's and looking up at him with that unashamed adoration that comes with being six. The similarity between man and boy—for Finn is a miniaturized version of his father—only magnifies her love. *I have a beautiful boy and a beautiful man*, she thinks, as she watches James's broad shoulders—a one-time rower's shoulders—and waits, more in hope than expectation, for him to look back and smile at her, for she has never managed to grow immune to his charisma.

Of course he doesn't and she watches as they slip out of sight. The most precious people in her world.

———————

That world crumbles at 8:43 p.m. James is late. She should have known he would be. It is an alternate Friday: one in which he is holding a constituency meeting, deep in the Surrey countryside, in a brightly lit village hall.

When he had first been elected, they had stayed there every weekend: decamping to a cold, damp cottage that had never quite felt like home, despite their extensive renovations. One election on, and it was a relief to give up the pretense that Thurlsdon was where they wanted to spend half their week. Lovely in the summer months, yes, but bleak in winter, when she would stare out at the bare trees fringing their hamlet garden and try to placate their urban children, who wanted the bustle and distraction of their real, North Kensington home.

They venture there once a month now, and James schleps down for a meeting in the intervening fortnight. Two hours on a Friday afternoon; he promised to leave by six.

He has a driver now that he is junior minister and should have been back by seven thirty—traffic permitting. They are supposed to be going to friends' for a kitchen supper. Well, she says *friends*. Matt Frisk is another junior minister—aggressively ambitious in a way that doesn't sit well with their set, where success is understood as inevitable but naked ambition considered vulgar.

But he and Ellie are near neighbors and she couldn't easily put them off again.

Sophie had said they would be there by eight fifteen. It was ten past now, so where was he? The October evening crept against the sash windows: black softened by the glow of the street lamps, autumn stealing in. She loves this time of year. It reminds her of fresh starts, running through the leaves in Christ Church Meadows as a fresher, giddy at the thought of new worlds opening up to her. Since having children, it has been a time to nest; to cosset with log fires, roast chestnuts, take brisk, crisp walks, and make game casseroles. But now, the autumn night was taut with apprehension. Footsteps tottered down the pavement and a woman's laugh rang out, flirtatious. A deeper voice murmured. Not James's. The footsteps rose and fell, died away.

She pressed redial. His mobile rang then clicked to voicemail. She jabbed the sleek face of her phone—rattled at her loss of customary self-control. Dread tightened her stomach and for a moment she was back in the chill lodge of her Oxford college, the wind whistling through the quad, as she waited for the pay phone to ring. The look of sympathy from a college porter. The chill fear—so intense in that last week of her first summer term—that something still more terrible was about to happen. Age nineteen and willing him to call, even then.

Eight fourteen. She tried again, hating herself for doing it. His phone clicked straight through to voicemail. She plucked at a piece of imaginary lint, rearranged her friendship bracelets, and glanced critically at her nails—neatly filed, unvarnished, unlike Ellie's gleaming gelled slicks.

Footsteps on the stairs. A child's voice. "Is Daddy back?"

"No, go back to bed." Her tone came out harsher than she intended.

Emily stared, one eyebrow raised.

"Just climb back into bed, sweetheart," she added, her voice softening as she chased her daughter up the stairs, heart quickening as she turned the corner and bundled her under the covers. "You should be settling down, now. He won't be long."

"Can he come and say goodnight when he gets in?" Emily pouted, impossibly pretty.

"Well, we're going out, but if you're still awake . . ."

"I will be." Her daughter's determination—the set of her jaw, the implacable self-belief—marked her out as her father's daughter.

"Then I'm sure he'll come up."

Sophie gave her a quick peck on the forehead, to curb further arguments, and tucked the duvet around her. "I don't want you out of bed again, though. Understand? Cristina's babysitting just like normal. I'll send Daddy up when he gets back."

———————

Eight seventeen. She forced herself not to ring his number. She has never been the sort of wife who behaves like a stalker, but there was something about this complete silence that chilled her. It just wasn't like him. She imagined him stuck on the M25, working his way through his papers in the back of his car. He would call, text, send an email, not leave her waiting—the au pair hanging around the kitchen, keen for them to disappear so that she can curl up on the sofa and have the house to herself; Sophie's carefully touched-up face becoming a little less perfect; the flowers bought for the Frisks wilting in their wrapping on the table in the hall.

Eight twenty-one. She would call the Frisks at half past. But that deadline came and still she didn't ring. Eight thirty-five, thirty-six, thirty-seven. Aware that it was bad form to do so, at eight forty she sent Ellie Frisk a brief, apologetic text explaining that something had cropped up in the constituency and they were terribly sorry but they wouldn't be able to make it, after all.

The *Times* had a piece on the Islamic State by Will Stanhope but the words of her old college contemporary washed over her. It might as well be a story about dinosaur astronauts, read to Finn, to the extent to which it engaged her. Every part of her was attuned to one thing.

And there it is. The sound of his key in the door. A scrape and then a hiss as the heavy oak eases open. The sound of his footsteps: slower than normal, not his usual brisk, assertive tread. Then the thud of his red box being put down, the weight of responsibility abandoned for a while—as glorious a sound, on a Friday night, as the slosh of dry white wine being poured from a bottle. The jangle of keys on the hall table. And then silence again.

"James?" She comes into the hall.

His beautiful face is grey, his smile taut and not reaching his eyes, where his light crow's feet seemed deeper than usual.

"You'd better cancel the Frisks."

"I have done."

He shrugs off his coat and hangs it up carefully, averting his face.

She pauses then slips her arms around his waist—his honed waist that deepens to form a V, like the trunk of a sapling that burgeons outwards—but he reaches back and gently eases them away.

"James?" The cold in the pit of her stomach flares.

"Is Cristina here?"

"Yes."

"Well, send her to her room, will you? We need to talk in private."

"Right." Her heart flutters as she hears her voice come out clipped.

He gives her another tight smile, and a note of impatience creeps into his voice, as if she is a disobliging child, or perhaps, a tardy civil servant. "Can you do it now, please, Sophie?"

She stares back at him, not recognizing his mood—so different to what she had expected.

He massages his forehead with firm, long fingers, and his green eyes close briefly, the lashes—disarmingly long—kissing his cheeks. Then, his eyes flash open, and the look he gives her is the one Finn gives when he is trying to preempt a telling off and plead

forgiveness. It's the look James gave her twenty-three years ago before confessing to the crisis that had threatened to overwhelm him,
that had caused them to split up, that still sometimes causes her to
shiver, and that she fears is about to rear its head again.

"I'm sorry, Soph. So sorry." And it is as if he is carrying not
just the weight of his job—undersecretary of state for countering
extremism—but responsibility for the entire government.

"I've fucked up big time."

———————

Her name was Olivia Lytton—though Sophie had always just
thought of her as James's parliamentary researcher—five foot ten,
twenty-eight, blonde, well connected, confident, ambitious.

"I expect she'll be dubbed the blonde bombshell." She tries
for acerbic, but her voice just comes out as shrill.

The affair had been going on for five months, and he had
broken it off a week ago, just after the party conference.

"It meant nothing," James says, head in hands, no pretense that
he is anything other than penitent. He leans back, wrinkling his nose
as he trots out another cliché. "It was just sex, and I was flattered."

She swallows, rage pushing against her chest, barely contain-
able. "Well, that's OK then."

His eyes darken as he takes in her pain.

"There was nothing wrong with that part of us. You know
that." He can usually read her so clearly: a skill honed over two
decades, one of the things that binds them so closely. "I just made
a foolish mistake."

She waits, poised on the sofa opposite, for her anger to subside sufficiently for her to speak civilly, or for him to bridge the distance between them. To reach out a tentative hand, or at least offer a smile.

But he is rooted there: head bowed, elbows on knees, fingers touching as if in prayer. At first, she despises this show of sanctimony—a Blairite trope, the penitent politician—and then she softens as his shoulders shake, just the once, not with a sob but with a sigh. For a moment, she sees her mother as her charming, rakish father confessed to yet another "indiscretion." Ginny's dry resignation, and then the quickly suppressed flash of pain in her marine-blue eyes.

Perhaps this is what all husbands do? Sorrow surges, then anger. It shouldn't be like this. Their marriage is different. Founded on love and trust and a sex life that she does her very best to maintain.

She has made compromises in her life, and God knows, she took a huge leap of faith when they got back together. But the one certainty was that their relationship is solid. Her vision begins to blur, her gaze filming with tears. He looks up and catches her eye—and she wishes he hadn't.

"There's something else," he says.

---

Of *course* he wouldn't confess to an affair without a reason.

"Is she pregnant?" The words—ugly but necessary—discolor the space between them.

"No, of course not."

She feels herself relax a little. No half-sibling for Emily and Finn. No proof of a liaison. No need to share him in any other way.

And then he looks up with a grimace. Her nails bite into her palm in sharp crescents, and she sees that her knuckles are ivory pearls thrusting through the red of her skin.

What could be worse than some other woman having his child, or perhaps choosing to abort his child? Other people knowing. The affair, a particularly juicy piece of gossip, dropped into the ear of a favoured few in the Commons tea rooms until it becomes general knowledge. Who knows? His colleagues? The PM? Other MPs' wives? What about Ellie? She imagines Ellie's silly, plump face alight with barely suppressed pity. Perhaps she already knows and recognized her lie of a text.

Sophie forces herself to breathe deeply. They can deal with this; move beyond it. They have experienced far worse, haven't they? There is no crime in having a quick fling. It can be brushed over, quickly forgotten, absorbed. And then James says something that takes this to a more damaging, corrosive level that strikes her in the solar plexus hard as she contemplates a scenario so terrible that, fool that she is, she hadn't quite seen coming.

"The story's about to break."

# THREE

## SOPHIE

It is the *Mail* that has the story. They have to wait until the first editions to learn quite how bad it is.

The PM's director of communications, Chris Clarke, arrives and paces their living room, phone jabbed to his ear or glued to his hand. His ratty face is tense with anticipation: small eyes narrowed either side of a sharp nose dulled with the grease of too many take-aways and the grey exhaustion of countless early mornings and late nights.

Sophie cannot bear him. His estuarine twang, his self-importance, his strut—the strut of a short man because, at five foot nine, he is dwarfed by her husband—the knowledge that he is indispensable to the prime minister.

"He has the common touch. Keeps us in check, knows what we lack, and how to counteract that," James once said when she'd tried to articulate her instinctive distrust. He's a for-mer *News of the World* journalist from Barking, and she has no barometer by which to measure him. Single, without children, but apparently not gay, politics genuinely appears to consume him. In his late thirties, he is that unfathomable cliché: married to his job.

"Fuck's sake." He is skimming the story now on his iPad, while waiting for the fat wad of a Saturday paper to be delivered, mouth twisting in a sneer as if there is an acrid taste in his mouth. Sophie feels a surge of bile rise up as she catches the headline—MINISTER HAS AFFAIR WITH AIDE—and the subheading: "PM's friend in trysts in the corridors of power."

She skims the first paragraph, the words coalescing into something solid and impossible. "Britain's most fanciable MP had sex with his female aide in a lift in the Commons, the *Daily Mail* can exclusively reveal.

"James Whitehouse, a junior Home Office minister and confidant of the prime minister's, conducted his affair with his parliamentary researcher in the Palace of Westminster. The married father of two also shared a room with blonde Olivia Lytton, 28, during the party conference."

"Well, that was fucking stupid." Chris's voice cuts through the silence as Sophie struggles to master her feelings and considers how to sound controlled and cogent. She cannot manage it and stands abruptly, revulsion swelling like a tide of sickness as she walks quickly from the room. Hidden in the kitchen, she leans against the sink, hoping the desire to throw up will ease. The chrome is cool to her touch, and she concentrates on the shine and then on a picture drawn by Finn—one of the few she has deemed good enough to be pinned to the fridge. It shows four stick figures with huge smiles, the father figure towering over the rest of them, 50 percent taller than his wife and 100 percent bigger than his son. A six-year-old's view of the world. MY FAMLY scrawled in magenta felt tip.

Finn's family. Her family. Tears brim, but she blinks them back and touches her wet lashes to prevent her mascara smudging. No time for self-pity. She thinks of what her mother would do: pour herself a double whisky and take the dogs for a bracing, blustery walk along the cliffs. No dogs here. No remote, coastal path on which to lose one's self, either, or hide away from the press who, if the past indiscretions of other ministers are anything to go by, will soon be circling outside their front door.

How to explain this to the children, expecting to go out early to ballet and swimming? The cameras. Perhaps a reporter. Finn can be fobbed off, but Emily? The questions will be endless. *But why are they there? Is Daddy in trouble? Who's that lady? Mummy, why do they want a photo? Mum, are you crying? Why are you crying, Mummy?* Just thinking of it—the fact that they will be exposed to this very public embarrassment and scrutiny, and that she will need to reassure them while the questions continue incessantly— makes her retch.

Then there will be the snippets of information heard and only half-understood on the playground and the looks of pity or ill-disguised delight from other mothers. For a moment, she considers bundling the children into the car and driving them to her mother's in deepest Devon, hidden down endless, high-banked lanes. But running away implies guilt and a lack of unity. Her place is here, with her husband. She fills a glass from the tap, takes a couple of sharp, hard swigs, and then walks back into the front room to discover how she can shore up their marriage and help rescue his political career.

———————

"So, she's a classic woman scorned?" Chris Clarke is hunched forwards, scrutinizing James, as if trying to find an understandable explanation. It strikes Sophie that perhaps he is asexual. There is something so cold about him, as if he finds human frailty inconceivable—let alone the messy foolhardiness of desire.

"I had told her our fling was a mistake. That it was over. She's not quoted directly, is she? So she can't have gone to the papers?"

"She works in Westminster. She knows how to get the story out."

"'Friends of . . . ?'" James looks pained as he glances down at the lines of type about himself.

"Exactly. 'He used her. She thought it was a proper relationship, but he treated her abysmally . . .' a 'friend' of Ms. Lytton said."

"I've read it," James says. "No need to go on."

Sophie sits then on the sofa opposite her husband, and to the right of the director of communications. Perhaps she seems masochistic, wanting to know each detail, but ignorance isn't an option. She needs to understand exactly what she is up against here. She tries to reread the story—taking in the "friend's" description of what Olivia endured, reading about a lift taken in the House of Commons. "He pressed the button between floors and the ride took some time." She can imagine the smirk as the reporter chose the double entendre, the hastily suppressed sniggers or raised eyebrows of some readers. But, although the words smite her with their crudeness, the facts in their entirety make little sense.

She looks up, aware that Chris is still talking.

"So the line to take is: You deeply regret this brief affair and the pain you have caused to your family. Your priority now is to rebuild those relationships." He glances at her as he said this. "You're not going to be springing any surprises on us, are you, Sophie?"

"Like what?" She is startled.

"Announcing that you're leaving. Putting out your side of the story. Moonlight flits?"

"Do you need to ask?"

"Of course I do." His gaze is appraising.

"No, of course not." She manages to keep her tone neutral, so as not to reveal that yes, of course she had thought of fleeing, of disappearing down a rabbit hole of lanes far away from London and her new, painful reality; or betray her anger that he has guessed this.

He nods, apparently satisfied, and turns to her husband.

"The problems, of course, are A) that you were in a position of power; and B) this allegation that you shagged on government time. At the taxpayers' expense."

"The party conference isn't funded by the taxpayers."

"But your business as a minister in Her Majesty's Government is. And the idea that you were getting down and dirty in a lift when you should have been helping to run the country looks problematic, to say the least."

"I can see that."

Sophie looks at James then, a sharp glance of shock that he isn't denying this, that he is acknowledging this description. The director of communications smiles and she wonders if he takes pleasure in belittling them like this. It is self-aggrandizing. By putting them in their place he validates himself and reiterates his importance to the prime minister, she can see that. But there seems to be more to it than that. More, even, than his journalistic revelling in a good story. For all his political dirty tricks—for he has a reputation for being ruthless, someone who will hold on to a kernel of gossip and threaten to wield it at the most effective moment, much like a government whip—he seems to be personally judgemental about this.

"So, the key is to refuse to comment on details. This is tittle-tattle, the details of which you refuse to be drawn into. In your statement, you will stress that in no way did this brief error of judgement affect your ministerial business. You will not be drawn into denials. They have a way of coming back to haunt you. And you will not elaborate. Stick to the line: deep regret, brief affair, priority your family. Deflect and dismiss but don't deny. Understood?"

"Of course." James glances at her and offers a smile, which she ignores. "And there's no need to offer my resignation?"

"Why would you do that? The PM will make it clear if he

wants that, but he doesn't abandon old friends, you know that, and you're one of his closest." Chris points to the iPad and the *Mail's* copy. "It says so here."

"Yes." James seems to visibly straighten. Tom Southern and he go back to Eton and Oxford, their adolescent and adult lives intertwined since the age of thirteen. This is the one positive to hold on to: the prime minister, known for being almost fatally loyal, will do everything he humanly can before letting his oldest friend down. Sophie clings to this thought. Tom won't hang James out to dry. He can't. It's not in his nature, and besides, he owes James too much.

"He reiterated that earlier." James clears his throat. "Conveyed his support."

Sophie feels her breath ease out. "So you've spoken?"

He nods, but refuses to be drawn out. Theirs is an exclusive relationship. The drinking rituals, the schoolboy debagging, the shared holidays in their twenties during which they'd plotted Tom's political career and one for James later, after he'd gained some experience in the real world, all melding the two men together in a way that twelve years of marriage and two children apparently still haven't done as indestructibly for him and Sophie. And the curious thing is that Tom—whom she still can't think of as the most powerful man in the country; whom she can still remember getting hog-whimperingly drunk with during one of their late-twenties holidays in Tuscany—is the more dependent one. It has become less apparent since he became PM, but still, she knows there is an inequality there, perhaps only discernible to her. Tom is the one who looks to her husband for advice, yes, but he also relies on James, she knows, to keep his secrets.

"With the PM's support, you should be fine." Chris is brisk. "Sex doesn't have to kill a career these days. Not if the issue is closed down quickly. Lying does. Or rather, being caught lying." He gives a sniff, suddenly fastidious. "Also, you're hardly some poor fool caught with your hands down your pants, filming yourself on a smartphone. There will be an element among the older male voters who will see a quick knee-trembler with a young filly as perfectly understandable." He sneers. "No one's business but yours as long as it's brushed aside swiftly and doesn't reoccur."

"What about an inquiry into my having a relationship with a party employee?"

Sophie's insides clutch tight. The thought of an ongoing internal investigation, pored over by the press, who could chivvy and harry and complain about lack of accountability or a whitewash, is chilling. It could destroy his career, but it would also wound them, stoking the subject when it needed to be buried deep.

"Did the PM mention that?" Chris is sharp, his ratty eyes—a pale opalescent blue—widening.

James shakes his head.

"Then there's no need. This is a foolish affair, quickly forgotten—as long as you've told me everything?"

James nods.

"Well. You're part of the inner sanctum. If this moves off the front page quickly, there'll be no need for anything further at all."

She feels like laughing. James will be fine because he is the right type, he has done nothing illegal, and he has the prime minister's patronage. She glances past him to the bookshelves on which Hilary Mantel's pair of Cromwell novels sit: stories of an era in which a mercurial king's favor was everything. More than four centuries have passed, and yet, in Tom's party, there is still a flavor of life at court.

She lets her eyelids lower, trying to block out thoughts of a 24/7 news agenda and the pack mentality that takes hold when a story gains traction on social media. News, these days, spins so fast. But all will be well, Chris said, and he is a realist, a cynic even. There is no reason for him to offer false reassurance. None at all.

She opens her eyes and finally looks at her husband.

But his classically beautiful face—with its high cheekbones, strong jaw, and those crinkled lines at the outer edge of his eyes that tell of a love of the outdoors and a propensity to laugh—is drawn, his expression closed to her.

He looks at the other man, and she spots something uncharacteristic: just the tiniest flicker of doubt.

"I just hope you're right," James says.

# FOUR

## JAMES
### 31 OCTOBER 2016

The sun is filtering through the bedroom curtains, and Sophie is still asleep when James comes back up to their bedroom. Six thirty, Monday morning. Almost ten days since the story broke.

It is the first time she has slept past five thirty in all that time. He watches her now, taking in her face, stripped of makeup, softened against the plump pillows. Her forehead is etched with lines and her tousled hair has a fine silver thread running from her temple. She still looks younger than forty-two, but this past week has taken its toll.

He sheds his dressing gown and slips back into bed, not quite touching her in case he wakes her. He has been up since five, poring over the newspapers that, thank God, have nothing on him—as if the press has finally accepted that the story has run its course. What was Alastair Campbell's rule? That if a story was on the front page for eight days then the minister had to go? Or was it ten? Whatever the figure, he'd avoided both, and there was nothing in the Sundays. No sniff of anything further to come on social media, not even on Guido Fawkes's blog, and Chris has heard nothing. All the indications are that the tabs have dug up nothing new.

Besides, they have a real story to latch onto this weekend. There has been a foiled terror plot, yet again. Two Islamic extremists from Mile End had been planning another 7/7-style attack and had been raided once they'd received supplies. The Met were paranoid about leaking details for fear of prejudicing the trial, but the papers were full of speculation as to the amount of damage the ammunition could have caused. He hadn't needed to lean on the chair of the Home Affairs Select Committee to help flame the coverage. Malcolm Thwaites, pompous ex–Home Office minister that he was, would be working his way through his contacts, raising the risk of allowing Muslim asylum seekers to stay in this climate, pandering to the dog-whistle fears of his constituents, and beyond them, of white, insular Middle Britain. The affair of a junior minister few had heard of outside Westminster would fade into insignificance compared to the perceived risk of hordes of potential terrorists infiltrating the country.

He yawns, letting some of the tension of the past week ease from him, and Sophie stirs. He won't wake her. Won't even risk slipping his arm around her waist, let alone down between her legs. She is still behaving in a way that is decidedly frosty, perfectly civil in front of the children and Cristina but chilly—and, yes, frigid—when they are alone. It is understandable, of course, but she can't keep it up. Sex is the energy that fuses them together. She needs it just as he does, or at least she needs the affection and the affirmation that he still wants her.

That is what has hurt her so much about his thing with Olivia. He can see that, he isn't stupid. He has been a shit, no question of it, and he has admitted it freely in those still, small moments in the night when she has finally let herself cry, and the rage she manages to control most of the time spills out in tight, sharp sobs. The trouble is he wants sex more frequently than her; would have it every day if at all possible. It is a release—just like going for a run, or even having a piss. Something purely physical, an itch that needs to be scratched, a need that has to be answered. And for quite some time, since the children were tiny, she no longer seems to feel that same urgent need.

He decides to risk it: to wrap himself along the length of his slight wife. She is still tiny, her shape even sleeker than when she was a rower in her college women's first eight. Her bottom is pert, her legs toned from her regular running, her stomach just a little slacker—silvered with fine stretch marks from bearing Emily and Finn. It isn't that he doesn't desire her. Of course he does. But Olivia was there, virtually offering herself up on a plate. Plus, she was undeniably gorgeous. Even now that he thinks of her as a bitch—for she had sanctioned the story in the papers even if she hadn't gone to them herself—he can acknowledge her beauty. A body untouched by motherhood: tight, high breasts and skinny legs, blonde hair that shone and smelled of citrus, and a mouth as capable of cruelty—for she is clever, that was part of the attraction—as it is of temptation.

It was the first time he had been unfaithful. Well, the first since their marriage. Their engagement didn't count—nor their

student days. He had raced through girls at college as if compelled. Things had changed for a while after he'd met Sophie,
and she, rowing, and finals had briefly combined to exhaust him.
Yet even then, he was open to opportunities. That was what Oxford was about, wasn't it? Exploration—intellectual, emotional,
physical—of all sorts.

He had gotten away with it—in the same way that, as the
only son with two older, doting sisters, he had always gotten
away with things as a boy. Soph had never guessed that there
were other women. He'd picked wisely: girls in different colleges,
different years, reading different subjects, making it all possible.
These were one-night stands that lasted two nights at most, for
it was variety that he craved—the endless, surprising difference
between one pair of breasts and the next; one woman's cry and
another's; one soft, damp cunt or crook of an elbow or curve of
a neck. For a young man who had spent five years of his adolescence in an all-male boarding school, and before that, boarding
at a prep, his first year at Oxford—and even more that glorious,
exam-free second year before he met Sophie—had brought immense, anarchic freedom.

On he'd romped through his mid-twenties, when they'd split
up for seven years, and through his late twenties. Years when he'd
worked as a management consultant, and his City salary and late
nights working and then drinking, meant there was almost a
surfeit of girls. And then, at twenty-nine he had bumped into
Sophie again in a pub in Notting Hill. She was twenty-seven
then, not a needy twenty—more self-assured and experienced,

something of a challenge, a bit of a catch. She'd played hard to get for a while. Wary, she'd said, of him behaving as recklessly as he had before, fearful that the crisis that caused him to dump her—for she had seen him at his most vulnerable and he couldn't bear that—would come back to haunt them. But despite her ambivalence, it seemed inevitable they would get back together. As he'd said in his wedding speech, trotting out a cliché he hadn't taken the time to articulate more freshly, it had felt as if he was coming home.

And he really thought he had satisfied his itch. That desire to sniff around. During their engagement, there had been a couple of friends with benefits: an ex-girlfriend who'd tried to dissuade him from marrying Soph in the months leading up to their wedding; a colleague who had become a bit of a stalker when she failed to recognize that he really *did* just want sex with no strings attached. That had shaken him a little. Amelia's clinginess, those tremulous eyes—limpid pools of tears that had filled whenever he had sprung out of bed, leaving her place for his, straight after sex—that final, irate phone call. Her voice rising in a hysterical crescendo of pain until he'd silenced her with the OFF button. That had forced him to draw a line under his behavior. Marriage, he decided, was when his fidelity would start.

And it had worked. For nearly twelve years, he had been completely faithful. The kids had made it easier. He had assumed he would be a traditional, semidetached dad, rather like Charles, his own father, and yet they had changed him entirely—at least for a good, long while. He hadn't felt it when they were babies.

Had been fairly ambivalent when they had puked and gurgled and slept. But once they had begun to talk and ask questions, then the all-encompassing love affair began. It had started with Emily but became more intense with Finn: this burden of responsibility, the need to be someone his child—his son—respected. Not just an admirable but a *good* man.

Sometimes he found them unnerving. Those big, questioning eyes, that extreme innocence, the total trust. In his professional life, he wasn't always entirely frank. He could get away with answers that didn't fit the question and yet still manage to mollify or beguile. But not with them. With them, he feared they saw right through him. For his children, he had to be better.

And for a while, for quite a while, he had succeeded in being this good man. He had behaved as he knew he should. Kept to those pledges made in that sixteenth-century church, in front of Sophie's father, Max, who had made little pretense of keeping them himself. He would be a good man for her and their children and a better man than her father. And until a month before their twelfth wedding anniversary, he had managed it.

And then, in May, he had been in the House, late at night. The new Counter-Terrorism Bill. A late sitting. He had been racing through the cloisters after a vote towards Portcullis House, his stomach caving in with hunger, hoping to find something healthy to eat. And there she was, returning to collect a bag from his office after a night out with friends. She was tipsy, slightly, delightfully tipsy. Not something he'd seen her like before. She had tripped on her heel as she'd passed and fallen against him; one hand reaching out for his forearm as her left foot had landed on the chill slate of the cloisters; a sheer stocking foot landing by his polished Church's; mulberry-painted toenails just visible through the toe.

"Oops! Sorry, James," she had said, and bit her bottom lip as her laugh faded for it was, "Yes, Minister" in the office, even though he knew they referred to him as James in his absence and he tried to get them to use their first names. She had kept her hand on his forearm as she had steadied herself, and slipped her foot back into the shoe, and he had found himself holding the crook of her other elbow in his hand, as she righted herself again.

"Are you all right? Can I get you a cab?" He began to walk her towards the bell in New Palace Yard, concerned, solicitous, for she was a young woman who needed to get home safely, an employee slightly the worse for wear.

She had stopped and looked up at him in the moonlight, suddenly sober and just a little knowing.

"I'd far rather have another drink."

———————

And so it had begun. The seeds of their affair sown that balmy, late-spring night as the sky turned navy, and he had limited himself to a single beer and she a gin and tonic, out on the Terrace Bar. The Thames had slipped past, and he had stared into its charcoal depths, watching the lights of St. Thomas's opposite—the hospital where his daughter was born—dapple the water. And he had known that he was letting go of his principles, that he was jeopardizing everything that made him the man he was—the better man he wanted to be for his children—and he had barely cared.

They hadn't consummated their relationship then. Didn't even kiss. It was all too public, and he was still telling himself he was resisting the inevitable. That happened a week later, after seven days of the most painful, delicious foreplay of his life. Afterwards, he had apologized for it being so rushed; for him needing to consume her—for it felt like that—so quickly and entirely. She had smiled. A lazy smile. "There'll be other opportunities."

"Like now?"

"Like now."

It had carried on, their fling, until three weeks ago. Intense, when there was the opportunity, but with physical breaks during the recess: a week in the South Hams near Sophie's mother; a fortnight in Corsica, where he had taught the children to sail and made love to Sophie each night. During that time, he had still thought about Olivia but seen their fling as a madness, something he could and *would* finish as soon as parliament resumed.

He had tried to distance himself once he got back; told her it was over after the party conference. He had called her into his office, hoping that, this way, she wouldn't make a scene and they could be businesslike. Professional. It had been fun while it had lasted, but they both knew it couldn't go on.

Her eyes had watered and her tone became clipped, a reaction he was familiar with and so was unperturbed by—the response of previous girlfriends, and on the very rare occasions when he had disappointed her, of his mother, Tuppence.

"So, we're all fine then?" he had made himself ask, only wanting to hear her say yes.

"Yes, of course we are." She gave him a bright smile: chin up, her voice all perky and plucky, though she rather ruined it when it wobbled. "Of course we are."

———

And that should have been it. Perhaps would have been if he hadn't been a fool. If he hadn't succumbed just the one last time.

He rolls towards Sophie, pulls her tight. He won't dwell on what happened in the lift. Hardly the most romantic setting, but then there was little that was romantic about their relationship. He doesn't need the *Mail* to remind him of that fact.

It must have been that that tipped Olivia over the edge, or rather his reaction to her afterwards. A flash of arrogance, perhaps, yes. But he'd thought it was a one-off, and that a bout of fast and furious sex didn't mean, as she predictably thought it did, that they were getting back together.

"Thanks for that. Just what I needed." Feeling light-headed, he was uncharacteristically crass. He could see that now.

"Does that mean . . ."

"What?" The lift had reached their floor, and as the doors

opened, he stepped out into the narrow corridor and opened the committee corridor door; his mind already on the day's events, uninterested in what she had to say.

Her eyes had swelled into pools of hurt, but he couldn't be bothered with it. They were supposed to be giving evidence at a committee and were now running late. He just didn't have the time.

Perhaps if he'd offered her a kiss, smoothed her hair, let her down gently. Perhaps if he'd been a bit less brutal, she wouldn't have gone to the papers. But he had just left her. Her hair less sleek; her tights, he remembered this now, snagged where he had pulled at them; had left her just staring after him.

Sophie stirs and rolls towards him, rousing him from the discomfort of the memory. He holds his breath, wary of causing her to shift away, feeling the familiar warmth of her body lying against his chest. Gingerly, he puts a hand between her shoulder blades then moves it lower towards the small of her back and pulls her into him.

She opens her eyes—a deep, startling blue—and for a moment seems surprised to be in such close proximity. Little wonder, as she has spent a week being as physically distant as possible.

"Hello, my darling." He risks a gentle kiss on her forehead. She draws her face away, her brow furrowing into a crease between her eyes, as if she's deciding whether to view this as an intrusion. He takes his hand away then places it behind her shoulder, lightly enclosing her within his arms.

"OK?" He leans forward and drops a kiss on her lips.

"Don't." She shrugs her shoulders, discontented, but doesn't move away.

"Soph . . . we can't carry on like this."

"Can't we?" She looks up at him and he can see the hurt in her eyes, and then, something more promising: a mixture of defeat and hope that suggests she doesn't want to continue in this state of chilly restraint.

He removes his arm, releasing her from the circle of his clasp, and shifts back to look at her properly. There is a foot between them and he reaches across it to stroke the soft down of her cheek. For a moment, she hesitates and then she turns her lips towards it, and, as if she cannot help but do so, as if it is a force of habit, lightly kisses the palm of his hand. Her lids close, as if she knows she is being weak to concede.

He draws her back to him. Holds her close, trying to convey through the force of his hug how much she means to him. Her shoulders, tense for the past nine days, are still tight, but her breath comes out in a rush, as if she is trying to relax, as if she wants that desperately.

"There's nothing in the papers today. It seems to be all over," he says, drawing back and kissing her on the top of her head.

"Don't say that. It's tempting fate . . ."

"Chris hasn't heard a murmur all weekend. And there's nothing today." He brushes over her superstition. "I really think we're safe."

"We need to listen to *Today*." She rolls away from him as the clock radio switches on automatically for the six-thirty headlines:

a predicted drop in interest rates; a British nurse with Ebola; another bomb in Syria.

They listen in silence. "Nothing," he says.

Her eyes well with tears, huge globes that topple. She swipes at them and gives a surprisingly noisy sniff.

"I've been so frightened."

"What about?" He is bemused.

"You *know*. In case the papers dig up any stuff about the Libertines."

"Pffsh. Not going to happen." He has boxed those days away, doesn't let himself think about them, and wishes she wouldn't. "My conscience is clear about what happened then. You know that."

She doesn't answer him.

"Soph?" He tips her chin; looks deep into her eyes; gives her his most persuasive, heartfelt smile. "Truly. It is."

For a while they just lie there—her in his arms, his chin on the top of her head.

"You've been my rock, you know?"

"What else could I be?"

"No, really. You've been my everything. You've had every right to be angry, but you and the kids have gotten me through this." He peppers her face with kisses: a light dusting just as she likes it. She remains unresponsive. "I owe you so much, Sophie."

She looks at him then, and he can see a hint of the young woman he fell in love with beneath the layers of distrust that have built up over the past week.

"If I'm going to carry on sticking by you—if we're going to

try and make us work—then I need to know that it's *completely* over," she says.

"We've been through this before," he sighs. "Christ, I'm hardly going to want to see the woman." He gives a bark of laughter. "Besides, our paths aren't even going to meet. She's on sick leave, and she'll be moved to another office when she returns—*if* she returns. There's no need for me to see her again."

"And I need to know that you won't do this again . . . I can't bear the *humiliation*." She gives a shudder and recoils from him, shifting up in bed and wrapping her arms around her knees. "I can't be like my mother." She looks at him, accusatory. "We said we wouldn't be like them—like my parents. When we married, you *promised* me."

"I know, I know." He looks down, conscious of the need to still play the penitent. "I don't know what to say to convince you. I've—we've—all paid for my behavior. It's not something I'm *ever* going to repeat.

"You are my world," he adds, sitting up and putting his arm around her shoulders. She doesn't move away from him, and so he slides the second, exploratory, around her waist.

"Don't," she says, resisting now and shifting to the edge of the bed. "I've got to get the children up."

"But you do believe me?" He gives her the look. The one she would normally find irresistible: a wide-eyed glance injected with a streak of disbelief.

"I do." She leans against him briefly, and gives a small, sad smile that acknowledges her weakness. "Fool that I am, I do."

He kisses her then—a proper kiss, mouth open with a hint of his tongue. A kiss that manages to be respectful while being far from chaste.

"It's over," he tells her, looking into her eyes and trying to convey a conviction he doesn't feel entirely. "Everything is going to be OK."

# FIVE

## KATE

I lay my copy of the *Times* down on the clear surface of my galley-kitchen counter and work through it methodically, then do the same with the *Sun,* the *Mirror,* and the *Daily Mail.*

Plenty on the foiled Mile End terror plot, more, too, on the all-consuming story of the week: an Egyptian beachside bombing. But nothing on James Whitehouse, "the PM's mate caught bonking," as the *Sun* described him last week; or "Liv's lover in the lift." I double-check the tabloids, pilfered from the clerks' office. Not one single word.

It's bizarre how swiftly that story has sunk: buried by proper, earth-shattering news, and yet its complete absence is unsettling. Something doesn't smell right, as my mother would say. The prime minister has said that he stands by his colleague. That he has the utmost confidence in him, that this is a private matter now resolved. But other junior ministers caught having sex with a junior member of staff would be hung out to dry. So what has inspired this loyalty?

It bothers me, this old boys' favoritism, but I don't have time to obsess. Nine o'clock on a Monday night, and just like every other night, I have a wheelie-case of documents nudging, like a loyal dog, at my heels. I scan through the notes for *Blackwell*, tomorrow's hearing at Southwark Crown Court. I'm prosecuting a recidivist sex offender who, at 2 a.m. one morning in March, abducted an eleven-year-old. His defense? He was being kind-hearted and the boy—paralytic on the four cans of the cider with which he'd plied him—is "a lying shit." Sounds absolutely charming.

I work efficiently, and despite the grubbiness of the evidence, the unrelenting sadness for the child, begin to feel lighter. Graham Blackwell, a twenty-five-stone, fifty-five-year-old man, will not endear himself to the jury. Unless something terribly goes wrong, I should be able to win. And then I turn to *Butler*, a case of relationship rape that will be more difficult to prove. The details swim up from the pages of notes, and I realize that my eyes are blurring with fat tears that pool and swell. I can feel them teetering on my lower lashes. I swipe them with my knuckles. God, I must be exhausted. I glance at my watch. Ten forty—relatively early for me.

I stretch, trying to energize my weary body. But I know this is less the bone-aching tiredness that comes from traipsing around the southeastern circuit, or the intellectual weariness of teasing out each legal loophole, and more an emotional exhaustion that blankets me like the velvet darkness of a starless night. Here in my quiet, rather lonely flat, I am tired of man's inhumanity to man. Or rather, his inhumanity to women and children. I am tired of such casual sexual violence, or as Graham Blackwell might put it, the refusal to give a shit.

Time to buck up. I can't allow myself to wallow. It's my job to catch out these bastards, to use my considerable powers of persuasion to do all I can to put them away. I pack up my files, slosh whisky into a tumbler, dig around in the freezer box for some fat ice cubes—I remember to make ice even though I forget to buy milk—and set my alarm for 5:30 a.m. The flat's cold—the central heating's on the blink and I haven't had time to get it fixed—and I run a bath, hoping it will warm my bones and unknot my tense shoulders; will envelop me in its watery caress.

The steam rises and I submerge my limbs. It almost scalds, but the relief is immediate. No one has touched me since last month's brief, unsatisfying evening with Richard, and I feel exposed and somehow vulnerable as I take in my nakedness and note how thin my thighs are these days. My hips protrude like tiny islands, my stomach is concave, my breasts tight. I am dropping a cup size each decade. My face might have improved—high cheekbones, arched brows, my once-hated nose no longer kinked but straight and petite (a thirtieth birthday present to myself, the most dramatic evidence of my reinvention and success)—but my body is more scrawny than lean. A bubble of self-pity wells as I remember the younger Kate and envisage an older one: a grey-haired husk of a woman as brittle and shrivelled as the beech leaves I scrunch through on my walk from the tube to my mansion flat. Desiccated.

Oh, for God's sake. Think of something else. I reach for the

newspaper by the side of the bath and scan through the news—
Egypt; the cloying fog; the planned arrival of Syrian refugees before Christmas—before my mind flits back to James Whitehouse
and the intensity of his friendship with Tom Southern, the PM.
They go back thirty years, plenty of time for secrets to be made,
shared, and kept. I wonder if the tabloid hacks are sniffing around
for them again, digging for a tale of class and corruption, determined to unearth some choice nuggets this time.

There's that infamous photograph that emerged in 2010, just
after the prime minister was first elected, of them both at Oxford.
They're posing on the steps of the grandest college, dressed in
the uniform of their elite dining club, the Libertines: midnight-
blue tails, velvet burgundy waistcoats, cream silk cravats blooming
like peonies against each blemish-free face. The photo was hastily
suppressed—news organizations can't use it now—but the image
persists of those preening, entitled young men. I see their smooth,
smiling faces now—the faces of men who will sail through life:
Eton, Oxford, parliament, government.

And then I think of the child in *Blackwell*, the case of tomorrow's repeat sex offender, and how his life chances have differed;
how his life has already been derailed. The paper dips in the water,
and I let the soggy mass slip from my hand to the floor as I find
myself ambushed by a wave of sorrow, an ache that engulfs me so
entirely that I can either succumb or suppress it. I sink deep into
the bath, welcoming the oblivion of the hot, greying water as it
closes over my face.

# Six

## James

### 1 November 2016

James walks briskly through Portcullis House, across New Palace Yard, and through Westminster Hall, taking care not to glance at the tourists who are peering up at the vast, cavernous space above them as it rises up to the fourteenth-century hammer-beamed roof.

His brogues click over the stone floor, carrying him away from the babble of accents—Czech, German, Spanish, Mandarin at a guess—and the careful overenunciation of a young tour guide, a recent politics graduate perhaps, who is delivering his spiel—the largest roof of its kind, the oldest part of the Palace of Westminster—as he shivers in his old fogeyish tweed jacket and tie.

Westminster Hall—chill, austere, redolent with history—is the part of the Commons in which the gravitas of his job as MP for Thurlsdon, junior minister in the Home Office, and a member of Her Majesty's Government always strikes James most clearly. The largest room in all of Westminster, it was saved at the expense of most of the rest of the buildings when fire raged through the palace in October 1834. There is no pretense in Westminster Hall, none of the overelaborate fleur-de-lis tiles or marble statues or garish murals. None of the color—that distinctive poison green for the Commons, the vermillion red of the Lords—that illuminates the palace, as if an interior decorator had been let loose with a 1940s color chart while on acid. Westminster Hall—all severe grey stone and rich brown oak—is as ungarnished and somber as Oliver Cromwell could ever have wished it to be.

It is bitterly cold, though. The sort of cold that demands people wrap up in furs in keeping with the hall's medieval heritage. An uncompromising cold that laughs in the face of modernity and reminds James—should he ever get above himself—of his current insignificance in the history of this place. He sweeps on past a couple of policemen warming themselves by a vertical heater in St. Stephen's Porch, and on through the warmer, more intimate St. Stephen's Hall, with its glittering chandeliers, bright stained glass and murals, its imposing statues of great parliamentary orators, resplendent in spurs and cloaks with marble folds. He passes the spot where the only British prime minister ever to be assassinated was killed, then has to duck around a bucket. The whole place is falling down.

No one spares him a glance here, and on he goes through Central Lobby, the heart of the palace, bustling with tourists, where a Labour backbencher, chatting to a member of the public, gives him a knowing, unfriendly nod. He hangs a sharp left, past another couple of policemen at the entrance to the area where the general public are forbidden: the relatively narrow

Commons corridor leading to the Members' Lobby, and beyond that, the Chamber itself.

He feels safer here. There is no way a lobby journalist could collar him now that the House is sitting, unless, glancing to the corridors leading up to the lobby where they are allowed to hover, he chooses to catch their eye. There is no need for him to venture here today. Home Office questions aren't this week; there is no debate that requires a large front-bench presence; it isn't PMQs. And yet he feels the need to brave the public spaces of the House, to visit the tearooms, to lunch at Portcullis, to sit in the Chamber. To prove to himself—and his colleagues—that, as he told Sophie, it really is all over and done.

Joining Tom for a secret gym session this morning has convinced him that Olivia and the subsequent fallout is a closed chapter. Chris had been incandescent when he heard about the meeting later, but James had snuck in and out of Downing Street by 6:15 a.m.

After forty minutes of bonding over the rowing machine, he refrained from giving his oldest friend a hug.

"Thanks for not hanging me out to dry," he said at the end of an ergo which stripped everything back to basics. Sweat glistened on his skin and he wiped his drenched forehead.

Tom, thicker in the waist since becoming PM, couldn't speak at first, he was panting so heavily.

"You'd have done it for me," he managed eventually.

The most powerful man in the country bent over the handles of the rowing machine, but when he straightened, his look took James back over twenty years. They could have been sprinting round Christ Church Meadows, pushing their bodies in joyous relief at the end of finals or in frantic desperation. James resisted that memory, but once again, Tom wouldn't let it drop. "Let's face it. It's the least I could do. Probably my turn to bail you out."

And so far today, it has all been fine. There have been a couple of jibes from the more sanctimonious Labour MPs—out-of-shape northerners who probably haven't had sex since the millennium—and some disdain from the more shrewish Labour women, but many on his own side have nodded in support. There have been kind notes, particularly from a couple of older politicians—former ministers who remember Alan Clark, Cecil Parkinson, Tim Yeo, Steve Norris, David Mellor. Not to mention Stephen Milligan, who auto-asphyxiated, trussed up in stockings. No one is pretending this government is going "back to basics." No one cares—so sharply—about individual sexual morality. There is a frisson of concern about his having dallied with an employee, but Chris Clarke's strategy has worked faultlessly. James's sense—and his instincts for this are usually sound—is that his dalliance might be a mark in the chief whip's apocryphal black book, or worth a paragraph or two in a future political memoir, but that, in terms of his long-term career, a line has been drawn underneath the affair.

The relief is immense. He pauses by the oak pigeonholes, which are perhaps anachronistic in this age in which his phone vibrates constantly with texts and emails, but still used frequently.

His is illuminated, revealing a message: a note—surprisingly unpatronizing—from Malcolm Thwaites. He pauses, looking towards the entrance of the Chamber beyond the principal doorkeeper, another anachronism in his black tails and waistcoat, who gives him a measured but courteous nod. The lobby is quiet and he stands in the calm of the antechamber, looking up at the bronze of Churchill, hands on hips, head jutting forward like a prizefighter. On the other side of the lobby is Mrs. Thatcher, right hand raised, index finger poised, as if at the dispatch box. His is a new brand of conservatism, and yet, he needs to channel their unwavering self-belief, to regain his chutzpah. He nods to the Iron Lady, turns, and gives the doorkeeper his most charming smile.

All will be well. Walking backwards, he glances up at the arch to the Chamber and the reddish patches left by the flames when the Chamber was bombed and completely destroyed in the Blitz. The roof to this lobby caved in, but you wouldn't know it. All was rebuilt just as his career—knocked off kilter but not irreparably damaged—will be. The key, in addition to being less aloof with his more tedious backbench colleagues, is to make something of this Home Office brief, a potential poisoned chalice, though Tom knows he can shine. He'll get back to the office now, and he strides down the Commons corridor, leaving the inner sanctum, the beating heart of this House, behind.

He crosses into the peers' lobbies—all thick red carpet and panelled walls, topped with the crests in peacock blue and gold leaf of attorney generals. An elderly peer totters to the printed paper office and nods. Neither speaks, the atmosphere as hushed as a Trappist monastery, though the High Victorian Gothic décor is far from austere. He prefers this sumptuousness and secrecy to the shiny openness of Portcullis, the modern part of Parliament with its vast fig tree–lined atrium, though it might have been better if *that* committee meeting had been in the modern part of the Commons. For a moment he considers how events could have been different. There, the lift doors are made of glass.

He shoves the thought aside and takes a shortcut down a spiral staircase and through a maze of admin offices before emerging into a yard at the far end of the building, sheeted in plastic and barricaded in scaffolding, right by Black Rod's entrance. The autumn sunshine is beating down, and behind him, the Thames sparkles and reminds him of the golden bits of Oxford. He has long since compartmentalized the not-so-golden bit. And then Tom had to allude to it this morning. *Let's face it; it's the least I could do. Probably my turn to bail you out.*

"Mr. Whitehouse?"

The voice drags him from his thoughts. A middle-aged man and a woman in her early thirties come towards him as he prepares to cross Millbank and stride down towards the Home Office.

"May I help? Can I ask that you make an appointment?" He glances behind him in the direction of the Commons, with its police protection and security guards. It's not that he is wary of meeting members of the public but he'd rather not, particularly since this man is making for him with the smirk of a nutter.

"We were hoping you could make an appointment with *us*," the man says, coming closer. The woman—not bad-looking (the assessment is automatic) though her ill-fitting trouser suit and lank haircut do little for her—follows a pace behind.

"I'm *sorry*?" James notes the twang of his voice but then the man flicks a Met Police ID card from his wallet, and James's smile hardens into a rictus grin.

"Detective Sergeant Willis. This is my colleague, Detective Constable Rydon. We've been trying to contact you, Mr. White-house, but your office seemed unaware of your whereabouts?" He says this with an easy smile though his eyes don't waver. His voice, stuffed with glottal stops, holds an edge.

"I switched my mobile off for an hour. Criminal behavior, I know." James chooses his words deliberately, trying for a smile that is unforthcoming. "Occasionally I do, at lunchtime. I just wanted to be able to think."

He smiles again and offers his right hand. The detective looks down at it as if it is something he would not normally encounter, and refrains from taking it.

James, affecting not to notice, moves his hand as if to guide them. "Perhaps we could talk elsewhere? In my office at the de-partment? I'm heading there."

"I think you might prefer that," the other man says.

His junior, slim and delicate-featured, nods, implacable. He wonders what it would take to make her smile, and at the same time, where the most discreet place would be.

"Perhaps you could tell me what you'd like to discuss?" James asks. His breath is coming quickly, and he concentrates on slowing it down.

"Olivia Lytton," DS Willis says, looking at him directly. He rolls back his shoulders, surprisingly broad for a slim man, and suddenly becomes more imposing. "We're here to ask you a few questions in connection with an allegation of rape."

# SEVEN

## Kate

### 9 DECEMBER 2016

Friday night and I am in a good mood as I make my way up the path to my oldest friend, Ali's, house on a suburban street in West London. It's been a week since Brian handed me the first set of papers for *Whitehouse* and I am still queasy with excitement at the thought of bringing this case to court.

"Oooh, fizz! Christmas? Or have you won a case?" Ali gives me a brisk kiss on the cheek as she takes the cold prosecco and the bunch of flowers I bundle into her arms.

"I've just been given a good one," I explain as I follow her through the hall of her Edwardian terrace. A forest of coats sways against me and I am enveloped by the smell of lasagna—onions, garlic, caramelized meat—as I move into her cluttered kitchen at the back of the house.

The house is busy with one child raiding a cupboard—"But I'm hungry"—another playing the piano badly, fingers floundering over the same bar then racing onwards, louder and apparently oblivious. Only Joel, the youngest at seven and my godson, is quiet as he works on the box of Legos I brought him in the hope of buying an hour's uninterrupted chat with his mother. Fifteen minutes after ripping it open, he has almost completed the apparently not-so-elaborate task.

Ali places a mug of tea in front of me and sweeps aside a day-old *Guardian*. She is busy, but then she's always busy—teaching four days a week, bringing up three children ages seven to thirteen, being a wife to Ed. She never needs to point out her busyness; it's just there. A fact. And one in which I often sense a strain of resentment as if *her* busyness is of a richer texture than mine. Motherhood, marriage, *and* a career—not a career as high-flying or well-paid as mine but still a career—drain her so that, by Friday night, she is probably not in the mood to listen to my triumphs, still less my problems. It's lovely to see me, but she could do without it at the end of a long week, really she could.

I imagine her thinking this, of course. She gives no indication, but I sense it simmering, implicit in her quick glance at my new handbag—oversize and of firm, rich leather—suggested by the utter exhaustion cloaking her face. It seeps out as she finally sits down, breath rushing from her like air from a deflated balloon, and as she scrapes her hair into a ponytail with quick, sharp movements and a grimace. It's even implied by her hair—fine grey streaks and dirty blonde strands where the roots need doing—and the fact that her forehead seems permanently furrowed between two unkempt brows.

"I like your glasses. Are they new?" I ask, wanting to say something positive.

"Oh, these." She takes them off and peers at them as if seeing them for the first time. One arm is bent and the lenses are smudged with finger marks. She thrusts them back on and flashes a look that manages to be both wry and defiant.

"They're ancient. Can't remember when I got them."

"You used to hate wearing glasses." I think back to the girl who wore contacts through her late teens, twenties, and early thirties, whom I'd thought so glamorous for expertly balancing a lens on her forefinger, and without a mirror, brushing it into her eye.

"Did I?" Ali smiles. "Well these are cheaper and a lot less hassle." She shrugs, not needing to state that she no longer has time for grooming or to recall that she was the one who once drew the looks—naturally slim, blonde, confident—while I was heavier and shier. A gallery of old Kates and Alis in our various physical incarnations—memories heaped layer upon layer on one another—hover like a string of cutout paper dolls.

"So, you're well?" Ali pushes her glasses onto the top of her head as she brushes aside random pieces of Lego. I wonder if she really wants to know. She seems distracted by the lasagna bubbling away in the oven; the second load of school uniforms sloshing around the washing machine; or the first, in the dryer, that rolls with a heavy regularity, a repetitive thud.

Her attention flickers. "I said not to eat anything." She stands and slams a low cupboard door shut as her eldest boy, Ollie, ten and apparently permanently hungry, tries to plunder it. "Dinner's in ten minutes."

"But I'm starving!" The boy stomps his foot, testosterone palpable as he runs from the room.

"Sorry," she says, sitting back down and fixing me with a smile. "Hopeless trying to have a proper conversation around here."

As if on cue, Pippa, her eldest, slopes in and curls around the back of my chair; sinuous as a cat. "What are you talking about?"

"Can you just go? All of you!" Ali's voice rises in exasperation. "Can you just let me talk to my friend for ten minutes in peace?"

"But Mum . . ." Joel looks aghast as he is unceremoniously shooed out. His big sister peels herself from the back of my chair and stalks out, her slim hips swishing in a parody of a model. I watch her, this girl-child, half in awe of the woman she will become, half fearful for what her future brings.

"That's better." Ali sips her tea with relief, emits a tiny, satisfied sigh. Why aren't we drinking the prosecco? It's a Friday night. Once upon a time we would have been three quarters of the way through a bottle by this point, but Ali has stashed it away in the fridge. I sip my own tea, too strong for my liking for she never gets it quite right, reach for the huge plastic carton of milk on the counter and pour a little more in.

"So, you said something about a case?"

So she *is* interested. I feel a wave of relief, and then my apprehension wells up inside me.

"It's a big one. A rape. Quite high-profile."

"Sounds exciting?"

I am torn. I am itching to divulge just a little. Not to run through the evidence, but to let her know whom we're talking about here.

"I can't really talk about it." I slam the possibility of disclosure shut and catch her expression: a be-like-that-if-you-want smile; a slight sigh; a distancing between us when we seemed, briefly, to be easing back into being our familiar, gossipy selves.

"It's James Whitehouse." I break my own rules, eager to regain that closeness, and more than that, to check her reaction.

Her blue eyes widen. I have her attention. "The minister?"

I nod.

"And you'll be prosecuting?"

"Yes." I roll my eyes. I still can't quite believe it.

Her breath eases out, and I wait for further, inevitable questions.

"So . . . do you think that he's guilty?"

"The CPS believes it has a strong case."

"Not the same thing." She shakes her head.

I wrinkle my nose and offer my usual, bland, straight-as-a-die response. "He says he's innocent. The CPS submits that there is sufficient evidence to convict, and I'll do my best to convince the jury of the case."

Ali pushes back her chair, picks cutlery from a drawer with a silvery rattle. Six knives, six forks, the cruets held in her other hand like a pair of maracas. She turns quickly, pushes the drawer closed with her hip.

Perhaps she's irritated by my use of legalese—inevitable, when it's the language I use in court. It's hard, when discussing a case, to slip into something more colloquial, just as I find it hard to shed my lawyerly precision, my tendency to cross-examine when trying to prove a point. I watch for the telltale signs that she's angry: a refusal to meet my eye, a tension around her mouth as if she's forcing herself not to speak. But Ali looks more thoughtful than cross.

"I can't believe it of him. I mean, I know he had that affair, but I genuinely thought he was one of the good guys. He seemed to be doing a good job—reaching out to Muslim communities rather than automatically pillorying them. And he just seemed lovely."

"Lovely?"

She shrugs her shoulders, momentarily embarrassed. "The one Tory I wouldn't kick out of bed."

I'm shaken by her tone but I tease, "Not really your type, is he?" He is as unlike Ed, her partner since our early twenties and now a rather earnest, balding head teacher, as it is possible to be.

"I just think he's beautiful." She looks at me, frankly, and all the baggage she wears so heavily—as wife, as mother, as teacher to small children—slips from her with this uncharacteristic admission. We could be getting ready for a college bop, freshers discussing which boy we had our eye on, both eighteen again.

I shrug and busy myself by clearing her table, troubled by her response on several levels. This is what we are up against. A man who will win over every female member of the jury by virtue of being beautiful; may win over some male members, too, for his looks are never going to alienate. The chiselled jaw, the high cheekbones, those green eyes, his height, his charisma—because that's what it is, this rare quality that marks him out so clearly—

are those of a leading man. And then there's his charm—for James Whitehouse has this in abundance. The effortless, unostentatious courtesy that is the trademark of an Old Etonian, that cannot help but flatter so that you feel, when their attention is on you, that they are genuinely interested; that they genuinely want to help. As Olivia Lytton found, it can be seductive. I have no doubt that, if he is put in the box, as he surely will be, he will use every ounce of this charm, every trick up his sleeve.

"Bit shallow of me to be swayed by his looks, isn't it?"

"Not shallow. I'm worried it's natural. That the jury will think it."

"I keep imagining his poor wife and family. He's a father and husband. I think that's what makes it so difficult to believe."

"Oh, Ali. Most rapists are known to their victims. They're not men with knives who pounce down alleyways."

"I know that. You know I know that." She starts slamming the cutlery down.

"You'll be telling me you don't believe in marital rape, next!" I laugh to cover my frustration, my disbelief that she can think the best of him.

"That's not fair, Kate. Not fair at all."

The temperature in the stuffy kitchen suddenly drops five degrees. She is red-faced, her eyes dark beads as she looks up at me. It strikes me that she is properly cross.

"I didn't mean to patronize." I row back, aware that the gulf is widening between us—a chasm that began with a chink when I got my first, and she her low 2:2; and that has widened as she entered teaching and I progressed to the Bar. She has long been chippy about feeling intellectually inferior and yet once upon a time, she would argue as passionately as me, would be joining me in lecturing about feminism and sexual politics and putting her point across, sometimes forcefully. Is it marriage, motherhood, or just age that has changed her? Made her more conservative. Less willing to believe that a good-looking—no, a beautiful—man, and an upper-class one at that, could be capable of such an ugly crime? We all mellow with age. We make compromises; bend our opinions; become less strident. Except that I don't. Not when it comes to rape.

I feel prickly, but it's unfair of me to direct my exasperation at her. This case—and the likelihood of James Whitehouse getting off—has affected me in a way it usually wouldn't. For, despite the heat of my fury, I am good at remaining emotionally detached. On the rare occasion I lose a case, it's my failure that bugs me as much as the implications for the complainants—the girls whose dress sense, levels of alcohol consumption, and sexual behavior are pored over in the witness box, as if we were prurient tabloid readers, and whose stories are still not believed after all that.

Usually, I bounce back from any loss: a fast run, a stiff gin, plenty more work in which to immerse myself, for the pressure of my job means that I cannot wallow in self-pity. I presented the evidence and the decision was out of my hands, now move on. That's what I always tell myself, and usually, it's what I manage to believe.

But not this time. This case is under my skin. And the odds

are stacked against us. Just like Ted Butler and Stacey Gibbons, there was a relationship here, though there was little that was domestic. An affair conducted in the workplace, in lifts and on office desks, over bottles of Veuve in hotel rooms and at her flat. And some of the evidence hints at a casual violence simmering beneath James Whitehouse's charming exterior; suggests—with his utter disregard for his one-time lover's feelings, his extreme sense of entitlement—he is a sociopath.

I can't discuss any of this with Ali. Can't share Olivia's witness statement. The details of exactly what happened. It's not that I don't trust her. It's not even because it's professionally unacceptable. Perhaps it's that I don't want to make myself vulnerable—don't want to admit that this high-profile prosecution of a charismatic, credible figure will be almost impossible to pull off. Or perhaps it's because I fear it's evident that I am losing my objectivity, and that's something that can never be questioned at all.

"Let's not argue." My dearest friend is holding out a glass of wine, a peace offering that I take gratefully.

"Come here." She opens her arms, suddenly maternal, and I give her a quick, tight hug, enjoying the warmth that flows from her, the familiarity of her small, soft body against my tall, lean one.

"I don't know if I can do this," I admit, above the top of her head.

"Oh, don't be ridiculous."

"I don't know if I can get him convicted." I pull away, ashamed at the admission.

"Not your decision, is it? Isn't that what you always say. That it's up to the jury."

"Yes, it is." The thought is bleak.

"I think you might have your work cut out." She takes a swig of wine. "Wasn't he having an affair with her, and didn't she go to the papers when he called it off to be with his wife and kids? Doesn't sound like she's much of a victim. More a woman getting her own back," she says.

"That doesn't mean she wasn't raped before that happened."

My voice sounds choked—the words hard, angry clots, and behind my back, my hands clench involuntarily into fists.

# EIGHT

## HOLLY

### 3 OCTOBER 1992

It was as if Holly was on a film set, or in an episode of *Morse*, perhaps. Yes, that was the view seen through her mullioned windows. A golden quadrangle, a hard blue sky and the dome of a library seen on the college prospectus and on the postcards of Oxford she had bought when she had come down for her interview. The Radcliffe Camera, or the Rad Cam, as she supposed she would soon call it. Eighteenth century. Iconic. Less a dreaming spire and more a honey-colored pepper pot. An image snapped by tens of thousands of tourists, every year, and now, it seemed, the view from her window.

She still couldn't quite believe it. That she was here in this room, or couple of rooms. For she had a "set": a large living room or study—with its oak-panelled walls, huge seven-drawer desk and battered leather sofa—and a small bedroom off it, a single bed wedged against more panels, cloistered away.

"You've done well in the room ballot," the porter had remarked, as he'd handed over a heavy mortise key, and she had. She'd come fourteenth, apparently, which meant a set of rooms on the first floor of the sixteenth-century Old Quad; not a room in the Victorian Gothic 'New' Quad; or exiled in the 1970s annex across town. The dark-stained stairs creaked as she climbed them, and she noted how they had warped and worn in the middle under the tread of centuries of students. And when she had pushed open the heavy oak door, which squeaked as if she were in a Grimm's Fairy Tale, she had almost cried out in delight.

"Bit different from home, isn't it?" Her father's voice broke into her thoughts. Pete Berry peered at the casement above a panelled window seat. "That looks like it'll get a bit drafty."

He thrust his hands deep into his pockets and rattled his car keys, rose onto the balls of his feet.

"Just a bit different." Holly ignored his criticism of the practicalities of her room as she peered at a sundial on the opposite wall of the quad: blues, white, and gold with a regal thread of red. Back home, she had half a bedroom, her side Spartan compared to her younger sister Manda's, with its mass of Rimmel makeup and plastic jewelry. There was no view from their window except the dark-red brick of the house opposite, the slate of the roof, and the clutter of chimney stacks, topped with TV aerials. The smudge of a charcoal-grey sky.

"Well, I'd best be getting off then." Her father was uneasy in these surroundings, perhaps uneasy in her presence. No use playing the proud father when he had disappeared six years earlier, leaving his wife and two kids. He was only here because she had had too much luggage to carry. She wished she had packed more lightly rather than deal with the embarrassment of their small talk in the Nissan Micra. His overt jolliness—a mix of pride and barely suppressed chippiness, perhaps even nerves—that filled that tinny space.

Her suitcase and rucksack sat between them.

"Well, bye, love." He came towards her gruffly, opening his arms. He expected a hug. She stood stiffly inside them.

"I'm proud of you." He pulled away. "No driving down cul-de-sacs for you, hey?" A driving instructor, he laughed at his habitual quip.

"No, I suppose not." She managed the expected smile.

"You be good."

Like you? She felt like asking, for it was his constant philandering—a compulsion to seduce the women he taught, and his surprising success at this—that had seen him abandon family life. She let it go. "I'll try," she said.

"Good girl." He rattled the keys in his pockets, again; didn't think to offer her any cash. She had a full grant, money was tight, and it wouldn't have occurred to him to do so. "Well," he said again. "Best be going, then."

She didn't suggest finding a pub for lunch, or even the local Wimpy bar. Down in the quad, her peers were streaming out into the autumn sunshine with their parents, a river of navy blazers and smart camel coats topped with shining, well-cut hair. A peal of laughter rang up: a father throwing his head back then placing an arm around his boy's shoulder. A mother put her hand to the small of her daughter's back; steered the tall, blonde girl towards the porter's lodge, past a trolley piled high with matching luggage. There was uniformity to these families. Slim, tall, well-dressed. Entitled. A sense that these students arriving to start college were at ease; that they knew they belonged here.

The thought of being seen with her dad—with his too-loud laugh, his black leather jacket, and his paunch hanging over his jeans—made her nervous. Every single thing about him would jar.

"Yes," she said, and swallowed for she still wanted to cling to all that was familiar while she could feel herself trying to repel it. "Yes, perhaps you had."

———————

Left alone, she could relax. Or try to. She lay on her bed—unmade, for she would do that in a minute—and stared at the ceiling, then sprang up because she was jittery, too excited to keep still, her stomach a jumble of nerves. She wouldn't venture out into the sunshine of the quad just yet, though, but would get her bearings; find the toilet—at the top of the staircase, she thought the second-year who had shown them up here had said—perhaps see if she could find her neighbors. On her way up, she passed a cubbyhole, set back in the paneling. A cupboard cut away to reveal a small fridge. She peered inside. No milk, but on the wire racks were three bottles topped with fat corks held fast with wire and decorated with gold labels. Even she, who had never seen a bottle of the stuff in real life, knew this was champagne.

A door above her opened and a face peered out. A boy, a young man really, older than her, with a mass of long, auburn curls, and a look of lazy amusement on his face.

"Plundering my supply?" His voice had a plum in it.

"No . . . honest." She straightened as if caught red-handed.

"Ned Iddesleigh-Flyte." He held out a hand. Bemused, she climbed the remaining stairs towards him and took it. "PPE. Third year. Where were you at school?"

She was bemused. "Liverpool," she said.

He raised an eyebrow. "I meant *which* school." A pause. "I was at Eton."

She felt like laughing. He was kidding.

"Really?" It was the best she could manage, and she hated herself for not coming up with a proper put-down: something that would nail him firmly in his place.

"Really," he said, though it sounded like *rarely*—a different word entirely from her guttural intonation that rose up with its second syllable and which she realized now she might have to abandon. His long vowels stretched through the silence as she thought of something to say.

"Anyway," he rescued her. "What's your name, dear neighbor?"

"Um, Holly," she said, bracing herself for the inevitable. "Holly Berry."

"You *are* joking?"

"No." She was used to this reaction; also used to trotting out the same embarrassing explanation. "I was conceived on Christmas Eve. My Dad has a sense of humor, or likes to think he has, anyway."

His smile widened and he threw back his head, like that father in the quad below: perhaps it was him she'd spied. "Well, it's certainly memorable. Holly Berry. Are you prickly?"

"I can be." Was that the best she could do? A childhood's worth of taunts surfaced, but her tongue lay fat in her mouth, incapable of forming a better retort. Blood flushed up her neck as the silence yawned between them, exposing her gaucheness. She needed to say something, anything, to wipe that smirk off his face.

He gave her that smile again: a wide, languorous grin from a boy who knew he had the world at his feet. Though he wasn't all *that*. Manda, who *was* experienced, or more experienced than her, wouldn't look at him twice with that shaggy mop of hair. She liked her men—and they *were* men—to look neat. But then Manda would never apply to Oxford. "Why would I want to go somewhere stuck-up like that?" she had asked Holly, whom she also viewed as stuck-up. She wanted to go to Manchester and had started a BTEC in business studies at the local sixth-form college. Studying English—reading English, whatever that meant—was a waste of time. Far better to start earning straight away or to do something vocational. Something that you knew would make you money.

Holly wasn't preoccupied with making money. She was reading English because it was the subject she was good at. "Exceptional," her A-level teacher had said, before suggesting to her mum that she might apply for Oxford. "Some of the colleges are becoming aware that they need to be diverse about their intake. I really think she has a chance," Mrs. Thoroughgood had explained.

She had gotten into her first-choice college. A choice she had made because it looked particularly pretty in the prospectus and was central and close to the libraries. Though she had realized the percentage of freshers from a state school like hers would be low, it hadn't occurred to her that she might meet someone like Ned. She had heard of Eton, of course, but only in the way that she had heard of the House of Commons or Buckingham Palace.

And now she had an Old Etonian as a neighbor. She needed to find someone more normal, more like herself. For though she had wanted to come to Oxford to leave her old life behind, now she needed to find someone familiar.

"Is there anyone else on this staircase?" she asked.

————————

Alison Jessop wasn't on her staircase, it transpired; nor was she reading English. But Holly gravitated towards her as inevitably as an iron filing to a magnet's strength. It was her laugh that caught Holly's attention: a warm, full-bellied sound coming from this small, pretty girl, flicking her hair and beaming up at a boy on the other side of the dining hall, across two rows of dark tables. Above her hung heavy oils of notable alumni—an archbishop of Canterbury, a prime minister, a Nobel Prize–winning novelist, and an actor. Either side of her were earnest boys—her fellow mathematicians, Holly later learned—with the pale complexions and pustules, the lank, greased hair of those who spent too much time in the library. Alison— with her guttural laugh and hot-pink top beneath her short, black gown—provided a blast of color, a hint of glamor against the somber wooden panels and gloom of a hall lit by flickering candelabras.

She was from Leeds. Her accent more muted than Holly's— generically northern to the southerners around them with their

*rarelys* and their *orfullys* and their *A*s that were lingered over, warm
and indulgent, compared to Holly and Alison's *A*s, which were
flat and short. Alison had gone to a private school, and so could
have fit in, but she played up her northern-ness. She didn't see
it as the badge of shame that Holly feared. "Nowt like pie and
gray-vee," she would say in a parody of the flat-capped, pigeon-
fancier others assumed her to be, as they queued together in the
canteen the next day; or as she demolished the plate of food with
a gutsiness that suggested she was ready to attack her life here at
Oxford with the same enthusiasm.

It should have grated—perhaps would have if she had been
thickset and crop-haired like Holly, or if she had looked as if she
had a whippet chained up in the quad. But Alison looked as if she
was born to wear a cocktail dress. Her face was angelic. Heart-
shaped with big, blue eyes and a Cupid's bow of a mouth, from
which an unlit cigarette often hung, the crumpled packet stuffed
in her back pocket. Her subject should have marked her out as
uncool, but her contradictions—that exquisite face with its dirty
laugh, the dry subject with the vivacious girl—were beguiling.
And she seemed to like Holly. "Thank fuck I've found you," she
declared, at the end of their first evening together, with the passionate ferocity that tended to characterize friendships in that
first week—alliances that many spent the next term, perhaps the
next year, trying to wriggle out of. She downed her snakebite
and black. "Time for another?"

Having Alison as a friend meant that Oxford seemed suddenly more manageable. The social side, at least. The academic

side didn't sound as if it would be too difficult. They were doing the medieval paper this term and Victorian literature. An author a week: Hardy, Eliot, Pater, the Brontës—Charlotte and Emily— Tennyson, Browning, Wilde, Dickens, the latter given two weeks in a rare concession to the volume of his work.

Reading the novels she hadn't devoured before she'd arrived was achievable; as was constructing the essays, for she was organized and systematic, working long hours and keeping to a realistic timetable for when she would need to start work on her weekly essay—8 p.m. the night before a tutorial scheduled first thing the next day. There was a maturity to the way she studied, honed during the past few years at school when her peers had shunned her and books were her comfort and her escape route from their sustained bullying. But navigating her way socially was far trickier.

And yet it needn't be, for now she had Alison, whom she might have found intimidating were it not for the shared geography which bound them, Yorkshire and Merseyside blanketed together as being part of a vast, unknowable grim-*ooop*-northness; the two of them black sheep in a uniform flock of white. Of course there were others who stood apart from the mass of hearty, public school southerners—the overtly campy guy who left to go to Bristol at the end of his first year; a token Asian mathematician. But they squirrelled themselves away. These boys kept themselves apart from those who slipped from libraries to bars to bedrooms, from tutorials to dining halls and out into the crisp moonlit nights. They would emerge, blinking, for their exams, but otherwise lived in the alternative universe of the college computer room where they found friends in similar rooms in other universities through the magic of Internet message boards.

But Holly and Alison were different. Female, for one thing, in a world in which their relative rarity in a male-dominated college made them interesting. And, in Alison's case at least, not socially inept. By virtue of her association with her funny, mouthy friend, Holly could navigate life at college and ride on her coattails, at least for a while.

———————

The Saturday of their first week—the improbably named noughth week—and the noise from the cellar bar flowed out into the quad from the bottom of the staircase. A deep-bottomed, rich, male laughter topped with something high-pitched and overeffusive: the sound of girls wanting to fit in.

The steps down to the bar dripped with condensation—the moisture from more than eighty students breathing in the same stale air. Holly pushed her way in behind Alison and was thrust against the damp back of a young man, T-shirt drenched in sweat. His buttocks, in jeans, were hot against her skin.

"Two snakebite and blacks, please," Alison called to the barman, an unshaven, disarmingly good-looking third-year. She reached into her cleavage and retrieved a crumpled five; shoved the three pounds change he gave her into a pocket of her jeans.

The floor was sweet and sticky, and Holly felt nauseous as

she moved through the tight-packed, pulsating bodies, the conversation ebbing and flowing then building to a roar. This part of the bar was thick with smoke, wreathing from the mouth of Ned Iddesleigh-Flyte, who gave her an ironic nod, and a group of third-year men, each dressed in a uniform of shirts, rolled at the cuffs and half-pulled from jeans that hung low at their waists, revealing a hint of a Calvin Klein waistband. Ned had a piece of string twisted around one hairy wrist.

Holly and Alison pushed on deeper into the bar, into the farthest section, beyond the pool table. It was late. They'd just made last orders, Holly insisting on working in the college library before Alison, bemused by her behavior—"You don't need to be such a spod"—had dragged her down here. The students in this dark part of the bar had had a long night. She slipped on a puddle of cider and jarred her hip on the edge of a dark wooden table; was briefly befuddled as someone grabbed her elbow and righted her with a casual arm thrown round her waist.

"It's a little fresher! Easy does it," went his cry, and she felt her body stiffen against the fluid brush of his fingers, the quick squeeze that she knew meant no harm but was still a surprise. *Fuck a fresher,* the mantra she'd heard bandied around in the dining room as the second-years had assessed the newcomers, filled her head. She glanced at the boy. Was that what he wanted? But he had already released her and was downing a pint—head tilted back, Adam's apple bobbing as the golden liquid slipped down his gullet. She watched, fascinated; the memory of his fingers imprinted on her waist.

"Come on! You'll miss the action!" Alison was calling back to her and thrust out a hand—the fingers square with chipped fuchsia nails. Holly took it and allowed herself to be pulled along in her slipstream, jostled and hustled through the crowd.

"You all right?" Alison called back, her face, flushed with excitement, gleaming with a sheen of sweat.

She nodded, forcing down any misgivings and giving in to a flicker of excitement building inside her; the sense that something new—and possibly illicit—was about to happen, for there was definitely something going on in the furthest corner of this stretch of the cellar bar. A crowd was gathered facing the wall, shielding a table, and a mantra was building: "Ros-coe, Ros-coe, Ros-coe, Ros-coe." The boy's name was being chanted, and then there was a drumming of several pairs of hands on the table and a great cheer erupted: a brutal cry of delight at the breaking of some final taboo.

"Fuck's sake!" The boy Roscoe staggered up and away. "I need some beer." His broad, pleasant face was flushed as he shoved past on his way to the bar, but behind his beam she sensed some embarrassment—though perhaps it was just the effect of the drink, held high and sloshed back from a plastic pint cup.

"Gi's a go." Another boy, broadchested as the first, called out, and his request was met with a rallying cheer.

"An-dy, An-dy, An-dy," the chanting resumed as the boy was thrust through his friends and hauled up onto the table. He looked around, grinning, delighted at being cheered by his teammates—for they were members of the college rugby team, she saw as she took in their tops emblazoned with their initials and the college crest.

"An-dy, An-dy, An-dy, An-dy." And then, as he lowered himself to lie down, his back on the table, "Go on, my boy."

She watched—curious at first, then bewildered, and then appalled as another member of the rugby team pulled down his jeans and boxer shorts and positioned himself on all fours above the laughing Andy. "Salis-bury!" The roar rose up as a third boy stood on a bench with a pint of beer and poured it down Salisbury's naked buttocks and into poor Andy's mouth.

"An-dy, An-dy, An-dy!" The drumming on the table almost drowned out the calls, but then there was a jubilant roar and he was heaving himself off the table, spitting beer and demanding a refill, while the half-naked Salisbury, who'd clambered off him, hauled his jeans and boxers up.

"Fuck's sake!" Andy half-spat his beer. "Fucking gross."

"Any more takers?" The ringleader—the lad pouring the pint of beer—looked around, and to Holly's bemusement, another rugby player—chest puffed out, hips rocking in a parody of a cowboy swaggering towards a fight—took Salisbury's place.

"What are they doing? Why are they doing this?" The words slipped out as she glanced at the flushing Andy, whose neck was caught in a headlock by other team members. They slapped his back as they thrust him towards the bar.

"They're anal chugging," Alison shouted in her ear. "It's what the rugby boys do."

"What . . ."

"I know. That lad, the one standing up, is a scholar. I saw his gown at dinner. He's supposed to be super bright." She raised her eyebrows then turned back.

Holly watched the boy Alison was talking about as he stood above his teammates, one hand tipping a plastic pint of beer, the other on his hip as though he were a farmer presenting his best beast at a show.

His face, on top of a thick neck, seemed free of malice: dark eyes glinting below a floppy fringe that was damp with sweat; pink lips, with perfect teeth, parted as he poured the amber beer then threw back his head and gave a roar.

Disappointment weighed heavy in her chest like a physical pain. These were supposed to be the brightest brains of her generation. Oxford the place where she thought she might discuss philosophy or politics—where she'd rant against John Major's government—not watch broad-shouldered lads with plummy accents drink beer from each other's cracks.

"Mad, isn't it?" Alison grinned at her and rolled her eyes, but there was nothing in her reaction to suggest that she was repulsed, more that she was intrigued by this aspect of student life.

Andy, the second boy to take part, was by her side now she realized, released from the throng and trying to meld into the back of the crowd. He was drinking determinedly, eyes fixed on the middle distance as he downed his beer, huge shoulders hunched forward as if to minimize his presence. She caught his eye and tried to convey her sympathy. He looked away but not before she saw him flush.

# NINE
## HOLLY
### AUTUMN 1992

Sophie Greenaway curled her legs beneath her in the capacious armchair and smiled at Dr. Howard Blackburn, the renowned medieval English scholar, as she looked up from the essay she was reading aloud.

It was the second week of Michaelmas term, and Holly watched their tutor watch the other girl, saw his eyes follow the easy flick of those legs in their black opaque tights as they crossed and uncrossed then languidly rearranged themselves, her feet tucked underneath her bottom. Most of the week, Sophie wore rowing skins: the regulation navy-and-pale-blue kit which marked her out as a member of the college women's first boat. But not, it would seem, for Howard's tutorials. For those, it was a short tartan mini, loafers, and opaque tights.

She was reading about courtly love. *Sir Gawain and the Green Knight.* The concept of loving with no expectation of consummation, of admiring from afar, of humiliating oneself in the adoration of a fair lady—and risking her disdain or disapproval—to prove one's chivalry. One's essential knightliness.

Sophie's essay wasn't particularly illuminating. Holly could detect nothing that she hadn't read herself in the *York Notes* she had skimmed before turning to C. S. Lewis and A. C. Spearing; nor was it in any way elegantly written. It was a solid essay. What she would later know as beta-minus material. But that didn't matter. What mattered to Holly was that Sophie looked as if she was the sort of woman who, six centuries earlier, would have had noble knights falling at her feet. While Holly would be a peasant, Sophie would be on the receiving end of courtly love.

She recrossed her legs and Holly was entranced. While Alison was pretty, Sophie had a different quality to her. A type of beauty that looked as if it had evolved through the generations, or perhaps her ancestors had been consciously bred to look like this, for hers was a look that belonged to a certain class. Legs that were effortlessly thin even at her upper thighs, delicate bones and arched brows, and thick dark hair that she flicked, to Holly's irritation, from side to side. Her eyes were a startling blue and so wide that she could use them to obvious effect—as she was doing now—to suggest innocence or incomprehension. If Holly had had to describe her in a single word, she would have picked "classy." But that was the type of word her dad would use. It didn't come close to capturing the essence of her.

Holly found it incongruous that they had been paired up like this for the term among the seven students reading English in their year at Shrewsbury College—medieval literature with Dr. Blackburn and then the Anglo-Saxon translation class. Sitting in Howard's study, Holly felt exposed. Her DMs were planted on the carpet between two piles of books that teetered like all the other piles in the room, those crammed on coffee tables or perched on the edge of the bookshelves that ran the height and breadth of one wall. She shifted back into the armchair, loosely covered in a plain, worn velvet. The fabric was soft beneath her fingers and she stroked it, eyes flickering from the books to the vast windows opening onto the quad, motes of dust floating in the sunshine, to the gaze of her tutor—a quizzical smile on his face—as he watched Sophie's legs crossing and uncrossing once more.

"And what about you? Do you agree with Sophie's interpretation of Sir Gawain's motives?" Dr. Blackburn dragged his eyes from her tutorial partner and fixed them on her.

"Um, well . . ." And suddenly Holly found her voice. She spoke of Sir Gawain's conflict between chivalry and desire, and as she gained confidence, she could sense that not only was Dr. Blackburn looking at her with more interest—"That's an unusual interpretation, but I like it"—but that Sophie, her beta-minus essay forgotten, was sitting up and joining in, was forcing herself to think beyond the pass notes she had copied verbatim, perhaps. In any case, the attention was collegiate, not unfriendly, and when they left the tute—as she found herself now calling it—it seemed natural that the two of them would have a cup of tea together in the tea bar. Besides, Sophie said she had a proposition for her.

The plan was that they would divide up the Anglo-Saxon translations and take it in turns to research the bulk of the medieval English essays. Sophie had an arch lever file of notes, given to her by an accommodating second-year whom she had plied with drink the week before.

"Are you sure that's all you had to do?" Holly didn't mean to sound intrusive and yet this goodwill seemed excessive.

"Holly! What are you implying?" Sophie gave her a knowing smile. "He doesn't need these essays anymore. And he said he knew what a bore the medieval paper is. God, we've so much to read for the Victorians that we're not going to be able to cover them properly unless we're efficient about handling our workload. Look, here's one on the Pearl poet—I can plunder that for next week—and then can you read the Malory?"

"I think *Le Morte d'Arthur*'s quite important. We should probably both read it, shouldn't we?"

"Bugger that. Life's too short. Honestly. I want to try for the women's lightweights and I won't have the time if I'm going to do the Victorians properly. If you could read the Malory and fill me in, I'll do the rest from pass notes."

"Well . . . OK."

"And I'll do my share of the *Beowulf* translation, I promise. Oh look, though." She gave a cheeky grin. "Jon's given me his translation here."

"Isn't this cheating?"

Sophie looked at her askance and smiled, though not unkindly. "Not at all. It's about being efficient. Everyone does it."

"I just thought . . ." and she almost stumbled on the words as she realized they sounded so gauche. "I thought that doing the translations and reading English literature from the start was important for our understanding of its development. I thought reading the whole canon was what this degree was all about."

"Well, if you want to spend time translating *Beowulf*, you do so." Sophie took a swig of tea, but she seemed more amused than irritated. "I don't think my doing so will make a jot of difference to my marks or to my university experience—apart from reducing the time when I could do other things."

"Such as?" Holly wondered aloud.

"Oh, you know. Rowing—and men." She gave a jubilant laugh. "That's what uni's about. Having fun. Making contacts. Doing sport. An extension of school in a way."

Holly shrugged. Her school hadn't been like that at all.

"My father always says you should assess the validity of any investment before deciding on the amount you invest."

"Oh. What does he do, your father?"

"He's an investment banker. And yours?"

Holly's heart sank. She should have seen that coming. "A teacher."

"Which subject?"

"Cars. He's, erm, a driving instructor." It would have been better if she'd confessed to this from the start.

"How sweet! And useful?"

"I suppose so. I don't drive."

"Didn't he teach you? Or did it lead to arguments?"

"No. He's not around much. My parents split up."

It felt strange to unburden herself like this: to divulge so much information in one whoosh when she was usually quite private, but this seemed to be the way at uni, she was discovering. Close friendships were being forged at a fevered rate, as if the brevity of the terms—eight or nine weeks—meant the usual, cautious way in which relationships developed had to be abandoned and the process speeded up.

"God, I wish mine would sometimes." Sophie put her hand to her mouth as if the words had slipped out without her meaning to. "Oops. Forget I said that. I didn't mean it."

"Really?" Holly was interested. Perhaps Sophie's life wasn't as perfect as it seemed.

"Oh just, you know, bit of a philanderer. Men, hey!" Sophie gathered her books together and thrust them into a bag, then picked the arch lever file of notes off the table and hugged it to her chest. The opportunity for sharing secrets seemed to have been slammed tightly shut, and the smile Sophie wore now was fixed, with none of the joyfulness of a few minutes earlier. Holly, gathering her notes together, took her lead from her.

"Yes, men!" she said as if she knew all about them, instead of still being a virgin who had only just turned eighteen. She ruffled her hair and pulled her baggy jumper over her jeans—a means of making herself blend into the background or at least of being sexually invisible—and followed her new friend out of the tearoom and into the soft autumnal sunshine outside.

That first term at Oxford was an education—not just in the texts of the Pearl poet and Malory, in the poetry of Christina Rossetti and Elizabeth Barrett Browning, but in life or the very real possibility of a different life. Looking back, it was as if her eighteen years had offered her just one version, and the old certainties—the food she ate, the way she talked, the way people thought—could be taken apart and reassembled so that life became brighter and harder, more textured and complex than ever before.

Later, she would remember that autumn term as a relentless feasting of her senses: a daily bombardment of new sights and smells and sounds that sometimes felt exhausting, so extensively did they challenge what she had once known.

This newness was everywhere. She could be wandering through Christ Church Meadows and see a cow staring at her through the dense November mist, its huge head contemplative and mournful—for, of course, students could keep Longhorn cattle on the Meadows and had been doing so since the fifteenth century; or she would run over Merton Street's cobbles and be surprised by a bowler-hatted porter, or a couple of boys, inexplicably in tails, staggering back to college, arms around each other's shoulders like the most amorous of lovers, an empty bottle in each spare hand. She could duck into the labyrinthine covered market and be surprised by the ripe reek of fresh meat and the sight of a deer, hanging upside down by its haunches, perfect except from the neat shot to its head. And then she would see the same species, hours later, in a deer park in the center of this city, flitting dewy-eyed and fearful.

That Michaelmas term was partly characterized by food—

jacket potatoes in polystyrene boxes oozing butter and baked beans bought from the kebab van on the high street when she missed hall, as she soon learned to call dinner. Vast quantities of lasagna and garlic bread, shoveled down by the rugger boys and boaties and by her and Ali, as autumn crept on and the nights turned cold. Steaming mugs of tea and toasted sandwiches in the college tearoom or the Queen's Lane teashop, where you perched on stools and people-watched through windows wet with condensation. Venison and port, consumed for the first time at a formal hall; so delicious she tried to steal the wine, in a crystal decanter, before being stopped by a college servant and having it removed, ever so gently, from her hand.

There was a new language to be learned: tutes—for tutorials; battels—the bills for each term; Mods—first-year exams; subfusc—the black-and-white dress worn for formal occasions; collections—the exams at the start of each term; exhibitioners—students who gained first-class marks in their yearly exam; scholars—students who achieved this in subsequent years. A new academic terminology to understand: Marxist theory; feminist theory; as well as the lists of the critics she would be reading, and the lecturers she would be listening to.

She bought postcards of the dreaming spires from Blackwell's and propped them on the mantelpiece above her fire; Blu-tacked a large print of Klimt's *The Kiss* in her bedroom, drawn to it by the opulence of the gold leaf and the quiet knowledge of being loved that played across the woman's face. Because it was what she thought she should do, she invested in a college scarf: a thick navy-and-pink weight of wool that she thought looked pretentious tossed over one shoulder and instead wound round and round her neck so that she breathed into it as she blew out and became snugly hot. She did not join the Oxford Union—the debating ground for past prime ministers and political leaders; and the environment where future politicians gathered, in their mustard cords and tweed jackets. Young men—and they were invariably men—aping the behavior of older ones.

She began to shed her baggy jumpers and started to wear hoodies and to try leggings with her trusty DMs, though her thighs were still wide and cumbersome compared to her friends'. Her glasses—dark-rimmed, NHS ones—were hidden when she wasn't in the library, and she experimented with kohl pencil, heavily applied at the corner of her eyes. She joined the student paper and began to review student drama; attended meetings of the Labour Party, and volunteered for the telephone counseling service, Nightline. She marched, angrily, to Reclaim the Streets, holding her rape alarm tight as if Oxford's potential rapists were primed at any point to pounce. After a couple of weeks, she stopped carrying it because her world of the quad and the high street, the pubs and the faculty, seemed so safe, so cosseted, compared to anything she had experienced back home that it felt like an affectation. Besides, although in a college with a mere eighteen girls in her year, she received little male attention. Ned would offer an ironic grin; the two boys reading English in her year would be perfectly friendly, but no one appeared to be interested in her sexually. Why would they be when there were the likes of Alison—who spent her nights drinking or clubbing—or Sophie, the epitome of an athletic young woman, to try their chances on?

It didn't bother her, or she told herself it didn't, and her passion was channelled into her close female friendships. The bond with Alison—so different from her in so many ways—grew stronger the night she found her slumped, unconscious, on the toilet, after a heavy session in the bar.

It was she who held Alison's long blonde hair back as her friend vomited into the pan; she who wiped her mouth with a paper towel and brought her a glass of water; who splashed her face, as tenderly as a mother would a child, and half carried, half guided her back to her bedroom; who sat up with her that night, terrified she would choke if she didn't keep watch.

Alison's jeans had been pulled down when she'd found her there and there had been something so vulnerable about her being so exposed like this.

"What if one of the lads had found me?" her friend wondered later.

"They'd have been embarrassed."

"Well, yes. But what if anything had happened?"

"Nothing would have happened. You weren't in a fit state to do anything and you were about to throw up."

"I don't know." Alison had chewed at a cuticle and Holly noticed that her once-neat nails were becoming bitten down, the quicks ragged. She gave a hard, bright laugh. "Not sure everyone would be put off by that."

If this bonded them—the more confident girl becoming more noticeably appreciative, the relationship equaling out a little—then it was through their Anglo-Saxon studies that she grew closer to Sophie. Every Wednesday, they would sit together in the college library swapping halves of translation, and laboriously copying them from each other before Sophie found a photocopier and so cut their sessions short.

Holly would watch her friend from the opposite side of the desk and wonder if her hair would grow that thick if she abandoned her masculine crop and how she could make her caterpillar eyebrows as elegant and refined. And what about her dress sense? Sophie wore short skirts or Levis, if not in rowing kit, and Holly wondered if a pair of these jeans, though way beyond her budget, would somehow make her legs look longer, or give her that elusive status—mark her out as being cool.

She would watch Sophie's looping writing—a swirl of purple ink spiraling from a fountain pen across lined A4—and compare it favorably to her own biro-ed mass of letters. Holly's work was neat—Post-its, fluorescent marker pens, a ring binder with different sections demarcated by card and plastic files that could be reinserted (she was a stationery junkie)—but her actual handwriting was a scrawl. It was as if there were so many ideas inside her head that they fought against each other to get on to the paper. A flurry of jumbled letters—a witch's hand or a substandard clerk's—was the result.

That hour spent comparing translations, checking that each other understood what the Green Knight was doing at a certain point, or whether they could discuss it convincingly, was one of the highlights of Holly's week. Before now, her cleverness had been a mark of shame—something she was secretly proud of, but which she knew she shouldn't advertise, not even here, where there was currency in suggesting that you crammed for your tutes—a week of work concertinaed into a few twilight hours.

But Sophie was frank in her appreciation of Holly's hard work—for, invariably, Holly did the lion's share, Sophie popping a note in her pigeonhole the day before, admitting that the early mornings spent rowing were taking a toll on her and she hadn't *quite* found the time to manage her half.

"Oh, you are clever," she would tell her repeatedly. "Not like thickie old me."

"Come off it. You're not thick."

"A solid Desmond, my father thinks."

"A 2:2?" Holly translated. "Well, that's OK."

"Exactly. Far better to enjoy myself. A solid degree, a rowing blue and a nice chap—hopefully a future husband—that's what I want to get out of being here."

Holly leaned back. There were so many parts of that sentence that were foreign to her—so many that struck her as completely wrong—and yet she couldn't help but smile at Sophie's frankness. There was something so uncomplicated about her, this fresh-faced girl, a former county runner and lacrosse captain and now-member of the college boat club's first eight, for whom life was about seizing opportunities and making the most of her advantages: those long legs crossed and uncrossed in front of poor old Howard; and, yes, the ability to flatter her tutorial partner into doing most of the work.

Holly knew she was being manipulated, but it was done in such a charming way that somehow she didn't mind. Sophie was steely: willing to get up for those chilly 6 a.m. starts on the river when most students were still hunkered under their duvets; persuading second-years to hand over their essays with no sense that she needed to reciprocate at all. Holly had no doubt that, at the end of the three years, she would have the rowing blue, the future husband—or a potential future husband—and probably, because luck always shone on the likes of her and she would know how to use it, a just-scraped 2:1.

It would be easy to envy her, perhaps even despise her. And yet Holly couldn't. Sophie represented a world that, even though she might profess to hate it, completely intrigued her.

"You know she's a Tory," she grumbled to Alison later, after she'd mentioned to Sophie that she was off to a meeting of the university Labour Party.

"Well, of course she is," said Alison.

"And she wants to live in a house off the Woodstock Road next year, or in Jericho—not off the Cowley Road like us."

"Why would she want to be in *east* Oxford? I expect Daddy's buying her a house."

"I dunno." She felt suddenly disloyal, thinking of the fragments of conversation that suggested Sophie's father wasn't emotionally attentive, that he lived a quite separate life from his family. "She hasn't mentioned that. Forget I said it."

Alison laughed. "You quite like her, really."

"Yeah. Well, you know . . . she's not *that* bad."

And she didn't find her bad at all. She would hanker after the snippets of information Sophie dropped about her life—the details of cocktail parties in other college rooms; the casual reference to drugs snorted by school friends elsewhere, though Sophie didn't touch the stuff, was far too preoccupied with being a wholesome, healthy rower; the tales—offered with an eye-rolling "boys will be boys" tolerance—of the elite drinking societies, to which her cousin Hal, a third-year in a different college, belonged.

"You won't believe what they got up to last weekend," she whispered, and Holly wondered if there was an element of Sophie that loved scandalizing her friend with the extravagance of the upper classes.

"What?" Holly's stomach tightened in anticipation at a tale that promised to be more *Brideshead* that anything she could imagine. These stories—told in a breathless hurry amid a run of giggles—were like the opening of *Decline and Fall*, with the added thrill of having happened in real life.

"The Libertines were at a lunch at Brooke's on Turl Street, and when they were finished, each of them ordered a separate taxi to take them down to the King's Arms."

"But that's a minute's walk away." Holly was befuddled.

"Exactly! A fleet of taxis queuing the length of Turl Street, each waiting for a minute's ride!"

"Weren't the taxi drivers annoyed?"

"They were each paid fifty pounds."

"Fifty quid's not bad for a minute's job."

"I'm sure they were fine." Sophie sounded airy.

"But they might have felt stupid."

"Oh, come on. Who cares? They did their job and were paid for it. God, sometimes, you're so *serious.*" She gathered her books in one swift movement that suggested the issue was closed and stood looking at Holly, who was still busy imagining the bemused taxi drivers. "Come on." Sophie's voice was tight with irritation. "We'll be late."

And so Holly trailed after her, reproaching herself for the crime of being insufficiently lighthearted, of failing to see the funny side in a group of indulged young men flaunting their privilege, agonizing over why she detested this sort of behavior, but still seduced by Sophie and the world she seemed to represent. She stumbled down the worn wooden steps from the library and into Old Quad, Sophie several strides ahead of her now, obviously displeased and apparently shaking her off before the tutorial where she would rely on her translation and revert to being all sweetness and light.

By the porter's gate, Sophie stopped and smiled up at a tall young man—a boatie from another college: one good at rowing, perhaps Oriel or Christ Church. He seemed to know her and bent down to give her a double kiss: one on each cheek.

The light flooding into the quad glanced off his thick hair, which flopped into his eyes, and his sharp cheekbones, illuminating his face so that Holly could see the curve of his mouth and his green-and-gold-flecked eyes. His shoulders, tapering to a slim waist, were those of a rower, and when he laughed—as he was doing now at something that Sophie said—the tone was rich but not braying. It spoke of class more than money, and of an innate, but not grating, self-confidence.

"Who was that?" she asked Sophie later, as they waited on the landing outside Howard's room and her friend watched this Adonis walk across the quad to leave the college. At the porter's gate, he turned and looked up.

"Oh that?" Sophie said, her eyes feasting on him though her tone suggested her feelings were terribly casual. "That was James Whitehouse."

# Ten

## Holly

### Autumn 1992

Holly's heart hammered thick and fast as she leaned against the tree trunk. Seven a.m. and her breath rose through the early morning mist and beaded into moisture that clung to each stark branch.

Her chest hurt. She had managed this run four times this week, but it wasn't getting any easier. Her body wasn't used to pushing itself—games being something she'd shirked as much as possible, her scholarliness a creditable excuse. "Well, I suppose you could miss it to prepare for your Oxford exam," Mrs. Thoroughgood had said, and her exclusion had become permanent because her presence on the netball field contributed little and was never sought by the team that was burdened with her.

Now, though, she was paying for that slothfulness. Her face, she knew, was a shiny red, and there was sweat clagging beneath her bra straps and dampening her armpits—even more of a reason to hide away. They hadn't come past yet. The men's first eight. And she'd make sure she was well on her way, or hidden back from the path, when they did. The fear of being seen was

the only thing that drove her on, that prevented her from collapsing in a pile on the grass where her body so clearly wanted
to give up. Of course, to prevent detection, she could just run
slowly back to college, face turned downward, weaving through
the smallest passages in the hope of seeing no one. But then she
wouldn't see them. She wouldn't see *him*.

A voice in a megaphone, the rhythmic slick of oars on water,
the hum of a bicycle strumming the towpath. She sprang back,
like one of the does in Walsingham College deer park, though in
damp, black leggings and cheap trainers, as ungainly as an overweight eighteen-year-old could possibly be. She flattened herself against the trunk, watching as the first boat seared past: the
epitome of synchronicity and power. Eight young men at the
pinnacle of their fitness working in unison, urged on by their
cox and the coach, whose bike sped alongside them. There was a
rhythm and a beauty to what they were doing: their oars sculling
the water without a splash; their bodies bending forwards and
leaning back in a seamless, continual motion. Even if she wasn't
interested in one crewmember—the stroke, the leader, the most
skilled and competitive—they were a joy to see.

She ran on, keeping her distance, though she knew they were
too preoccupied to see her, and would pay less attention to the
floundering fresher who possessed not one item of college sports
kit than to the swans who hissed, imperious, from the banks of
the Isis, and rose from the water in a flurry of hard-beating wings.
At some point, the boat would turn and come back, would streak
back up towards the boat club and she would have the chance

of watching his face, tense with effort and concentration, as he shifted forwards and leaned back, driving his teammates onwards, setting the pace. She would try to time her running so that she could manage to see him before she lumbered back towards where she'd left her bike. Her breath became more ragged, her chest aching, as she pushed herself onwards. How to time it so that she would just glimpse him?

And then they had sped past, and she was pounding along the sandy path, back towards the colleges, a shot of adrenaline searing through her as she reeled from her hit for the day. They would train again tomorrow and she would be here, though there was a tutorial at nine and she could feel an essay crisis looming. Still this—seeing him—would power her through, would make her write her essay on sensuality in *Middlemarch* more sensitively and with more authority. University was about education, but an education is gained in so many ways.

Sometimes, she wondered if she was becoming obsessed. But her behavior seemed quite in keeping with the feelings of these literary heroines. The physical excitement she felt when she saw him, the way in which her breath grew lighter or her stomach tipped over, was what infatuation was about. Even hearing his name was enough to make her feel light-headed. "Oh, really," she'd say if Sophie mentioned him, and would adopt the casual nonchalance her friend had once shown. She made sure she was never around the two of them, would duck her head on the rare occasions they were together and he entered college. And he was, she was sure, completely oblivious of her.

Just the once, he caught her eye. She was racing to her room and heard footsteps thundering down the stairs from Ned Iddesleigh-Flyte's above her. Two pairs: Ned's, from the sound of it, and someone unknown's. They sped past as she reached her door and stood back to let them bound past.

"Cheers," Ned called in passing. *Chairs*, she mouthed, as the second figure barged past. "Sorry—*sorry!*" He held both palms up and flashed her a smile, his green eyes emitting warmth and the confidence that he would be forgiven—of course he would be forgiven—then bounded ahead without waiting for an answer.

"That's all right," she called down the stairs. Her voice sounded high-pitched, weak, and ineffectual, as it petered down the staircase. She waited, but there was no reply.

---

Things could have become trickier when Sophie became involved with him. "Seeing him" was how she rather coyly put it, for no one would ever claim to be going out with James Whitehouse. It wasn't just that he was someone who would ever be possessed by anyone, it was also that no one wanted to appear less than cool.

In fact, their relationship made things easier. He rarely came to college, except late at night, and so there was no risk of being seen, of her infatuation being guessed at. And yet Sophie couldn't resist confiding in her, hinting at her insecurities, seeking reassurance about whether this meant he really liked her. And, of course, regaling her with the latest exploits of the Libertines, of which James was a member, all whispered in the breathy knowledge that she shouldn't really be sharing this but she was going to do so anyway; all divulged, in part, out of a desire to shock.

Sophie chatted too about the New Year's Eve party she would be throwing at her parents' home in Wiltshire, while they were in London. James, she very much hoped, would be going, and the set she hung out with in college—girls studying classics and history of art who came from the same sort of background: fathers in banking; houses in the country; ponies and tennis lessons; skiing holidays; a private education culminating in boarding for the sixth form at a good public school. Holly had nothing against Alex, Jules, or Cat; was sure they were perfectly nice, though they had made little effort to be friendly to her. She didn't expect to be invited, and yet it smarted as the term progressed and it became increasingly clear she wouldn't be. She waited, half-hoping that the issue might be raised, but as the details changed from a party to a dinner party, it dawned on her that she had never even been considered.

Should she raise it as a joke? And then she imagined Sophie's pity. "Oh sorry. It didn't occur to me you'd want to come." Or, even more bluntly: "Oh Holly, it's not your sort of thing *at all.*"

———

As the term raced to its end, she realized that she had entered into an unspoken contract with this girl who both entranced and appalled her. She would increasingly shoulder the workload—do the weekly translation and make notes for the essay that she would photocopy at the newsagents in Holywell Street—and in return Sophie would allow her to vicariously experience her life.

And that was fine. The casual kindness was enough—the requests for reassurance, the snippets of gossip, the acknowledgement of her across a packed dining hall with the kind of radiant smile that stopped her in her tracks and warmed her. That said that even if she wasn't the right type, she was a friend of sorts.

And then, one evening, she came across them both in the gateway to the college and managed a "hello," the syllables thick in her throat so that she almost had to cough them up. She barely looked at him, was just aware of his presence, his broad shoulders in a charcoal wool jacket—not his rowing kit, for they were going to dinner—collar turned up, framing the hint of a smile. She smiled at her friend, her face flushing as she mumbled some nonsense about needing to find a book in a pigeonhole, and quickly ducked out of sight.

"Who was that?" she heard him ask Sophie, as she busied herself in the porter's lodge, searching for the nonexistent hardback.

She waited, her ears straining to hear her answer, avoiding the porter's eye.

"Oh, that?" said Sophie. "Just my tutorial partner. No one important."

And she took James's arm, clinging to it as if she was a delicate specimen who needed protecting, and swept off into the night.

# ELEVEN

## SOPHIE

### 13 DECEMBER 2016

Court Two of the Old Bailey is not as Sophie imagined it. She had anticipated something intimidating and impressive, not this tawny, oak-panelled room that looks distinctly shabby, as if its glory days are long past.

She can barely believe she is here, in these surroundings that remind her of the Commons: the same poison-green leather on the seats emblazoned with gold, the same wood—forming five sturdy thrones and a crest. The same nod to past grandeur glimpsed in the carved wooden wreaths of flowers and grapes, coated in dust, that drape above each door.

She perches on the edge of a bench, high up in the public gallery, and tries to distract herself from the fact that her husband is sitting in the dock below, flanked by security officers, showcased behind sheets of bulletproof glass. He looks vulnerable from this angle. His shoulders are as broad as ever, but his hair thinning just a touch at the top, she notices for the first time. A wave of fear ambushes her. Her knees begin to quiver and she puts her palms down on them firmly, hoping that the teenage tourists, glancing at her with frank curiosity, won't wonder why she is quaking. Stupid. Of course they'll guess. She places her handbag—X-rayed, opened, pored through—on her knees and when that doesn't quite stop the juddering, crosses her legs, and hugs them close.

A loud gurgle from her stomach. She can sense the acid swilling though she hasn't eaten this morning. Little wonder that she has lost nearly a stone in the six weeks since James's arrest. This is only an initial appearance—the plea and trial preparation hearing—so how emaciated will she look by the trial next year?

She swallows, trying to dislodge the sharp plum of pain in her throat. She could wail. She, the most calm and controlled of individuals, who was brought up to temper any unpleasant feelings with dry humor or to keep them firmly suppressed. Her insides have hollowed out and a potent bank of emotions presses up: horror, incredulity, revulsion, and above all a deep, all-encompassing shame. She clamps her lips tight. It frightens her, this intensity of feeling. Only once before has she experienced anything similar and then it was a shadow of this. She dabs at her eyes with a tissue. Letting her emotions overwhelm her isn't an option. She has the children to think about and, of course, James.

But she knows now, with a certainty that she hadn't before today, that she can't attend each day of the trial. Just running the gauntlet of the photographers outside the court has shown her that she can't. Maintaining her smile while James's fingers almost crushed hers, his fist such a clamp of iron she nearly winced. She had sensed his nerves then, something he hasn't admitted to, even in the still, quiet moments of the night when she lets herself shift into the warmth pooling from him in bed and whisper: "Are you OK?" He hasn't shown a chink of vulnerability since being charged nor has he raised the possibility of being convicted. If they don't speak of it, perhaps it cannot happen. And it has seemed so far-fetched. That cliché: a living nightmare.

It all feels very real now. As solid as the sturdy oak that stretches everywhere. The witness box, the jury benches, the judge's bench, the counsel's row, upon which James's barrister—a stout, somewhat formidable woman called Angela Regan—and the prosecuting QC, a Ms. Woodcroft, are piling lever arch file after lever arch file of evidence.

Her husband will stand trial for rape. She tastes the squat word, ugly like the offense itself. She knows it is happening, and yet, despite the reality forcing its way upon her as she stares down at him in the dock, as she drinks in the details of the court, the patrician gaze of the judge—who, in her normal life, she could imagine talking to at a drinks party—it still doesn't make sense.

He is innocent. Of course he is innocent. She knows that, has known it ever since that terrible Tuesday when he was arrested. She knows all the flaws in his personality, and he could never be capable of this. So how has the situation escalated this far? She thinks of recent party investigations, one presided over by a lawyer who'd been at school with James and Tom, the other by a friend from Oxford—men who could provide a patina of independence and still guarantee the right conclusion—and she wonders why that couldn't have happened in this case. Tom

owes him. Oh, how he owes him. But once the police were involved, even the prime minister's close friendship, those ties that
have bound them for more than thirty years, haven't been tight
enough to protect him.

"So if we can agree on that week in April?" James's QC, Ms.
Regan, cuts through her thoughts. Her voice, with its Belfast
accent, an almost masculine gravel. She and the judge are referring to "the housekeeping"—as if James's case is something to be
tidied away.

The hearing seems to be coming to an end. There is a date set
for April, bail is confirmed, and now, John Vestey, James's solicitor, is pushing back his seat and allowing himself to smile as he
whispers something to the QC.

Sophie stares up at the ceiling as they gather their documents
and the court clerk asks them to "be upstanding." It is high and
formed of eighty-one opaque glass panels. She counts, trying to
impose order: a neat nine by nine. The sky is a thick grey, bland,
oppressive, uninviting, and a blur of a bird flutters above it, a dark
smudge mocking the humans below—mocking her husband,
granted bail but not granted any real freedom. The limpid light
barely filters through and she craves sunshine and openness, lush
green fields and the quiet contentment of an empty mind.

April means they have more than four months of this limbo,
but now she just wants to get on with it. To put an end to this
encroaching sense of dread. She has already had six torturous
weeks in which to prepare herself and to consider and reconsider
her options. Six weeks of long runs along the Thames, and fren-

zied gym sessions that exhaust her body but not her mind. Long enough to assess and reassess her relationship and to ask herself: what do I really want here?

The answer she has fumbled towards—for nothing is a certainty now, nothing has been certain since that terrible evening in October—is that she wants to keep her family intact. She wants James. Despite the humiliation he has heaped on her, her anger at his infidelity and at his selfishness in putting them through this, she still wants to be with her husband. She has never doubted his innocence, so why would she not be with him?

She needs him, of course, and sometimes she hates herself for this dependency. Perhaps it is hardwired into her DNA? This need to hold on to her man, a feeling she knew acutely as a student when she guessed, of course she guessed, that he was unfaithful, whatever he chose to think. Or perhaps it developed when she saw the impact of her father's infidelity, not least the financial insecurity that came when Max left Ginny just before her fiftieth birthday. All three of his daughters had left home and so there was little financial recompense despite her choosing to be his wife as her career. Her mother claimed to be perfectly happy, but the former rectory was sold and she had downsized to a cottage in Devon. Her life was more emotionally stable—with none of those heightened periods of self-loathing that had occurred every time Max had found another woman and that had characterized Sophie's childhood—but she had lost her home, her social life, and her status. Somewhat reclusive, she lived alone, with her dogs: a black Labrador and a liver-colored springer spaniel.

Sophie doesn't want that. She is too young to dedicate herself to her children or to become a country-living eccentric. Nor does she want to become the sort of woman her friends shy away from—the attractive divorcée. Never invited to dinner parties for fear she can't be trusted with their husbands. As if her own ex-husband's infidelity were contagious or her neediness, and a ruthlessness about remarrying, clung like a musky sexuality.

Perhaps it would be easier if she had some sort of a career. But she didn't go back to her job as a junior editor in children's publishing after having Emily, the childcare eating up most of her salary; James, whose mother had never worked, more than happy for her to focus on their babies and him. She suspects that was a mistake. Children's literature was the one thing that had interested her in her degree. She had even written a dissertation on the use of menace in Narnia, exploring Lewis's use of the priapic faun myth and the theme of abduction. Incredible to think she could write about such a thing. She had briefly hoped that she might stumble upon the next J. K. Rowling, but then she had drifted into preschool literature where the only jeopardy was the difficulty of pulling on an odd sock or of finding a lost dinosaur, and it was hard to justify leaving her baby in a nursery to edit such things.

Besides, marriage and a family were what she had always wanted. When she was a little girl, she repeatedly painted pictures of herself in a wedding dress. A husband—and a good-looking, high-achieving husband—was on her wish list along with children and a period property with stables for horses and a vast walled garden. It was what she had experienced in her childhood and what she was brought up to aspire to. Well, she has achieved two of the three.

Even at Oxford, finding a husband had been a priority. Perhaps it shouldn't have been. She looks at photographs of herself then and wonders why she wasted so much time worrying about being alone and obsessing about holding on to James? She was quite a catch, but then he had finished with her at the end of her first year and they didn't see each other for seven years. And she had managed. There were other boyfriends—kind, good-looking, fun—whom she had finished with when it was clear they weren't husband material. There were even periods, a couple of months on two occasions, when she was on her own, and she had coped with it.

But she hadn't liked it, and if possible, she doesn't want to have to manage again. James has been her priority for too long. A boyfriend and then husband whom she knows other women covet, but who chose her, and who has been faithful throughout their marriage before this blip—this terrible, destructive thing that has threatened to rip their marriage apart. Hearing Olivia giving evidence is the thing she fears the most. Having to listen to that bitch detail the *event* and hear her describe their relationship before this happened—for she fears she will be led through all of this by James's barrister—how they met, where they first kissed, how frequently they had sex, whether this was a proper relationship (a five-month affair, as James had said) rather than a hurried, violent fumble, an uncharacteristic one-off.

James's defense, of course, is that this was consensual sex: sex

Olivia agreed to, and which they both sought despite his knowing it was morally reprehensible. "Classic woman scorned. A love
affair that went wrong," as Chris Clarke said in the early days.

This isn't rape, but neither was it about love, and it infuri-
ates her that it might be dressed up as this. This—and she thinks
she knows her husband well enough to understand this—was all
about sex.

Of course, she has made James tell her all about it. It was
John Vestey, his solicitor, who suggested it. Better that there be no
shocks in court, that, if she comes—as Chris Clarke thinks she
should, as she knows she might eventually have to—she will be
forearmed, forewarned.

And so he has told her the facts of their affair. Where. When.
Why. How many times. "I see," she had said, trying to keep her
voice calm. "And what about what happened in the lift?" The
temptation to scream about the fucking lift was almost overwhelming, but she stayed in control, as she always did. She and
her children—they were her children at the moment, not his—
needed her to stay calm. She imagined a veneer of serenity encasing her, a hard, impenetrable varnish.

She hated listening to the answers—his calm assertion that it
had been a moment of passion, a madness though entirely consensual—but she made herself sit there, fury wedged tight in her
chest. Her eyes burned but she was too angry to cry. She didn't
ask him if he loved Olivia or if Olivia had ever thought she loved
him. She pretended the question was irrelevant but, the truth was,
she didn't want to hear.

# TWELVE
## KATE

The courtroom is quiet. Quivering with the weighted anticipation that comes in the second before a Wimbledon player serves for the championship or a fly-half lines up a match-winning kick that will win the rugby world cup.

We have gone through the administration—the choosing of the jury; the organization of our work desks; the last-minute horse-trading between myself and the defense barrister, Angela Regan, so we agree on what can and can't be brought as evidence and so there will be no further disclosures at this eleventh hour. We have coughed and shuffled and sought to endear ourselves to the judge's clerk, Nikita, a young Asian woman, who, by virtue of her closeness to the judge, is one of the most important people in the room. We, with our juniors—Tim Sharples and Ben Curtis, who have done some of the background work, the drafting of statements and liaising with solicitors, and who sit beside us—have marked out our territories, physically, intellectually, and legally, as carefully as tomcats out on the prowl.

His Lordship, Judge Aled Luckhurst, QC, has spoken to the jury, explaining their responsibility in judging this case. The man being tried, he reminds them, is a high-profile individual whom they may recognize from the newspapers. There are a couple of blank faces at this—the young black guy in the back row, and a grey-haired wisp of a woman dressed as if the past three decades have passed her by entirely—but most of the jurors brighten at this news. Fresh and alert on this Monday morning at the start of their two weeks' jury service, they know full well that James Whitehouse is a junior minister in Her Majesty's Government, although they may not have known, or cared, about his title or role. What they do know is that he is the politician who is accused of raping a colleague in a House of Commons lift. They watch him shrewdly. Does he look like a rapist? What does a rapist look like? He looks less like a politician than one of the new breed of top public-school actors.

They have struck the jackpot in the lottery of jury service. Short of a trial involving a television celebrity or a gruesome murder, they could not have landed a more interesting or gossip-worthy case. But His Lordship suggests they should be impervious to this fact. "We hear a lot about rape at the moment in parliament and the papers," he intones, his voice more patrician than ever. "We all have prejudices and you must make sure you do not let prejudice, preconceived ideas, or conjecture influence you in the least." He pauses, letting his words hit home, and, though he has said this over a hundred times before, the formality of his language, and the authority he exudes—through his wig, his voice, his position high on the bench on his throne—creates an intensely solemn moment. No one seems to breathe, no paper rustles. "This case must be tried solely accord-ing to the evidence."

He pauses and there is that heavy anticipation, that frisson of apprehension and excitement. You can see the enormity of what they are being asked to do weighing them down. A young Asian man stares, eyes widening; a woman in her thirties looks stricken with fear. His Lordship elaborates, explaining that though they may have read about the case in the newspapers or on the Inter-net, they are not to do so from this point. Nor, and he looks at them down his nose, over half-moon glasses, are they to conduct their own research. Most importantly, they are not to discuss the case outside the jury room, not even with family and friends. He smiles here, for he is a very human judge, one whom I admire and the jury will grow to like; in his early fifties and so not one of the judiciary who seems divorced from the real world, even if he refers to 'the Internet' as if he regards it with distrust. I suspect he knows more about the net than many of the jurors. He recently presided over a lengthy fraud trial of two City bankers, and be-fore that, the trial of a pedophile ring that met in an Internet chat room. He knows all about the work of the Criminal Internet Retrieval Unit, which can unearth documents apparently erased from hard drives, and though he may not use WhatsApp and Snapchat, himself—preferring to sing in a Bach choir and grow orchids in his spare time—he knows exactly how they work.

The jurors smile back at him and nod, these twelve good men, though seven are women. A jury that's not ideal, as women are more likely to acquit a personable man for rape. Two or three are making notes: the rotund man in suit and tie on the far right of the front bench, whom I suspect will become the jury fore-man; and two of the women, both in their thirties, whose gazes flit from the defendant to the judge. An Essex boy—goatee, gelled quiff, cable cardigan, impressive tan—stares at the man in the dock behind me, a hint of menace simmering just below the surface. I look down at my notes, hands soft in my lap, and wait for my moment to come.

With a nod from the judge, I stand, positioning myself with my head up and my body at ease. My left hand holds my opening speech, at which I will barely glance, my right a disposable foun-tain pen with purple ink, my tiny act of individuality to counter the innumerable conventions of the court. I won't need this pen for my speech but it and my sheaf of paper are props to prevent me gesticulating wildly. The last thing I must do is fidget and risk distracting the jury or irritating the judge.

I hold the judge's gaze and then turn to the jurors and make eye contact with them all. I am going to speak to these people, concentrating on wooing them above anyone else. Like a lover intent on seduction, I will use the tenor and tone of my speech and the way in which I hold their attention to persuade them. I will use every trick in the book.

Because on this opening day, everything is unfamiliar and disorientating for these jurors: the wigs, the gowns, the language that could come from an eighteenth-century textbook—*my learned friend; Your Lordship, if I may interject? An issue of disclosure? Well, there it is. I am mindful to suggest an adjournment.* Mens rea. *The burden of proof.*

By tomorrow, they will be used to the canteen, will know where to go to the loo, and how long they will have for a cigarette break. They will realize how hard they will have to concentrate—will agree that, as the judge says, "five hours a day is quite enough for all of us." By then, they will have understood the legal definition of rape and the concept of consent and their eyes will no longer widen, their bodies freeze in surprise when words like penis, penetration, oral, and vagina are used.

But for now, they are keen pupils at the start of the school year—in polished shoes and smart uniforms; with new folders and pencil cases; excited and apprehensive about what the week will entail. And I will settle them in, will reassure them that we can do this together, that they will understand the terminology as well as the magnitude of what the British justice system is asking them to do. I won't bamboozle them with law. Most crimes center around dishonesty, violence, and lust—the last two in full play here. Juries sometimes surprise me with the astuteness of their questions and they will be fully capable of understanding the question at the heart of this trial: at the point of penetration, did James Whitehouse understand that Olivia Lytton did not consent to sex?

I begin to speak, still ignoring the man in the box behind me, whose eyes I imagine boring through my black gown, my waistcoat, my tailored shirt, and into the soul of me, but taking heart from the fact that his wife, whom we had thought would be unfailingly supportive, is not in the public gallery high above the court. My voice is low and reassuring, caressing the words, and only interjecting a note of sorrow and indignation when strictly necessary. I reserve my anger for my closing speech. I may need it then. For now I will be calm and steady. And this is how I start:

"This case is centered on an event that took place between two individuals. James Whitehouse, who you see behind me in the dock, and a young woman called Olivia Lytton.

"Mr. Whitehouse, as His Lordship has said, may look familiar. He is a member of Parliament, and until he was charged with this offense, a junior minister in the government. He is married with two young children, and Ms. Lytton was his parliamentary researcher who started working for him in March of last year.

"By May, the two of them had embarked on an affair, despite his being married. It was a consensual relationship and Ms. Lytton believed she was very much in love. The relationship ended on October sixth when Mr. Whitehouse told her he needed to be with his family. And that might have been that. Except that on October thirteenth, a week after their affair finished, they had sexual intercourse once again in a lift off the committee corridor in the heart of the House of Commons.

"There is no dispute that this event took place. Both sides acknowledge that. What is in dispute is the nature of it. Was this, as the Crown submits, something sinister—an act forced upon Ms. Lytton by the defendant? Was it, in fact, a rape? Or was it, as the defense will submit, an act of passion, a frenzied bout of lovemaking by two individuals caught up in the moment?

"You will hear evidence from both sides, but for you to reach this verdict you must agree on three things. One, did penetration by a penis take place? The answer is yes. Neither side disputes this.

Two, at the point of penetration, did Ms. Lytton consent? And, three, at the point of penetration, was Mr. Whitehouse aware that Ms. Lytton did not consent?"

I pause, push my heavy-rimmed glasses up my nose, then look at the jury, managing eye contact with each and every one of them, trying to impress upon them that they must concentrate but also reassure them that they can do this. I smile as if to say that this is simple.

"It really is no more complicated than that."

# THIRTEEN

## KATE

### 25 APRIL 2017

Day two and Olivia Lytton—"the complainant" in the language of the court, the "blonde mistress" as she was once described by the *Sun*—enters the witness box. The jury falls quiet, for my opening was the warm-up. Olivia is the main event, as far as we are all concerned.

A couple of the women stare at her, eyes narrowed. The elderly woman, who had looked as if she had no knowledge of the case yesterday, is peering at her through wire-rimmed glasses, and one of the thirtysomethings—straightened hair, heavy brows, foundation troweled so that her face is an orangey-pink—is perfecting a scowl. She is one of the women who have been glancing at the defendant in the dock as if she cannot quite believe that he is there, almost as if she is starstruck. I keep my gaze neutral, and when she catches my eye, give her a bland, businesslike smile.

Olivia looks terrified. Her eyes glimmer, the possibility of tears not far off, and her skin has an unnatural pallor as if her spirit and not just her blood has been drained. When I met her in the witness room yesterday, she spoke clearly and quickly, betraying her intelligence, her anxiety, and a simmering anger. She was brittle, holding her body stiffly like a fragile twig about to break.

"The odds are against us, aren't they?" she had asked, rattling off some statistics about conviction rates in a direct challenge.

"We've got a strong case and I aim to persuade the jury he's guilty," I said, looking her in the eye and trying to convey the strength of my determination—not just the CPS's—to acquire a conviction.

She smiled weakly, her mouth twisting to one side, a look of sad resignation that said: *But that's not enough, is it?* She's a Cambridge graduate and not stupid. But you don't need to be clever to acquire her knowledge. Being raped will soon erode your belief in fairness and justice and being treated with respect.

In court, though, there is no hint of such brutal awareness, and she looks the picture of innocence, or at least more innocent than you might imagine a young woman in her late twenties who has embarked on an affair to appear. She is wearing a simple shift dress with a Peter Pan collar. I wondered if this was pushing it too far, but it works well. She's sufficiently slim to pull off the androgynous, waif-like look, and it has desexualised her body. Those small breasts—bitten and grabbed, the Crown will submit—are swamped by navy fabric, her long legs obscured by the stand. No glimpse of anything that could be perceived as overtly, tantalizingly sexual here.

James Whitehouse can't see her, of course. The stand is cordoned off so that she can be seen by the jury, the judge, and counsel but not by the defendant. There's a move towards using video evidence of vulnerable witnesses in sexual assault cases; the complainant's testimony relayed in grainy black-and-white images that flicker and jump like a crudely edited amateur video as it lurches between the disturbing and the mundane. Olivia could also be questioned via video-link, but has bravely agreed to give evidence in court. That way, the jury can sense the full trauma of the ordeal, will catch each intake of breath, spot her shoulders shake. And though it will be distressing and might seem cruel, it is in the spaces between her words—the silences that swell as she fumbles for a tissue or responds to His Lordship's suggestion that she has a sip of water—that her story will emerge most clearly. It is through this vivid and compelling evidence that we have the best hope of convicting him.

I watch the jurors watching her now, assessing her dress, the shine of her hair, trying to read into her expression—distinctly apprehensive, though she is trying so hard to be brave. She catches my eye and I smile, hoping to convey my reassurance, to let her know that she will survive this, that it will be bearable if not OK. I know she is preparing to relive the most horrific event of her life with all its intense shame, anger, and fear. It takes real courage to do this, to stand up in court and accuse someone you once loved of this vicious crime, and she may feel guilt at this apparent betrayal. I imagine her palms pricking with sweat, her underarms growing damp as the court clock ticks, regular and insistent, marking the silence. She is about to reveal herself as emphatically as if she were cut to the bone.

I wonder if she is thinking of him behind the screen, if she imagines his gaze focused in her direction. She sounds intensely nervous. Her voice, that of a Home Counties Sloane, so quiet that when she confirms her name I have to ask her to speak up.

"Olivia Clarissa Lytton," she says, more firmly, and I smile and turn to the jury. Ms. Orange Face's eyebrows have shot up. Yes, we all know it's a ridiculously posh name, but don't hold that against her. Rape, like domestic violence, happens across all classes, could happen to each and every one of us.

"Ms. Lytton, I am going to ask you some questions and we are going to take things slowly. Now, if you could just keep your voice up a little?" I try to settle her in, maintaining eye contact and smiling encouragement, trying to make her comfortable. It's important. An uneasy witness won't tell their story well and there's little worse than a witness with a suddenly blank mind.

I phrase my questions simply and ask them one at a time, leading on things like date, location, time, and names, but otherwise allowing her to talk about the events at her own speed and in her own words. I develop a rhythm: question; answer; question; answer. Maintaining an even tempo as if we were going for a gentle afternoon's walk and a single fact was being thrown down with each step. When did you start working for Mr. Whitehouse? In March. And what was your role in his office? Did you enjoy it? And what did that entail? Short, easy questions that are uncontentious and allow me to lead her a little, because they are not in dispute, and Angela Regan, a formidable advocate, will not need to bluster and interject. "And I think that when Mr. Whitehouse gained his ministerial job, you

still worked for him in his Commons office? Yes, that's right?"
And so we go on.

We hear a little about the long hours she was expected to
work and the general culture within this and the departmental
office. They all respected Mr. Whitehouse: the civil servants calling him "minister," though he preferred "James."

"Was he friendly?"

"Yes. But not overly so."

"Did you socialize together?" I give her a smile.

"Patrick and Kitty—the staff in the private office—and I
would sometimes go for a drink, but James never did."

"And why was that?"

"He had a heavy workload or he would say he needed to go
home to see his family."

"His family . . ." I pause. Let the fact that he is a married
man with two young children just hang in the air. "But all that
changed, didn't it?" I go on.

"Yes."

"On May sixteenth, you did go for a drink together."

"Yes."

"I think you'd been for a drink with friends earlier?" I pause
and smile to reassure her that I am not revealing anything shocking. We all go for the odd drink, my demeanor and my calm,
no-nonsense tone says.

We establish that she had a couple of gin and tonics with
former colleagues from the Conservative Central Office at the
Marquis of Granby, and that, feeling "a little light-headed," she

went back to the Commons, just before 10 p.m., to pick up a forgotten gym bag. And it was while she was walking through New Palace Yard that she met James Whitehouse. "That's marked A on the first map in your folders. The outside space between Portcullis House and Westminster Hall," I tell the jury, holding a document up.

There is a rustling of papers, an increase in interest on the jurors' faces as they open their ring binders of evidence and search for the map. Everyone loves a map, even though there's no real need for anyone to look at one at the moment. But I want the jurors to visualize Olivia and James meeting at this point they see marked with an X on a map in their ring binders. They need to get used to the physical layout of the Commons—a labyrinth of back passages and secret corridors that lends itself to illicit meetings, both political and sexual. I want to plant the seed of this idea now.

"And what happened next. Did you speak to him?" I ask.

"Yes," Olivia says, and her voice wobbles. I look at her sharply. She can't turn flaky now. We're not close to the meat of the evidence. I smile encouragingly though my smile contains a hint of steel.

"I saw him coming towards me so I said hello and I stumbled a bit. I think I was nervous. The House wasn't sitting and I hadn't expected to see him. I was just rushing to collect my bag."

"And what happened, when you stumbled?"

"He helped me. He sort of held my upper arm to steady me and then he asked if I was all right, something like that."

"And had he ever helped you like that, held your upper arm before?"

"No. He'd never touched me. It was all quite proper in the office."

"Did he carry on touching your arm?"

"No. He dropped it once I'd gotten my shoe back on."

"And what happened then?" I continue. Any slightly tipsy young woman might scurry away, but that's not what happened here. I can't lead her on that, though. I must wait for her to place the next piece in the jigsaw of her story.

She smiles and her voice quivers at the memory.

"He asked me for a drink."

———————

I lead her on. Question; answer; question; answer. Maintaining the rhythm. Keeping things slow, even, and pleasant; pacing my speed to match the movement of the judge's pen.

We confirm that the relationship started, and that, after a week, it was consummated. Ms. Orange Face narrows her eyes further. *They had sex, yes. That is what this case is about. Get over it.* I don't convey this irritation, of course. I remain serene, my gaze moving from one juror to another, but not settling on any of them for any length of time. I am too busy drawing out my chief witness, who has grown in confidence. She stands more at ease now, her voice no longer so high-pitched.

I don't want her to go into details of this relationship. That will only open her up to Angela questioning her about their previous sexual history, something, the Crown submits, that's totally irrelevant. We have agreed on a series of set words to convey that it happened, and now it is time to move on to what happened in the lift.

But Olivia resists keeping it this factual and clear-cut.

"I didn't want it to end," she adds, when I ask her to confirm the relationship was finished on sixth October. Her voice drops to a near whisper. A curtain of hair swings in front of her face.

I don't ask why this was, and am preparing to move on, but she seems determined to be heard on this.

She tilts her head up, her hair swishing against her cheek. Her eyes are moist, but her voice rings out, clear in the simplicity of her statement.

"I didn't want it to end because I was in love with him."

# FOURTEEN

## SOPHIE

### 25 APRIL 2017

Sophie is shaking. In the sanctity of her home, she has begun shaking; her body betraying her in a way it would never do in public, limbs knocking together, jangling, undermining her habitual self-control.

Her stomach falls out of her as soon as she reaches the downstairs loo, handbag thrown on the floor, its contents splayed across the Edwardian tiles—lipstick, purse, diary, mobile phone. The phone's face shatters with the sudden drop: a slim line running in a neat diagonal then dispersing into tiny shards just held by the cover's tension. Gathering the items together, she traces the line with her finger, entranced and unthinking, then winces at the pain caused by a tiny sliver of glass.

She begins to weep, her shoulders hunched around her, the sobs muted until she reaches her bedroom, for Cristina might be in her room on the next floor and Sophie cannot bear her gentle, insistent support. The au pair has been so eager to show her sympathy. Those tremulous brown eyes threatened to overflow with tears as she left with the children for school this morning, and

Sophie wanted to scream at her to pull herself together, to show some self-restraint in front of the children as she was having to do, as she continually had to do. Where was the self-absorption she had expected from a teenage girl and that they had experienced with Olga, their previous au pair, who would empty the freezer of Ben & Jerry's, scooping the ice cream straight from the tub into her vast, gaping mouth, and then put the near-empty carton back?

Cristina has witnessed the whole unfolding of this hideous mess: was at home that night, back in October, when the story broke, has lived with them through the door-stepping by the paparazzi that first terrible weekend, and even—bless her—opening the front door and lying on her behalf.

"Mrs. Whitehouse and the children are not in," she told one photographer who was more insistent than any of the others, hanging around after James had gone into Westminster on the Monday and laying siege to them in their own home. And she and Emily and Finn had hidden upstairs in Em's bedroom at the back of the house as this slight eighteen-year-old, with her charming French accent, deviated from the instructions she had given her—"Just tell them we're not here then close the door politely but firmly"—and began to beseech them, her voice spiralling in indignation. "Pleez. Pleez. Mrs. Whitehouse eez not here. Pleez. Can you just leave them alone?"

She listens, now, a sob in her throat. "Cristina?" she calls up to her bedroom. Silence. Her body aches with the relief, the utter relief, of being on her own. She shuts the bedroom door and leans against her radiator, feeling the warmth seep into her back, pulling her knees up, and holding them tight towards her, as if she is being held tight and warmed; as if, she acknowledges as she gives herself up to the shaking that courses through her body so that her knees knock against one another uncontrollably again, she is back in the womb.

She lets herself sit like this for a good five minutes, the tears tracing lines down her cheeks, though her sobs remain muted. Having spent forty years learning to control her emotions she feels self-conscious, and yet the relief of letting go! She reaches for a tissue and blows her nose noisily, swiping at her wet cheeks then risking looking in the mirror to find her face blotched, red, streaked with mascara. She looks a mess. She walks to the bathroom, splashes herself with cold water, and reaches for the cleanser. Laboriously sweeps away the detritus of the morning—mascara, foundation, eyeliner, fear, guilt, shame, and this intense, gnawing sorrow—with a large flat cotton-wool pad. Pats her skin dry, applies moisturizer. Stares blankly at a face that is no longer the one she knows, or rather, one she would rather not recognize. Begins the process of constructing it—and herself—once more.

She had gone to the court in disguise and left just after Olivia said that she was in love with her husband; after she prompted a little hush of sympathy, some of the jurors looking rapt as her voice, fraught with emotion, rang out around the court.

James didn't know she was going to be there. After the pre-trial hearing, she told him she wouldn't attend. That she couldn't bear to sit, hearing the evidence, whatever Chris Clarke might deem necessary for his political rehabilitation after the case had come to an end.

"You can't not stand by him!" The director of communications had been incandescent, spitting tiny globules of phlegm.

"I am standing by him but I don't have to sit there, lapping it all up," she had said. "Besides, if I'm there, it will just mean another picture." Chris, his face flushed an unhealthy red, had grunted and conceded, with visible reluctance, that she had a point.

She was surprised by the intensity of her fury and by the inner strength that surged up inside her at their insistence. "The trouble with women," James once told her, making the sort of sweeping generalization he would never make in front of female colleagues, but did at home, "is that they lack the courage of their convictions. Mrs. Thatcher aside, they don't have our self-belief." Well, she had stood firm on this. James was disappointed. That was his word, said with cold eyes, and a certain sanctimony, although what he had to be sanctimonious about, and here a surge of anger reignited, she did not know, but, of course, he respected her decision. How could he not? He loved her; wouldn't want her to suffer any further humiliation. And perhaps, in the end, he was relieved. For just as he had refused to see her in the full throes of labor for fear it would affect their sex life, perhaps he thought it would kill it entirely if she had to hear every detail of his relationship with another woman.

Because how could any relationship survive hearing the most intimate details of another like this? You can survive infidelity if you can convince yourself, time and again if necessary, it need not be repeated. She knew this because her mother had lived with her father, because James had been repeatedly unfaithful when they first went out. She had refused to acknowledge it, ignoring the smirks of those girls who thought they might drag him from her, never once confronting him—for that would force him to make a choice between her and them. And you can survive repeated infidelities, she knew, if you can tell yourself that these affairs are devoid of emotion. That they are purely physical and that it is you, and only you, whom your husband loves.

But can your marriage survive if you are forced to listen to every detail of the liaison? If that relationship is picked apart like roadkill ripped by carrion, and if your marriage is then put under the spotlight—its flaws, its robustness implicitly questioned and found wanting after all? If you learned that another woman loved your husband, and, worse, that she believed *he* loved *her,* or at least, that he had intimated he felt something? For a five-month affair with a colleague, with whom he works closely and whom he admits he admired, is not a one-night stand. Is not entirely devoid of emotion, not if it's conducted by someone like James, who can be ruthless, yes—and she thinks of his cocktail eyes; his tendency to analyze a room and assess who will be the most interesting, the most useful, and to extricate himself from less helpful conversations—but who can also be so very tender.

Could her marriage survive her listening to all this? Her hearing that it wasn't just her whom he made love to, really made love to, or that the sex—even the rough sex, for that was how she thought of this allegation—reflected the sex that she had had with him? That there were distinct parallels between the way in which he kissed, sucked, tweaked, played with them both and that the most intimate part of her relationship was not as unique as she had always thought it? That their relationship—the thing that she had always put first, before *even,* and this shamed her now, her children—was not as special as she had once thought?

The risk of discovering this is what made her dig her heels in and insist she stay away. That and the inevitable humiliation, the prospect of being scrutinized by judge and jurors and those in the public gallery—a peculiar mix of law students, foreign tourists, and day trippers who have discovered that they might find more compelling drama here in this courtroom, than at home on their television screens.

She has always been lucky, someone whose life has been as bright and solidly precious as a fat gold ingot. Her middle name is Miranda—she who must be admired—and she has taken it for granted that this is the most apt of names. But in the past six months, her luck has deserted her and the admiration she has long accepted has been replaced by an almost gleeful pity. The envy she is used to, which peaked when James was elected and started taking the children to school once a week, has curdled into faux sympathy and outright suspicion. The coffee-morning invitations have dried up, and she was asked to leave the PTA ball committee in case the substantial sums fundraised petered out. The stream of requests for playdates with her children has abruptly stopped. And if this has sapped her self-esteem, corroded her spirit, hurt far more than she has admitted, then how much worse to have to endure this humiliation in court?

And yet, when it came to it, she could not keep away. The desire to hear what happened and to understand what her husband was up against became physically overwhelming—a sharp pain to be coughed from her chest, that could not be contained. And so she did something entirely uncharacteristic: pulled a wool beanie on her head, dressed down in trainers and jogging bottoms, and thrust on the horn-rimmed glasses which James despised and which she only wore when she made the long drive to Devon. Dressed like this, she had gone there and hidden herself away.

Unlike the pretrial hearing, when she had marched to the court entrance, clutching James's hand and braving the throng of photographers, she slipped straight to the queue for the public gallery and waited with a couple of broad-shouldered, bomber-jacketed black youths who talked of their friend's previous stretch and predicted his next sentence in language she could only guess at. "A four, man?" "Nah, a two."

The larger cracked his knuckles and bounced on his toes, testosterone and adrenaline firing from him, his energy so contagious she couldn't help watching, even though she was trying to avoid their attention.

"Yo' phone."

She started as he pointed to her electronic device, his voice a disarmingly sexy bass, his gaze not provocative but serious.

"Yo can't take yo' phone into court. Yo need to leave it outside." And she, having forgotten, felt ashamed, for he was chivalry itself once she stopped behaving as if he was to be feared, and directed her to the travel agent down the street where you could leave your gadgets for a pound, and where, he told her enthusiastically, he had left his.

In the end, she only managed half an hour of listening to Olivia. Perched high in the public gallery with a group of American law students whose terrorism trial had been adjourned, she was unable to see her, though she knew her from the papers and from previous news footage: a tall, sylph-like figure, a blonde version of herself, or herself as she had been fifteen years ago.

She could hear her, though, and sensed her through every catch of her voice and through the jurors' reactions: intrigued, scandalized, and then sympathetic as she told of how she had fallen in love. And she had watched her husband, apparently forgotten in the dock, but listening intently to every word that Olivia said and occasionally taking a note that he would hand to his solicitor.

And then Olivia confirmed details of when their relationship had started and ended, and she remembered assuming that James was just working late. And suddenly, the air was oppressive and she was pushing past the American girls' long denimed legs and their big white sneakers, mouthing apologies as they glanced up at her, bemused. She was desperate not to be noticed by the court as she tried to open the oak door to the gallery silently, and managed to slip away.

She hailed a black cab on Ludgate Hill after retrieving her phone, and now she is here: safe back home. Her experiment in watching the case incognito apparently not discovered, but she is still filled with a profound sense of shame. She doesn't know how she can ever go back. How she can sit in court and listen as the evidence grows more explicit, the details more murky. For that is what she is going to have to confront, isn't it? The fact that her husband, her loving husband who adores their children and is almost universally admired, has been accused of something indecent; something abusive; something she does not want to hear. A rape, for goodness sake. The worst crime she can conceive of apart from murder, and something she cannot make fit with her knowledge of him.

She starts to throw clothes into a holdall. Ridiculous, she knows, and yet the flight-or-fight reflex is kicking in properly. She cannot stay here, in her tasteful bedroom with its muted greys and whites, its Egyptian cotton with a high thread count and its touches of cashmere, its clean, clear surfaces for what James calls her unguents and potions, and her collection of jewelry—pared down, with the heirlooms from her grandmother hidden away. "Let's have a bedroom like a hotel room," her husband once said, making a rare foray into her realm, their home's interior design. "It will feel more decadent. More naughty." And he had snaked a hand up the front of her shirt. Now she wonders which hotel rooms he was thinking of and with whom he spent time there.

She races to the children's rooms; heart jamming away, a tight hammer striking against her rib cage. Wrenches drawers open and empties them of jeans, tops, hoodies; pants and socks; pajamas; a couple of books; favorite soft toys. In the bathroom, she scoops up toothbrushes and toiletries, then Calpol, Benylin, ibuprofen. From the hall, three pairs of wellies, her walking boots, hats, gloves, waterproofs, waxed jackets. In the kitchen, children's water bottles, fruit, and the sort of contraband that is usually rationed: crisps, cereal bars, bags of sweets left over from parties, chocolate biscuits. At the fridge she pauses then unscrews a white wine bottle and very deliberately takes a large, hard swig.

By 3:30 p.m. she is parked in prime position outside the children's school, the nose of her car pointing westwards. The roads will become gridlocked in the run-up to rush hour and she wants to whisk them away. She checks herself in the mirror and notices that her eyes are alight with what she hopes Emily will interpret as excitement, but which she recognizes as adrenaline. In the lines crinkling at their corners—dehydrated from lack of sleep, roughened by crying—she can read only fear and pain.

Finn flies out first, his face breaking into a smile as he barrels into her legs, her small ball of passion.

"Why's Cristina not picking us up?" Emily, bag knocking against her ankles, is more circumspect.

"Because I am." She smiles. "Come on, get in the car."

"Where's Daddy? How was his day in court?"

She pretends not to hear as she herds them into the four-by-four, negotiating a route through her one-time friends, those feline-eyed mummies who cannot help but look up, ears pricked, eyes glinting, as Emily's too-bright voice rings out, loud and clear.

"Not here, darling," she mutters, almost jogging to the car,

and resisting the temptation to be curt. She makes her ⟨
eyed. "Here we are. In we go then."

Her hands are shaking as she thrusts the key fob into th⟨
tion and starts the car; her pupils, caught in the mirror, are⟨
buttons. She has a distinct sense of observing herself, of kn⟨
ing, objectively, that she is too hyped to be embarking on a lo⟨
journey with two young children and yet realizing that she has t⟨
do it anyway. She takes a quick swig of a water bottle, the liquid
spilling down her chin in a wet beard, flicks the indicator, and
draws away from the curb.

A shining black tank of a car—all chrome bumper, gloss, and
anger—blares as she pulls in front of it. She swerves, narrowly
avoiding a crash, and holds up her hand in apology.

"Muuummm!" Emily's voice escalates into a cry. "I'm doing
my seat belt."

"I'm *sorry*." She is as close as she ever comes to shouting. Her
voice wavers. "I'm so very sorry, OK?"

The car thrums with silence.

"Mummy?" Finn asks at last, as they crawl onto the main ar-
tery out of West London and then up and away, leaving the tower
blocks and all uncertainty behind them. "Where are we going?"

She feels the tension begin to ease from her for a second because she has predicted this question and has prepared her answer.

"On an adventure," she says.

# FIFTEEN

## HOLLY

### 16 JANUARY 1993

The college library smelled of books. A smell that was dry and sweet, as if the scent of parchment had been distilled to that of clean, crisp straw. It didn't smell like a bookshop—a place in which the scent of the books was muddled by the rain on customers' coats or the fug that they brought with them: the tuna sandwich gobbled on entering the shop and quietly belched, or the beer, still warm on the breath, that had been swilled at the King's Arms moments before.

When Holly first entered the mid-seventeenth-century library, it was the scent of these books that struck her. A smell unmarred except by a hint of instant coffee that wafted from the chief librarian's sturdy pottery mug. Next, it was the books themselves, stretching from the thickly carpeted floor almost all the way up to the barrel-vaulted ceiling, its panels painted the delicate pale pink of a baby's fingernail and a soft, mint green, divided with gold, and studded at each intersection with a white ceiling rose.

There were ten shelves or more of these books, reaching all

the way up each bookshelf from the leather-bound encyclopedic tomes at the bottom to the paperback textbooks that you needed a wooden ladder to access—the struts creaking as you shifted your weight on the way to the top. There were sixteen bays in all, each lined with these shelves and divided into English literature; French, German, and Italian; Ancient Greek and Latin; philosophy, politics, and economics; geography; theology; music; history of art; law. History had its own college library as if the subject matter was so immense it could not be contained within these shelves. She didn't know if the chemists, biochemists, and mathematicians borrowed textbooks, but she rarely saw them here and imagined that most of their knowledge was gained not in such a quiet, studious space, but in the forensic environment of a lab.

It was early morning: eight thirty. One of her favorite times of the day, when the library was almost empty—only herself and the chief librarian, Mr. Fuller, a scurrying figure she had nicknamed Mr. Tumnus, after the faun in *The Lion, the Witch and the Wardrobe*, and who emanated tension if a student dared to talk loudly, or worse still, entered the library to find a friend, not a book. He liked her, though. She watched as he gave her a quiet nod and then busied himself with the set of small oak drawers in which the books were indexed—the authors alphabetized and then the titles. The university library, The Bod, had an electronic catalogue, but these things took time and there was no hurry here for such a system. Though the books were pristine, a soft layer of dust coated the screen of the library computer. Order was preserved by index cards. Some yellowed with the titles typed fifty years earlier, others handwritten. The system had worked for a hundred-plus years and there seemed no need for it to be altered. There was still a role for those small oak drawers.

The librarian trod briskly down the carpeted corridor to shelve returned books and to rearrange a pile pulled out overnight and then abandoned. But apart from the tread of his brogues and intermittent *tsks* at the apparent selfishness of the students, the library was silent. Just Holly and those tens of thousands of books.

She stretched out, enjoying the shaft of sunlight that streamed through the vast east-facing window beside her and dappled her notepad, motes of dust dancing in the brightness, the shadow of the tracery stonework demarcating her book. A staircase criss-crossed inside the windows of the college on the other side of the square, and she spied the smudge of a figure running down it and wondered, yet again, at the exquisite beauty of this place and at its mystery—all those lives, all those *stories* being played out alongside each other in libraries, dining rooms, and boat houses; bars and nightclubs; museums, gardens, even punts.

If university was a place of discovery then there were thousands of lives being reinvented or found: narratives written and rewritten; sexualities tried and discarded; political allegiances tested, altered, and abandoned over the length of an eight-week term.

The freshers who smiled proudly for their first formal group photo were not the same students who threw their mortarboards into the air and pelted one another with eggs and flour—some self-consciously, some with the sheer thrill of relief—as they left the Exam Schools, three years later. Life—intellectual, social, and sexual discovery—would have embraced them all.

And she was ready for all this. Already, just one term in, she could feel herself altering: her accent softening as if the warmer Oxfordshire climate was melting her lilting cadences; her self-belief increasing as she let her guard down, just a little, and allowed herself to believe that she had just as much of a right to be here as anyone else. The thought caught her short. Did she really believe that? Well, yes, just a bit. She still felt an imposter, but maybe others did, too? "I'm the token girl mathematician," Alison had admitted glumly, late one night, as she had pored over a textbook that might as well have been in Russian for all Holly could make of it, then drew a neat black line through her calculations. "Brought in to meet some gender quota." And then. "I feel such a fucking fraud."

Holly was happy here, though. Her chest constricted and swelled in one fat throb as the thought reverberated through her. At Oxford, she could be entirely herself. Particularly here, in this library, where the whole point was that she could immerse herself in this womb of books and no longer have to pretend that she wasn't clever. At school, she had been consistently bullied for being bright until she had shrunk in on herself, no longer offering answers to the teacher's questions; hunching her shoulders and fixing her eyes on the floor as if to make herself invisible. If there was a crime worse than being bright, it was failing to disguise the fact under layers of sarcasm and thick mascara. At her school, the overriding aim was to get a boyfriend, and being clever could only work against that.

And then, in the final year, with it known that she would apply for Oxford, she had become defiant, had begun to speak up again and to acknowledge her cleverness, though tentatively at first. This is who I am, she effectively said, every time she found herself raising a hand to respond to Mrs. Thoroughgood's questions on free will and determinism in *The Mill on the Floss* or on Bertha Rochester as Jane Eyre's doppelganger. She saw the end of school then, could count the remaining months and *smell* the freedom that would soon be hers; could sense the escape from the girlish cliques, the continual bitchiness, the insidious belief that if you weren't pretty or slim or wore a sufficiently short skirt or tucked in your tie in precisely the right way—skinny with the fat tongue thrust between the top second and third buttons, you had no worth. On the last day of her exams, she had stalked into the Shakespeare paper, her thighs rubbing together under her frumpishly pleated skirt, her tie unashamedly fat, and she had written her heart out. Her worst tormenter, Tori Fox, had asked how she had found it, and she still hadn't dared to tell the truth; hadn't risked confessing, "Actually, it was pretty easy." But when she had gotten her four straight As, they all knew.

She stood up to stretch and to glance out of the window again, at one of the finest views in Oxford. The Gothic tower of St. Mary's offset by the classical Radcliffe Camera; a thrusting phallus of a spire outshone by a rotunda, study trumping worship; self-containment beating self-aggrandizement, over and over again. Perhaps that was why she felt so content here in this spot on the west side of this cobbled square where she was surrounded by libraries with the square's center showcasing the prettiest of them all. All of this beauty and history and tradition existed to celebrate and facilitate studying. She need never feel apologetic about wanting to read a book—or be herself—again.

And so none of her social fears really mattered. She knew she would never be part of Sophie's clique, but perhaps it wasn't a huge issue. She had friends outside her college: those earnest, ambitious boys on the student paper, who talked of applying for work experience on broadsheets or at the BBC—perhaps had even already done so—and Alison, with whom she could down a pint of cider in the college bar, and who she knew still unaccountably liked her, even if she was too inhibited when she dragged her to the Park End Street nightclubs; her clothes wrong and her movements stilted; her body too gauche to really let herself go.

She was free of the fear of being deemed wanting for here, she was finally realizing, there were a few other people who were sufficiently different, enough for her to feel as if she could somehow fit in. For the first time in her life, or the first time since very early childhood, she belonged. And she could relax. The low-level anxiety that had coursed through her veins every day at school, and that had only ebbed away on the bus home, as she sought comfort in a Twix gobbled in a rush of relief at having survived another day, had disappeared and would only surface intermittently, when she sought Sophie out among her other friends. It was a new and completely wonderful feeling. This strong conviction. This sense of being happy and at ease.

# Sixteen

## Kate

### 26 April 2017

Day three and Olivia Lytton looks more as if she is dressed for a job interview. Gone is the Peter Pan collar; in its place a crisp white shirt and well-cut navy jacket and skirt. Her hair, which she repeatedly tucked behind her ear yesterday, has been held back with a nest of grips. The effect is to make her look both younger and less elegant. Her cheekbones are more pronounced. She is less attractive, more severe.

She is even paler this morning. I would guess that she has barely slept and her eyes are lit by an artificial brightness, powered by adrenaline and the bitter filter coffee bought from the court's canteen. Olivia's eyes have hardened. Ali, in a rare undiplomatic moment, once told me that no one could properly understand the pain of giving birth until they had experienced it. In the same way, Olivia could not hope to predict quite how terrifying giving evidence would be. Despite the court's best efforts to be gentle, I know of few chief witnesses in sexual offense cases who have managed to come through this experience unscathed.

The court is nearly full now. I rearrange my side of the bench, building a fortress with bundles of documents, neatly aligned pens, a jug and glass for water. I am defending myself with books and files, as the jury settles themselves into their now familiar positions and a clutch of journalists—not just the jaded court reporter from the news agency, with his shiny suit and greasy tie, but the safe hands from the broadsheets and tabloids—sidle onto the press benches and fling their pads down.

Jim Stephens from the *Chronicle* is here—an old-school hack fuelled by beer and fags, his face puce beneath that raven-black hair that perhaps comes from a bottle. One of the few who re-member working on Fleet Street when it was Fleet Street, it would be easy to dismiss him compared to the hungry graduate trainees working alongside him. But I read him; and I rate him.

For the third day, Sophie Whitehouse hasn't arrived.

"Done a runner," Angela Regan whispers, her mouth set in a line of condemnation. My junior, Tim Sharples, a languid fellow with a good line in black humor, catches my eye.

I look at the QC, sharply.

"Scarpered off to her mother's in Devon." Angela's tone is grim. This doesn't look good for her client: this pointed, con-tinual absence of his wife. I busy myself with searching for a document in a ring binder, double-checking out of a needless nervousness, biting back the trace of a smile that Angela, a street fighter of an opponent, must know is playing across my face.

And then there is a hush, which grows into a heavy cushion of silence. The rustles stop, and all I can hear is the rhythmic ticking of the clock. We are all poised. I stand, an actor on a stage, until His Lordship indicates that we should get started. I turn to Olivia. For it is time to draw her on, now, to tell the heart of her story.

"Can I take you back to October thirteenth?" I say, my voice moderate and reasonable. "The date in question. I think you were due to attend the Home Affairs Select Committee together?"

"Yes. James was due to give evidence on the new counter-extremism strategies we were about to start implementing."

"In everyday English, I think those are ways in which the government aims to stop potential terrorists?"

"Yes." She straightens. She is on safe territory here: civil-servant speak, which is uncontentious. "Normally this would be evidence given in private to the Intelligence Select Committee, but there was a slight turf war between the committee chairs."

"I think the meeting was first thing in the morning. So what time did you set off?"

"Just before nine. James was jittery and said that he wanted to talk to me over a coffee."

I push my glasses up my nose and turn to look at the jury. The officious, middle-aged man, his belly straining against his ironed shirt and a smart navy tie on today, smiles, anticipating my next question—for it is a courtly dance I am playing here and the jury is beginning to predict my every move.

"You say he was jittery? . . . Why was that?'

"There'd been an unfavorable comment piece in the *Times*. It was by a journalist he knew and rated. A contemporary from Oxford; he thought he liked him. It was quite poisonous, and he didn't seem able to laugh it off, like he usually did. He kept repeating the most damaging phrases, as if he couldn't shake them from his mind."

"I think we have the article in question here." I flip to the relevant page in my file. "I think you'll find it's document three in your bundle of evidence." A rustle of action and a frisson of excitement among the jury at being asked to do something. Frankly, I'm amazed the judge has ruled the article admissible; it's so potentially prejudicial. But I argued it is relevant because it prompted James Whitehouse's anger before the alleged rape and explains his state of mind.

"Here it is!" I hold the document in my left hand, brandishing it firmly and looking around for confirmation. "It's from the *Times* of that morning, October thirteenth, and it's written by a Mark Fitzwilliam. He's a comment writer on that paper. It's about the impact of the terror legislation, but the part we are interested in starts at the second paragraph, and you may think, constitutes an attack on the defendant."

I glance at Angela, but she lets this go, as discussed pretrial. We are all agreed the article is pretty bloody damning. I clear my throat. "If I may begin":

When James Whitehouse came into government, many hoped he would be a fresh broom to sweep aside some of our more draconian antiterror legislation. But the close personal friend of the prime minister, and long-standing member of his kitchen cabinet, has surpassed his predecessor by rampaging through our nation's civil liberties like a member of the Libertine Club intent on trashing an Oxford restaurant—smashing its windows; defacing its walls; soiling its carpet with magnum upon magnum of wasted, emptied champagne.

As a member of the notorious dining club, James Whitehouse was famed for his breathtakingly arrogant disregard of those who owned or worked in such establishments. Why should he care about the disruption, the grievance, the headache of righting the chaos he and his friends had wreaked when a fistful of fifty-pound notes would always provide a ready solution? Born with a silver spoon in his mouth, he had no insight into the effect of his behavior on those whose livelihoods he trashed. In the same way, this Old Etonian shows a blatant disregard for the impact of the antiterror legislation on law-abiding British Muslims that he champions now.

I pause. "You say he was 'a bit jittery'? Is it fair to say that this article also made him angry?"

"Your Lordship . . ." Angela rises, for I am leading the witness.

"I'm sorry, Your Lordship." I bow to the judge. "Let me rephrase the question. Could you describe Mr. Whitehouse's response to this article more fully?"

"He was angry," Olivia confirms. She deliberates, and I catch a glimpse of the thoughtful young woman who would have been destined for a good career before it was derailed by sex. "Short with me, but also somehow seeking reassurance. It was as if he had forgotten the distance that he'd put between us and wanted to recapture our closeness. It was clear that this had affected him sharply. He seemed vulnerable, for once."

"'It affected him sharply.' How could you tell this?"

"His body language was stiff: ramrod straight and I had to half-run to keep up with him. Usually he brushed off any criticism, but as we marched to the committee room, he kept quoting parts of it, as if it had really got under his skin."

"If I can stop you, what time was this?"

"At about nine fifteen. Normally, the minister would sweep in just before the start, so he didn't have to chat to the backbenchers unless he wanted to. And he didn't want to that morning. When he saw the committee members huddled together outside room fifteen, the Lloyd George room, and glancing at him as he arrived, he said something like, 'I can't deal with this,' and he charged off down the corridor in the other direction."

"That's towards the press gallery, to the east?" There is a rustle of the jurors' folders.

"Yes, that's right. It is."

I direct the jurors to the relevant map, another corridor stretching away from the central staircase and leading to our crime scene, for which they also have photographs: an unprepossessing, brown-carpeted lift.

"And what did you do when he charged off like this?"

"I followed him."

"You followed him." I pause, letting the fact sink in with the implication that she was just being a good employee, attentive to her minister. "He said, 'I can't deal with this,' stormed off, and you followed him." I tilt my head to one side, sympathetic. "Can you remember what he said?"

"He was still muttering under his breath and then he stopped by the door leading to the press gallery and the lift, and turned to me and said, 'I'm not breathtakingly arrogant, am I? Do you think I'm arrogant?'"

And Olivia stops abruptly, for she is like a runner who has been pushing herself to exceed her personal best and finds that she has surpassed herself and is breathless, her face flushed, her energy almost spent.

"And what did you say when he said that?" I keep my voice matter-of-fact, and glance down at my open file, as if the answer is of no particular significance.

"I said he could be ruthless when he needed to be. Cruel sometimes, even."

"And how did he respond?"

"He didn't like it. 'Cruel?' he said, and then, 'I'm sorry.'"

"And what did you say to that?" I ask, for we can all imagine how she felt—the jilted lover who finally receives the long-awaited apology.

"I said . . ." and her voice dips, but the court is quiet. We are all straining to capture her every word, and they are words that could damn her.

"I said that, sometimes, arrogance could be devastatingly attractive."

———

On we march through the evidence that could be construed as damaging. He flings open the door from the committee room corridor to the press gallery, stops outside the lift, presses the button, and she enters first.

"And what happened next?"

"We kissed. Well . . . we sort of collided."

"You sort of *collided*?"

"I suppose we both moved together at the same time."

"*You moved together at the same time.* There was a strong attraction there, then, although he had 'finished with' you, that was the phrase I think you used, just over a week earlier?"

"We had been involved for five months. . . . We had been lovers," and here she looks at me, a little defiant, and I wonder what she thinks of me; if she imagines me as a woman who has never known an irresistible sexual attraction—that melding of mouths and limbs, the jigsawing of bodies that shrinks one's world to just the two of you, and in those most intimate moments, makes the rest of the world disappear.

I smile, waiting for her to continue. For this is what the jury needs to hear to understand how she got herself into this situation in the first place. They need to sense her emotional confusion to appreciate that, despite feeling humiliated and bruised by his treatment, she could not fail to respond when the man she loved so passionately moved towards her for a kiss.

"You don't just switch off your feelings for someone when they finish with you. Not after that short a time. Not if you'd wanted it to continue," she says. "Or at least I don't. I still found him very attractive. I still loved him."

"Can you describe the kiss?" I need to push her on this.

She looks blank.

"Was it a chaste peck on the lips?"

"No." She looks at me, perturbed.

I smile. "Well, is there a word you might use to describe it?"

She looks embarrassed. "I suppose you would call it French kissing."

"French kissing?"

"You know. Passionate kissing, with tongues."

"So you kissed, with tongues, and can you remember what happened then?"

"His hands were all over me. Touching my breasts and my bottom . . ." She falters.

"And then?" I probe gently.

"Then he . . . he . . . He wrenched at the top buttons of my shirt to get into my bra . . . to my breasts."

I pause, letting the room take in her humiliation, the casual violence of the moment. Perhaps I seem cold, pushing her to relive it all, and yet I am not. I can imagine all too clearly and I want the jury to imagine what she felt then and what she is feeling now.

"Can we take this in stages. He was touching your breasts and bottom and *wrenched* your shirt to get into your bra. Did he get into it?"

"Yes." She is close to tears. "He grabbed one of my breasts—my left breast. Pulled it out of my bra and began to kiss and bite it . . ." She nods and swallows. "He kissed it quite savagely."

"What do you mean by that?"

"I mean that he gave me a love bite, but quite a harsh one."

"I think you received a bruise as a result, just above your left nipple?"

She nods, close to weeping.

"In fact, we have a photograph which you took on your iPhone later that week. It's photograph A in your bundles," I tell the jury, and I hold an A4-sized photo up for them to see. It shows a fat greengage of a bruise, two centimeters by three—a yellowy-brown by this stage, less angry than the reddish-black it must have been in the immediate aftermath of the attack.

"If you look closely on the left of the bruise," I tell the jury, my tone ever so matter of fact, "you can see a slight indentation. The defense's case is that this is a usual discoloration on a bruise but the Crown submits . . ." and here I pause and shake my head ever so slightly, "the Crown submits that they are caused by teeth."

I wait for the inevitable gasp. The jurors don't disappoint. Several glance at the dock and Essex Boy eyeballs James Whitehouse clearly, chocolate eyes not moving from his face.

"And where were you when this happened?" I go on, for I must continue before Olivia loses momentum.

"In the lift. It's a tiny wooden lift. It says it can hold six people, but it can't possibly. I had my back to the wall and he was in front of me, so I was pushed . . . well, trapped against it. I couldn't move past."

"You couldn't move, but you must have done something?"

"I think I yelped in shock and tried to push him. I said something like, 'That hurt me.' And then, 'No. Not here.'"

"You said, 'No. Not here.' And why was that?"

"A kiss in a lift was one thing—something I found exciting—but this was different. Too full-on. Too aggressive. He might have meant the bite to be passionate, but it shocked me. It was painful: not something he'd ever done before. And it wasn't appropriate. He had yanked my breasts out and bitten me, but we were meant to be preparing for a select committee. The lift runs from the press gallery to New Palace Yard, where the ministers' cars wait. It's a shortcut to the committee room corridor. Anyone could have called the lift at any moment and found us there."

"So would it be fair to say that you were scared of being discovered?"

"Yes."

"And that you were preoccupied with being late for the meeting?"

"Yes. But it was more than that. I hadn't known him to be as forceful as this and he seemed not to be listening—a little like he was a man possessed."

"Like a man possessed." I pause as the reporters keep their heads down—their headlines and their opening paragraph written for them now—and as the judge takes a note, his black Parker scrolling. The pen stops, and so I can begin again.

"So, in this state, what did he do when you said, 'Not here,' and tried to push him away?"

"He ignored me and grabbed my thighs and my bottom."

She stops and I tilt my head to one side—a picture of sympathy for the evidence is going to get even grubbier now, the detail more embarrassing and explicit, and yet we need to hear it. The jury senses it, too. Some of them are leaning forward. All of us are rapt, knowing that the kernel of this case—the evidence that my learned friend will dispute and seek to undermine in cross-examination— will be found, bound hard and tight, in her next words.

"And what happened then?"

"He tugged at my skirt so that it rode over my bottom and up round my waist. Then he thrust his hand between my legs."

"If I can ask you to be a bit more specific. You say he thrust his hand *between your legs*?"

"On my vagina."

I wait three beats. "His thrust his hand *on your vagina*." My voice softens, quietens, becomes as gentle as cashmere as I wait for the impact of her words to resound around the court.

"And what happened then?" I say it so quietly.

"He pulled at my tights and knickers and . . . yanked them down. I remember hearing the tights laddering and the elastic on my knickers ripping."

"If I may stop you there, we have a photograph of the knickers as evidence. If you look at photograph B in your bundle," I tell the jury. "You can see the ripped elastic."

A flurry of turned pages and a photograph of a wisp of black lacy nylon—the sort of knickers a lover might wear. The waistband at the top is frayed, the seam pulled loose at the top of the pants as if they have been wrenched in a hurry. It's not incontrovertible evidence—and the defense will argue they were already ripped—but I feel a rush of sympathy for Olivia who will never have envisaged that her underwear would be pored over like this or make it into print. She is flushing now, crimson blooming on her cheeks, and I push on, for the evidence will only get harder, her experience worse.

"So, he yanks down your tights and knickers . . . and what happened then?"

"Then he put his fingers, two of his fingers, his middle and his index, I think, inside me."

"And what happened then?"

She looks outraged that I am so relentless. "I struggled and tried to push him off again, to tell him to get off me. But my back was to the lift wall, his weight was pushing against me, and he just wasn't listening to me."

"So he had two of his fingers inside you." I pause and speak only to her for a moment, deepening my voice, indicating that I know that the next part will be difficult. "And what happened next?"

"I realized his fly was undone and his boxers were pulled down and I saw his . . . well, I saw his penis poking out."

"Was it flaccid or erect at this point?"

Her look is one of intense shame that she has to point this out. I tilt my head and remain impassive. Her voice dips. "Erect," she manages to say.

And still I push on. "And what happened then?"

"He sort of lifted me up, against the wall, and he shoved it inside me," she says, and her voice cracks with pain and perhaps relief that she has got the worst over. "He just shoved it inside me even though I had said I didn't want it."

"You said that again here?"

"I said something like, 'Not here. Someone might see us.'"

"Just to be clear: you indicated that you didn't want this. You said, 'Not here.'"

"Yes." She is emphatic.

"And what did he say?"

"He said . . ." and her voice breaks now and she can barely get the words out, they are so painful. "He said . . . He whispered . . ." Still a pause—and then out the sentence floods and her voice rings clear though I anticipated a whisper. "He said, 'Don't be such a prick-tease . . .'"

The words whip around the court—the c and t, two hard consonants that smash into the silence.

"And then?"

"He just kept going."

"He whispered, 'Don't be such a prick-tease,' and he just kept going," I repeat, more in sorrow than in anger, and I pause, letting the jury take in her unrestrained sobs that now fill the windowless courtroom—soaring up to the ceiling and bouncing off those oak benches with their fir-green leather seats.

The judge looks down while he waits for her to compose herself. The jurors put their pens down and lean back. One of the older women—sensible short grey hair; a wide, open face—looks close to tears; while the youngest—a slight, dark-haired woman whom I imagine is a student, watches, her face shrouded in the most exquisite pity. They wait, and they tell her with their silence that they have plenty of time.

Olivia is not in a position to answer calmly just yet, but it doesn't matter. Those tears, and our understanding silence, will prove more eloquent than anything she has to say.

Judge Luckhurst looks at me and Angela from over the top of his spectacles as her sobs become louder and more ugly—a throaty cascade that shows little immediate sign of abating, although she wipes ferociously at her eyes.

"Perhaps this might be a good time to adjourn?" he suggests, his voice gentle. "If I could see you back here in twenty minutes, at eleven o'clock?" He is gracious to the jury.

His clerk, Nikita, stands as he does. "Silence. Be upstanding in court."

———

I am trembling when I reach the Bar mess to grab a few moments in which to compose myself. Olivia did well. I could not have hoped that she would have done better although I can predict the points that Angela will push at in her cross-examination. The bruise: a sign of passion, not violence? The prick-tease jibe: is she sure she remembered correctly? That it wasn't just a "tease"—something that might be whispered lovingly? Those words: "Not here. Someone might see us." Not—as I had hoped she would elaborate; though it was not there in her initial evidence—a more emphatic, unequivocal "No."

The CPS solicitor, Jenny Green, appeared pleased outside court, and I think Olivia will have played well to His Lordship—although the decision, of course, is not his. I should feel buoyed with relief, but the adrenaline is rushing from me, and I feel momentarily drained. The inevitable anticlimax, perhaps, after a good performance, but there is also something else beyond this and the low-lying anger that helps power me through such evidence: a residual sadness that hijacks me like a stubborn bully I cannot shift.

I slump in my chair and take a swig from a bottle of water—tepid now and tasting of nothing. My cuticles, I notice, are ragged.

I need to put myself physically back together. I cannot let myself slip. Just one minute of introspection and then I must refocus. I close my eyes, wallowing in the dizzying blackness, shutting out the sound of my fellow barristers bustling in, and try to draw on my inner strength—that shard of steel that my ex-husband, Alistair, once insisted I had instead of a heart. How little he really knew me; how little anyone knows me, except, perhaps Ali. I see Olivia in that lift; and shove aside the memory of someone else.

"Looking thoughtful, Kate," Angela—her grey eyes sharp in her doughy face—is brisk as she sweeps aside a paper cup half-filled with cold coffee and slams down her slab of papers. The room is filled with the bustle of counsel scouring laptops, analyzing court papers, or reliving the horror of representing certain defendants. "By this point he'd drunk fourteen pints of lager and a bottle of vodka." "But he's impotent—so that's his defense."

I am aware that Angela's eyes are still on my face. Her presence—her papers, her laptop, her capacious bag plonked right opposite me—feels oppressive.

"Always thinking, Angela," I retort, for my learned friend is ruthless in court and I can't betray any weakness. I push away from the table to escape the fetid smell of the room—canteen food congealing on a plate; the windows need opening—and prepare for the next part of the case.

Sometimes, I think as I shuffle my papers together, ensuring that the documents are just so, the jurors must question how I can pry like this. How can I probe into the most distressing moments of a woman's life and appear so very detached? How can I niggle away at the details—where exactly did he place his fingers? How many? For how long? Where was his penis? Was it erect or flaccid at this point? A pause, just to exploit her anguish. And what did he do then?

*Where is your milk of human kindness?* That's something Alistair had also hurled at me as our eighteen-month-long marriage imploded—a casualty not just of my inability to open up to him, and of too many late nights working, but of an obsession, in arguments, with being utterly ruthless in winning each point.

I know that, in the early days, I thought I had to just keep the questions coming until I ground the witness down and unearthed the salient fact. That's fine if it's the defendant in the box, but how can I do this to another woman? Reduce her to a humiliated heap of messy tears?

I do it because I want to get at the truth, and by getting at the truth I can do my best to ensure each rapist, or murderer, or abuser is convicted. I can't guarantee it. That decision lies with the jurors, but I do everything I can to ensure that's the case.

And how do I deal with knowing, and repeating, and rehearsing such graphic details? From mouths and tongues that probe, unwanted, to a penis rammed into each and every orifice—for hands on breasts or even vaginas are at the milder end of the spectrum of what I hear. I deal with it just as a detective or a forensic pathologist or a social worker does, or should: I practice detachment, developing a neutral façade that is as much of a disguise as any gown or wig.

Of course it doesn't mean that I don't feel. I just choose

to contain that emotion, or rather to channel it into righteous anger—cold, forensic, focused—rather than the white-hot rage that would boil over if I gave it half a chance.

"His hand was on your vagina?" I repeat, keeping my voice disinterested and low. A pause and she confirms it. I wait three beats. "And what happened then?"

To be fair, I sometimes wonder why so many of us women allow ourselves to wander so directly into the path of danger. Why return to a man who has made an unwanted advance or send a text with a kiss or a smiley face emoji? Why *engage* when it's the last thing you feel?

But the truth is, women are often scared of antagonizing their assailants or they feel conflicted; not so very long ago they may have been charmed by them. And we women aim to please. It is hardwired into us that we should placate and mollify—bend our will to that of men. Oh, some of us have fought against that, and we're seen as hard-nosed, difficult, assertive, shrewish. We pay the penalty. Why don't I have a proper, live-in partner? It's not just because I'm unsure if I can trust anyone sufficiently. It's because I refuse to compromise. I refuse to woman up, you might say.

And so, yes, a young woman whose boss has touched her up, or whose supposed friend has kissed her might well seek to minimize what has happened. To think the best: that it was an out-of-character mistake, best forgotten or brushed over, whatever the pounding of her heart—and the shot of fear coursing through her—might betray.

But she is a fool, and it is no wonder.

Men can make fools of us all.

# Seventeen

## James

### 16 January 1993

They had reached the stage of the evening when it was imperative that they empty the restaurant of all the champagne on the premises.

That, to James's increasingly inebriated mind, made complete and utter sense.

"Here, Jackson." He leaned back in the elegant dining chair and gesticulated to the maître d' of the Cock restaurant, who looked as if he was having a tough night, though why, when he would be amply reimbursed for any damage the Libertines might commit, James couldn't for the life of him understand. He stood up and flung a strong arm around the man's shoulders, to Jackson's apparent discomfort. Having your gaff wrecked by the Libs was a badge of honor among Oxford restaurant staff. Or it should be. Part of university folklore. Tradition. James was a strong believer in tradition, or rather, he was when he had drunk such an excessive amount that he needed something as concrete as this to hold on to, rather than grasping at more nebulous concepts and sounding vacuous.

He didn't drink excessively these days. Rowing precluded

that. You didn't become an athlete—a stroke for the men's heavyweight blue boat—by sating your body with alcohol nor by shirking training or ergo practice thanks to the mother of all hangovers—something he would experience tomorrow, he knew. Which was why it made sense to stop the drinking now and dispose of the remaining Bollinger by some other means. No use leaving anything for other punters to drink, not that any other punters would be visiting this fine establishment in the immediate future. Perhaps they *had* rather trashed it. His shoe slithered on a sliver of glass beneath his chair as he took in the table strewn with smashed goblets, domes fractured into shards, splinters dusting the lone breadbasket and glinting on the pats of butter. The plates, slick with gravy from the duck, had been whisked away, but the side plates had been smashed. Tom standing on a chair and Cassius on the table, which creaked as it took his hefty weight, holding the crockery up high and then throwing them down like a bunch of Greek tourists. Jackson and his staff, including two young waitresses who looked at them wide-eyed, had left the debris—jagged pieces of china and finer parings. He supposed it made sense to wait until they'd seen the full extent of their destruction. The clutter now looked pitiful, though those crashes had been satisfyingly noisy at the time.

His stomach fizzed. That would be the burgundy on top of the champers, the duck, and the Dover sole. God, he felt sick— a physical nausea and also something verging on self-disgust or distaste. Of course, his body would bounce back from this night of excess, but he was proud of its definition—those abs made getting laid with whomever he wanted a foregone conclusion. He slid his hands under his waistcoat to surreptitiously check his definition was still there.

"This won't do!" Tom, more bladdered than usual, more intoxicated than James, was weaving his way towards him, hips banging against the edge of the table, his broad, pleasant face a cheery red. You wouldn't know there was a sharp brain beneath the sheen of his skin and that foppish hair. He was on course for a double first for he had the critical ability to judge the exact amount of work required to excel. James had shared tutorials with Tom in the summer term of their second year—a time *he* had spent rowing, punting, and, pre-Sophie, getting laid with as many different girls as possible—and had relied on Tom heavily but had still been surprised by the extent to which his friend had blagged it. Neither of them frequented the Union—old fogeys, has-beens who *never had been,* in Tom's words—but despite this, he sensed that Tom, with a place lined up at the Conservative Research Department post finals, could do as he intended and forge a stellar political career.

Not that you would think it now. "This won't do at all." Tom slammed the flat of his palm down on the table with a frenzied beam then sniffed. He had snorted a couple of lines of coke, which helped explain his uncharacteristic volubility. "We need more champers, don't we, Jackson?" He clamped the maître d' in a forceful hug. "More champers. More champers. More *Bolly!* We need more Bolly and we need it now!"

There was a general braying of agreement from George,

Nicholas, and the Honorable Alec, the chaps at their end of the table; and a rallying cry from the other end where Hal was dozing on the floor, his midnight-blue tails dusted with glass and his shirt rucked up from its waistband to expose a delicate, pale arc of stomach flopping out. A dark stain bloomed at his crotch and he gave a low and fruity belch.

"Let's not drink it." James offered a note of caution. "Let's waste it!"

Tom's face broke into a smile of comprehension. "Come on, Jackson. All the Bolly. All the Bolly-olly-olly. Let's drink it and then let's piss it up the walls."

The maître d' put his hands up in a mild plea.

"Come on, man? What's the problem?" Tom protested, as Nicholas roared and George undid his fly, preparing to take him literally. "We won't really piss it—put your todger back, George. We'll pour it away." And they half hustled, half jostled the man to the champagne fridge and watched as he withdrew the remaining ten bottles to add to the twenty already quaffed.

"Come on, man!" George, his penis stuffed back in his pants, the zip hastily pulled up, was in a hectoring mood. "Open it, open it, open it! Christ. What's wrong with you? Talk about fumbling . . ."

". . . And pour it away," Tom roared as Jackson, his hands shaking as he fiddled with the muselet, finally popped the first cork and began to empty it down the kitchen sink, the bubbles fizzing against the stainless steel. One of the waitresses ducked away, but the elder—a dark-haired girl, pretty in an obvious sort of way—stood by her boss, handing over bottle after bottle, her face rigid with disapproval. Small-minded pettiness. Well, bugger her. She was never likely to be able to do the same.

"And the next!" James cried. "Come on, my good man . . ." He stood close to the maître d', conscious of towering over this slight man—five foot eight at most—and of the potential threat of his presence. He stepped back a little. No need to be thuggish. It wasn't his style. The plate smashing and window breaking he accepted as inevitable—part of the tradition of the Libertines, the havoc central to the ethos of the club, the general sense of entitlement and invincibility over those who had attended minor public school, or who'd been to comprehensives and whom he barely knew and certainly never mixed with. But there was no need to be boorish. He left that to the likes of Hal and Freddie who were coarse in their brutality; could not conceive of being civil as they were recklessly violent. James always made sure he apologized profusely for their destruction, was the first to whip out his fistfuls of notes, and collate the money to compensate for their damage. Courtesy cost nothing, his mother had always taught him, and did much to ease problems and endear oneself.

"And the next!" chorused Tom, Nick, and Alec. "All the Bolly! All the Bolly! All the Bolly! All the Bolly!" Their voices surged into one great roar as they stomped over the broken crockery and swayed against the burgundy velvet curtains, which Cassius grasped, the velvet falling over him like the end of an act as the pole was wrenched from the wall.

"Gentlemen, please." Jackson's face was stretched tight, his voice fraught with panic as he glanced at the chunk of plaster protruding above the pole and the flakes of paint snowing down.

"Whoops!" Tom, as delighted as an errant schoolboy, beamed then turned to the maître d' with the solicitude that would allow him to smooth many political differences in the future. "I'm terribly sorry, my dear man. We will, of course, reimburse you."

Jackson still looked unsettled, but demurred, exhaustion glazing his face, the awareness that his restaurant would be out of action for a few days and the upheaval this would require apparently registering, though James was sure they had trashed it before.

"All the Bolly, all the Bolly!" Alec, coked up as usual, continued to chant, and they jostled their way to the kitchen and the mass uncorking. Like effervescent urine it frothed and foamed, fizzing down the plughole in one long golden stream.

"In years to come," Tom flung a conspiratorial arm around his best friend, "we will be able to say: we were rich enough to pour our Bolly away . . . gilded youths, yup?" He gave a discreet belch then laughed and pressed his wet lips to James's cheek.

James extricated himself—not drunk enough to enjoy being kissed by Tom. He thought of other lips.

"We need some women." The need was urgent.

"Women!" Tom shook his head. "The trouble with women is they're such fucking hard work."

George, bent over a line of coke he had managed to assemble on the table, threw back his head and laughed.

"Spike their drinks," said Sebastian. "Get them so mullered there's no need for foreplay."

James shivered. "Not my scene. I like them to appreciate what I'm doing."

"Jim doesn't need that," Cassius drawled, as he watched him with barely concealed envy. "Touch of the Errol Flynn about him."

James shrugged. No need to deny or confirm Cassius's supposition. Hung like a Vittel bottle, as a girl once said.

"Extra double shots of vodka," Seb persisted. "That's what the rest of us have to do if we're not going to stick to buggery. Spike their drink and fuck 'em hard."

He emptied his glass in three swift gulps, his Adam's apple bobbing furiously, then looked at James directly, his pale eyes in his pudgy, still-unformed face fixed, hoping for a reaction. "Or slash their bike tires so they can't get away. No choice but to stay and get fucked."

James didn't smile. For a second he felt revulsion towards this Christ Church man, the wealthiest member of the club—his family had made millions through retail—but the one he knew the least about; his new money of too shiny a lustre, and not as trustworthy as the old money that bankrolled most of them. Then he shrugged. Seb was callow—a sexually inexperienced first-year trying too hard to be a man—but he was harmless, no? The boy smiled, rubbery lips pulled tight, but his eyes still cold, and again James felt a shiver of unease, a need to distance himself, perhaps get more drunk, or high, if he couldn't go out and find himself a woman. To seek a fresh sensation that wouldn't just distract but overwhelm him.

He nodded to George, and for once, bowed to the inevitable, snorting up the clean, sharp coke then waiting for the hit and, Christ, it was good and he felt good. He felt fucking invincible. What was he doing listening to Seb's shit when he could go and get a girl now? More doing, less talking, because he was fucking gorgeous, wasn't he? They all knew it: the Libertines, Soph, and every other girl in Oxford. He was a fucking love god and he could go for hours. Hung like a Vittel bottle, with the stamina of a rower, the tongue of a lizard, the lips of Jagger . . . well, no, not Jagger, fucking ugly bloke . . . but he was shit hot in bed, he knew that, and he was funny, too; he was a fucking catch, and much as he loved these guys, well, loved Tom at least, there were places to go, girls to see, the night was young and there was a whole night of loving ahead of him if he could scale Soph's college wall—the spikes by the bike shed—and hammer on her door; or find someone fresh because that was what he craved right now: a new mouth, new breasts, new legs to wrap around his waist or cradle his ears, a new way of whimpering when she came, because of course she would come, this imaginary new girl who was replete with possibility—because he was shit hot in bed, hung like a Vittel bottle . . .

A giggle—not the manly laugh he was known for but something younger and more joyful, his laugh as a seven-year-old before he was sent off to prep school and learned to man up—slipped out. A laugh of complicity and intimacy because he loved these guys just as he loved his girls, didn't he? Well, no, not quite in the same way as he loved girls, he wasn't *gay*, for God's sake, but he did love Tom. His best friend since their first year at school. He'd do anything for him. Well, almost anything. *God*, how he loved him. He'd tell him now just how very much he loved him . . . his dearest friend; the best of chaps . . .

"Here, Tom." He flung his arms around his shoulders and pulled him to him, proffered the kiss that he'd shunned from his friend earlier. "Let's go and get some women."

"Women. The trouble with women is . . ." Tom began.

"Yeah, yeah. I know. The trouble with women is they're such fucking hard work," he finished, and that giggle emerged again—high-pitched and joyful—because it was fucking funny. He was fucking funny. Why didn't they all realize how funny he was?

"The trouble with women is . . ." Tom repeated.

"They've got no backbone!"

"No." Tom looked confused. "They've got no cock."

"Well, that can be rectified," he sniggered.

"The trouble with women . . ."

The answer was so blindingly obvious, James couldn't help but butt in, his laughter blasting the words straight out of him. "The trouble with women is they don't know what the fuck they want!"

He doubled over and thought, *Now, why aren't the others laughing?* Instead of smashing plates, or in Seb's case, trying to grope that poor girl. Pretty in an obvious way—skirt up to her arse, forehead crinkling as if she was seriously pissed off with him, though Seb was harmless, or he was pretty sure he was harmless, and she was dressed as if she was asking for it . . . skirt up to her arse and blouse cut low.

"Oww!" The girl squealed and her black eyes glared at Seb, who must have pinched her bum, he was looking so sheepish and holding his hands up in the air if he was innocent, though he'd clearly sidled up behind her.

"Gentlemen. You will have to leave, I'm afraid." Jackson's face was crumpling in on itself like a rotting plum as he came towards Seb and it occurred to James that the girl might be his daughter. They had the same eyes—hard, dark blackberries in a clafoutis face—and he looked as if he wanted to hit him. "I really must insist that you leave the premises. Enough is enough. I mean it, now. Enough is enough."

He pulled himself up to his full height, and for a moment, the air shimmered with the possibility of violence—a tension that radiated between the maître d' and Seb, taut and tight. No one spoke—the strain spreading throughout the candlelit room as James tried to work out how the atmosphere had changed quite so quickly from something fun and jovial—the good-humored destruction of the Libs who were gents, really they were—to something rather distasteful and socially awkward. The very opposite of the atmosphere they always managed to create.

He opened his mouth as he tried to think of something suitably solicitous, but Tom stepped in.

"My dear man, of course we will. A thousand apologies. Do

tell us what we owe you?" And then to Seb, "Come on, man. Let's get some air. Time to call it a night, hey? Time to go home."

But Seb was having none of it. "What the fuck! A chap pays a girl a compliment. Tells her she's a bit of a looker—though I take *that back*, I take that back *right now*—and she objects. Can't take it. Can't take a compliment. What rot! What fucking rot." He looked around, incredulous, and for one terrible moment it looked as if his eyes were filling with tears.

"My good man," James was stuffing notes into the maître d's hand—£100, £200, £300—not enough to touch the damage but enough hopefully to distract him.

"It's fucking rot, I say." Seb would not be quietened, wasn't going to be ushered out gently, and suddenly there was a smash and a slivering of yet more glass as he lifted a chair, and before any of them realized quite what was happening, hurled it through the window and out into the street.

"Ha!" Into the dazed silence came a whoop from Hal's end of the room where the Hon. Alec began clapping, slowly at first and then ferociously. "Bloody good show, man, bloody good show."

But it wasn't, was it? As George and Nick and Cassius and a dopey Hal, roused by the explosion of noise, joined in the applause and in the destruction; and Jackson moved into the foyer towards the restaurant's phone, James locked eyes with Tom. A night in the cells wasn't an option, would be a crushing embarrassment. They were invincible, yes, but neither of them needed this. And—and here he was dimly aware of the coke affecting his usually measured thinking—it *would* be them, wouldn't it? The

Libs who, Icarus-like, flew closest to the sun? Far better to slip away now, to let the younger chaps—those wreaking havoc now and smashing more glasses and, oh God, George was getting his cock out again while Hal was parking a tiger, a thick stream of vomit splaying from his flabby lips—take the rap.

All this was transmitted in one quick glance; a locking of eyes that required no further confirmation. And then they scarpered, slipping from the scene as Jackson was on the phone to the police and the poor waitress stood cowering beside him, flattening herself against the wall as they squeezed past. James mouthed a sorry—for it cost nothing to be civil, his mother always said, it helped smooth things over, for no one wanted any difficulty—and then they were out into the freezing January night.

"Fucking hell." Tom ran his hands through his light-brown fringe, a compulsive gesture James recognized from his rare moments of high tension: the time, age seventeen, when he thought he'd got a girlfriend back home pregnant; that late afternoon at school when they'd been caught smoking spliffs and for a brief moment in the headmaster's study it looked as if they would be expelled.

"Shh." His warning ended with a giggle.

"I know. Fucking *hell*!" Horror and delight, shock and awe were caught in his voice and then they were off—as a distant police siren began to wail up St. Aldate's towards them and down the high street.

*We are invincible, fucking invincible*, James thought, and then, *they're getting closer*—as they raced the sound, coattails flying, hearts thudding, legs burning as if straining to do the mother of all ergos or the final torturous length of a rowing race.

His heart was throbbing against his ribs, this great muscle that never let him down, and he flew, one last surge of energy pushing him over the cobbles until they reached the sanctity of Tom's college, Walsingham. The oak gates were locked and so they breached the wall, tails ripping as they negotiated the spikes, palms stinging as they grazed on the stone, but it didn't matter for they were half shushing, half laughing. They were invincible, really they were. They had outwitted them all; they had made it. They were safe. Home.

He paused as he scaled the spikes, high up on the wall, close to the navy sky, the stars, the heavens, and, yes, the leering gargoyles. King of the castle and of all he surveyed. He caught his breath as he leaned against a tower, feeling the solidity of the stone beneath his fingers, the warmth of it, and its age—here for four hundred years or more. Invincible, in a way they would never be.

"Are you coming or what?" Tom, safely down, called up; his eyes glinted, pools of warmth and trust. God, he loved him; would do anything to protect him. They'd been buttressed against the world since that first term at school; bound together through sport, prep, adolescence, that headmasterly bollocking; shared first experiences—the drug-taking (the spliffs and coke), and he supposed, in their joint masturbatory fumbles, sex.

The night loomed down on him all of a sudden, and he let go, landing lightly in the shadows where the night porter, ensconced in front of his portable TV in the lodge, was unlikely to

spy them, where their footsteps—tapping against the concrete—
seemed to melt away.

"Nightcap?" Tom flung an arm around him, his breath warm
on his cheek.

"Nightcap," he agreed.

# EIGHTEEN
## KATE
### 26 APRIL 2017

Twelve o'clock. Day three and Angela Regan, QC, is tapping her fountain pen lightly on the top of her file: *Ra-tat, ra-tat, ra-tat, ra-tat*—the tattoo of a drum on a battlefield at daybreak as the uneasy peace snaps at dawn.

She leans forward, her bosom resting against the file, the knuckleduster of a diamond that crowns her right hand glinting in the light. Midfifties, with working-class Northern Irish roots, she is an inspired choice. If James Whitehouse spent his adolescence playing fives and saying Latin grace, Ms. Regan was navigating the Ardoyne area of sectarian Belfast—and plotting her way out fast.

She smiles at Olivia now and places her surprisingly small hands beneath her bosom. Her smile is brisk and doesn't meet her eyes, for she's no hypocrite. Any warmth will vanish more quickly than frost on a courtroom window once she gets to the heart of the evidence.

Olivia looks straight ahead, as if determined not to be cowed by this woman whom she detects is less than sisterly. Chin up, she places her hands in front of her in the witness box, catches my eye, and gives a somewhat shaky smile.

"Ms. Lytton. I'll try not to keep you long but there are some points we need to check," Angela begins, her tone sleek and designed to lull Olivia into a false sense of security, though Olivia, on the defensive, must know that Ms. Regan intends to catch her out.

"We have heard that you were in a sexual relationship with Mr. Whitehouse, is that right?"

"Yes."

"And how long did that last?"

"From mid-May to the sixth of October when he finished with me. So a little less than five months."

"And I think you told us that when you *collided* with him in the lift you *still loved him?*"

"Yes."

"So at what point did you fall in love with him?"

"I suppose right away. He has that effect on people. He's very charismatic. You—I—became infatuated with him."

"But on the date in question you had split up, hadn't you?"

"Yes," she nods.

"And how did that make you feel?"

"How did it make me feel?" She looks bemused at so obvious a question. "Well . . . I was *distressed.*"

"And why was that?"

"Because I was in love with him . . . and because I didn't see it coming. At the party conference we had spent the night together.

Then two days later, when we were back in London, he ended it." The incredulity—the pain of his behavior—is caught in her answer. She looks down, aware that she has revealed too many messy emotions and departed from her sober, sanitized script.

"Moving to the date in question, were you still distressed then? Just a week later?"

"I was upset, but I was determined to be professional. I made sure it didn't affect my work and that my colleagues—and James—were unaware of it. That was the last thing either of us would have wanted," she says.

"But you still had strong feelings. You have told us that you still loved him, haven't you?"

"Yes. Of course I was still affected. I was still upset."

"And you were angry, weren't you?"

"No." The denial is a little too quick to be entirely convincing. A simple *no* can reveal so much with its one, plain syllable and this suggests that Olivia felt a glimmer of rage.

"Really? The man you were in love with had finished with you *out of the blue* and then wanted you to behave in a way that was entirely professional? You would be forgiven for feeling just the slightest bit angry, wouldn't you?"

"I didn't feel angry."

"If you say so." Angela flicks her hand in a gesture of evident disbelief. "If we can go to the day in question, you said that you were in the committee corridor, and Mr. Whitehouse was preoccupied about a comment piece in the *Times* that accused him of being arrogant?"

"Yes."

"And you told him—ah, here it is—that 'Arrogance can be *devastatingly attractive.*' What did you *mean* by that?"

"I meant what I said . . . That arrogance can be an attractive quality."

"You meant that *you* found *him* devastatingly attractive, didn't you?"

"I suppose so."

"You *suppose* so?"

A pause and then, "Yes."

"And after you say that he opens the door from the committee room corridor to the lobby staircase, he calls the lift, pushes the button to open the door, and I believe you go in first?"

"I don't remember."

"You *don't remember?*" Angela is all mock-incredulity and looks at the jury to register the apparent flakiness of the witness. She turns back to Olivia. "Well, if I may refer to your statement, which I have here, you say very clearly: 'He called the lift and I went in first. He followed.'"

"Then I must have done," Olivia says.

"So you tell him you find him *devastatingly attractive*, and you then lead the way into the lift that he's opened?"

"I didn't lead the way. The door opened and he ushered me in."

"But you didn't resist?"

"No."

"You didn't question why he was doing this?"

"No."

"Even though you needed to stay on the committee room corridor and you had a meeting to go to in less than fifteen minutes, you didn't question why he was doing this and you didn't resist going into the lift at any time?"

A pause. Then, "No," Olivia reluctantly says.

Angela waits, her forehead creased in a V, then looks down at her papers as if searching for a credible explanation. When she speaks, her voice is low and her tone oozes incredulity and a hefty dose of contempt.

"What did you think he was *doing*, calling the lift?"

"I don't know."

"Oh, come on. You're a highly intelligent woman. You had told this man with whom you'd had an affair that you found him devastatingly attractive, and then he calls the lift and you enter first *without question*." A pause. "He was taking you somewhere *private*, wasn't he?"

"I don't know . . . perhaps," she says.

"*Perhaps?* There was no reason for you to get in that lift together. The meeting you were about to attend was in that corridor, wasn't it?"

"Yes."

"And your offices were in an entirely different building?"

"Yes."

"And I think that that lift only leads down to New Palace Yard, where you could turn right and go back to Portcullis or left towards Central Lobby. Nowhere that had any bearing on your meeting? Nowhere that you needed to be?"

"Yes."

"So what were you *thinking of*, getting into the lift?"

There is a long pause while she lets Olivia endure the agony of being unable to come up with an innocent explanation. Angela is cruelly feline—a cat toying with a vole, permitting the possibility of escape, tossing it in the air before sinking her claws in.

The blow is vicious.

"He was taking you somewhere private, wasn't he?"

The silence is painful—long and taut before Olivia breaks it in a voice so quiet it is almost a whisper. "Yes," she says.

"So he ushers you in, and once in the lift, you kiss."

"Yes."

"It was a passionate kiss, I think?"

"Yes."

"A French kiss. With tongues?"

"Yes."

"'His hands were all over me,' you said. So you enter the lift with this man you have told us you still *loved*, that you found *devastatingly attractive*, and you kiss passionately."

"Yes."

"He puts his hands on your bottom."

"Yes."

"And opens your blouse."

"Yes . . . He wrenched it open."

"Wrenched suggests some force. Were there any buttons missing?"

"No."

"Was it torn?"

"No."

"So perhaps it's more accurate to say that in a moment of passion, he pulled it apart?"

Olivia's face contorts with the struggle of remaining calm in the face of such disbelief. She compromises. "He pulled it apart *forcefully*."

"I see." Angela lets her skepticism tinge the court before moving on.

"So he pulled it apart *forcefully* and he gives you what might be called a love bite above your left nipple."

"He bruised me and it hurt."

"We will submit that it is the nature of such bites to bruise and many might describe it as a bite of *passion*." Angela glances at the jury. We've all been there, her look says. "But it is only at this point that you say"—and here she looks down at her notes, drawing out the tension and the possibility for bathos—"it is only here, when he has kissed your breasts, passionately, that you say, 'No, *not here*.' That's right, isn't it?"

A pause and then a reluctant, "Yes."

"I'm just checking your statement. You don't say, 'No, don't do that. I don't want it.' You don't even say simply, 'No.' You say—at this point when he has opened your shirt, forcefully or not—it is only here that you say: 'No, not here.'"

"Yes . . . I was worried someone might see us."

"You were worried that someone might see you."

"It would have been acutely embarrassing."

"And that was your concern: that *someone might see you*. Not that he was doing it—this man you still loved, with whom you had had a sexual relationship and had willingly entered the lift. Your concern, as he pulled open your blouse and put his hands on your bottom, was that *someone might see you*?"

"He had shocked me with the bite, but, yes, that was my main concern *at that point*."

A pause. Angela looks down at her notes again, shakes her head as if she cannot quite believe that she is hearing this. Her voice slows and is lowered.

"Are you *sure* that's what you *really* said?"

"Yes."

"That you said, 'No, not here.' At this point?"

"Yes."

A very lengthy pause. Angela shuffles some papers. Looks down as if composing herself. Olivia looks discombobulated— left hanging and waiting to be challenged. She knows that something is up.

"This wasn't the first time you'd had sex with Mr. White-house in the House of Commons, was it?"

The reporters on the press bench scrabble to attention. You can almost see their ears prick up as their pens race across their notepads. Only Jim Stephens, sitting back, looks characteristically languid, but I know all the damning quotes are being jotted down.

The color rushes to Olivia's face. Her eyes flit to me, but I can't help her and look away. During the lengthy legal argument on day one, Angela made a section 41 application to cite previous sexual history, arguing that two incidents were identical to that in this case, and I agreed to the material being included, because the last thing I needed was for James Whitehouse, if convicted, to use its exclusion as grounds for appeal.

"I don't know what you mean." Olivia's voice is a semitone higher than usual.

"Oh, I think you do. If I can ask you to cast your mind back to the night of September twenty-ninth—that's a fortnight before the day we're talking of. You met Mr. Whitehouse in his office. It was just after nine p.m., wasn't it?"

"Yes." She is meek.

"You were due to go to a friend's leaving party. Your colleague, Kitty Ledger, was waiting for you in the Red Lion, but I think you were late for her, weren't you?"

"A little, yes."

"And why was that?"

Silence.

Angela turns to the jury and virtually rolls her eyes.

"The reason you were late was because you were having spontaneous sex with Mr. Whitehouse in his office, weren't you? Oral sex, which you performed, I believe, and then sex on his desk. Sex that anyone could have walked in on, that anyone could have spotted. Passionate, risky sex of precisely the kind in which you indulged in the lift."

The reporters are scribbling frantically and some of the jurors are glancing at her, wide-eyed. You can sense the sympathy seeping away from the older women as they recalibrate their opinion. Orange Face is delighted at this turn of events, while the elderly woman watches through narrowed eyes.

"I think there was another occasion, too, wasn't there?"

Olivia doesn't answer, is looking down, blood flooding her neck.

"On September twenty-seventh—two days before the one we just spoke of?"

Still no answer.

"There's a BBC recording studio tucked away at the end of the lower reporters' gallery and at around nine p.m. you met Mr. Whitehouse there, didn't you?"

A squeak from Olivia: a sound that seems to escape involuntarily.

"*Did* you meet Mr. Whitehouse there?"

"Yes," Olivia eventually says.

Angela gives a small sigh. "And there you had passionate, risky sex. Just straightforward sexual intercourse this time, but sex anyone could have walked in on at any moment." She shakes her head. "There seems to be quite a pattern of reckless sex in the work environment happening here."

But if the jurors think that Olivia will take this further dose of humiliation meekly, they have underestimated her.

"No."

"No?" Angela raises an eyebrow, on certain ground.

"On those first two occasions, it was consensual sex. Sex that we both wanted. We are talking about something very different here." Her voice wavers and cracks, fury and fear coalescing, and then it falters and comes to a standstill, as if she lacks the power to argue against this ferocious opponent; as if she recognizes that she has been damned by her frank admission of desire.

"You had sex in the House of Commons on two occasions

barely a fortnight before this incident in the lift. Risky sex that anyone could have walked in on, that anyone could have spotted, didn't you?" asks Angela. She pauses, letting the tension stretch. "A simple 'yes' will suffice."

———————

Judge Luckhurst suggests now might be a good point for a break. "Ten minutes—no more," he tells the jury. Angela, I'll wager, is furious. She has ensnared her victim and wants to go in for the kill.

When Olivia returns, she seems more composed—no sign of tears, a taut, pale face—but Angela is merciless. She has scored a killer point, overridden Olivia's perfectly accurate distinction and will hunt her down until there is nothing left of her allegations but a bloodied carcass, no use to anyone at all.

She downplays the casually dismissive, "Don't be such a prick-tease."

"Are you sure he didn't say, 'Don't be a tease.' or 'Don't tease me'? That's the sort of thing some lovers say to one another, isn't it? Particularly if they're the sort of lovers who thrive on the illicit nature of an office romance; the sort who love the riskiness of sex in an office or in a lift?'

She pooh-poohs the idea that her knickers were ripped. "They're a rather flimsy piece of underwear and cheaply made. There's no proof they weren't torn by you, or torn already."

"They weren't. They were relatively new." Olivia is close to tears.

"You could have ripped them while pulling them off."

"No, I didn't!" she insists.

The atmosphere quickly turns oppressive.

"I didn't want it. I said I didn't want it," Olivia insists at one point, her composure slipping completely; her sheer anguish exposed.

Angela looks at her over her glasses. "You are clear about that, are you?" she asks, boxing her in.

"Yes."

"That you said that you didn't want it?"

"Yes."

And my heart clutches tight for now I know that Angela has something concrete with which to catch her out again and all I can do is sit and listen, powerless to mitigate the next blow. Judge Luckhurst looks up, too, alert to every counsel's trick, familiar with the traps we set; and so do the jurors—in delicious anticipation of the next twist.

Angela sighs, as if it is painful for her to inflict this, and she reaches for a statement. She passes it to Olivia, via the usher; reads out the declaration of truth; gets her to agree that, yes, this was a statement made at the police station ten days after the meeting in the lift and this is her signature and they are her own words.

Angela looks up, gestures at the document. "On page four, paragraph two—please correct me if I read this incorrectly—you say: 'I told him to get off me. He shoved himself inside me even though I kept saying, "Not here."'"

She pauses and looks at the jury.

"In court you have just said, 'I didn't want it. I said I didn't want it'; but in the statement I've just read out—given to the police soon after the event—you merely say, 'I told him to get off me . . . I said, "Not here."' You didn't mention—in your statement given ten days after the event—that *you said you didn't want it,* you merely indicate that this isn't the place. And you only mention it now, several months later, when you find yourself entangled in a court case and appearing in front of us here."

She looks straight ahead at the judge, this formidable woman protected by her books and files and the garb of the court, holds her head high, keeps her voice deep and controlled, and delivers her killer accusation. A rhetorical question to which Olivia is not expected to reply.

"You're not reliable, are you? You loved this man. You'd had sex not once, but twice before with him in the House of Commons; and distressed at him having finished with you, you told him you found him attractive, entered a private space with him, and kissed him—fully intending to have sex with him again."

And Olivia is left floundering, mouth goldfishing open, as Angela finishes this section of her cross-examination with a triumphant flourish.

"The words you used in that lift could be interpreted as an invitation. You're not in the least reliable. In fact, you're lying!"

# NINETEEN
## HOLLY
### 5 JUNE 1993

The music filled the quad, throbbing from the far staircase where the junior common room bop was in full flow. Saturday night, the sixth week of the summer term, an event where anyone single could be part of a sweaty, friendly mass, and those who fancied it, could cop off with one another, hands circling the sweat-drenched backs of T-shirts and squeezing buttocks in something that could morph into a clumsy first grope.

The couples peeled away as the night went on, retreating to corners where they perched on chairs or one another's laps, bottles of beer drained or knocked over as they settled down to the more exquisite business of learning new lovers' faces: cheeks, necks, mouths. The unchosen few ignored them and carried on dancing, right arms breaking the air in a rhythmic salute; bouncing on the tips of their toes, bodies straining up in one big celebration of being eighteen or nineteen—for most were first-years with nothing more to preoccupy them than whether they would pull at the end of the night. The music swirled and rose: an anthem that built to a crescendo they could all shout out loud in one great affirmation of joy. Holly mouthed the lyrics—the words, not quite known, catching in her throat—and Dan, a friend she knew from the student paper who had invited her to Walsingham College for this bop, lowered his salute until his finger was jabbing at her. He spun her round, then sang into her hair, his breath sharp with beer, his hands light on her waist brushing up against her breasts, and she was perturbed; her sense of feeling flattered giving way to embarrassment and shame.

"Too dizzy, sorry," she said with a smile and broke away. And she was, the spinning, on top of the two pints of cider that fizzed and sloshed in her stomach, was turning her head. She pushed through the fug steaming from all those hot bodies, the air stale and sweet, and made for the quad. The noise pulsed behind her, thrusting her forwards, encircling her before being absorbed by the rough, golden stone. The boom lessened as she walked quickly towards the porter's lodge, boots clipping irregularly, for she felt an irrational need to escape from this college and Dan who, she belatedly realized, might be interested in being more than friends.

She kept her head down, concentrating on the flagstones and trying to walk straight for she risked stumbling onto the lawn, with its strict notice to keep off the grass, and her feet were definitely weaving. The June night had cooled, pimpling her skin, for she only wore a vest top, and she stopped to put on her denim shirt, tied around her waist. The euphoria of being part of one happy group had vanished and she started to hum, her voice low and tuneful, to try to recapture a joy she could no longer feel.

Her dizziness was lifting. She risked looking up at the cloud-less night sky that stretched, midnight blue and brilliant, and tried to find the features in the face of the creamy full moon that hung high above. Venus winked and Holly blinked back. For a moment, she just gazed up: letting herself be overwhelmed by the darkness that soared beyond the golden spires. The feminist literary theory she devoured meant she saw phallic symbolism everywhere, but the penetrating towers seemed pitiful, risible even, compared to the grandeur of the night sky. She staggered a little, overwhelmed by the velvet richness and the immense beauty of a full night sky pressing down on her.

The college clock tolled twelve—the chimes long and so-norous. She must find her way out, but taking a left turn, she discovered she was in the college cloisters: a magical courtyard with oak doors set deep into the walls and a moonlit patch of lawn, framed by arches, enclosed. Was she lost? She didn't know this college. It was far larger than hers—grander, with its deer park and fellows' garden—and slightly disorienting. Perhaps she was trespassing, although Dan had invited her—had been quite insistent she attend. As always, she felt an imposter. Dan, Ned, Sophie, Alison even—though she would never admit to it with her proud northern-ness—could justify being here but she still sometimes felt a fraud: someone who had managed to slip in, perhaps to fulfil some state school quota, and who wasn't entitled. It was only a matter of time before she was found out.

She skulked into the shadows, away from the faux windows that framed an impossibly pretty view, and leaned against the pale Headington stone. In the shadows, she could exist, observing without being noticed. Not quite part of it but still present, on the edge. She tiptoed, hugging the shade of the walls, enjoying the calm, feeling herself sober up as the cool night air forced her to think. She had been rather stupid. Perhaps she should turn back, pretend she had got lost while looking for the loo, find Dan again, maybe even let him make another pass at her, for her virginity was becoming more of an embarrassment than her background, and must be just as obvious, something she feared everyone could guess.

Could she do it? With him? She thought of her unthreatening friend: silky-haired, skinny, slight, with a smattering of acne still around his jawline. Good with words, or with the written word at least. She liked that about him: the way in which he could sculpt a sentence, his unerring ability to capture a story with a few choice words. He was clever, and she valued cleverness, even if he had been clumsy this evening. Perhaps he was just nervous and this was his way of trying to show he wanted to sleep with her, or at least that he didn't find her physically repulsive? Perhaps it would be better to do it with a friend? Someone with whom it needn't mean anything, with whom she had invested nothing; and who would allow her to hold on to her romantic ideals—for she knew the first time was meant to be painful and messy and an anticlimax, and she wouldn't want to experience that with someone for whom she actually cared. She reached inside her denim shirt and rearranged her breasts, exposing some cleavage created with the help of her new Wonderbra, something that undermined all her feminist principles and yet marshalled her puppy fat and sculpted it into something that suggested perhaps she wasn't really so virginal. Glancing down at the two soft pillows, she felt guilt and an unfamiliar pride. *This is me. These are part of me—perhaps as much me as all the thinking, all the literature.* She undid another button, and with her pale orbs leading the way, turned back towards the junior common room, apprehension brewing; a broiling mass of anticipation that eddied and swirled as she retraced her steps.

A figure ran from the far side of the cloisters. She heard the footsteps before she saw him—the hurried jog of someone fit, feet bouncing off the flagstones, and then his breath, curiously intimate in the silence, as he came hurtling round the corner and almost crashed straight into her.

She stopped, her body as rigid as one of the does in the deer park the other side of the walled garden. Though she could hear him coming she hadn't anticipated him bounding up to her so fast, filling her space with his bulk and his energy so that there seemed no room for anyone else.

"Christ—sorry, *sorry!*" He was equally shocked, the darks of his eyes swelling above his high cheekbones as he grabbed her upper arms to steady them both. Her heart thudded hard against her chest, fear and adrenaline mixed with a sharp pang of lust. He gave a quick smile, his charm automatic, though his breath was thick with whisky and he swayed, unsteady on his feet. What must it be like to know that, however you err, you will always be forgiven? For your charm to be so intrinsic, so overwhelming, that you know you can rely on it entirely, even when drunk? Sophie had told her about the Libs pouring bottles of Bolly down the sink, but even now, she couldn't believe he—a disciplined rowing blue—had taken part. He wasn't *boorish*, she thought, drinking in his smooth skin, and she became suffused with tenderness. Perhaps he didn't want to be part of the club? Perhaps, like her, he wasn't a party animal—though he was dressed in the ridiculous kit of the Libertines? He was wired, she realized now—a palpable nerviness pulsing through his body and she wanted to hug him, to reassure him everything would be OK. She thinks all this, aware of the warmth, the grip of his hands on her upper arms, just inches from her breasts.

"It's all right." She looked down, afraid that he might detect her reaction.

His pupils seemed to focus. "Do I know you? . . . Molly? Polly?"

"Polly," she agreed. Of course he wouldn't know her name. He wouldn't know her.

"Pretty Polly."

She laughed, embarrassed at the compliment and at his painful attempt at wit.

"I do know you . . . or at least I should." James's voice was liquid as he leaned closer, scrutinizing her features. "Pretty, pretty Polly."

"Not really." She could feel her cheeks burning and tried to look down but his eyes drew hers back.

"Yes, really," he said and smiled.

Almost imperceptibly, they were moving closer. One hand snaked to the back of her neck. Shivers shot from his fingers as he stroked the short down on her nape: a part of her that never felt feminine, for the crop she had hoped would look gamine was anything but.

"The baby dyke look?" Sophie had once asked, with the casual thoughtlessness at which she excelled. "Are you?"

"No. No, I'm not." Holly had shaken her head, embarrassed at not wanting to be thought gay, for that was fine, *really*, that was *fine*; relieved that her friend hadn't detected her feelings for *him*.

She closed her eyes briefly and for a moment imagined that she was someone else observing them: two students caught in slow motion, moments before their first kiss. For that was what was about to happen now. Mad though it seemed, there was that peculiar tension in the air—a friction that could be broken, just, but was far more likely to stretch into a kiss. Every love story demanded it: that ineluctable coming together; that falling into one another's arms; mouths and limbs meeting and melding; eyes closing in delicious expectation; a slight smile playing on parted lips.

Her eyes flicked open. He was still staring at her and his eyes had deepened, an unmistakable desire hijacking any brief speculation about her identity. Did he know her? She doubted it. She was just another tipsy student, ill met by moonlight, he a randy rower. His fingers stroked her cheek before he leaned towards her again.

His lips were soft, and that first kiss surpassed all expectations. It was wondrous. She looked up, searching for his warm green eyes and he opened them and smiled back at her, then leaned down again, his arms circling her back and waist, pulling her close. His breath was warm against her mouth and she breathed him in as he kissed her again, tongue darting against her lips so that flickers of pleasure fired in unexpected parts of her body: a private firework display.

This is magical, she thought, still the observer looking in, even as she was held in the moment. His passion was infectious and her heart quickened, growing in excitement, as his lips hardened and became more determined, tongue probing her mouth. He was like a wave now, a force that had caught her up and was pushing her along, irrespective of whether she could handle the drama or pace.

"Perhaps I should go," she began, though she did not know where she would go, or if she even wanted to. She just wanted to take things a bit slower, wanted to take stock of where his hands were now going—one creeping up the bottom of her shirt, his broad thumb stroking her nipple, the other somehow riding beneath her pelmet of a skirt.

"Really?" His eyes widened into a little-boy-lost gaze; and she saw gold flecks in the green, and incomprehension. Had anyone ever said that to him before?

"Really," she repeated, and smiled to placate him.

"I don't think so," he said, a growl in his voice, a sound that spoke of unbridled confidence. "I don't think you really want that at all." And he kissed her more savagely this time so that her lip felt grazed. Lust, she told herself and felt a jolt of surprise—and perhaps pride—that she could have this effect on him even as she felt a lurch of fear, a sense that things were tipping out of her control.

"No, really." She gave a little laugh now and pulled back. For how could he be so arrogant as to guess what she wanted? It riled her. Or perhaps it was the game of seduction. His eyes softened, and she longed for a repeat of their first kiss—something teasing and yielding. Could he kiss her like that again?

He bent down, kissed the tip of her nose. "That better?" he added.

"Much better." So he understood her. Her relief was immense. She kissed him back, her lips lingering, enjoying the moment: the moonlight on their upturned faces; the quiet chill of the cloisters; the combination of excitement and apprehension that was surging in her, urging her to be bolder than she had ever been before; to ignore any thought—loyalty to Sophie, fear of being discovered, anxiety as to what he might think of her—and just give herself up to the sensations pulsing through her, and which threatened to overwhelm.

His fingers played with her hair, and his mouth snaked up her throat to her ear, light kisses dusting their way up. And then he pulled her tight in a bear hug so that her ribs felt crushed and her breath was forced from her like air wheezing from an accordion.

And he whispered something in her ear. She froze, chilled by the quiet menace of the words for his voice was still quietly caressing. Did he really say that? She tried to hope that she had been mistaken.

But yes, she realized, he had.

———————

And then everything changed. She managed to endure it by resorting to her stock role of observer. By imagining herself watching another girl experiencing it—a Tess Durbeyfield, perhaps—and observing her pain. She focused on a gargoyle—a mocking grotesque with hands half-covering his eyes, his mouth downturned and gaping at the horror—carved high up in the corner of the wall. See it from that figurine's eyes, she told herself, as her back was thrust against the cold stone. Just another event in the history of the university—something that must have gone on for centuries, the gentlemen of the university taking their pleasure from serving wenches or boys. Nothing personal and perhaps she had encouraged it, parading her ridiculous breasts; looking at him, frankly, with blatant desire. Her fault, or partially her fault, for though she initially struggled and told him *no*—her mouth slipping from his as she tried to get the words out—he mustn't have heard her and she was quickly silenced: his mouth overwhelming hers, the size of his body muffling her sounds. Because he wouldn't be behaving like this otherwise, would he? If he had known that she really hadn't wanted it? She stared at the gargoyle, tears blurring his horrified leer and bulbous nose, though she could still see his hands on his eyes, his thumbs pressed hard in his ears. Hear no evil. See no evil.

---

She managed it. She almost managed it—except it was impossible to remain disconnected, to spin some story, when the most intimate part of her was ripped and her body seared with pain. She couldn't help crying then, the tears sliding down her cheeks, though she didn't cry out—she was too overwhelmed by this point, too appalled at the entire submersion of herself, the sense of being so impotent.

When he was done, he pulled away and apologized. Not for the act, but for the fact she was a virgin.

"First time? My God, I'm sorry." He looked at the blood trickling down her legs and blotching him. "You should have said."

He tucked himself away, the evidence of her deflowering and shame hidden in his dark trousers. "I'd have taken more time." He looked flushed and unsettled, evidently didn't come across many virgins. "Fuck," he concluded.

She didn't say anything to help him out and so he ran a hand through his hair before looking up beneath that fringe and giving a winsome grin. "Fuck," he repeated—then dropped a kiss on her forehead, pulling her towards him so that she could feel his heart thudding against hers, strong and vigorous. He tried for friendly. "Still—no hard feelings, hey?"

Her throat seemed to have closed over and she stood, unmoving and barely breathing in his arms, just wanting to be released; to get away so that she could scrub herself clean of all taint of him.

"No hard feelings," she managed.

———————

It was Alison who found her the next morning. She had scurried back to college, keeping to the shadows, avoiding eye contact with any swaying, loving couples, and had slipped through the college's ancient gates when another student let her in with a late key. Had hidden herself away.

She ran a bath, deep and hot, not caring that it was antisocial to do so this late, the pipes creaking and moaning as they disgorged themselves and the sound of the rushing water reverberating behind the wooden paneling. Her skin flushed a porcine pink as she scalded herself; thighs smarting with the heat and her insides stinging as she pushed the soap inside her. Sinking deep underneath the water, she clawed at her neck, her breasts, and collarbone—anywhere he had touched—and scrubbed her hair—fingers digging into her scalp through the crop he had stroked and clutched, like a mother combing her head for nits. Her fingers dug in an obsessive, itching motion, until she felt a sticky wetness and saw that her scalp was bleeding, her nails red.

Later, she lay curled in her bed, smothered in a sweatshirt and jogging bottoms—infantilizing clothes that hid those troublesome breasts, that troublesome body, away.

She felt numb. Though her insides stung, her heart was a hard, heavy pebble. She was spent with crying. Guilt and rage would come later. Would surface at the least expected times. But for now, she was too exhausted.

She didn't move for breakfast. Down in the quad she could hear the chatter of fellow first-years returning from the dining hall; full of toast and porridge, or a plate of fried eggs and bacon swilled down with tea and filter coffee; paid with a slip of pink paper worth 50p. There was a Nightline meeting she had planned to go to at ten but she didn't move; nor did she meet Alison for lunch, as arranged. The thought of bumping into anyone—not least Sophie, lovely, blameless Sophie—made her want to heave.

At half past one, there was a sharp banging on her door. She gripped the duvet, her ears pricked, as it continued: an insistent rapping, the sound of someone who wouldn't go away.

"Who is it?" Her voice was unlike her own, quiet and with a noticeable quiver, as she left the safety of her bed and crept towards it.

"Alison. Are you ill or something? Or are you in there with Dan? If so, I'll bugger off."

She wrestled with the key and pulled the door open, the effort of opening the door—and of opening herself up to someone else; of revealing her secret—almost more than she could bear.

Her friend's mouth dropped, betraying her shock as she took in Holly's face: swollen, she knew, and tear-stained; her eyes bloodshot; features scrubbed of any makeup; childlike and bare.

"What happened to you?" The words came out as a whisper, as if by saying them quietly, they could disbelieve the answer. She put out her arms to hold her, but Holly shrank away.

# TWENTY
## HOLLY
### 19 JUNE 1993

She returned home to Liverpool soon after that. Slunk back. Her body language, when her mother, Lynda, met her at the station, spoke of dejection and failure, for that was exactly what she felt. That she was a failure for being unable to negotiate her way sexually and socially; and for being unable to communicate something so crucial—the fact she did not want her body to be invaded by another—adequately.

"Too snobby," she explained whenever anyone asked why she wouldn't be returning in October. Manda, who could barely disguise her glee that the sister who had dared to overreach herself had had her wings melted by the sun, kept pushing. "Leave it, will you," Holly answered. "It just wasn't for me."

"I think she was just homesick," her mother had elaborated when her friends probed. "She found it a bit different down south." Far better to do a course at Liverpool University where she could return home whenever she wanted, for something had shaken her up, Lynda wasn't stupid; she could see that. A boy. Or a man, more likely.

And so she had started again. September 1993. Liverpool University. The reports from her Oxford tutors had been exemplary, though she hadn't done as well in her exams as expected. She had a full grant and there was no question of this being withheld now that she was changing direction and studying law.

"Far better to do something vocational," she told Manda, who had nodded before pointing out that she had said this all along.

"No point namby-pambying around with novels. I wasn't going to achieve anything like that."

"Whatcha want to achieve?" Manda had chewed on a piece of gum and affected a nonchalance belied by her interest in this newly career-minded sister.

"Oh, you know," she said, affecting a flippancy she did not feel, for to speak from the heart would be to expose herself. "Bringing down the bad guys. Getting justice." And for the first time since she had arrived home, she gave a proper smile, one that reached her eyes and lit them so that her severity, her seriousness, briefly disappeared.

When she enrolled for her degree, it was under a different name: Kate Mawhinney. Kate, a harder, sharper form of her softer middle name, Catherine, and Mawhinney, her mother's maiden name, which Lynda had recently reverted to after discovering that Pete and his twenty-eight-year-old girlfriend were going to have a child.

Holly Berry—a joke of an individual with a joke of a name— was shed entirely, like a skin shorn from a bedraggled, raddled sheep to reveal a clean, brutally cropped one.

Her metamorphosis continued. The hair she had cut just before going down to Oxford grew back, and over the years, grew
lighter, the Sun-In that Manda had liberally applied that first summer being replaced by highlights that were so convincing only
her mother and sister ever remembered that she wasn't a natural
blonde. She shrank: those problematic breasts and the stomach
that bulged beneath them melted away and her body was honed,
contained, controlled by weights and running. The war with her
body was constant. Her soft yieldingness, her unnecessary sexi-
ness fought until she became almost androgynous; her look slight
and fierce. Her heavy near monobrow was pruned and plucked,
and as she grew increasingly willowy, her cheekbones emerged—
high, sharp, and distinctive while her once-plump cheeks were
pared down, her face becoming a heart.

"She's a looker," Lynda remarked at her daughter's graduation, as she photographed her outside the city's art deco Philhar-
monic Hall, her mortarboard perched jauntily on her head, but
her smile still a little severe. "If only she'd realize and let someone
take her out."

For her Liverpool student years were almost entirely devoid
of boyfriends. Kate Mawhinney being a woman few would dare
to ask out so complete was her contempt for men. Which was
why it was such a surprise when she gained a boyfriend, who
briefly became a husband, when she started Bar School in London. Alistair Woodcroft, a genial young man who deferred to
her at all times, and was never taken on by chambers after his
pupilage.

She had so wanted to trust someone again, to drop the brittleness that she knew had entered her soul, and to let herself be loved just a little. But she couldn't handle the intimacy, though she managed the sex. She didn't want him to pry into her deepest thoughts or to try to *help*. And so she snapped; scored points; put him down; pushed him away whenever there was a risk of him getting too close. She would see his eyes flare with hurt and she would stay late in the wine bar or the office, only creeping home when she knew he would be asleep, or pretending to be asleep.

The marriage lasted eighteen months and left her with two things: a disinclination to live with anyone ever again and a new name, with which to begin her legal career. She liked it for its simplicity—the hard, no-nonsense consonants, the three stolid syllables, the impression of sturdiness.

Kate Woodcroft had arrived.

# Twenty-one

## Ali

### 26 April 2017

Ali slumps at the kitchen table and wriggles her toes in her black, opaque tights, pushing her heels down firmly. The house is quiet for once. Ten p.m. The packed lunches made and kitchen tidied—or as tidy as it will ever be. The children are asleep, Ed is away, and although she knows she should try to catch up on some sleep, she needs to summon up the energy to go through the palaver of getting ready for bed. Besides, it is so rare to have a moment just to stop. To have the time to think.

She takes a sip of her tea: decaffeinated Earl Grey, milky and comforting, the adult equivalent of the warm milk that Joel still clamors for at bedtime and which she makes if she is in a good mood. Not something that happens much these days. She reaches for yesterday's *Guardian*. She rarely gets the papers during the week, but this was a freebie picked up on an emergency super-market run. Perhaps, for once, she can catch up on world events.

She skims the front page and turns to page three—home to the more salacious stories, even on a broadsheet. It's a report on the opening day of the James Whitehouse trial. That's the case that Kate mentioned the last time she was here, in this kitchen: the massive, high-profile case that was supposed to crank her career up a gear. The thought winds her. She hasn't seen her in over a month—no, nearer six weeks. This must be why. A twinge of guilt. She should have texted good luck. She glances at the clock; as ever the friend who feels she has the less important job, who is wary of disturbing. No, if she's working, it'll only distract her, and anyway, it's probably too late.

She scans the first three paragraphs, drinks the story up greedily, absorbing the allegation in seconds: "lover," "lift," "House of Commons," and that sinister detail that stops it being just a juicy bit of gossip, "rape." Clever Kate, to be given such an important case, though she still finds it hard to believe he is guilty. There he is, in a four-column-wide photo, his expression a compelling mix of seriousness and clear-sighted confidence. No smile, no hint of smugness, just that sense of intrinsic self-belief. He knows he is innocent, his expression suggests, and so the jury cannot help but be convinced.

Her scalp prickles with unease. If he is innocent, then Kate is prosecuting a blameless man. How can she do that? It's something she has never understood about barristers—their blithe explanation about guilt needing to be proved not innocence—for she knows miscarriages of justice can happen. She hopes James Whitehouse *is* innocent. He has a wife and children, doesn't he? What must it be like for them at the moment? She can barely imagine his poor wife's horror. But if he didn't do it, then Kate must lose, and she will be devastated.

She skims the copy. Only two years older than her, Old Eto-nian, Oxford—she vaguely knew that. Not accompanied by his wife. Curious that that's mentioned. Her interest in his family, and in particular this wife, intensifies. Now who would that be? She reaches for her iPad and taps in the key words, feeling faintly grubby for she knows she partly wants to see if he is married to some appalling Sloane and half-hopes she is ugly—though she knows she is being unsisterly and it's most unlikely.

And here his wife is, mentioned in some detail. "Mr. White-house's wife, Sophie, granddaughter of the 6th Baron Greenaway of Whittington" and a photo of her, clasping his hand and look-ing haughtily towards the camera—long dark hair flying, wide blue eyes lit with a potent combination of contempt, resentment, and perhaps, just a flicker of fear.

Her insides loosen and her heart ricochets. She knows that face. She knows that woman. More mature here, yes, and more groomed, but still instantly recognizable. Last seen across a col-lege dining hall, dressed in rowing kit no doubt, or a strappy top and tiny cut-off jeans. It would have been post-finals: that balmy June when they did nothing but punt and picnic in the university parks. She can see this girl now: head tossed back as she laughed, playing croquet in the quad; voice rising confidently above her peers—a beautiful voice, well-modulated, honeyed, but occasionally marred by that ever-so-slightly-too-loud cry of laughter. A cry of entitlement.

Sophie Greenaway. That's who this is. One of the beautiful ones who had slipped effortlessly into college life, who barely wasted their time with those not from their background, who knew intrinsically, without it needing to be spelled out, almost as if they could *smell* it, who wasn't destined for their set. The girls who read history of art or English or classics: nothing precise or *useful*, still less scientific, because gaining a career immediately after university, still less paying off any debts, wasn't a priority. Oxford was about the experience, the all-round education—though some managed to become accountants or management consultants, hard pragmatism asserting itself in their final year.

Sophie would have barely glanced at Ali, or Alison as she called herself then, in the mistaken belief that it sounded more adult. So why did Ali remember her better than the other girls who would have ignored her? Why sense some connection there?

She knows the answer before she makes her way to the downstairs loo where her matriculation photo is hung in a way that, she hopes, seems ironic.

And there it is. The proof she is desperate not to see. Hidden among the open faces of all those eighteen- and nineteen-year-olds with their heavy fringes and their soft, mousy hair; those identically dressed teenagers in their subfusc, the uniform of exams and matriculation—the formal ceremony at the start of their degrees. White shirts, white ties, black ribbons for the girls, black gowns, black mortarboards, upright on most, tipped jauntily on the more confident.

There they are. Two girls, their faces the size of fingerprints, dotted at either ends of a row stretching the length of the chapel, standing, she remembers it now, on a bench. Girls who were physically dissimilar—one plump, one slim—but who read the same subject and shared the same optimism, that sense that they were about to embark on a glorious three years. Like divers primed at the edge of a pool, they were poised for the most marvelous adventure. The faces of Sophie and Holly shimmered with hope, not fear.

She looks at those faces now and she knows that there shouldn't be a present-day connection. Natural justice tells her this—though she knows little of the ethics of the Bar.

Had Kate spoken to her about this? Her mind reels back to that conversation when she told her she was prosecuting James Whitehouse. Did she ever mention Sophie? Say anything like, "You'll never guess whom he married?" Or even venture that there was some sort of tenuous connection? She roots for that snippet of conversation, that sentence of admission that will tell her everything is all right; that Kate has this in hand; that everything is above board and she knows what she is doing. And yet she knows, with a chill certainty that makes the base of her spine tingle, that this never happened. That Kate never brought it up.

Her stomach closes in on itself as she worries away at the reason for this omission. Why would Kate not say something? Perhaps she didn't know that James Whitehouse was married to the Sophie they knew at college? Although hadn't Sophie gone out with a James even then? She remembers a tall, broad-shouldered rower; thick hair shielding his eyes, flopping against his forehead;

someone who would never have glanced at them on the rare occasions when they spied him running from Sophie's room. The
figure shimmies into view, forcing aside the flotsam and jetsam
of life, from the deepest recesses of her memory. That must have
been him.

Perhaps Kate just hadn't realized; had somehow not made the
connection; or, if she had, hadn't thought it significant. She hadn't
known *him* even if she had known his student girlfriend, and so
any link would be negligible, wouldn't it?

And yet this doesn't ring true. Kate with her color-coded
Post-its and her intricate essay plans; her sustained and forensic approach to cases; her always-impressive memory would have
winkled out this connection. Would have discovered—even if she
hadn't initially remembered—that the man she was prosecuting
had married a girl who had read the same subject as her at college and who had been her tutorial partner. That there had been
a link between them; however tenuous, however brief.

So why didn't she bring it up, or think it worth mentioning?
There is one possible, perturbing, reason—the reason Ali's insides
are lanced with a frozen poker, fear shooting from her heart and
down each limb.

She leans against the toilet wall, scrutinizing all those faces
and recalling names she had forgotten about until this moment;
individuals she habitually dismissed in one black-and-white blur
of familiarity, but who had been there, witness to those golden
years. Except that they hadn't been golden for Kate—or Holly
as she was at that time—had they? And she sees her dear friend,

swamped in that unflattering hoodie, her eyes shot with red, and with an unfamiliar deadness to them.

And she remembers what happened to her.

———————

She had never told Ali who it was. When Ali had found her that lunchtime after the attack, she only admitted that it had happened. Someone from a different college, she said, and Ali had briefly thought it must be that boy from the student paper she had mentioned, Dan. Then she met him, a couple of days later, and Ali couldn't square it. Couldn't imagine this skinny, silky-haired boy with his fine, long fingers and his nervousness around her friend—in whom he was clearly very interested—as an aggressor, as someone capable of such an act.

For a rape had clearly taken place. Ali could see that. You didn't have a reaction of this kind if you thought the act was consensual. A drunken knee-trembler you went along with because it was easier than saying no was one thing. But an act that led her to scour her body, to plunge herself into painfully hot water—for she had admitted obsessively washing herself afterwards—was entirely different. There was no ambiguity there.

She had told Holly to go to the police, or to contact the college's women's officer, though neither of them knew quite what she would do or if she had ever been confronted with this kind of problem. What about the junior dean? A young French lecturer, supposedly more in touch with student issues than many of the desiccated academics in her quad. But Holly had shaken her head vigorously. "It might have been my fault," she had whispered. "Perhaps I gave out the wrong signals. Perhaps I *was* ambiguous?" She had looked at Ali for reassurance she couldn't give, though she had tried. "Of course it wasn't you; of course you didn't." The words felt ineffectual. It was inevitable Holly had blamed herself. Because why, according to her thinking, would someone do that unless she had encouraged him?

She had remained steadfast in refusing to go to the police and Ali had understood that. Who would want to make a scene about it? To draw attention to herself? To risk having to retell her experience with the likelihood she would not be believed? Women had only recently entered the college and there was a sense that they shouldn't rock the boat. Why would she want to be forever known, by the college authorities, by her tutors, by the other students, as the girl who had cried rape?

She had shrunk into herself, this girl who had briefly blossomed. Who had evolved from the shy, slightly suspicious, sometimes-chippy student into a girl who had grabbed everything Oxford had to offer and clasped it tight with both hands. She stopped writing reviews for *Cherwell*, and attending Labour Party meetings; gave up singing in the college choir, where her voice was a deep, sought-after alto; abandoned her all-night stints for the telephone counseling service; and retreated to her space at the end of a long oak table in the lower reading library, where she sat, protected by a defensive barrier built out of textbooks. If she ventured out at night, she clutched a rape alarm—a hard funnel that let out a high-pitched blast—but she rarely went beyond the library. There she hid, just the top of her head glimpsed behind her bookish barricade.

And when the second year began, she never returned. She wrote to Ali. *Seems Oxford wasn't for me. I couldn't hack it. Only you know the reason.* And that last sentence, and the memory of finding her afterwards, and of Holly protecting *her* earlier in the year—when she had found Ali semiconscious on the toilet and had pulled up her knickers, wiping the sick from her mouth, holding back her hair—meshed them together far more intensely than all the good times. She wrote straight back and they had kept in touch, and when they both migrated to London, their friendship deepened and strengthened even more.

She was Kate by then. Had become Kate during her absence: a harder, more elegant, almost unrecognizable version of Holly. It had happened gradually, but by the time she had started her pupilage, the metamorphosis was complete. This new version was more confident than the girl who had run back home to Liverpool, her voice deeper and more gentrified, all hint of an accent gone—the odd lilt only returning on the very rare occasions she got drunk and maudlin. She was glossy, poised, and rather humorless. Highly focused on her work, with her poor boyfriend, or husband as he quickly became, very much her second priority. Ali had felt rather sorry for him: a perfectly lovely chap who lacked Kate's clear ambition, her drive and tenacity. He was clearly a gentler character who she imagined had never suffered a setback in his robustly middle-class life.

They didn't speak of what had happened that night—for why would she want to be reminded? Only once, early on, had Ali raised the subject and she had been emphatically rebuffed.

"And are you OK? About what happened?"

Kate had stared at her with wide, cold eyes. "I really don't want to talk about it."

"Of course not. I'm sorry." She had fumbled her way towards another topic, averting her eyes so that Kate wouldn't spot her observing her flush.

"That's OK." Kate's voice let in a chink of light, as if she was relenting, her tone so soft that Ali had to listen intently to catch what she was saying. "I just can't go there."

But if mentioning it was entirely unnecessary it was still there: an unacknowledged undercurrent. Hovering when Kate broke up with Alistair, when she went through her many barren periods, and when she lurched from one to another briefly held affair.

It might have happened over twenty years ago, but Holly's rape helped meld Kate into the woman she was. The catalyst that made her pursue a career as a criminal barrister, and the reason she preferred to prosecute. Ali sensed this, though Kate had never acknowledged it.

And now, is it possible that her private pain has overridden her professional judgement? Is it conceivable that James Whitehouse is the man who raped her—and she has a very personal reason for prosecuting him? All Ali knows for sure is that, twenty-four years ago, Kate knew the woman who became his wife; that this is a fact she hasn't disclosed, and there has to be some reason for not doing this. The question niggles like an insect bite she knows she mustn't scratch, but which becomes more distracting the more she tries to resist it. She must think in tiny, logical steps. James went out with Sophie, Kate's old tutorial partner, so perhaps he may have met her; he was certainly at Oxford at the same time as her. But it's a huge jump from that to accusing him of her rape.

She leaves the downstairs cloakroom and the photo with those youthful, trusting faces; tries to think calmly as she boils a kettle, and craving certainty and comfort, makes another mug of tea. It is *just* possible that Kate would keep quiet about a connection because of this sinister, shaming reason. She has never once revealed the name of her rapist and her intense privacy might explain this refusal now. But there's a steeliness, a stubbornness, and a ruthlessness to her friend, as well, and if—and it's a huge if—it was James Whitehouse who had raped her, then she is perfectly capable of pursuing him for what he did to her that night—perhaps little caring if he is also guilty of this rape.

And where does that leave the poor woman accusing him now? If Kate is not focusing on her case, but is driven by something else entirely? Her life will be ripped apart in court, for God's sake. She takes a deep breath. Surely Kate, forensic, disciplined Kate, won't let herself be hijacked by her emotions, but will manage to channel her anger and use it to win her case?

And what about Sophie? Ali's heart swells. Poor, poor woman. Not some silly Sloane but someone she once knew, a woman not so unlike herself, with this terrible question at the heart of her marriage. What must it be like to live with—to sleep with—him? A memory rises of Sophie rushing through the lodge, pink spreading through her cheeks as she referred too frequently to "my boyfriend." Now he is being tried at the Bailey and she isn't going to watch. Does she suspect he's done it before? Even if she doubts him, she must be praying he gets off this time.

And then she thinks of her dearest friend—of Kate—and how, if she loses, she won't just have lost a hugely high-profile case. She will have lost the chance of avenging her own rape, of destroying him just as he almost destroyed her.

If he gets off, it will tear his alleged victim apart. It might Sellotape Sophie's world together.

But what will it do to Kate?

# Twenty-two
## Kate
### 27 April 2017

He looks just the same as he did then. If anything, age has not withered him but made him even better looking, one of those men who improve, like a cheese or a fine red wine. The smile lines at his eyes and the faintest dusting of grey at his sideburns suggests a certain gravitas, and his jawline is firmer, more determined. He has managed that clever trick of looking experienced and still youthful at the same time.

His body is that of a young man, of course. Still that rower's torso—the broad shoulders and the definition at the waist, those Westminster lunches creating no hint of a paunch, or if one ever threatens, he must exercise it away. Though he may have practiced excess with the Libertine Club, I've never thought this was truly him. Someone who rowed for an elite crew and managed a first, and who was catapulted into a junior ministerial rank within five years of being elected, after a lucrative career in an entirely different area, is someone who exercises strong self-control and is capable of great discipline.

I merely glance at him, of course, as I enter the court. The last thing I want is to make eye contact. The fear that he might somehow recognize me still hovers, though I have reinvented myself so drastically. Even my profile's different. The nose I disliked even before he'd kissed the tip of it, and grew to loathe after that, straightened by such a skilled surgeon I can't find the girl I was when I catch myself in a mirror and have to peer even harder when dressed in wig and gown.

But, as the case has continued, it has become clear he sees me purely as Kate Woodcroft, QC. And, as my fear has eased, I've realized that of course he wouldn't detect me. I was entirely unmemorable. Anonymous—"Polly or Molly?" he asked, our encounter another notch on a bedpost. A run-of-the-mill conquest to be chalked up with all the others, if he ever even thought of it again.

I breathe deeply, sidelined by a sudden quickening of my heart, a fierce shot of anger. How dare he have forgotten about it, I think irrationally, or have no sense of the damage he inflicted so casually? With each brutal thrust, he stole my trust in others and my sense of the world as an essentially decent place. The pain of the rape quickly faded; the sickness from the morning-after pill lasted just one day; but the memory of his violence—the wrenching of my skirt, the burn of his lips, the phrase he uttered—that bitter aftertaste has lingered. I thought I had suppressed it, and then Brian handed me the court papers, and the memories were sparked again.

I shuffle my notes, wondering what he thinks of me—this sharp-faced woman in a wig. I cannot know if he looks at me with interest, for there is no reason for me to look at him. Though this whole trial revolves around him, one of its paradoxes is that for the bulk of the evidence, he can be ignored. We—the counsel for the prosecution and the defense—will spend hours not deigning to acknowledge him as we listen to the witnesses who take the stand to give their version of events. He need not even be called—though of course Angela will do so; it would be madness not to. Up until now and for a little longer, it is the other witnesses who will command the bulk of our attention, and not him, at all.

It is Kitty Ledger who is to give evidence next. Kitty is Olivia's close friend, who works at Conservative Central Office. More pertinently, she is the woman who spoke to the *Daily Mail* when they first approached Olivia about rumors of an affair. Despite what Angela Regan might allege, and James Whitehouse believes, Olivia didn't go running to the tabloids herself, but rather let Kitty respond when reporters got a sniff of the story. Angela Regan will seek to savage her for this, and for the fact that it was she who encouraged Olivia to go to the police. My job is partly to establish that she had no animus against this powerful, attractive politician—the close friend of the prime minister, who is a man whose party she seeks to promote, for she works in the electoral events department, and whom she knows, intellectually, she should do everything to bolster. So why did she help set in motion the train of events that have put him in the dock at the Old Bailey? She can only have done so because she knew it was morally right.

She is a good witness. One glance as she enters the witness box tells you that—a stocky, dark-haired young woman in her late twenties with a no-nonsense bob; a demure, navy dress; and an imperturbable manner. In another life, you could imagine her as the headmistress of a prep school, or the matron in a busy A&E. She is a coper. The sort of slightly bossy friend who would never get herself in tricky situations, but would know how best to respond if others were involved, and who, in a crisis, would automatically take charge.

I look at her now and see that while she might be unimaginative, this young woman has a clear moral code. A sense of right and wrong honed, I imagine—and yes, there's a small, diamond cross around her neck so I may be right—by a childhood of Sundays in church. I can't imagine that anything has gone drastically wrong in Kitty Ledger's life, but I can see that, if it had gone wrong for another woman, she would want to put it right.

She speaks clearly and confidently to confirm her name and relationship to Olivia. I establish that her friend first approached her the day after the incident in the lift.

"Can you describe how she was?"

"She was jangled, teary. Normally she was quite blasé about things, or she had been before their relationship ended. But now she was distressed."

We have already established that this occurred a week before Kitty spoke to the *Daily Mail* to confirm their story. In agreeing to this, was Olivia out for revenge?

"No. She *was* angry with him"—I see Angela make a note

out of the corner of my eye—"She felt used. But it was more than that. She blamed herself for the fact he did this to her as much as hating him for his behavior. She said she felt dirty. As if it was all her fault."

We go through the fact that Kitty had probed her friend for details. I can see her doing so: brown eyes widening with the horror of it; arm around her friend like a protective older sister; her tone alternating between outrage that he could have done this; and a gentle, persuasive sympathy.

"Who raised the question of rape?" We need to tackle this head on.

"I did." Kitty is unapologetic, head held high, chest out. "After she'd told me about him ripping her knickers and showed me that bruise, after she told me what he'd called her." She looks revolted. "I said, 'You do realize what he's done, don't you?' She nodded and started crying. She wouldn't say the word."

"And so you did?"

"Yes." I sense a frisson run through the court. "I said, 'He raped you. You told him you didn't want it repeatedly, and he ignored you. That's rape.'"

"What happened then?"

"She cried some more. She said that she had thought he'd loved her. That she couldn't believe he would do that to her. 'I know it's hard to believe,' I said, 'I can barely believe it myself, but James *has* done that to you.'"

"Did you discuss what, if any, action she should take?"

"I suggested she go to the police. She was very reluctant at first. I think she wanted it all to somehow be made better. She wouldn't go for over two weeks."

"That was on Monday, October thirty-first. Nine days after the story was in the paper."

"Yes." She refuses to be cowed by this. "I only spoke to the paper when I was approached about rumors of their relationship, and I confirmed that they'd had an affair, making no mention of this."

"I think they quoted 'a friend' as saying, 'He treated her abysmally. She was in love with him, and he's abused her trust.' Was that you?"

"Yes. It was."

"What did you mean by 'he's abused her trust'?"

"That he had let her down. Treated her badly. I didn't allege rape, or even assault. She was very anxious that I not do that, and, of course, legally I couldn't. I think she somehow still hoped he would apologize and that they would make up."

"That they would make up?" I raise an eyebrow. We need to confront this implication that Olivia was being manipulative, and that she went to the papers—via Kitty—hoping to prompt a loving reconciliation.

"Not that they would get back together, but that they would be able to work together. She was finding it impossible to work in his office once this had happened."

"But that didn't happen?"

"No. He was furious about the story in the paper, which made out she was vengeful. He refused to take her calls or even acknowledge her. And she came to realize that he would never apologize for what he'd done. He couldn't see he'd done anything wrong. That's why it took some time to go to the police. She needed to properly process what had happened and accept it couldn't be resolved or made better before she went to them."

---

Angela tries to make short shrift of her, of course. She takes a more dogmatic approach than with Olivia. One heavyweight fighter limbering up to score some blows against another, and they will not be glancing blows. My learned friend's posture changes, shoulders more firmly square, chest out. Two women of the world, her stance seems to say, both assured of themselves; neither prepared to be underestimated, each fighting for their perception of the truth.

This Kitty is a calculating figure, in Angela's version of events. The sanctimonious friend who disapproved of Olivia's affair with a married man and was keen to swoop to judgement; the do-gooder with a grudge against the junior minister whom she once admitted was "ravishingly gorgeous," but who failed to acknowledge her—and why would he?—on the occasions when they'd met. The young woman who introduced the idea of rape, and first mouthed that ugly word, who tried to shame the politician in the papers—"Abused her trust? That was code for he *raped* her, wasn't it?"—who *kept on and on* at her distressed friend until, a fortnight after the incident, she finally cracked under the pressure of her incessant questions and went to the police.

His Lordship interrupts to tell Angela to ask questions and not make comments; ensures that Kitty can come back to each point put to her. The allegations swirl, risking clouding Kitty's evidence, a blur of muddied water puddling round. Angela scores a few points: yes, Kitty disapproved of the affair and didn't have a high opinion of James Whitehouse, though Kitty's take—"I thought him a cad"—makes some jurors smile. She intimates there was something prurient in her interest. "Why were you so quick to chivvy Ms. Lytton into believing a worst-case scenario? Why interfere?"

And yet I'm not convinced this mud sticks. I watch the jury, trying to anticipate their response, and I spot the likely foreman frowning at Angela at this point and Ms. Orange Face rolling her eyes as if to say, *Do me a favor, pur-lease.* It helps that Kitty seems unquashable. No one likes a bully. And though Kitty is hardly an underdog—too establishment, too educated, too damn posh— there is something endearingly plucky about the way she refuses to be cowed by my fellow counsel, this weighty woman swamped in black.

"No," she insists at the climax of it all. "I told her to go to the police because he *raped* her." And her voice—the voice of a young woman who has had a charmed life, yes, but would never consider agreeing to another's viewpoint if it didn't suit her; the voice of a woman who won't be cowed into saying something she doesn't believe entirely—rings out loud and true and clear.

Essex Boy smirks—a smirk that holds the threat of menace and is directed at the dock, where James Whitehouse is sitting, and not at the woman in the witness box who helped put him there. Next to me, Angela plunks herself down—all gown and self-righteousness with just a hint of bad temper—her mouth a tight, impenetrable line. She knows she could have done better for her client; that she did not handle this witness in a way that helped his case; that Kitty's confident assertion—"He raped her"—has reverberated around the courtroom and will be a piece of evidence the jury remember during their deliberations. My heart swells, and I begin to hope.

---

The day stretches; a short day because the judge has a pretrial review and a couple of sentences to deal with this afternoon. "If you don't mind, we will have this afternoon off and arrive bright and early tomorrow," he tells the jury, and they beam like children told that school has been canceled, for the case is beginning to weigh on them—the need to concentrate on the evidence; to listen attentively as each strand of the story is unraveled and the different versions lie like pieces of wool and embroidery silk; threads of the wrong color and texture that can never be woven into a convincing whole.

First, though, they need to listen to James Whitehouse's police interview: the words spoken by him after he was approached by two police officers and cautioned. Detective Sergeant Clive

Willis, the officer in charge, takes the stand; head held high, voice ringing clear, for this is the most high-profile case of his career.

My junior, Tim, should be reading out the police interview, but he's been called out on another case so DS Willis and I will be playing the parts of the officer and defendant; me voicing the words in as brisk and neutral a tone as possible, reading through the slightly edited interview at my customary, page-a-minute pace.

DS Willis is a perfectly pleasant man but it's fair to say that he sounds like a detective when giving evidence, with that peculiarly deadpan delivery—as if he cannot conceive of, still less risk uttering, something exciting. The questions he asked a senior politician about a serious criminal offense appear of no more interest than the shipping forecast or his shopping list. Nevertheless, the words contain their own drama and my scalp tightens as he reveals what he said to James Whitehouse when he was cautioned—words that every member of the jury will recognize if they have ever watched a detective programme on the TV.

"You do not have to say anything. But it may harm your defense if you do not mention when questioned something which you later rely on in court," he incants and his voice finally rises with confidence and a sense of occasion. "Anything you do say may be given in evidence."

I wait, just for a couple of seconds, and let the significance of the words press upon the jurors, watch them brighten in recognition as the phrases swell and ripple around the room.

"And where did you arrest him?" I ask.

And DS Willis puffs out his chest, the drama of the moment and the incongruity of the setting recalled and relayed. "Just outside the Houses of Parliament."

———————

Though we finish at lunchtime, I feel exhausted by the time I have raced through the police interview. Perhaps it is the process of reading aloud for half an hour or perhaps the effort of not betraying my frustration as I recite James Whitehouse's suave, credible version of what occurred. My mouth fills with cotton wool as I articulate his words, feeling the cadences of his sentences, noting the ease and fluency with which he spins his story. He explained it so effortlessly, that it's all perfectly credible.

For his claim is that Olivia is lying, of course. She never told him to stop as they made love in the lift. She initiated it—just as she had done so many times before. He is sure this is all a misunderstanding that can be smoothed over. And then a hint of his ruthlessness: the officers are aware that he had finished the relationship—he was a married man; it had been a foolish mistake; he owed it to his wife and children—and that she had taken it very badly. She had gone to the papers. Frankly—and it pained him to say this, he said it more in sorrow than anger—he was now concerned for her mental health. It hadn't been as robust as he'd assumed; a bout of anorexia in her teens; the rampant perfectionism that made her a superb researcher, but indicated a lack of balance; and now that her going to the papers hadn't paid off—that he hadn't left his wife as she'd wanted—this patent *fantasy*.

His blithe dismissals tumble from my mouth. Does he believe them? A politician who is so self-assured that his version of the truth is entirely subjective. His truth the one that he *wants* to believe? Or is this the smooth response of a liar who knows that he lies? We shall find out soon. For tomorrow, the press benches and the public gallery will be packed for the main event, and I will test these claims in my cross-examination. Tomorrow, James Whitehouse will give his evidence. And I shall face him at last.

# Twenty-three

## Sophie

### 27 April 2017

The Devon mud pools in the lanes like spilled hot chocolate, running off the hills and dripping from the hedgerows where the hawthorn and brambles gleam.

The children love it. The clay-rich puddles that spread across the potholed road and that cry out for Emily and Finn to splash one another with water—fat globules that pearl on waterproof trousers and coats. "He got me. Hey, you got me!" Emily's self-righteous tone morphs into delight as she retaliates and splatters her brother, red Hunter wellies stomping then cancanning as the puddles race across the muddied tarmac then eddy and whirl.

Sophie watches, not chastising them for once, not telling her daughter to try to keep clean, for what does it matter? They are showing an almost hysterical abandon—Em regressing to being a little girl, Finn far bolder and freer than he ever is at home. They are living by Devon rules now—the rules of their mildly eccentric, real-ale-drinking grandmother, for Ginny has given up the G&Ts from which she drew her name and now brews her own nettle beer. Or, rather, the usual rules have been relaxed to the point of being abandoned. No school, no routine, no Cristina, no Daddy. Only their mother remains a constant; and even she, as she would be the first to admit, is not behaving like she usually would.

They have been down here for two nights now. It is less than forty-eight hours since Sophie unexpectedly picked them up from school and brought them on this surprise Devon jaunt. The fourth day of the case, the third of evidence. A day when her husband's terrifyingly expensive QC should rip the case against him more decisively apart. Oh God, she hopes she does. Her fingers cross in an involuntary tic and she uncrosses then crosses them again. There's no need to be superstitious, and yet she can't discount a thing, will cling to every single crutch.

"Come on—let's get to the beach," she calls to the children, for she craves real exercise: a vigorous walk, not their aimless ambling. They lollop, wellies banging against their legs, feet starting to drag as the novelty of their splashing wears off and they grow warm.

Emily stops and holds her hat out for Sophie to carry.

"No. You wanted to bring it. You carry it, Em."

Her daughter gives a moue of disgust, rosebud bottom lip jutting out. "No," she insists.

"All right, then," she sighs, taking the soft wool with its bright Fairisle knit, and squeezing it into her coat pocket to Emily's evident bemusement. She doesn't want an argument. All her emotional energy is focused on holding herself and the children together and on getting through the next few days.

Because tonight she will have to return to London. Angela wants to put James in the box, and if he gives evidence she must be there for him—at home even if she cannot make it to court. That's the deal she struck, after a forthright conversation with Chris Clarke, who made it clear that if she continued to absent herself, her husband's chances of political rehabilitation following an acquittal would grow even more slim. She was so close to saying she didn't give a damn about James's political rehabilitation at the moment. She is far too preoccupied with news of the trial and whether he is likely to get off.

She winces. The inside of her mouth is sore as if she has an ulcer. But no, she has been chewing it. She runs her tongue over the rough, broken edges; tastes the salt of her blood.

It's no wonder she's so stressed. Once the children are in bed, she logs on to the *BBC News* and the online newspapers, reading everything she can on the case in which James's alleged crime is trumpeted loudly and Olivia is granted total anonymity: name-less, faceless, her job unidentified—which causes some gaps in the papers' narrative as to how Ms. X, or "the alleged victim," as they keep referring to her, came to be in that lift. Sophie has been obsessing about the evidence. Some—the bruise; even the ripped tights—she can just about discount. James is a passionate man. A love bite given a little too hard; tights tugged; knickers ripped—they're all possible; all understandable, none of them sin-ister since they occurred in the heat of the moment. He desired Olivia, after all.

She swallows, trying to stay rational, congratulating herself on remaining calm and on not thinking about the knickers: black, flimsy, unashamedly sexy—the sort of obvious underwear that would turn James on. She curbs herself from obsessing about that, but she can't stop fixating on one detail. That horrible phrase: *Don't be such a prick-tease.* Not the sort of thing James would *ever* say. So why can't she shrug it off? Perhaps it's the fear that others will imagine him saying it, will think him capable of being that vicious and vulgar? Or perhaps it's because he *has* used that word as a casual dismissal. Not to her, but of fellow men. "He's such a prick," he has said of Matt Frisk and Malcolm Thwaites. Perhaps even of Chris Clarke. An airy dismissal. But never used in relation to women or in a way that was sexual. Never *prick-tease.* It's not the same, is it? In any way at all?

She needs to stop this. "Come on. Let's run," she calls to the children, then powers up the sand dunes, trying to shake this niggling anxiety. The wind is picking up now—a brisk inshore breeze that ruddies Finn's cheeks and makes Emily smile, unself-conscious, as they scale the slippery dunes then charge down to the sea.

She picks her way through the shore's debris—driftwood, fishing rope, the odd message-less glass bottle—then gazes at the view, trying to empty her mind of worries. A small island rises from the water, cut off from the land at all but low tide. Burgh Island: the spot where Agatha Christie hid herself away to write *And Then There Were None* and found the seclusion demanded by the novel. If only she could cut herself off in the same way.

She has tried. Oh, how she has tried. There are no shops in

the crease of this valley and there is no Wi-Fi; and so, during the day, she has managed to avoid all news and emails, to pretend—at least to the children—that the events in court two of the Old Bailey do not exist. She is not managing today. Last night was spent hunched over her laptop, a large G&T at her side—for her mother has not abandoned her old tipple entirely—a cold knot in her stomach as she read on, compulsively. The fear spread through her bowels and down her limbs. What was described—the bruise; the ripped knickers; that horrible, menacing put-down . . . well, it chilled her entirely.

She will leave the children here. No need to take them back to London. To force them to experience what she must go through. The possibility that he will not be acquitted, the fear—which inhabits her every waking moment—that Olivia's testimony will be believed and her husband convicted of rape.

Her throat thickens. She cannot believe it. She will not *let* herself believe it. James might be a passionate man, an assertive man; even a forceful man, sexually—someone who wants sex more frequently than her and will sometimes *pester* her for it, if she is completely honest. But he has always stopped whenever she has said no; has always accepted when she hasn't wanted it.

The children race across the beach. Two flashes of red and blue like kites caught on the breeze and blustered, wheeling and whirring in a blur of fierce energy. Her heart swells, and the sight of them steadies her for these are *his* children, and they reassure her so that she is suddenly filled with certainty. Someone involved in their creation could never be capable of rape.

This nightmare is the revenge of a woman scorned who went to the papers, and then found herself in far deeper waters—the Crown Prosecution Service pushing a case even though, as she implied yesterday in cross-examination, or so Sophie chooses to read in the evidence, she later had reservations about this.

"I loved him and I wanted him." That was what Olivia had admitted, when questioned about the moments in the lift. Sophie knows what it is like to feel such desire for James. She understands, too, her intense, flinty jealousy at the thought of him with another woman, and the humiliation that would have provoked her to fatally, stupidly, seek the sweet, quick gratification of revenge.

The case should never have been brought. That is the line they will be pushing when he is acquitted. She can hear Chris Clarke practicing it. Honing a terse statement that will lay the blame with a CPS that had the audacity to pursue a groundless case because it was deemed politically expedient while countless *real* criminals have gone undetected and unpunished.

She walks more briskly, buoyed by this idea, and thinks of some of the things she experienced before her marriage. The blurring of consent in her days of sixth-form parties when boys would try anything and sometimes it was easier just to acquiesce. She is not saying that those boys were in the right—and she would hate this to happen to Em—but these days she could accuse them of rape, or at least of sexual assault, when what they were guilty of was a selfish exuberance and what she was guilty of—for she was complicit in this, too—was a lack of communication. An inability to stand up to them and say, "I don't want that. Please, don't do that to me."

She is all too aware of the legal definition of rape. That it can only be proved if the jury is satisfied that her husband knew, at the point of penetration, that Olivia did not consent. And why would James continue if he knew that? He might be passionate, reckless, assertive, but he is not brutish; and Olivia has admitted that she wanted him; that they collided, the kiss being consensual; that she willingly went in the lift.

Her heart lightens as she runs through these facts. This is an instance of political correctness gone mad. She can imagine the *Daily Mail* leader after his acquittal, and she tries to smile as she walks the stretch of the beach towards her children, who are now throwing slivers of slate at the gunmetal sea. Her husband is far from perfect. He gave mixed messages. He was unfaithful, yes; callous even, for she has no doubt he had no intention of resuming his relationship with Olivia and that he was using her in that moment. But he is not a rapist. Common sense—and the law—dictates that he has to be let off this life-destroying charge, doesn't it?

She will feel better when she sees him—when they talk face-to-face, and she can read the expression in his eyes clearly. Newspapers will always sensationalize and focus on a detail that distorts things. *Don't be such a prick-tease.* She tastes the menace of the words on her lips.

"Mummy, Mummy!" Em's voice drags her from her thoughts, as she reaches them, scavenging on the shoreline. She is holding out what looks like a tiny cockleshell, except that it is blooded.

"Look!" Em gives a smile that looks unfamiliar. "My wobbly tooth came out!"

She takes the pearly nub from her daughter, further evidence that she is losing her last traces of babyhood, that she is growing up fast.

"Will the tooth fairy find me in Devon? Will she be like Father Christmas?"

She looks at Em closely. She is nine. Too old to believe in either the tooth fairy or Father Christmas, although she is canny; knows she will only get shiny pound coins and fat stockings if she plays along with the myth. Or perhaps she is like her mother—determined to believe something because it's the happier, if less credible, explanation? Emily believes in the tooth fairy, just as Sophie believes that James couldn't have used that phrase, because it's what she so desperately wants to believe.

She clears her throat. "I'm sure she'll find you," she says, overbrightly. "Perhaps you could write her a letter to put under your pillow explaining that it's still you even though you're down here?"

"But she'll know that anyway," Finn says, his face cloaked in a six-year-old's confusion. "She'll recognize the tooth, remember? Because she's Tabitha, Em's special tooth fairy."

"Oh, of course she will." She had forgotten the tangled web she'd spun when the last tooth was lost in Cornwall, the previous summer. "Silly mummy to forget."

The lies we tell, she thinks, to ease things, to make life more palatable. Father Christmas; the tooth fairy; a husband who would never knowingly rape someone—and he couldn't, she just knows he couldn't; would never utter that phrase to another woman, a woman with whom he had previously had sex.

She wraps her arms around her daughter, feeling her ribs beneath her fleece—no hint of a dip of a waist, no sense that she will one day be a woman—and breathes in the smell of her soft hair, wanting to physically stop her growing older.

"What's that for?" Em wriggles, spiky and suspicious.

"Do I have to have a reason?" She pulls away with a smile, saddened by her daughter's response but conscious of remaining perky. "Oh, perhaps I haven't hugged you enough today."

"Or me." Finn worms his way between them, sibling rivalry and his need to be loved the forces that drive him; that ensure that, time and again, he is at the heart of any embrace.

For one long, sweet moment they stand there, as the tide licks around their wellies: Em's hands round her waist; Finn's head nuzzled between her breasts; her arms close around them. Then she pulls away. Mustn't scare them. Mustn't overwhelm them with emotion, draining their love from them, but must pull herself together for their sakes. And for her sake.

"Come on," she orders, looking up as she brushes down her jeans, giving herself a moment to avoid Em's quizzical gaze, to compose herself so that she is their firm, no-nonsense mummy. "Let's wrap that tooth up safe and head in. Time for hot chocolate. It looks like it's going to rain."

On cue, the charcoal sky rumbles and the sand is splattered with fat droplets that dot-to-dot, turning the blond sand golden. The children look up, wordless, then start running in.

"Who's first back?" Sophie calls.

Emily is in the lead, Finn frantic to catch up, as always. A squeal then a bubble of laughter drifts down the beach.

She must try to mimic their childish ability to live in the moment, to clutch at moments of happiness, standing here, in the rain on this Devon beach. And so she follows, feet sinking into the mounds of sand, cheeks licked by the now-slick rain; trying to ignore the all-pervading sickness at the pit of her stomach; the phrase that echoes like a mantra. A fixed smile on her face; her heart, a pebble of grief.

# Twenty-four

## Kate
### 27 April 2017

It is late afternoon before I pick up the call from Ali. I noticed her number flash up on my mobile as I made my way to Inner Temple just after seven this morning. The sky was a noncommittal blue as the Strand roused itself from an uncomfortable night's sleep. I bought a double-strength cappuccino for myself, and a hot chocolate with extra sachets of sugar to place by the olive-green sleeping bag curled up in a shop doorway. The girl didn't stir and I scrutinized her small, hunched figure to check that she was breathing because the night had been cold—temperatures dipping below freezing. My toes in my thin tights and court shoes were numb as I bent down, the chill of the grey pavement running through me. Only when I noticed a faint movement—the tiniest of shivers—did I move away.

I didn't have time to listen to Ali's message then. I was too focused on thinking about Kitty Ledger's evidence, and on a quick pretrial preliminary hearing I had to do at ten. The icon for my answerphone registered a small red dot, but I filed the fact that she had left a message neatly away. I spent the afternoon preparing for my cross-examination of James Whitehouse and it was only after I'd finished that I pressed the dot—expecting a chirpy suggestion of dinner or perhaps meeting for a drink, for it has been over a month since I saw her and she is good at keeping in touch, far better than me, with my tendency, when work overwhelms, to shut down my social life and be reclusive. There were three missed calls—odd, since she knows I don't take social calls when in court—and three short messages. I played them back, my breath quickening as her voice, taut with anxiety, and increasingly querulous as if desperate for reassurance, filled my head.

"Kate. It's about your case. James Whitehouse. Can you call me?" Then, "Kate. Please can you call? It's important." Finally, at 6:03 p.m., about the time when I think she'd usually be picking Joel and Ollie up from after-school club, a message that is more businesslike, her voice irritated but with a touch of hurt that I have been ignoring her all day. "Kate. I know you're busy but I need to talk to you. Can I come round this evening?" There is then a small sigh, as if I am one of her children, and she cannot contain her disappointment. "I think it's important, Kate."

———

And so she must know. I look out the window of my Georgian office, and across the court towards others in this rarefied setting. The pane is splattered with a flurry of raindrops, the evidence of the brief hailstorm that drenched me as I had ducked out of my cab and back into chambers, struggling to maneuver my wheelie case of documents as the storm clouds turned the late-afternoon sky a deep plum, like a bruise that takes time to fade. I watch the drops trickle down now, and I think of how I would peer out of the library windows at college—those elegant panes of glass that offered a view into other worlds, that let me look down onto those who weren't able to enter—and of how my elevated position here lets me do the same. Enclosed in the heart of the British legal establishment—in the heart of this maze of Georgian buildings—I am completely safe.

And then I think of how James Whitehouse must have thought he was similarly protected in a much more fortified, rarefied place: the House of Commons. Secure at the very heart of the political establishment, involved in devising and voting through our legislation, for heaven's sake. I think of the protection his position affords him, and then of how he may finally be unmasked, caught out by the very laws he and his predecessors helped to create. How his ministerial status does not preclude him from having to stand in the dock at the Old Bailey, as accountable as the most prolific, apparently amoral recidivists. The criminals who break the biggest taboos in society—the murderers, the pedophiles, and the rapists.

I think of how justice is not always done. Of how a recent CPS report admitted that in three quarters of cases there are issues with disclosure: the crucial question of whether all the evidence needed for the administration of justice, evidence that may help the defense or undermine the prosecution, is provided, and whether this disclosure comes too late or is incomplete.

All of us working in the criminal justice system know of trials that have collapsed because it emerges, late in the day, that a star witness has contradicted themselves and is not as trustworthy as presumed; or because information suddenly emerges—perhaps gleaned from social media—that contradicts the Crown's case. We all fear that unreviewed evidence may be sitting in a box some-where; the police disclosure officer and CPS lawyer not having had the time to review it and put it on the schedule of unused evidence. Since such potential evidence is sent to lawyers, it is not impossible that some material becomes lost—left in a post room, abandoned by a courier. Miscarriages of justice may be occurring in the welcome rush to speed up the judicial process.

But it cuts both ways. If there are issues with disclosure, a case can be thrown out in legal argument before we even get to offer the evidence, meaning that those we are sure are as guilty as hell sometimes "get off" on a legal technicality. And I think of how I cannot bear this to happen here. How, even if there is a modicum of doubt in Olivia Lytton's case—for she admits she entered the lift with James Whitehouse, that she kissed him will-ingly, even, initially, that she welcomed it—there is the evidence that mounts up: the bruise on her breast; the wrenched tights and ripped knickers; that phrase with which he dismissed her, as pain-ful as the thrusts in its utter contempt.

I can hear him whispering it now, in that honeyed voice which carries the potential to be loving but was anything but in this instance. "Don't be such a prick-tease." And I know, right down to my bones, that he said it to her there in the lift.

It's not the sort of thing witnesses make up.

And, besides, it's exactly what he said to me.

———————

We meet at my flat in Earl's Court. Somewhere Ali rarely comes, a schlep from Chiswick, though I am on the right side of town. I have picked up a few M&S salads, though I'm not hungry. My stomach is a mass of anxiety, bile swirling instead of the pangs of hunger I would normally feel by eight. I pour myself a large goblet of wine and watch the white spikes cling to the inside of the glass. It is cold and tastes of nectar. An aromatic Sancerre. I take another greedy gulp and perch on the edge of my armchair, the burnished leather still glossy for, like all my furniture, this is relatively new—not the lived-in leather armchair I crave, that smacks of age and casual dishevelment, that tells of a long lineage. The seat is overstuffed, and I find it hard to relax.

Or perhaps it's difficult to relax because I know that I have done something wrong—at least according to the code of conduct of my profession. I knew it as soon as Brian handed me that printout of the legal documents—my billet doux despite the lack of pink fabric ribbon—with *R v Whitehouse* on the cover sheet.

The prosecution has to disclose anything that might undermine their case or help the defense right at the start of the judicial process, and they have a continual duty to do so throughout the trial. And I think it's pretty clear that prosecuting a defendant you know—even if he might not remember that he knows you—is an abuse of process. And if you believe that he raped you? Well, you can see how that might look.

The Bar Standards Board—the body that prosecutes barristers—doesn't stipulate outright that you mustn't prosecute someone you know. Perhaps it doesn't feel it needs to, but it is pretty unambiguous about barristers needing to behave in such a way that justice is not only upheld but is seen to be upheld. By not revealing the connection, I am possibly breaching its code in three ways: by not observing my duty to the court in the administration of justice; by not acting with integrity and honesty; and by behaving in a way that undermines the profession in the eyes of the public. I suspect the Bar Standards Board would take a pretty dim view of me.

I start shaking then. Properly shaking. A compulsive trembling which is utterly alien to me, and which I have only experienced once before, as I scrubbed myself raw in that college bathroom. A distillation of true fear. It continues for around five minutes, my wineglass quivering in my hand before I manage to set it on the table, stem banging and threatening to smash, knees knocking despite my attempts to hold them together, to quell them. I tell myself to breathe, to get a grip; that the thing I now fear the most—being betrayed, being exposed—will not happen because Ali loves me and I can make her understand. I can persuade her, for persuasion is what I excel at. And even if it weren't, she would see, wouldn't she? My breathing quietens. She will see. Of course she will. She has to see.

For I should have disclosed the fact that I know him—or I

knew him, of course I should. I should have willingly passed the case over to a colleague and trusted that they would prosecute him as assiduously as me. And yet, given that choice, I couldn't do it. I couldn't relinquish control and trust something as important as this to someone else. For in relationship rapes, the chances of securing a conviction are slight and I couldn't risk not tipping the scales of justice. I could not trust that anyone else would prosecute as passionately, as wholeheartedly, as me.

Because what I am concerned with is natural justice. With trying to bring someone to account for a crime they committed over twenty years ago—and ensuring they cannot commit it ever again. And I have a less edifying motive. I have felt such pain and self-loathing because of this man, have felt violated by that act, diminished, reduced, irrevocably altered; my trust that he would stop when I asked him shattered like a wineglass hurled on ancient flagstones, crushed to smithereens. I've never been able to trust anyone entirely after that, never been able to give myself completely. I don't want him to get away with doing that to Olivia or any woman in the future, but nor do I want him to get away with doing it to me.

———————

Ali is flushed when she arrives. Hair a little mussed, her face red either from racing from the tube, or more likely, because she is steeling herself for what she has to say.

I go to kiss her when I open the door, but she deflects me,

bending to put her bag down and shrug off her coat, then turning to hang it on the pegs in the hallway. She is unusually silent. Normally she doesn't stop talking when we meet, as if aware that we both have limited time, and we need to cram as much news into our allotted two or three hours as possible. Silence is a luxury that comes with everyday familiarity, but even when we briefly shared a flat or lived alongside each other in college, we were never silent. We were both too busy; her too naturally extroverted and me too enamored of being in her company.

She looks at me coolly now. Not a sentiment I would ever attribute to her for she is the warmest of friends even if our lives have recently felt more distant. And there is something else in those big blue eyes, a hint that she is hurt, perhaps. Aggrieved.

The milk of human kindness that Alistair so painfully accused me of lacking flows through Ali's veins and I try to read sympathy in her eyes for she is nothing if not compassionate. I smile a smile that is more nervous than I would wish. It holds none of the self-belief I convey in court. She glances down, her mouth in a twist, and doesn't reciprocate.

"Would you like a drink?" Alcohol has always eased our most difficult conversations. When I told her I was leaving Alistair, and when we first met after I left Oxford. It was eighteen months later and I was no longer Holly, but Kate by then, and she was visibly perturbed by the change in me. I was all angles: sharp elbows and knees and cheekbones like blades beneath newly bleached, straightened hair. She hadn't recognized me in the pub and we covered up our mutual embarrassment and confusion by ordering vodka and oranges and slinging them back, the burn of the spirit soon loosening our tongues. "Another?" she had asked, and, "Why not?" I had replied until we had downed six shots in quick succession and the swirly carpet was rearing up, the smoky room bearing down. We had staggered from the bar, ignoring the catcalls that followed and laughing with the abandon of young women who have escaped unwanted male attention, as we burst into the cold December night.

"Why not?" she says now, affecting nonchalance, and perches on the edge of my sofa, her hands in her lap and fingers threaded through each other like a basket weave. I place a wineglass in front of her, generously filled with the golden Sancerre. She glances at it, then picks it up and takes a sip, her face relaxing as the liquid slips down so that it is a somber Ali in front of me, but no longer a cold one. I sit on my chair to the side of her and wait for her to speak.

"I'm worried about you," she says at last.

I look down at my toes in their opaque tights, not wanting to risk incurring her anger, waiting for her to finish.

"James Whitehouse. I know he's married to Sophie—the Sophie who did English in your year, your tutorial partner?"

I sense her eyes on me, and look up, tentative.

"I can't work out why you wouldn't have mentioned the connection. Was it . . . it wasn't *him* who did it to you, was it?"

I meet her gaze.

"Oh, Kate." Her look softens, eyes brimming with tears now, and she shifts forwards as if to hug me. I can't bear it, would almost rather the harsh burn of her anger than the warmth of her touch.

"Don't."

"Don't what?"

"Touch me." My words come out wrong, my voice tight as a vise.

A flash of hurt crosses her face, and I look back down, hands in my lap, shoulders hunched forwards; trying to contain my emotion. The second hand on my watch ticks: one, two, three, and I wait.

"I can't believe it was him," she says, as if seeking reassurance that it wasn't.

I remain silent. There is little I can say.

She looks agitated, her cheeks flushed, for the truth seems particularly unpalatable. Her fingers twist until she thrusts her hands beneath her thighs.

"All these years, it never occurred to me it might be him . . . I mean, we didn't *know* him, did we? Did you know him?"

"No." I clear my throat.

"He was never in college, really, was he?"

"No." I'm not sure where this is getting us. "It didn't happen in our college and I didn't need to know him."

"No—of course not . . . Oh, *Kate.*"

I wait, not quite sure what she wants from me. I cannot rail or weep about this, now, for I have boxed up my anger, and if it occasionally takes me by surprise, it is not for public consumption—not even with the woman to whom I am closest and with whom I couldn't share it then. My colleagues sometimes call me the Ice Queen—a compliment of sorts, for a barrister has to be capable of putting emotion aside and being forensic, detached, even severe. I am icy now. Cannot let myself show anything as messy as grief or fury. Somehow I expect her to know this, and hope she will let the issue drop in a show of sympathy.

But, of course, I have underestimated her.

"Kate, should you really be prosecuting him when he did this to you?" Her voice is beseeching, but she has pinpointed the kernel of the problem: the probable lack of impartiality given that I am prosecuting a man who raped me for exactly that crime. "I can totally see why you'd want to do it, but how could you have got yourself into such a position? Shouldn't you tell the judge or something?" And she looks at me as if I have the power to right all this now, though I can't without the trial being abandoned and a fresh one ordered; one prosecuted by someone who cannot care as much as I do; one which will ensure Olivia has to go through this whole ordeal again.

She does not see this, does not realize, either, that if I confess to this prior knowledge, the trial will be stopped on the grounds of abuse of process and my entire world will come tumbling. The only other option is to hold my hands up and claim that I have only just realized the connection. But who on earth will believe me?

I must tread gently here for I have a choice. Do I lie and try to convince her that my experience is irrelevant, that as a professional I can put it aside; or do I tell the truth and try to appeal to her sense of natural justice and compassion? She wouldn't betray me; I know that, however clear her moral vision, her need to do the right thing. But I need her to understand my stance, or at least be convinced of the reason to stay silent. I don't want her to think me corrupt but to realize that, in that moment of accepting the papers from Brian, I didn't feel I had a choice.

I begin to talk and I find that my voice is trembling as I try to explain why I took the decision to accept the brief, even though I knew I could lose everything. The spectre of me sitting in front of a disciplinary tribunal hovers, just out of eyeshot: the prospect of me being barred from working. I think back to the moment when Brian handed me the documents and I could—perhaps should—have said, very calmly, "No thank you." Why didn't I? Because I am a control freak who couldn't bear to pass up the opportunity? Because I wanted to wreak my revenge? My accepting felt involuntary. I held out my hand and took it and it felt as if Fate intervened. *Here you are*, she said. And I know this sounds like madness: the ramblings of a schizophrenic who pleads diminished responsibility; who argues that a voice in her head told her to do something. But, in that split second when I took the papers, I wasn't thinking rationally.

"Can you imagine if something happened to Pippa?" I say, and I am aware that this is dangerous ground, my asking my closest friend to imagine the very worst thing happening to her daughter. "If, God forbid, she was assaulted."

She looks sickened.

"Wouldn't you do everything possible to avenge that—

especially if you thought there was a good chance the man who hurt her might get off?"

She nods.

"I haven't got a daughter and I never will," I say. "But the girl I was—that naïve, idealistic, *virginal* student who was so excited by life—is the girl I want to avenge, the girl I want to help."

I pause and my voice comes out in clots now, the pain suddenly building until my words are ragged, and I sound like someone else entirely. "He has done so much damage," I try to explain. "He damaged *me*, and what he did has stuck with me and still affects me, over twenty years later, when I should be completely over it."

"Oh, Kate."

"I try so hard to be happy—and sometimes I manage it. I feel real happiness when I've won a case and I see a sunset over Waterloo Bridge; or when I'm in the warmth of your kitchen; or the odd night with Richard when I let myself just relax and enjoy being with him. But then I'll be lying in bed and some memory will rear up: the tone of his voice; the shock of having my shirt wrenched open and my knickers shoved down; that grip of fear as my back was rammed against the wall of the cloisters and I realized that I couldn't get away.

"Taking the brief was rash and I'm never rash . . ."

"No, you're not," she agrees.

"It was the least sensible thing I have done. But I have accepted it now, and I have to see it through. Don't you see that he has got away with so much? Not just with me but with Olivia, too? I *know* he raped her—there are too many parallels with my case. And he'll get away with both rapes if I hold up my hands now."

"But if you admitted to knowing him and the judge ordered a retrial, with another barrister, he might still be convicted?"

"He might. But Olivia might well feel she couldn't go through another trial. And I would feel I'd let her down immeasurably if that happened, or if someone prosecuted him without my knowledge of what he was capable of; of what he did.

"I will be ruined if I confess, but he will be politically rehabilitated and his star will rise." My voice goes up in desperation, and I look at her, suddenly frantic, for I need her to see how unjust this probable ending will be. How he—a man born lucky—will continue to thrive and excel; once more the golden boy for this will be seen as a blip, a madness brought about and prosecuted by vengeful women. An unfortunate stain that will be eradicated over the years.

I am gesticulating now, catching at the air with my hands as if hoping to grab hold of some certainty. My eyes bright, filled with the threat of tears.

And my oldest, loveliest friend turns to me and quietly nods. Just the gentlest of nods: complicit, understanding. And I gulp down my gratitude at her making this choice. Of her unconditionally backing me.

# Twenty-five

## Sophie
### 28 April 2017

James is nervous. Sophie, who thought she knew her husband entirely, has only seen him this rattled on one previous occasion.

And just like then, he must be more credible, more *persuasive* than he has ever been before.

"You pulled it off then," she wants to say, only neither of them want to be reminded of that time. And besides, the stakes here are higher. This time his run-in with the police has ended in court.

You wouldn't guess at his nerves. He is not a person who betrays his anxiety, and he is not an anxious person. His innate self-belief, his confidence in his ability to achieve, overriding any troubling thought. She has always envied him that: this characteristic that is more intrinsic than the confidence she can shrug on when required, like a superhero's cloak that gives the veneer of impermeability or at least competence. He knows he is impressive. Self-doubt—which she increasingly identifies as female—has never troubled him. He will be acquitted, he reassures her, because he is innocent and because he has the utmost faith in the jury.

Nonetheless, he is not his usual urbane self. There is a tension in his jaw, which juts so that he looks far more chiselled than usual, and he is particularly focused as he dresses—the tie in a fat Windsor knot; the double cuffs fastened with simple, unobtrusive links; his white shirt new, not one of the six she has had dry-cleaned.

Perhaps he has been like this every day of the trial. She has abandoned him so she wouldn't know, but Cristina intimates that he is more nervy this morning. "It's good you are back," the au pair offers when they meet briefly in the kitchen, for Cristina is keeping a low profile and is largely out of the way. Sophie sips a black coffee she does not want and watches the girl compile a breakfast of fruit and yogurt and honey, marveling at her ability to eat for Sophie's stomach is corroding.

"He is much better now you are back. I think he needs you," Cristina adds, as she ducks from the room, her tone matter-of-fact and nonjudgemental. And it is true, Sophie thinks, as she watches James give her the sort of smile he might give a civil servant, one that doesn't reach his eyes, but is made for courtesy's sake.

He takes the coffee she offers and sips, his Adam's apple bobbing.

"Bit cold."

"I'll make another."

"No." His tone is sharp and he corrects himself, smiles in amelioration. "No. It's fine, really. I'll do it."

He begins to dismantle the coffee machine, and she waits,

imagining the grains splattering onto those pristine white cuffs and the re-dressing that must come.

"Actually, would you mind?" For a moment he looks helpless: like Finn when confronted with his football boots, unable to fathom how to do them up.

"Of course." She goes to place a reassuring hand in the small of his back but he shifts away, almost imperceptibly and yet emphatically.

"I'll be in the front room, thinking."

There is no need to mention that, of course, she'll bring it through.

His uncharacteristic display of nerves forces her to be calm. Just as she has managed that veneer of serenity around her children, so she manages it for him—being the type of steadfast, self-assured woman he so desperately needs her to be.

She is buoyed by his behavior last night. They were both exhausted: she by the drive back and her apprehension at seeing him after poring over the evidence, and he by the strain of sitting in court. His face was cloaked in grey and she felt an overwhelming and unexpected tenderness as he took her in his arms. How could she have doubted him? How could she have allowed herself to think he could say those terrible words, and worse, how could she imagine that he hadn't cared enough about Olivia's feelings? How could she even have half-formulated the suspicion that perhaps he was capable of rape?

She feels disloyal just thinking it now. She had sunk into his arms and really held him, conscious that it was unprecedented for him to need her so entirely. His shoulders relaxed, just a little, and she had stood, feeling the warmth of his body flowing through hers and enjoying his dependence, brief and uncharacteristic, and all the sweeter for its novelty.

And then they had made love. Properly made love in a way that they hadn't since the story broke. Not sex fueled by anger or a need to assert that they were fine, that they would be fine; or sex entered into because it was the easiest way to distill the anxiety, the fear and the doubt that had enveloped them for the past five and a half months: sex as a pure physical relief. No, they had made love. A tender lovemaking that communicated his need for and reliance on her; that exposed him at his most vulnerable—his face soft; no artifice; no need to impose a certain image. And afterwards, as she lay there, aware that she should get up, but wanting to luxuriate in their closeness, she felt that he had told her, as perfectly and completely as he could without words, that he was innocent. A man who could make love like that, with the utmost tenderness and consideration—her husband, her children's father—could never be capable of something as ugly and brutal as rape.

———

She walks the few steps from the taxi to the approach to the Bailey holding his hand. Head up, shoulders back, chest out, eyes fixed on the paparazzi, who rush at them when they see them approaching. Don't let them ask her a question.

"Sophie—Sophie. This way."

A middle-aged man in a trench coat—scruffy hair, scruffy suit, a drinker's red face—invades their space, clutching a notebook. "Does the PM still have full confidence in your husband, Sophie?" His voice is abrasive, energy and anger packed tight in there.

She shoots him a look that she knows is withering. She can do withering. How dare he shout at her? As if she is a dog, teased with a stick. And then John Vestey sweeps them through a door and they are safe, James's hand still tight around hers. She gives it a squeeze, conscious of its warmth, and the uncharacteristic smear of sweat. He releases her fingers.

"OK?" he asks, eyes fixed on hers, as if she is the only person that matters.

She nods and steps back, allowing him to chat with his solicitor, remaining silent, loyal—not required to join in the conversation but unquestioningly there.

Behind the door, she imagines the photographers comparing shots and that reporter concocting some words. Why ask her about James and Tom? The press are obsessed with their relationship and each time they raise it she fears they're digging around about the Libertines. Her palms prick and her heart beats faster, a rhythmic hammering that rings in her ears as she tries to calm herself, to steady her breathing, and drown out a question.

*What exactly do they know?*

———

High up in the public gallery, she focuses on her husband, trying to convey the strength of her support for him though she knows he will not look up and see her. He looks authoritative in the witness box and for a moment she hopes the jury will be fooled into thinking he is just another witness; one who offers a different version, an alternative narrative, and not the man being tried for rape.

There is a sign pinned to the wall, warning the public not to move during the judge's summing up or to lean over the railings. She ignores it, peering down until she feels disorientated, blood galloping through her head and introducing a new sense of panic that momentarily thrusts out her disarming thoughts until she feels as if she is toppling. She sits back abruptly, welcomes the hard certainty of the bench.

To try and steady herself, she scrutinizes the heads of the barristers, shuffling papers around in the still few seconds before the judge intimates that the case should resume and her husband give his evidence. She watches his QC, Angela, and tries to take some comfort in the breadth of her shoulders, the expansive way in which she fills her gown. Ms. Woodcroft is slight in comparison, though not short. A blonde ponytail peeping from behind her wig; a diamond band on her right hand; the most ridiculous shoes—patent courts with gold braid on them—the sort of shoes a female sergeant of arms might wear.

She is fussing slightly, this woman; double-checking something in an arch lever file, the edge of which is thick with colored Post-it notes; the pages bright with the fluorescent underlining of certain sentences. Her left hand scrawls furiously, a fat fiber tip pressing down. Along the bench, Angela has an iPad—as does her junior, Ben Curtis, no traditionalist. She is sharp, has a formidable memory, James says. Sophie finds his QC intimidating; knows instinctively that they have nothing in common; that she does not warm to her. It doesn't matter. She doesn't need to like her; she just needs her to get her husband off.

A hush falls on the court as the judge enters, a ripple of quiet like the stilling of a pool of water, and then James begins his evidence. He speaks well; his voice low and warm, with his habitual self-assurance, but not one hint of arrogance. This is James at this best: the approachable politician, setting out his story in his most persuasive way.

She still finds it difficult to hear. Angela tackles the infidelity head-on, and she listens as her husband explains that his affair with Olivia wasn't something that he embarked on lightly.

"I knew it was wrong," he admits, the fingers of his hands touching in that Blairite trope again, lightly pressing together—here is the steeple; here is the church.

"You were a family man?" Angela prompts.

"I *am* a family man. My family—my wife and children—mean everything to me. It was deeply wrong of me to betray that trust and to become involved with Ms. Lytton. It was wrong and weak and I feel profoundly guilty for the pain I have put them through every single day."

His QC pauses. "And yet you still put them through that pain?"

"I did." James gives a sigh that seems to come from the depth of his body, the sigh of a man tormented by his failings. "I am not perfect," and here he holds his hands up in supplication, "as none of us are. I respected Ms. Lytton as a colleague and, yes, I admit I was attracted to her, as she was to me. In a moment of weakness, we began an affair."

Sophie's eyes brim now, her chest filled with self-pity and a growing sense of humiliation, and she tries to focus on someone other than him. The jurors perhaps, whose gazes vary—the middle-aged man sympathetic; an elderly woman in the back row and a young Muslim girl, sporting a dark headscarf, noticeably less so. She watches John Vestey, and the female solicitor from the CPS, a dowdy woman in a cheap grey suit who leans back, arms folded, making no attempt to pretend she thinks James could be innocent, or perhaps she is just bored. And she watches the prosecuting barrister, Ms. Woodcroft, rifle through her notes as Angela leads her husband on, occasionally jotting the odd note in one of her blue legal notepads; and there is something about the way in which this woman inclines her head and in which she scribbles furiously that reminds her of someone else.

———

The feeling builds through the stuffy next half-hour as James's evidence continues. Perhaps it is easier to fixate on this woman than to tune in to her husband's version of events, which seem designed to convey that, though he was married, his relationship with Olivia was respectful, consensual; his parliamentary researcher someone he cared deeply about. He sent her flowers; took her out for dinner, and in late July, bought her a necklace for her birthday. Her heart judders hard at this revelation—an acute physical pain followed by a difficulty in breathing as the extent of her husband's deception is laid bare; his ease at living an entirely unknown life.

"And what was this necklace like?" Angela's question grabs her attention.

"It was a key," James explains. "A play on words. She was the key to my parliamentary office. I wanted to show that she was valued, that she was integral to the success of my job."

"You didn't think she might see it as the key to your heart?"

"I suppose that there was the possibility for that interpretation." His forehead furrows. "I don't think I consciously intended her to think that. Perhaps I was naïve, but well, I was a little smitten . . ."

His words wind her: five blunt wounds. Her heart closes over and she wants to feel nothing; to be entirely numb.

Angela pauses. Lets the significance sink in.

"You were a little *smitten*?" Her tone is interested but non-judgemental.

"Well, more than a little. She is a very attractive and intelligent young woman."

"And so you bought her a necklace. What was it made of?"

"Platinum."

"So a very generous gift?"

"I suppose so."

"Far more generous than a usual gift for a colleague?"

"I didn't think of her as merely a colleague by then."

"You were lovers?"

"Yes, we were."

"She has told us she was in love with you. But were *you* in love with her?"

"I think that's a possibility." He pauses and it feels, to Sophie, as if every person in the court leans forward to catch his next words, spoken so softly and with such apparent sorrow that he seems to be confessing a secret. "Yes, I think I was."

———————

She forces herself to listen as she hears how they spent the night together on Olivia's birthday. She had been at her mother's in Devon, had managed to speak to James briefly in the early evening after walking to the top of the nearest hill and catching a signal. He had sounded wistful and she had felt a nudge of guilt about abandoning him to his departmental papers while they all lazed around, going for swims, playing on the beach. "I'm so sorry," she had said, imagining his pang of frustration at being left alone in the sticky capital for a fortnight. "We could come home early but the kids would be so disappointed, and so would Ginny. They do love it here."

She remembered feeling the warmth of the day on her neck and being distracted by the sea, glinting at the end of the valley and merging with the sky at a barely perceptible horizon. She had hoped she wouldn't have to leave and drive home.

"Of course you must stay," he had said. "It's just I miss you."

"Ah, we miss you, too," she had replied.

Olivia must have been waiting as he took that call in St. James's Park, perhaps rolling her eyes in impatience. And yet he hadn't given the slightest indication that his evening held anything more exciting than his interminable red boxes and a salad and steak. The lies had tripped off his tongue, or rather the omissions. For the second time in minutes, she marvels at his dual life and how it came so easily to him. It reminds her of that other time, more than twenty years ago, when his explanation didn't convey the whole truth; was viscous; slippery in its omissions. And yet it did the job, was never aggressively questioned. Perhaps—like Emily with her tooth fairy, like her in Devon last summer—they were all just willing to be convinced.

She shrugs the thought aside and tries to focus on his answers once more; to will him to continue to come across as his personable self—flawed, yes, but all the more human because of this. Her nails pinch hard white crescents into her palm, the pain a welcome distraction from the dull throb in her chest, the overwhelming desire to cry.

And then Ms. Woodcroft interrupts.

"My Lord. My learned friend is leading the witness."

The judge raises a hand and lowers it as if disciplining an exuberant puppy he really does not have the time for. Angela smiles—Sophie can hear the smile in her deep vowels; and her heavy condescension—and carries smoothly on.

But Ms. Woodcroft's interjection preoccupies Sophie—the

tone, the timbre of that voice, well modulated, deep, like an
expensive claret one wants to linger over. A voice replete with
privilege that hints at a fine intelligence and exclusive education, so why is there something about her—a quality of intensity,
perhaps—that reminds her of someone she hasn't thought of for
over twenty years?

It must be her habit of writing. That feverish, left-handed
scribbling, as if her thoughts are so voluminous it is a race to
get them all down. Holly wrote like that, but so must plenty of
people, particularly tenacious barristers for whom any chink
in a narrative must signal another opportunity to prise a story
apart. She can almost see this woman's brain bulging beneath
that wig, concocting ways in which to trip up her husband
under cross-examination, though so far James doesn't seem to
have put a step wrong. He even has the less visibly impressed
jurors—that older woman, the Muslim girl—watching him
with less antagonism, while the rather obviously pretty younger
women—eyebrows dark arcs, tans from a bottle—seem to have
succumbed to his charm. They are lapping up his words—at
least at this point, while it's a tale of infidelity, a messy, modern
love story, and nothing more sinister. No mention of bruises or
ripped knickers. No suggestion, yet, that he might have said,
"Don't be such a prick-tease." She must stop it! There's no point
in repeating those horrible words.

She leans back, tells herself to relax. Forget about Holly. And
she must listen, must force herself to drink it all in. And so she
turns back to James; to her cheating husband, whom she is begin-

ning to loathe herself for loving, and who she is starting to like just a little bit less . . .

His evidence continues. She still closes her mind to much of it and lets his words wash over her like water applied to a thick block of parchment. They are getting closer to the kernel of the case: the incident in the lift. And she senses that she must conserve her energy for that moment when she will hear her husband's version of that event, spoken under oath. Her attention must be pin-sharp then.

Ms. Woodcroft speaks again. Another point of law, another weary dismissal by the judge. How could she have reminded her of Holly? This barrister has sticklike arms, no hint of a bust, slight shoulders. A skinny bird of a woman. Studious. A little neurotic? Not someone who will land a lethal blow on her husband, who will cut through his easy charm—for he still comes across as relaxed, despite taking the process seriously; and it is only she— alert to every tic—who can sense, in the slight tightening of his jaw, the tension in him. His voice brings her back to the present. His deep, persuasive voice that often holds the potential for a laugh, but then slips into one of confident authority. His tone is somber now. The politician taking responsibility for his failings but careful not to say anything to implicate himself at the same time.

"I'd like to take you back to what happened in the com-

mittee room corridor, on the morning of October thirteenth,"
begins Angela Regan, and she smiles at him, easily.

"Ah yes," says her husband. "After Ms. Lytton called the lift."

---

Later, Sophie wonders quite how she sat through it all, craning
over the side of the gallery, trying to imagine the thoughts of
the jury, those twelve diverse individuals who will decide her
husband's fate. She wonders how she dealt with the frankly in-
quisitive glances of those around her—who had recognized her,
there on the front row, and had shushed and exchanged mean-
ingful looks as she sidled past them. Shame seeps through her,
angry and hot. To think that she once enjoyed being looked at,
as a young woman at Oxford. This is a different kind of look: a
gossip-fuelled, judgemental, overtly bewildered analysis. *That's his
wife. Is she married to a rapist? Did he do it, after all?*

She tries to block them out; and almost succeeds, for James's
evidence is compelling. A very different narrative to that she has
read in the papers. An account she so desperately wants to believe. This is a version of events in which the woman who has
ripped her marriage apart called the lift and told her husband he
was "devastatingly attractive"; in which she ushered him in and
he—preoccupied by the *Times* article and grateful for some privacy in which it might be discussed—had naïvely, unthinkingly
followed.

"I know it sounds ridiculous," he says with the self-deprecating smile she knows so well, the one that works with the mothers at the school gate, with the children's teachers, with constituents. "But I just wanted to talk to her. She had always been a good sounding board. I suppose I doubted myself—found myself questioning if my manner could be construed as arrogant—and I thought she of all people would put me straight."

"But you didn't talk?" Angela prompts him.

"No, we didn't talk." He shakes his head, as if at a loss to explain how he could have found himself embroiled in this situation. "She reached up to kiss me and I found myself responding. It was a moment of madness, of sheer weakness." He pauses and his voice trembles, pregnant with a sincerity that comes easily. "It's obviously something I deeply regret."

His counsel pushes on, taking him through his version of the kissing, the bottom touching, the blouse opening. "I never wrenched her blouse open," he elaborates, and he looks around the court as if the idea is preposterous. "As I remember, *she* helped *me* unbutton it. I'm not brutish. Not the sort of man who would *ever* wrench a woman's clothes off. That's not my kind of thing."

He is clever, thinks Sophie. Careful not to say what she knows he thinks: that he is not a man who ever *needs* to wrench a woman's clothes off, that Olivia was practically panting for him.

"And what about the laddered tights?" prompts his barrister.
"They were very fine tights. Fifteen denier. The sort of tights that easily snag."

"That must have happened when she tugged them down and I tried to help her." He pauses, almost risks looking rueful.

"I'm afraid things got a bit frenzied in the heat of the moment," he says.

"And the knickers, with their ripped elastic? Can you say when these were damaged?"

"No. They may have snagged as she pulled them. I can't remember hearing them rip but, as I say, it was somewhat frantic. From memory, it was Ms. Lytton who pulled them down."

She wants to retch. She can see it all too clearly. She has been in a Commons lift, a tiny, rickety affair whose oak walls are so close together it's impossible not to nudge against those standing beside you. When they kissed, they would be thrust against each other, the space encouraging a tight embrace. Olivia would be helping him undo her buttons, perhaps even unbuttoning them all; tugging at her tights; yanking her pants. And James, frantic, desperate, perhaps gentlemanly at first but then unable to resist trying to help her, would be piling in.

And, at the same time, her skin tightens with the realization that what her husband says is not quite right. It's nothing major, just the tiniest frisson; a sense that things are out of kilter; that the exact truth isn't quite being conveyed. He has said he would never wrench a woman's clothes off—yet she can remember occasions where he tore her clothes in the hurry to get to her. A bias-cut slip of a dress whose straps he broke at a ball; a blouse with a complicated front opening he couldn't wait to get into; a skirt whose buttons he popped as he pulled it open. Moments from long, long ago, when he was an impulsive, passionate young man—twenty-one, twenty-two—and evidence of the strength of their mutual desire, for she had wanted him just as badly. But just because he has long since stopped behaving like this with her doesn't mean he hasn't with Olivia. He is more than capable of wrenching, whatever he says.

She cannot think. Barely listens as he explains away the bruise as just an overexuberant love bite.

"Had you given her one before?" asks Angela Regan.

"Yes," admits her husband. "It was something she wanted when we made love; just something I did in the throes of love-making."

She shakes her head, trying to order her thoughts. She knows he has lied before. He did it to the police in 1993, and he lied to her about Olivia. Sophie has had continual, irrefutable evidence of his lies ever since the story broke. He is professionally evasive, too. It's part of the political game, together with the manipulating of statistics, the massaging of figures, the deliberate omission or burying of facts that may undermine an argument and must be smoothed out of the way.

But lying in court about not wrenching her clothes? That's a new step for him, isn't it? Or perhaps not. Perhaps he thinks it no worse than an omission or a half-truth? *I'm not the sort of man who would wrench clothes off now.* What else is he lying about? That put-down? Or whether Olivia said *no*? A kaleidoscope of possibilities cascades before his voice wrenches her back to the present, crucial moment in time.

For it is the evidence that she has most feared and yet that she feels compelled to listen to; and like her prurient neighbors in the public gallery she cranes forward as Ms. Regan addresses the thorny issue of consent. The court stills; the air taut with an uncanny silence as the QC rises lightly on her toes before lowering herself and coming to the legal heart of the case.

"Ms. Lytton's evidence is that you said, 'Don't be such a prick-tease.' That would suggest that you knew she didn't want sex. Did you say that?"

"No. It's a foul phrase." He is appalled.

"Did you say, 'Don't tease me?'"

"No!" He is adamant.

"What about, 'You're teasing?'"

"I *may* have said that," he admits, "as a lover's endearment. But it was long before we got to this stage. It's possible I may have murmured it when she reached up and gave me that first kiss."

"Ms. Lytton's evidence is that she said, 'Get off me. No, not here.' Did you hear her say that?"

"No, not at all."

"Is it possible she could have said it and you didn't hear her?"

"No. We were in close proximity. There was no way that if she said something like that—or indeed anything—I wouldn't hear. Besides"—and here he pauses as if what he has to say is delicate and it pains him to point this out, though he must do—"she gave every indication that this was something she very much wanted. At no point did she lead me to believe that she didn't consent."

There is a sharp intake of breath from someone behind her, but Sophie feels her breath ease from her. She watches as he takes his time to address the jury, eyes moving from one to the other, for he knows that this is the crucial moment, the evidence he needs them to remember when they are back in the jury room determining his fate.

They are the words that Sophie needs to hear him say. He speaks in a tone of the utmost sincerity, his voice deep and reassuring. At this moment, when he is at his most persuasive, she should believe him entirely.

And yet, perhaps because she has heard that voice so many times before and she knows it can be switched on for moments of high drama, he fails to quell her sense of unease. It builds, this churning disquiet, as he reiterates his point, pausing to let the magnitude of his words resound around the room.

"I know for *definite* that she never asked me to stop," he says. "At no moment was I under the impression that she didn't want it."

And Sophie, knowing her husband—his love of sex, his self-absorption, his relaxed attitude to the truth, his *slipperiness* (and it pains her to pinpoint all this now)—is left with an unpalatable feeling.

She is not sure if she quite believes him.

# TWENTY-SIX

## KATE

And so we reach the moment I have been waiting for. The moment I have envisaged ever since Brian handed me the case papers; and that, on some more visceral level, I have been anticipating for over twenty years. The burden of expectation presses down. My hands shake as I rise to begin my cross-examination, and I feel that curious tightening over my scalp that comes in the few moments in life when we experience pure fear. It happened in those cloisters, when it became clear there was nothing I could do to stop him; and it happened when I realized Ali had guessed at the connection, and I knew that everything I have worked for, my stellar career and this chance to bring him to justice, could all come tumbling down.

I breathe deeply, imagining my lungs expanding and pushing down to my diaphragm, drawing in as much oxygen as possible. It doesn't matter that the court must wait. The jurors sitting up straight, for they are attuned to the rhythm of the trial now and they sense that this is a critical moment, one during which their eyes will flit from me to the defendant as if watching a tennis rally—the sort that makes spectators gasp in anticipation and hold their breath. And I will make him wait. It may seem like a petty power play, but everything has been about him today: we have been immersed in *his* story. Now is the time for me to offer an alternative narrative. To cast doubt on every single thing he says.

---

My problem is that James Whitehouse's entire persona is persuasive, reasonable, credible. Each trait, from the fingers placed together in prayer to his calm baritone, a voice that soothes with its richness and effortlessly imparts authority, lulls you into feeling that it is only right that he should be believed. I must limit the amount he speaks, and not give him an inch—ask closed, leading questions that do not permit him the luxury of explanation, of commanding the airtime and conveying his story. Despite my anger, boiling hard and fast now, this is not the forum for histrionic showdowns. He will be rational and forensic, and I need to remain as clinical and controlled as him.

"I have just a few points to clarify," I tell him with a brisk smile. "This issue of the blouse being opened. Ms. Lytton says *you* wrenched it open, but you have suggested that *she* helped *you* to unbutton it." I pause and glance at my notes, making a show of my desire to be accurate. "You said, 'I'm not brutish. Not the sort of man who would *ever* wrench a woman's clothes off. That's not my kind of thing.'"

"Yes. That's right," he says.

"You're a strong man, Mr. Whitehouse. A former Oxford row-ing blue. An athletic man, dare I say. Have you never wrenched a woman's blouse in a moment of passion?" I ask, for it is worth hoping that there will be a flicker of unease in his reaction, the hint of a memory, or even some foolish touch of machismo that leads to a moment's hesitation. But if I half expect him to recall my rape, or something similar, I am being naïve.

"No." He wrinkles his nose, cautiously bemused that I could suggest a thing.

"Not even in a moment of heightened passion? Such as the moment with Ms. Lytton in September—when you had consen-sual sex in your office?"

"No." He is on firmer ground here.

"What about when you helped tug her tights down and ripped her knickers, in the lift, as you admit you did?"

"Your Lordship," Angela is on her feet. "There is no proof that my client was responsible for any damage."

Judge Luckhurst sighs and turns to me. "If you could rephrase your question, Ms. Woodcroft?"

I pause. "You have admitted that you helped tug down the tights and knickers; that things 'got a bit frenzied in the heat of the moment.' It's perfectly possible that in this frenzied moment you wrenched down her tights, isn't it?"

"No."

"That, in the heat of the moment, you ripped her knickers."

"No."

"Really?" I affect to look unconcerned, but inside I seethe

for I know he is lying about this. He wrenched my shirt open, all those years ago; I still remember the strands of thread and the two lost buttons that popped as he grappled with my Wonderbra. "That's helpful. I see."

I clear my throat and make a rapid assessment. Rather than going through reams of evidence about the bruise—"just something she liked in the heat of the moment"—and facing this wall of self-assurance, I must head straight for the nub of the issue. Bounce my narrative off him and hope to unmask him—in my utter disregard for his answers—as the liar he is. But first I need to expose his arrogance—because the man the jury needs to see is one who puts his needs entirely above all others, impervious to the desire of any young woman who says no to him.

"If we can turn to the incident in the lift, we know that you and Ms. Lytton had had sex in the Commons before."

"Yes."

"On two occasions: September twenty-seventh and September twenty-ninth, I think?"

"Yes." He clears his throat.

"And so you might have reasonably expected that she would be willing to do this again? To have sex in another Commons setting?"

"Yes." He is a little more cautious, the syllable drawn out to indicate that his answer is circumspect.

"When you entered the lift—which you say she called, and which she entered first, having indicated that she still found you attractive—I dare say you thought that sex might take place."

"Not initially."

"Not initially? It was a swift encounter, wasn't it? Over in less than five minutes. 'A bit frenzied,' you admit, so not much time for foreplay?"

He clears his throat. "It became pretty clear, pretty quickly that it was going to happen, but I didn't enter the lift thinking that it would happen," he says.

"But you must have thought *something* might happen. You weren't going in for a *meeting,* were you?"

There is a stifled snigger from one of the jurors.

"No." His tone hardens, for he does not like to be laughed at.

"No," I agree quietly. "So you enter the lift and immediately collide and kiss."

"Yes."

"Her blouse is opened—wrenched, she says; opened by both of you, you say—and you put your hands on her bottom."

"Yes."

"And her knickers are tugged down by both of you. You helped, you admit."

A pause, and then, "Yes."

"And while this was happening, you were in 'close proximity,' you say?"

"Yes."

"It's a very small lift. Little more than a meter wide, less than that deep. How close would you say you were, exactly?"

"Well, we were kissing and . . . being intimate . . . so face-to-face."

"So, very close? Ten or twenty centimeters apart—or perhaps less?"

"No more than thirty centimeters."

"No more than thirty centimeters," I repeat. "So if she had said, 'Get off. No, not here,' you'd have heard her?"

"Yes."

"In fact you have told us, 'There is no way that if she said something like that—or indeed anything—I wouldn't hear her,' that's what you said."

"Yes." He juts his chin forwards, on the defensive, perhaps not sure where I am going here.

"And you are not a brutish man. Not someone who would *wrench* clothes aside, you say, even if you might help *tug* in the heat of the moment. So you would have stopped if you'd been aware of this?"

"Yes."

"And yet she told us, here in this court, that she did tell you to stop."

"No."

"She said, 'Get off. No, not here.'"

"No."

"Not once, but twice."

"No."

"She broke down crying, here in this court, as she said it, didn't she?"

"No." His voice hardens, guttural, like a fist.

"You were face-to-face with her; in a clinch; no more than thirty centimeters away. She asked you to stop, and you still carried on."

"No." His voice is tight, but I choose not to look at him; look straight ahead, instead, at the judge—not deigning to recognize James Whitehouse for this is war now, and I am not going to pretend it is pleasant in any way.

"She said it again, and you chose to ignore it again."

"No," he insists.

"You entered her even though you knew she had said no twice."

"No."

"In fact, you knew she wasn't consenting because you said, 'Don't be such a prick-tease.'"

"No."

"What does that phrase mean, Mr. Whitehouse?"

"What?" He is momentarily thrown by this change of pace.

"It's particularly unpleasant, isn't it?" And here I have to rein myself in, to make sure the anger that is rising doesn't engulf me. "It means 'don't excite me sexually and fail to follow through.' It acknowledges a reluctance to continue, a lack of consent, doesn't it?"

"That's academic. I didn't say it," he insists.

"But you did say, 'You're teasing,' didn't you?" I glance at my notes. "My learned friend Ms. Regan asked, 'Did you say, 'You're teasing?'" And you replied, 'I may have. . . when we first kissed.' You sensed her reluctance," I push on, biting down on each word. "You knew that she was withholding consent then."

And there it is: a hint of anger, for his jaw juts. He is fighting some internal battle.

"It was something that was meant to be endearing." His voice is as tight as an overwound watch. "Just something we said."

"You sensed her reluctance, and then you raped her because when she said, 'No, not here,' you chose to disbelieve it."

"No."

"You thought she didn't really mean it."

"No."

"Or rather you *didn't care*. You knew she had said no, but you ignored her lack of consent because you thought you knew better." And here I look at him, at last, directly, in a challenge, and I wonder if I see a flicker of recognition, but no, it is just a flare of anger.

I turn to the judge, not giving James Whitehouse the chance to answer.

"No further questions, My Lord."

# Twenty-seven

## Kate

### 1 May 2017

The jury is sent out late on Monday morning, after closing speeches and Judge Luckhurst's reminder that they take their time to weigh up all the evidence. He repeats the stricture he gave them at the start of the trial, that "it is the Crown who brings this case and the Crown who has to prove it. Mr. Whitehouse doesn't have to prove a thing." He summarizes the most salient points in our arguments and reiterates the definition of rape, hammering home that it is consent that is at the heart of this case; the crucial question—one person's word against another's—of whether James Whitehouse could reasonably know at the point of penetration that consent wasn't given.

The jurors are alert during this master class in jurisprudence, chests no longer caved in or bosoms easing onto the desk in front of them. Backs are straight; notes taken—for they are the diligent students listening to their headmaster, keen to accept this responsibility, to step up to the mark. For over a week, they have watched as highly educated professionals have sought to persuade, cajole, and argue; to perform to the best of our capabilities and impress them; and—yes—to score points off one another. Now, for the first time, the power is entirely with them. The judge will determine any sentence, but the decision, the choice over whether James Whitehouse is innocent or guilty; a rapist or a lover; someone who called his victim a prick-tease, bruised her and yanked down her underwear; or someone who merely laddered her tights and gave a love bite in the heat of that moment? That decision is entirely theirs.

I retire to the barristers' mess. DC Rydon and DS Willis are heading to the canteen for a coffee, but I decline their offer to join them. They make me nervous, and I crave either silence or the distracting black humor of my colleagues railing against the inefficiency of the judicial system or the sheer ineptitude that stymies us each day. John Spinney, from my chambers, is incandescent about a child abuse case that was adjourned because an engineer removed the equipment required for the video link for the victim, from court, overnight. "Have they any idea how difficult it was to get this highly vulnerable nine-year-old girl here in the first place?" David Mason is offloading about a defendant who pulled every trick in the book to suggest he was physically incapable of standing trial, but managed a remarkable recovery once acquitted. Caspar Jenkins is spitting about a pretrial preliminary hearing that had to be adjourned because the court documents hadn't been uploaded electronically.

It is cathartic, this expletive-loaded conversation; the almost-competitive telling of worst-case scenarios; this sense that we are all battling against bureaucratic incompetence, and working with

some morally devoid individuals; and oh! how we need this ca-
maraderie, as well as our more highfalutin quest for justice, and
the high of getting the right, the *just*, result to drive us out to
each godforsaken court in our circuit each day.

I listen to their banter and take a call from Brian about a murder trial scheduled for later in the year in Norwich. I don't do
murders, but there's a sexual element. The defendant is charged
with killing the man who repeatedly abused her as a child, thirty
years ago. I am being asked to defend, and feel easier, begin to
imagine how my mitigating arguments might play out. He emails
the preliminary documents across, and I try to immerse myself.

An hour ticks by. Will they come back before lunch? Unlikely, and it's almost a relief when one o'clock comes and I know
they can't be recalled for the hour when the judge is dining. Tim
asks if I want to pop out for a sandwich, but I decline. I don't eat
during the day—too little time—and there's too much acid in
my stomach, which is gurgling and swishing at the moment, fizzing away. I run on nerves and adrenaline, the low-level need to
be alert to rush from one court to another with half-minutes to
spare; the demand that I think clearly and swiftly; the imperative
that I never drop my guard; never stop listening or questioning
how best to break through a narrative and tease out a different
story.

And then, at a quarter past two, comes the adenoidal voice
down the tannoy: "Will all parties in the case of Whitehouse
come to court two immediately." A taste of bile spurts in my
mouth, and I try to calm the adrenaline—that curious combi-

nation of excitement tipping into fear—that surges inside me
as quick as a sprinter straight off the blocks. My hands, as they
gather laptop, papers, bag; as they cram the wig back on my head,
are shaking and I race to the loo, suddenly desperate to wee, and
afraid that I will be distracted if I don't. Alone in the cubicle, I
rest my head against the door, ambushed by the memory of what
happened in those cloisters: the scrape of stone on my back, the
pain of his movements; the heft of his body shoved against me;
that internal burn. I see the gargoyle, hands covering its eyes and
mouth, and more recently, my older self, convulsed with grief as
I slid under my greying bathwater. I feel the howl I gave as I lay
in that bath, and that has threatened to burst out, time and again,
over the years.

I slide the bolt open. I must hold on, though my insides feel
like falling out and my legs are water. I concentrate on trying to
think rationally as I clatter down the stairs behind Angela, who is
walking at her usual magisterial pace. They can't have come to a
decision yet; they won't have come to a decision yet. Though we
all know of quick decisions—seventeen minutes for an acquittal
is my fastest yet—these are few and far between. They have been
out for an hour and twenty minutes. Long enough to have made
a show of arguing if the decision is unanimous, not long enough
if there is a sizeable amount of doubt in many minds.

How long will they take? It will have taken up to half an hour
to return to their room, elect a foreman, and take a show of hands;
and then it will take time to dissuade those who think he is innocent for I am trying to persist in believing that I will get my guilty

verdict. That Essex Boy, the Asian man, and hopefully my tubby foreman will win over Orange Face, her comely sidekick, the elderly lady who couldn't conceive that a man of his status could be so unchivalrous, and the obese middle-aged matron who kept rearranging her bosom as she gazed, starstruck, at him.

Do they all need winning round? After all these years of waiting for jury's verdicts, I still find them hard to read. Urban and female-dominated juries are more likely to acquit. Juries in rape trials don't like to convict. All of this is stacked against me. And yet there was that sharp intake of breath when Olivia revealed that put-down; the sympathy that met her evidence, the suspicion—that I sowed in the jurors' minds—that James might be the sort of man to wrench clothing. That nasty insult: *Don't be a prick-tease.* Not the sort of expression a young woman giving evidence in a rape trial is likely to make up. Not the sort of thing she would want to repeat.

———

We pile into court: counsel, judge, defendant—his jaw set; his face a little drained of color. High above us, I sense, from the rustles, the public gallery filling, and I wonder if Sophie is up there, stomach as tightly knotted as mine. Fear must be coursing through her veins as she waits to discover if her husband is a rapist, and if her world is about to irreparably change.

And then a moment of anticlimax. No jury shuffles in. There is merely a note, handed over by the usher.

"The jury would like to know if they could have a copy of Ms. Lytton's statement," the judge reads. He gives an indulgent chuckle. "Well, I'm afraid the answer to that is *no*."

The usher bows her head and scurries out; Nikita tells us to be upstanding in court, and we do; and then we hurtle back; back to the stuffy robing room and a wait, the length of which we cannot predict or control.

"I'd have thought it was pretty cut and dried," Angela sniffs, as we climb the marble stairs. I try to detect a flicker of doubt, but her face is as impervious as ever. I cannot answer, my throat nursing a lump, my mind crammed with thoughts I don't want to acknowledge—of a jubilant James, acquitted; of me, diminished, disbelieved, defeated by him once again.

"You're very quiet?" Angela sounds sharp, cocks her head—a jay eyeing an earthworm. Her dark-grey eyes are more than usually perceptive.

And I can only nod, trying to shake my ricocheting thoughts away.

---

The afternoon stretches like a cat rolling on sun-drenched concrete. Justice takes time, and these jurors—assigned to jury service for two weeks, and taking their duties seriously—are in no rush to hurry things.

The steel hands of the clock in the robing room judder—three thirty; three thirty-five; three forty; three forty-five. Any minute now the tannoy might sound. Four hours, now four hours and five minutes. Is that enough time? Sufficient for these twelve people to analyze the evidence and to come to the right, the only *just*, verdict?

"I bloody well hope they don't sit late. I need to get away sharpish." Angela stalks the room, breaking off a finger of a chocolate biscuit with a crisp snap, and a silvering of the wrapper.

"Repulsive." She swigs warm black coffee from a paper cup and continues to pace. It matters to her, this result. It will not help the practice of Angela Regan, QC, if she cannot manage to get James Whitehouse acquitted. But it cannot matter one iota as much as it does to me.

I have tried to remain positive, though in the dead of night, the chill certainty of defeat engulfs me. Now, hope is easing with every minute the jury takes. I always knew a conviction would be hard. Rape is a particularly nasty crime, and if it's not stranger rape—a rape of the kind we have been implicitly warned about in stories, and then more explicitly in early girlhood, the man in an alleyway who holds a blade to our throats, or pins us down— if it's a rape committed by a personable, attractive, dare I say it, middle-class professional who has already had a relationship with the complainant; the sort of man you might acknowledge in the street or at the school gate; that you might be happy to have for dinner or to introduce to your kids or parents; if it's *that* sort of rape and *that* sort of man, then it's a huge thing to do as a juror, to cast that particularly dirty, intransigent stain.

Beyond a reasonable doubt: that's the burden of proof the

jurors need to apply before they can do this to someone. And it's far less damaging, far more *understandable* to give him the benefit of this doubt—to mark it down as a bad sexual experience, unpleasant, certainly, morally questionable, but not illegal. Not, by any stretch of the imagination, rape.

But then, as Angela becomes increasingly irritable, I let myself hope that I am being unduly negative. Perhaps there are only one or two jurors unconvinced of his guilt. The judge could call them back now, and give a majority verdict direction. Tell them that he would accept the verdict of at least ten of them, though it would be better all round if it were unanimous, if there were never any room to argue there was dissent or ambiguity. That some persisted in believing he was innocent to the very end.

I spool through my arguments: the closing speech I first sketched out on receiving the brief, and most of which I retained. There is no silver bullet. No forensic evidence that points unequivocally to the truth for the bruise, the tights, even the knickers can all just be explained away. I know he's guilty; '*Don't be a prick-tease*' nails him even if I didn't know of his past guilt. But for these jurors, there's just one woman's word against one man's. Two narratives that start off the same and then diverge. A few small discrepancies—did she or he call the lift? Did she or he kiss first?—and then one crucial, glaring, irreconcilable difference.

If they believe Olivia, I will feel not just ecstatic—of course I will be ecstatic—but *vindicated*. James Whitehouse will be exposed as the charming, ruthless, utterly narcissistic man I know him to be. If the jury believes *him*, Olivia will have been branded a liar. And I—well, I cannot bear to think of what this means for me, and what it says about my skill, my judgement and willingness to let my personal prejudice, my lack of objectivity, override my professionalism so that I have become obsessed with bringing James Whitehouse down.

---

"Could all parties in Whitehouse come to court two immediately."

Four fifteen p.m. Four hours fifteen minutes. The woman on the tannoy sounds bored, with no awareness of the potential drama of her announcement, its effect on Angela and me as we spring up, grab papers and laptops, cram on our wigs.

"Verdict, or sending them home for the day?" my opponent asks, more even-tempered now for there is nothing we can do to influence events, and at least something appears to be happening.

"The latter," I say, though I am not quite sure how I will bear a night of agonizing over whether they will come to the right verdict as they turn the evidence over in their minds.

But in court two, the atmosphere is dense with the pressure of expectation. The press benches are filled; the print journalists knowing they must move fast to meet their first-edition deadlines; the broadcasters thinking of the six o'clock bulletins in which a conviction would be placed high. Jim Stephens is in his front-bench seat. He hasn't missed a day. My throat thickens as I see the way he watches the usher. She nods to Nikita. We have a verdict. I swallow. We have a verdict.

The jurors shuffle in and I try to read their faces. Most are inscrutable, but none refuse to look at the defendant—something they do if they have decided to convict. Orange Face has the trace of a smirk on her lips, but that's habitual; and the officious middle-aged man whom I have predicted will be the foreman is somber for he is about to take center stage.

"Please answer my next question, either 'yes' or 'no.' Have you reached a verdict on count one?" Nikita asks. The air stills as the foreman looks down at a piece of paper in front of him. For a split second, I imagine Sophie Whitehouse and wonder if she is leaning over the front row of the public gallery, watching this man who has marshaled a decision on her husband's future. Or perhaps she is watching her husband and wondering if she really knows him at all.

It seems incredible that they have come to a decision, and yet, 'Yes,' the foreman says, and there is a collective intake of breath. My fists clench and my knuckles whiten. This is it. One of those pin-sharp moments that shape your life. Like that June night in the cloisters. The rasp of stone on my back; the pain as he entered me. *Don't be a prick-tease.* His voice soft yet I could feel the menace there.

"Do you find the defendant guilty or not guilty of count one?" Nikita asks, and I find I am holding my breath and digging my nails hard into the palm of my right hand as the foreman opens his moist, pink mouth and his voice comes out far too brazenly loud and clear.

"Not guilty," he says.

A woman in the gallery cries out in relief; and another—Kitty? for Olivia is not in court—calls "No!" The cry is guttural, instinctive; the *no* of a woman who knows that a miscarriage of justice is taking place and there is nothing she can do at all.

It's the cry I want to make, that I will echo oh so loudly in the sanctity of my bathroom later, but for now I am silent. Just the smallest nod of acknowledgement. A neat, grim nod as if I am filing the verdict away.

Beside me, Angela turns and permits herself a smile. It's a good result, I see her mouth. My face tightens into a mask. I remain calm and professional, but inside, my heart roars and roars.

# Twenty-eight

## Sophie

### 1 May 2017

James is jubilant. Sophie can feel the excitement emanating from him—muscular, sexual, infectious. He is a young man, again, at the peak of his physical and intellectual power. James as he was when his crew won head of the river, who would scale a college wall to surprise her late at night, and then make love until two in the morning despite being up a few hours later for rowing. The James who snatched a first despite leaving his revision as late as possible, and who won his admittedly safe seat with such a massive swing that it confounded the psephologists; the man who demanded attention at the school gate; throughout Westminster; and even in this court.

"My darling." He is ardent, his kiss passionate, his grip almost painful as he grasps her around the waist, and pulls her towards him in one effortless movement, so neat it is as if they are choreographed.

"Would you look at my wonderful wife?" he asks John Vestey and Angela, as he kisses Sophie fiercely, then releases her to make his way out of the building where he will make a brief statement in which any jubilation will be tempered by his gratitude for the fairness of the British judicial system, the insight of those men and women of the jury who unanimously recognized his innocence, and his concern that this case was ever brought to trial.

The crowd of reporters and cameramen jostle as he stands on the stretch of pavement outside the court. It is all too much: the shafts of the cameras thrusting forward; the gaggle of reporters with their bulbous microphones and spiral notepads; eyes lit with the need to grab a telling quotation; to capture each word that spills from James's lips so that it can be blazoned across a front page or played repeatedly on the rolling news.

"Over here, Sophie; over here." There is an incessant whirring and clicking as these men behind the cameras—and the bright-jacketed women with their microphones, who seem equally if not more pushy—call and cajole. She spies Jim Stephens—always in the thick of things—and shrinks away, her relief at the verdict, so intense she feels it is a physical clutch of her heart, compromised by an almost overriding need to escape.

Later, she sees the news and barely recognizes herself—the rabbit-in-the-headlights expression, the minimizing posture. *But I felt elated, didn't I?* And yet she knows this is not the case. The sheer weight of relief allows no room for lightheartedness; for the jubilation her husband is experiencing. She is drained; disorientated after months of anticipating the very worst, and also conflicted. Questions she wants answered still niggling away.

She steps back, trying to absent herself from the crush. It is James they are interested in; brow furrowed, voice deep as he speaks eloquently and briefly. Chris Clarke had advised that any statement should be short and nontriumphant, merely thanking those close to him for their support and stressing his determination to focus on his constituents and his party's work in government; for there is still so much to do.

But her husband does not understand her desire to flee. He is referring to her now, thanking her for her "continued, unflinching support." She doesn't think of herself like this and guilt tugs as she thinks of her doubt, sparked as she pored over that evidence in Devon, which has only intensified over the past few hours.

"These last five months have been a living hell for my wife and children. I want to thank them for standing by me and for trusting I was innocent of the terrible crime of which I was accused," he continues, and the words wash over her, anodyne, slick, pre-scripted. He had refused to countenance, at least publicly, the possibility of going down.

And now his tone grows deeper with just a flick of disquiet, a hint of blame. "There are serious concerns about why this case was brought to court. Questions the police and Crown Prosecution Service will, in due course, have to answer. We all want the perpetrators of serious offenses to be brought to justice; none of us wants public funds wasted when it is clear that it is a case of a brief relationship that has turned sour, nothing more or less. I am grateful that the twelve members of the jury unanimously accepted that I was innocent. I now ask for a little time with my family and then I am keen to get back to the job of representing my constituents and supporting this government in all they must do."

And then he nods and John Vestey makes it clear that there will be no questions, thank you very much, Mr. Whitehouse really has to get away, and they are being ushered into a black cab that has swept up—no ministerial car any longer, or not for the moment—and falling against the seats, James gripping her hand.

London flickers past as they drive down Ludgate Hill towards Blackfriars and Victoria Embankment, the steel-grey Thames swimming alongside them as they head west towards home, but first past the scene where it happened: her husband's affair. The House of Commons sits bathed in a sheen of golden light, and Big Ben thrusts, proud and resplendent, its clock tower—all brick shaft and cast-iron spire—piercing the soft pale blue of a dusky sky.

Pedestrians scurry as the cab scoots round Parliament Square, then past Westminster Abbey and down Millbank—taking the tourist's route for a woman who is so disorientated she feels as if she is seeing the city she knows so well afresh. After living in a tunnel of fear for so long, she is almost agoraphobic—the brightness and bustle of central London too sharp and intense; the cars too close; the tourists with their cameraphones—not interested in them, she knows, but *still*—clicking away, bearing down on them.

James's phone pings. It has been ringing almost incessantly with congratulatory calls that he takes, but this is the message that matters. A text from Tom. He smiles, indulgent, and—atypically—shows her. "Many congratulations. Welcome back. T."

He hasn't received a text from the prime minister since he was charged. Hardly the most secure form of communication, and Tom wouldn't want it to emerge that he was supporting an alleged rapist, though he has conveyed his ongoing support through Chris Clarke. "A friend of yours says: Chin up, almost over"; "The big man has the utmost respect for you." These snippets and a handful of snatched conversations have had to be enough to sustain. For there have been no late-night chats in the den at Downing Street, no games of tennis at Chequers, no relaxed kitchen suppers with Tom and his wife of eight years, Fiona. They have been virtually *personae non gratae* for a solid six months. But now the door to their social and political rehabilitation has been opened, and more than a chink.

"It's the least he could say," she manages, as she reads the text, and dwells on this former, hurtful exclusion. She doesn't add, "after what you did for him," but the words hang in the air.

He smiles, magnanimous now, able to make allowances, and she is surprised at how moved she is by this promise of resumed friendship. A fat sob takes her by surprise; her habitual self-control compromised so that her breathing becomes ragged, gasps fluttering as she tries to still it; eyes pricking with tears she blinks away.

"Come here, my darling." In the back of the cab, he takes her in his arms, and she lets herself give in to the force of this relief for a moment; feeling the strength of him; the firm beat of his heart through his charcoal wool overcoat; the warmth of his torso and its familiar firmness, hard against her chest. She slips her hands beneath his coat, feels his white cotton shirt where it is tucked into his waist; strokes his back, much as she might with Finn or Emily, to try to convey the comfort and reassurance she needs herself. To reconnect.

"Everything is going to be OK," he whispers into the top of her hair, and she feels a shiver of unease.

"Don't say that," she whispers into his shoulder, her voice just discernible. "You said it before."

He pulls away—his face quizzical as he fails to countenance the memory. "No." He is clear and precise. "Everything. Really. Will. Be. OK."

There is no point dissenting. Nothing will ever truly be the same again—she knows that, instinctively, in this moment—but this isn't the time or the place to risk an argument. Not here in this taxi, with the driver watching them in the mirror, hazel eyes framed by a rectangle of glass, knowing that the fare he picked up from the Bailey is the Tory MP who has just been cleared of rape—the one that BBC Radio *5 Live* will be talking about any moment for the five o'clock news bulletin is coming up. She can hear the music rolling up to the news on the hour as James speaks.

But her husband takes control, as he always does. Presses the button to speak to the cabbie, who makes a fair stab at pretending he hasn't been watching them.

"Could we have Radio Four instead?" He leans back, expansive, and listens as news of his acquittal tops the news bulletin. The words wash over her; the authority of the newscaster making it somehow more official, lulling her, briefly, into the sense that—at least to the outside world—everything *is* OK.

"Come here. I love you." He flings an arm around her, again, his lips curling into an expression of intense relief that she understands—of course she understands—but is half-appalled by. There are no words to explain, no reason to demur. And so she does what she so often does: gives herself up to the force of his personality, of his sentiments, and tries to still the relentless scurrying of her mind.

———————

The children are delighted, of course. They rush at him as Cristina opens the door, James having breezed past a couple of waiting photographers, polite but definitive—"I've said all that needs to be said. Now, I need some time with my family." Finn's face is an oval of joy; Emily's more wary for she has some inkling of what has been happening—not the nature of the charge, for they have glossed over that, said merely that a poorly lady has made things up about Daddy—but the fact that her lovely father has been in court.

Sophie watches as he pulls them to him as if his life depends on it; eyes tight shut as his head nestles between two domes of soft, light hair. She swallows, trying to dislodge the hard lump that seems permanently at the back of her throat, and to prevent the tears that spill now—in the safety of their own home—for she mustn't let the children see her upset. Somehow, they might sense that they are not just tears of relief, but of trepidation for the coming, unchartered days and weeks.

He looks at her over the top of Emily's head and smiles with eyes filled with distilled love, and she finds herself smiling back. The response is automatic. This is James at his very best. James, the loving father and husband, for whom his family's happiness is paramount. The James he would always like to be. The only problem is that his is too large a personality, and he is too complex, too conflicted, too *selfish* a man to be this James entirely—and so James the politician, James the philanderer, creeps in.

"Mummy hug, too?" Finn, always the most inclusive of children, the most loving, turns to try to pull her into their group embrace. He has regressed over the last week and in his childishness shows how clearly he wants them to be together. She lets herself be half pulled; her boy's arms tight around her waist; her daughter's resting on her back; James's mouth crushed against her hair.

"All home. All one family." Emily seeks to put the world to rights, her view black and white, with no room for dissent.

"All home together," James agrees.

*If only things were that simple*, she thinks, and simultaneously, *try to hold on to this moment.* The fact that your children have been spared seeing their father branded a rapist and sent to prison; that they will never experience the desertion of losing a father; need never feel any sense of shame.

You need no more than this, she tells herself, as she enjoys the warmth for a moment: the closeness of her children's small hands around her, holding her tight. And yet, there is that building disquiet. Those questions she cannot quash, and with them, the desire to push her husband away firmly. To experience only her children's embrace.

———————

She challenges him that night—once the children are in bed. She almost doesn't, tries to just drink the champagne he opens and enjoy the moment. A moment steeped in gratitude more than elation and clouded by exhaustion—the strain of the past few months a debilitating drain on her body, like the aches felt a day or two after a marathon or a rigorous boat race.

James remains on a high. Taking congratulatory calls; arranging a private meeting with Tom—all terribly hush-hush; he will be smuggled into Downing Street first thing—stopping to spin her in his arms as he paces past, then finally collapsing next to her, champagne flutes refilled and his expression still joyful as he leans in for a kiss.

He is all tenderness as he takes her in his arms and begins to unbutton her blouse, nuzzling her neck in a way that she usually loves, but which she now associates with other women. She reciprocates with a tight, closed mouth before extricating herself and wriggling away.

"What's wrong?" His handsome face is a question mark, and she almost relents and leans back into him, tells herself not to ruin things. But this is the moment, and if she doesn't say anything, the questions will eat away, incessant, and corrode their marriage like the rust blooming on the planters Cristina left out in the rain.

"There's no easy way to say this . . ."

"What?" His face crumples. Perhaps he thinks she wants to leave him?

"I need to know what exactly happened . . . I can't help thinking about what really happened in the lift."

"What?" he repeats. "You know what happened in the lift. I just stood up in court and told the whole world."

"I know what you said in court, yes . . ." She twists to face him, feet planted firmly on the floor in front of her, hands cradling her elbows as if she could comfort herself by rocking. "But I need to know what really happened. Was it exactly as you said?"

"I can't believe you can ask that." He bends and picks up his phone from the lounge table, shaking his head as if immensely saddened by her question. "After all I've gone through. After all you've heard me admit to, you doubt me?" His voice hardens. "I didn't think it of you. I'm off to bed."

"Just tell me that she never told you to stop." She can hear a strain of desperation in her voice but she needs to know. "That she *really* never said, 'No. Not here.' That"—and here her voice cracks with the weight of her unease—"you never said, 'Don't be such a prick-tease.'" The terrible words spill out in a rush. "That you never said *any* of it."

"What do you think?" He looks down at her, his voice calm again, and reasonable: the James who is utterly in control and will argue at his clinical best.

"I don't know. I worry that it's possible she said something about wanting you to stop and that you ignored it because you didn't think she meant it." The words that have reverberated around her mind fall into place in this neat, easy line that lies between them. Craving reassurance, she waits.

But he sits back down on the sofa, with an ironic shake of his head and a glance of what looks like admiration.

"You know me too well."

"What do you mean by that?" Something jars inside her. *I know you can be economical with the truth if it suits you*, she wants to say. *I know you've done it before*—but she can't quite go there.

"She *may* have made some sort of half-hearted attempt to fob me off."

"What?" She hadn't wanted him to agree.

"But she didn't mean it."

"How can you say that? How can you presume to know what she thinks?"

"Because I know she didn't mean it. She was always up for it." He takes in her crumpled face, for his words have punched her in the stomach, hard. "I'm sorry to sound crude, but I'm trying to be straight.

"It was what she was like: always pretending to resist but then coming round. It was a game to her. It seemed to make her feel wanted. She wasn't always like that, but she was in these risky situations—whenever we had sex and there was a chance that others might come in."

She sits stunned. It is too much to take in: the admission of habitual risky sex, the reference to Olivia's desire, the details of their game playing. She gropes for the nub of the issue amid the fog of his speech.

"But perhaps she didn't want it this time?"

"I very much doubt it."

"And she *told* you she didn't want it?"

"Well . . . she *may* have done."

"Did she or didn't she?"

"All right. I think she said it once, OK?" His voice rises in exasperation. "Hey, let's drop it, shall we? I didn't expect the third degree."

But she won't drop it. She is dogged now.

"You *think* she said it?"

"Christ. What is this? Another cross-examination? Look, she said it just the once, pretty half-heartedly, OK?"

His admission winds her, and when she speaks, her voice is quiet, almost disbelieving. "But, in court, you told them she didn't say that. You said that she never said it."

"Oh, don't go all puritanical on me."

"But that's what you said."

"Well, perhaps I misremembered."

"You *misremembered*?"

"I didn't *lie*, Sophie."

She is silent. Trying to think carefully. An error in remembering; an omission; a lie—all shades of inaccuracy.

"What about 'prick-tease.' Did you say that to her as well?"

"Ah well, there you've got me." He has the grace to redden.

"I may have done. But she wouldn't have taken offense. She was always teasing."

"Did you or didn't you?" She is crying.

"And what if I did?"

For a moment, their eyes lock and she sees raw anger in his; knows hers are clouded with hurt and confusion: the realization that everything she assumed about him has been wrong. He smiles quickly, trying to neutralize his anger, suggesting it can all be smoothed away.

"Listen," he says, and he gives her a look of contrition: a look she would usually succumb to. "In my police interview, I may have *misremembered* events. Rather than cloud things, I stuck to my statement in court. She said no, half-heartedly, just the once, and I knew she didn't mean it because I knew *her*, I knew the context—that she'd wanted it so many times in similar risky situations before. Equally, I may have used that phrase—all right, I did use that phrase—because she teased a lot, and she *liked* the idea that I saw her as that—that I saw her as a prick-tease, even. Frankly, that's what she was. But I denied it in court because I didn't think it relevant, and I knew that if I changed my story, having not mentioned it previously, it would only have muddied things.

"But none of this matters, don't you see?" He smiles, confident that he is winning her over, that he is as persuasive as ever—and she is bemused at this self-belief. "I knew the truth and that was that, whatever I may have said, and whatever she may have said briefly, half-heartedly and just the once, could be disregarded because at the point of penetration—the point at which, legally speaking, consent *matters*—she truly wanted me."

"But you didn't tell the entire truth, did you?" She speaks carefully, as if trying to get to the bottom of an argument between Emily and Finn, for she feels woozy and is fumbling her way to her own understanding here.

"I told the truth, near enough. Or the truth as I saw it."

Her head is reeling. "But it doesn't work like that, does it?" Of that, she thinks she is clear.

"Oh, come on, Soph. The truth was that she'd wanted sex several times before in similar, risky situations, and that I thought she was up for it this time. If I failed to mention something in court—or even contradicted her—well, I was only telling the truth as I saw it then.

"We all adjust the truth from time to time," he goes on. "Look at what we do in government, manipulating statistics; putting a positive spin on things; omitting figures that undermine our arguments; pushing the envelope just a little. Look at what we do with budget statements—all that double accounting. Look what Blair did with the Iraq dossier."

"That's irrelevant." She can't be deflected like this. Knows he's playing games; is trying to wheedle his way out of this; to outfox her as he does in every argument. "We're not talking about anything like that here."

"So you wanted me to confess to something that I knew wasn't relevant—and that would increase my chances of being branded a rapist and sent to prison? Is that what you wanted? For me to do that to us—and to Finn and Em?"

"No, of course not." She backtracks, for she hadn't wanted that at all. "I just think you should have told the truth!" The words burst from her, as fresh and unsullied as newborn babes. Her heart aches at the realization that he has twisted the truth to suit him, that he lied in court, and that he thinks it is acceptable to do this. She knows every flaw of his personality—every last unpleasant nuance. And yet she no longer recognizes him.

"Look." His smile is tight now, a grin bared with a determination that she listen to him. "Even you bend the truth from time to time."

"I don't!" Her panic is rising.

"Yes, you do. You've told your mother you'd love her to come and stay when it wasn't convenient; you told Ellie Frisk you admired her dress at the State Opening though you whispered to me that it aged her. You even told Emily that having your ears pierced before the age of sixteen increased the risk of them turning septic."

"That's rather different," she says.

"In what way? You said those things to ease a situation—or in Emily's case to scare her into accepting your point of view. All I did was tell the truth as I understood it so as not to confuse the jury, but to ease their understanding; to clarify things."

She is appalled. His understanding of the truth is so different from hers that she wonders if she is going mad.

"No, you didn't." She struggles to find her bearings, for hasn't he acknowledged that he knew he had a choice of whether to tell the truth and he chose not to do something that would increase his risk of going to prison?

"You told them a version that suited you when you were on oath, when you'd promised to tell the truth in court. You . . ." she deliberates over whether to use the word but there is nothing else that conveys the strength of his behavior. "You *lied* in court, James. You committed *perjury*."

"And what are you going to do about it, Soph?" His eyes are cold now; his mouth set.

And that is the question. What *is* she going to do?

"I don't know. Nothing." Her insides hollow. She is utterly pitiful, feels her resolve crumbling, for she will not destroy the family she has worked so hard to keep together—not after all of this.

He raises an eyebrow. It is rare for them to argue like this, and usually he would open his arms, not allow their bad temper to continue. He does not open them now nor would she go to him if he did.

Revulsion bubbles up at the realization that he may indeed have forced Olivia into sex. That he *raped* her. The room sways; the edges becoming less defined as the boundaries of their lives give way. He may persist in believing he did nothing wrong, but Olivia didn't consent to sex in that lift at that moment—and his admission that she said "No, not here," and his jab "Don't be such a prick-tease" suggests he knew it.

She manages to leave the room, legs wobbly, eyes blurring; her one thought that she must get away before she breaks down completely. The downstairs cloakroom is small and dark, but it has a lock that rams shut; will keep her enclosed and contained.

She sinks onto the closed loo seat and lets her horror engulf her; feels a wail rise up that she silences with a fist. Her hand grows wet, her cheeks slippery, as she regresses and feels her adult self disintegrate. Her husband is a stranger. Not only a narcissist who dismisses the truth if it suits him, who thinks it is flexible, but— and the horror comes crushing down on her—someone who is guilty of rape.

Hunched in the dark, she forces herself to analyze if he ever did this to her. No, he hasn't. The relief is enormous: a wave that sweeps her up and allows a chink of hope that he isn't entirely amoral; that this ugliness hasn't spread to their relationship and contaminated it.

But if he hasn't forced himself sexually, he has imposed his needs over the years, so subtly she has barely registered it. Because it has always been James who decides things.

As the tears run down her face, she counts the ways. He was the one who finished the relationship at Oxford and determined its pace when they met in their later twenties, so that she feared initiating anything in case she drove him away. He was the one who suggested she give up her job after Emily was born, and put the arguments so forcefully it seemed easier not to resist. He was the one who made her an MP's wife by making it clear from the start that he would be going into politics; who applied for that constituency; who even decided the area of London—as close to Tom as possible—where they should live.

Their friends have been largely his friends, she sees now: Alex and Cat quickly abandoned for Tom and his political allies. The holidays they take are those he prefers—with Tom in Tuscany, before they had children; once he became an MP, in Cornwall for fear an expensive foreign holiday would seem anti-austerity. She would be a vegetarian, but she eats red meat with him and even the way she dresses is subtly influenced by his preference that she always makes an effort, that she is understatedly sexy, never frumpy. In Devon, she wears old jeans and sweatshirts, doesn't blow-dry her hair, consciously chooses not to wear makeup. She relaxes in a way she just wouldn't for him.

The compromises have largely been on her part, not his, she sees that now. None of these suggestions have been dictated, none coerced. He just stipulates what he likes, and it has been easier to bend to his will and go along with it. No wonder she didn't challenge him properly before the trial. She has sleepwalked through their relationship and only been forced to confront the worst when it was revealed in court, incontrovertibly there.

She wipes her face; feels its heat; wonders when she became so malleable, so weak in their relationship. A memory strikes her of being a second-year student, sculling alone on the Thames. A late spring afternoon: the sun low, the water quiet except for the soft plop of an otter; the cut of the blades puddling on the water and leaving a trail triangling back to where the boat had been. She had just mastered this skill and she felt poised, hands lightly on the oars as she pushed the blades firmly through the water to propel the boat forwards, then let them glide, before dropping them square and anchoring the boat again. Power surged through her feet, legs, glutes, back, and arms, but she felt no pain. She was invincible. Happiness flared in a way it hadn't since the previous summer, before the tragedy; before she was dumped by James.

That girl has long gone. And the woman who replaced her can't conceive of such uncomplicated happiness. Her heart throbs with a sense of loss, and acute, inconsolable pain.

And deep down inside her a question nudges. What is she going to do now, knowing what he has told her: that he lied about raping Olivia—and that he has gotten away with it?

# TWENTY-NINE

## SOPHIE

### 2 MAY 2017

The next day, they decamp to his parents' home in deepest Surrey. A few days away is what is needed, for Sophie feels besieged. Unable to walk to the local shop where the front pages of the papers trumpet the news of his acquittal; ill-prepared for the smiles of congratulation from their neighbors and the texts from fellow mothers who profess to be "so *relieved*" when the week before they had kept their distance, staring and whispering about her when she had marched onto the playground to grab her children and whisk them away.

Woodlands, Charles and Tuppence's substantial home near Haslemere, provides the privacy they so desperately need—down a private road, with a lengthy drive; sitting squat in its own two acres of perfectly manicured grounds; fringed with pines and conifers which keep the world at bay. Sophie had always thought these evergreen sentries parochial and forbidding—trees that signal her father-in-law's "not on my front lawn" mentality—but now she sees the point. An Englishman's home is his castle—drawbridge up; ramparts manned; arrows poised so that its inhabitants may be protected from barely whispered innuendos and prying eyes. The world has not just pressed its nose to the window of their marriage, but shouldered the door; and now it is time for some backup in the formidable form of Charles and Tuppence Whitehouse, the sort of law-abiding individuals on whose property one does not trespass, and down whose drive one would not venture unless one has been invited or has a very good reason indeed.

James visibly relaxes here: shows boundless patience as he takes the children out onto the tennis court, testing Em's backhand while simultaneously teaching Finn forehand; managing the children's varying abilities with tact and ease.

It helps that his mother adores him. Tuppence, a handsome woman with a tight grey perm and a string of pearls at her throat that she pats when anxious, is not the sort to give in to emotion, or not according to her two daughters. And yet when their younger brother, her only son, comes home she softens—her sunken cheeks dimpling; her grey eyes lightening; her shoulders relaxing so that you can see beyond the somewhat haughty sexagenarian and glimpse the full-lipped beauty she must once have been. She basks in his presence, becoming girlish, almost skittish; and when she clutches him as they arrive, the emeralds in their Art Deco setting standing proud on her fists as she grips his shoulders, Sophie sees the depth of the fear that has consumed her—and that has kept her far from court, sequestered away. Her darling boy, a rapist? The possibility has shimmered, mocking Charles's innate self-belief in the "right way of doing things"—which includes stocks and shares and church on a Sunday and putting money in a trust for the grandchildren and golf three times a week and winter sun and a quick snifter before dinner—and ushering in a whole new world of court cases and press conferences and concepts like consent and blame, that she would really rather not have to think about; but which, being more imaginative than her husband, creep up on her in the still, small hours of the night.

Now, though, Tuppence can relax. Her boy is safe. She stands watching him chase the children over the immaculately striped lawns of her garden, while Sophie—desperate to be busy, to preoccupy herself in this substantial 1920s house that she can never feel quite at home in—prepares a pot of tea. She acts on autopilot, speaking monosyllabically when required but feeling entirely detached as she runs through her argument with James until she can no longer think. Her limbs are heavy and it is an effort just to place one foot in front of the other, and to keep her sorrow in check.

It takes a while, then, to notice that her mother-in-law is nervous. She keeps patting those pearls in a staccato rhythm and a nerve twitches beneath her left eye.

"Will you leave him?" The question takes Sophie by surprise.

"Because we wouldn't blame you if you did." Her mother-in-law gives a pinched, tight smile as if it pains her to say this. "Of course we'd far rather you didn't. Much better for the children." She nods as James tips Emily upside down so that her long hair swings free and her mouth opens in a squeal of delight.

Sophie can imagine the peals of laughter; that gurgle particular to preteen children that she hears less and less these days, for she has not been able to protect Emily from every whisper in the playground, and she fears she has understood far more of what has happened than she has admitted. That, just as she knows the tooth fairy doesn't really exist, so she senses James isn't entirely innocent. Still, her adoration for her daddy seems undimmed.

They are playing tag now, James giving both children a head start before he charges after them; Finn aping a footballer as he whoops round the garden, arms stretching out like an airplane. Em darts into a copse beyond the herbaceous borders. Spring is here, spied in the ceanothus and tulips, in the vibrant carpet of bluebells, but the sun is watery and glows opaque through a flannel-grey sky.

She warms the pot, while she considers what to say to her mother-in-law, whose words jar like an outburst from a drunk. But Tuppence continues, regardless.

"I sometimes wonder if we spoiled him. Let him believe that his opinion was always right? I suppose school inculcated that feeling—and Charles, of course, never brooking an argument. Perhaps it's a male thing? That complete self-belief: the conviction that you never need doubt your opinion. The girls don't have it and neither do I. He was like it as a little boy: always lying at Cluedo; always cheating at Monopoly, insisting he could change the rules. He was so sweet, so persuasive, he got away with it. I wonder if that's why he thinks he still can?"

Sophie is silent. Their conversations are usually about books, tennis, or the garden and she has never known her mother-in-law to open up like this. Nor would she have anticipated this soul-searching. It makes her uncomfortable and resentful. She has enough to contend with without accommodating Tuppence's need for reassurance; and, in truth, she *has* questioned whether there was a flaw in her mother-in-law's parenting.

She throws tea bags into the pot, pours on boiling water, while she works at remaining dispassionate. What does Tuppence want? To be told that she is not at fault? For Sophie to lay the blame firmly with her husband and his choice of expensive schooling? Much as Sophie likes the woman—for she is fond of her; she can't *not* be, though she is hardly effusive with the children—she is unable to absolve her in that way.

But her mother-in-law evidently requires some response.

"I'm not intending to leave him, no." The words leave Sophie's mouth without her having had time to come to a proper conclusion and, somehow, force the decision. She clears her throat, swallowing her doubt down and quashing the possibility. "It's best for the children, and they're the main consideration, as you say."

"You are *good* for him, you know." Tuppence looks at her with what must be admiration. "I hate to think of what he might be like if he didn't have a wife like you: someone so bright and attractive." She pauses, perhaps imagining a clutch of brief, unsatisfactory affairs.

The onus on Sophie to keep her husband in check weighs hard, and she feels a sudden surge of fury.

Tuppence, oblivious, continues, "He does know he's lucky to have you, you know. His father and I have made that clear."

"I'm not sure that he does." She will not swallow this portrayal of a contrite son and counts to ten to banish the expletives that would shock her husband's mother. When she speaks, her voice is quieter but with an unmistakably bitter trace.

"As you say, it's what's best for the children. It's not about me."

"I didn't *say* that." Tuppence is perturbed.

"You effectively did."

The air quivers with more emotion than their exchanges have ever held before, Sophie's anger straining their civility to breaking point.

She checks the table, laid for afternoon tea—the fat teapot and jug of milk, bone china cups, a lemon drizzle cake made with Emily this morning—and forces herself to sound contrite.

"I'm sorry to snap. We'd better get them in. Tea's ready."

And she goes to the back door to call her family.

# Thirty

## Kate

### 26 May 2017

It is over three weeks since the trial and I am standing on Waterloo Bridge, the place that usually lifts me. The end of the week and the pavements are emptying as my fellow workers race to make the most of a balmy weekend.

I'm watching a stunner of a sunset: mango sorbet, shot through with raspberry ripple and laced with streaks of caramel. The sort of sky that makes people whip out their smartphones to capture its glory, or just stop, as I am, and stare.

Beside me, a young Spanish couple is kissing. This is a sky to make you want to do that: grasp the person you love and be spontaneous, show the intensity of your feelings, your giddiness and excitement at the inexplicable beauty of life.

No one's wrapping me in a passionate clinch. *Earth has not anything to show more fair,* and yet the sunset and the view leaves me numb. St. Paul's, Canary Wharf, and the concrete sprawl of the National Theatre to the east; and the giddy Ferris wheel of the Eye to the west all pass me by. I can't help but home in on a golden Gothic building, perhaps the most iconic part of the river: Big Ben and the House of Commons. The mother of parliaments.

Even without this visual reminder, James Whitehouse is always at the back of my mind, and as I lie in bed at night, right at the forefront. My debilitating grief has diminished, but it still consumes me, a dull ache that becomes pin-sharp to ambush me at the very worst of times.

No one would know this, of course. I am as coolly competent as ever, though in the immediate aftermath my anger was palpable. "It was always going to be a long shot, convicting the PM's best mate, and at least you kept them thinking," my junior, Tim Sharples tried to reassure me, straight after the verdict. I remember trying to ram my wig and documents into my case, and atypically swearing as the zip jammed. The effort of not crying, as Angela swanned out, and Tim watched, unable to think of a quick line, felt immense. "It's just one case," he said, though we all knew it wasn't just one case. It was supposed to be the case that would confirm the wisdom of me making QC so early; that meant no one would raise an eyebrow at the speed of my appointment. "There'll be plenty more."

There are, and I have done what I do: dust myself down, and carry on working, prosecuting those accused of the foulest of sexual crimes. I am hungry for work because if I fill every crevice of my brain, I can try to stop obsessing about the quality of my cross-examination and the parallels between Olivia's and my experience. That's the theory. In practice, it rarely works.

I look up, and check that the kissing couple hasn't noticed

my bright eyes, which sting with self-pity. Of course not. Faces pressed against one another, they are wrapped up entirely in themselves. Besides, I am unremarkable, even in court. *Polly? Molly?* A wave of hate swells and I wonder if that journalist, Jim Stephens, is delving into James's Oxford past. Were there other girls like me? There were rumors of parties where drinks were spiked. Omerta of the Libertines? But someone, somewhere, must have an incriminating photo? I offer a prayer, eyes squeezed tight, that James will get his comeuppance; will experience the most intense humiliation. That he won't get away with doing this, to me and Olivia and whoever else it may have happened to, in the long term.

The sun has disappeared now—a hot ball of fire that has slipped from sight, leaving the sky bereft and no longer dazzled, the raspberry pink fading to a pinky-grey. Life moves on, or so I keep telling myself, though it's something that, with my obsessive mind-set, I'm struggling to believe.

And yet, rationally, I know it's true. There's a fresh bout of news and even a new political scandal. Malcolm Thwaites, Tory chair of the Home Affairs Select Committee, has been caught paying young male prostitutes for sex. The details—threesomes, poppers, explicit texts—make James Whitehouse's sex in a lift, for that, the jury ruled, is all that occurred, look positively tame. And the timing is fortunate. What a coincidence that another political sex scandal should be exposed the weekend after the prime minister's best friend was cleared. Politics is a dirty business and I could almost feel sorry for Mr. Thwaites. I give it less than a year before James Whitehouse is given a junior ministerial role and welcomed back to the lowly ranks of government again.

I must not let myself get bitter. I can feel the sour taste of it in my mouth, sense it seeping through me. Somehow, it seems preferable to despair. I know my anger needs to be boxed up—hard; finite; precious, like an indulgent cocktail ring buried deep in a drawer and rarely worn. I can't manage that yet. In the meantime, I run. Six a.m. sees me streaking down to the Chelsea Embankment, over the river and through Battersea Park. The day is brim-filled with possibility then, and seven kilometers in I feel a brief, sweet shot of serotonin. In the evening, I do less well; tend my pain with baths and gin.

I walk slowly back towards the Strand. Gin and a bath tonight, a run early tomorrow morning. The bank-holiday weekend stretches, a desert of loneliness except for the oasis that is Ali. Thank God I've been invited to Sunday lunch at hers, again.

I long for the fierceness of her hug as she greets me in her narrow hall; crave her warmth; her quiet sympathy; the knowledge that she is angry, too—her fury erupting in the swear words she used prolifically as a student, but since becoming a teacher and mother, she has largely put away. The night of the verdict she came round and stayed; held me as I shook with grief; listened as I raged against him; stopped me from obliterating myself with drink. We talked as we should have talked twenty years before, and when I finished—my throat hoarse, my body aching with exhaustion—she lay down next to me and curled behind me as I tried to sleep.

I have seen her every week since then and her family must be sick of me, must wonder why the previously elusive Kate now sits red-eyed in their kitchen; why their mum seems to have someone else to worry about these days.

But I need her. It is only with Ali that I can be myself completely. It is only she who remembers Holly.

# Thirty-one
## Sophie
### 22 July 2017

When the letter comes with the invitation to her college gaudy, she initially dismisses it. A Saturday night in July, a night away from the children, the best part of a weekend devoted to something entirely for herself.

Besides which, she would have to brave seeing people, risking the likelihood of them gossiping about James or ostentatiously avoiding doing so. Her husband and his court case, and by implication the state of her marriage, the elephant blundering around the room.

But she doesn't throw the heavy card with its embossed college shield and cursive font in the bin or place it in the fireplace, and so it sits on the mantelpiece, the RSVP date a couple of months away.

"Why don't you go?" James asks. "The children can stay with my parents." Because, even with Cristina on hand, there is no question of him looking after them for the weekend.

"I couldn't," she says, reluctant to point out the obvious: that *he* is the reason she will no longer put herself in new situations, situations in which she will have to sound assertive and perky as she gives new acquaintances, or old ones, a résumé of her life. Yes, she's married to James; they live in North Ken; have two gorgeous children. A version of the truth, but one painted in primary colors with broad brushstrokes that allow no room for nuance or detail: a version Finn or any other six-year-old could create.

And yet the possibility of returning to her old college remains; the invitation taunting her from its spot beside a silver picture frame on the mantelpiece. Sophie Greenaway, it says at the top of the invitation, and she finds herself rooting out old photos of that girl. There she is with Alex and Jules in their lycras, flushed and exuberant after the rowing race, Torpids; and, here, sitting outside the King's Arms, at the end of finals, her relief palpable, her gown splattered with the traditional eggs and flour. She rifles for more—a second-year party in that shared house in Park Town, her swigging a bottle of Bud as she tossed her hair back, the look on her face a challenge: come and get me if you think you're good enough. The photo grounds her in the mid- to late nineties—silver hoops in her ears; a leotard-like "body"; lips slick with lip gloss and brows not tamed with tweezers; a self-confidence she can barely recognize.

James is absent from most of these photos. Their Oxford life was one that was played out at night, largely in his college, and only in her first year. Though she associates Oxford with him, she spent more of her time there alone. Shrewsbury College was *her* college, and there is a strong part of her that hankers after that girl who wasn't defined by a charismatic boyfriend; and who, now, wants to reclaim her. Wants to recapture the spirit of Sophie Greenaway.

It tallies with her desire to become more assertive, to build a stronger self away from James's shadow, for her old self has fractured since the court case, and she is changing more evidently than he. Their marriage is a precarious construction. On the surface, all might seem stable. They are courteous to one another, perhaps excessively, cautiously so; and he is unusually attentive— listening to her opinions, or giving the semblance of doing so; buying her flowers; keen to indicate that he is interested only in her; that there is no future Olivia in the wings.

And yet, the foundations of their marriage are no longer strong; the map by which they have negotiated it no longer certain. Her husband is a stranger, or rather, she is having to accept a darker, half-recognized version of him. At times, her anger is a fist that unfurls as she derides herself as someone so weak that he knew he could confess to lying and be confident that she would not betray him. At other times, she tries to kid herself about his behavior, to demonize Olivia or indulge his sophistry. To forge an explanation that allows him to be mistaken rather than callous and cavalier.

It is bearable for James, she thinks in her deepest moments of self-loathing. He doesn't recognize that he did anything wrong. He genuinely seems to believe that Olivia was playing a game and his version of the truth is the only one that matters. Whereas she is tormented by his admission—those crucial details of what happened in the lift.

His life is returning to normal, his constituency work preoccupying him as well as his behind-the-scenes advice to the prime minister, the bond still strong although Tom is sufficiently politically astute not to be seen with him in public yet. Even that will change. "It will come," James reassures her, his smile stoked by an inner confidence; an awareness of the skeins of history that bind them tight.

She is the one who must brave the outside world: the smiles at the school gate, the faux congratulations from other women whom she knows wished her ill, as well as those that she hopes are more genuine. Her part of London is a village, and she imagines the whispers following her at the gym, the chemist's, the deli, the coffee shops, the dry cleaner's. She avoids all of these. *Act naturally*, she tells herself. And yet shame floods her veins. She is tainted by association. He may have been acquitted—an innocent man, a free man—but the whole world knows he has cheated, while she knows he has lied and raped.

Most of the time she carries this knowledge quietly, her heart aching with a sad resignation. And then it threatens to erupt— that closed fist searching for something to strike at, wildly—and she has to exercise aggressively, pounding the streets or using a rowing machine set up in the spare room when she began to shun the gym. Only then, when she feels her heart strain, fit to burst, and she pushes herself until her chest burns, does she gain some sense of equilibrium; physical exhaustion, and the near-unbearable sensation of almost blacking out with the effort, forcing all other sentiments away.

A therapist is helping a little, too. It was Ginny's idea. Something Sophie would never have considered, would have viewed as hugely self-indulgent had her mother not confessed to seeing someone after Max left and revealed that she found it useful. "Just having someone nonjudgemental to talk to might help," she had said.

James knew but pretended he didn't.

"I don't want to hear any details." He had looked severe. She had been bewildered. Why on earth would I tell you, she had wanted to say?

Of course there is far too much that she cannot tell. Huge truths that remain unsaid. Strings of words considered and dismissed out of hand before each session. My husband lied in court about raping another woman and I don't know what to do about it.

All of which makes it challenging when faced with Peggy, her grey-haired, apparently humorless therapist. The first session passed in near silence, Sophie censoring each brief sentence; as did the second until Peggy raised an eyebrow at some brief reference to her father, and Sophie filled the best part of an hour with tears. Great ugly sobs blotched her face and left her clutching a clump of sodden tissues, confounded at the intensity of emotion that her memories unleashed. "I'm so sorry," she kept saying, as she blew away the snot that bubbled up. She was as inconsolable as Finn when his team was defeated at football. "I don't know what's come over me."

As part of boosting her self-esteem, Peggy challenges her to go to the college reunion.

"What's the worst thing that could happen?"

"They could not like me. They might *judge* me," Sophie whispers, thinking, *if you knew, you would judge. You would think*

*me weak; complicit in what he has done; as self-serving and morally*
*compromised as James.*

"Or they might not," Peggy says, and tucks a hank of her bob
behind her ear. Sophie waits, watching her therapist watch her
and hoping that she will soon break the silence that grows embarrassing the longer it stretches.

Peggy shrugs; is disobliging.

"I suppose they might not," Sophie eventually says.

————————————

And so that is how she comes to be back at Shrewsbury College. She is in a room in Old Quad. A superior room to the one
she had during finals—dark oak panelling, a huge partner's desk
topped with aged green leather, and in the cell-like bedroom, a
single bed.

She traces her stomach—concave now since the stress of the
past ten months has eaten her up so that her hip bones protrude
and her little black dress no longer clings but hangs from her,
exposing the glockenspiel of her clavicle and ribs. Her palms are
moist, and as she washes her hands, she watches her loose rings
glint in the running water, the gloss of her newly manicured nails
gleam. They are the hands of a different woman entirely: those of
the old Sophie, whose biggest preoccupation was when to fit in
her gym sessions and what to cook if they were inviting friends
for dinner. Or how best to handle the disparity in the size of
sexual appetite between herself and James.

She shrugs the thought aside, and with it the memory of compromises made, and leans against the window to watch as her peers stroll across the quad for drinks before dinner. They are all forty-two or forty-three, at the prime of their life but also conscious that they have responsibilities—children, mortgages, aging parents—and will soon be hurtling towards middle age. And yet they are aging well. That's what relative wealth and a decent education does for you, she thinks, although such things have never been in doubt for her. She has always assumed that she will remain slim, active, fit, just as her going to university was taken as read. Upright, self-confident, self-assured, they look as if they still have the world at their feet—just as they did nearly twenty-five years ago, when they first entered this quad, some conscious of being the brightest stars of their generation, others taking it for granted. "Lucky buggers," her father, uncharacteristically dropping her off at the start of that first term, had said.

Now they are old enough to have weathered difficulties and harbored secrets, to have suffered divorce, bereavement, infertility, redundancy, depression. The stresses and strains accrued over forty years. She knows one of their year has died—an accident with a rifle in a safari park—and that another has suffered from cancer. But is there anyone else who has been charged with a criminal offense? She scours the figures—some with the makings of a paunch, a couple more sleek than she remembers—and she doubts it. A drunk-driving offense, perhaps, or a white-collar crime like fraud? No one else will have a husband who has undergone a trial for rape.

Her hands start to shake now. What was she thinking of, coming here? The painful memory of the end of her first summer term weighs upon her, magnified through the prism of James's case. She remembers the dread of something terrible happening to him and his intense fear after being questioned by the police; recalls the horror as the news spread through the university; her uncomprehending distress when James very quickly pushed her away.

Why has she risked stirring up these memories as well as exposing herself to condemnation? Once the drinks start to flow, there is bound to be someone who takes great pleasure in being controversial. Who asks, of the case, "And what did you think, Sophie? Did you always think he was innocent? Was there never any doubt in your mind?"

She has prepared herself; practiced the laugh to ward off the conversational tumbleweed; rehearsed her lines, even. "Of course I never doubted him. Do you think I could stay with him, if I did?"

She will play the loyal wife, as she reassured his mother, as she needs to do for his children.

She hasn't worked out a different role yet.

---

The candles cast soft pools of light around the mahogany tables and illuminate the faces of those talking over them, flattering them so that the years erode and they could be a decade younger:

no longer students, but late twentysomethings for whom university is still touching distance away.

They have moved on to the port. A full-bodied, semidry vintage that slips down all too easily and that she knows she drinks out of nostalgia. One balmy summer's night, after trying it for the first time, she had lain in the center of Old Quad, ignoring the tiny signs about not stepping on the grass. The sky was pricked with crystals and the buildings stretched to the heavens. She remembered the damp of the dew against her bare legs; the way her skirt rode up; and someone—possibly Rick from their English group—bending over and giving her the gentlest kiss. For a split second, it had felt intensely romantic and then she had felt a surge of nausea.

Whoever it was had laughed, pulled her to her feet, and led her to a toilet at the bottom of a staircase where he had waited, patiently, while she was efficiently sick.

"You should have some water," he had said, when she emerged, shame-faced and grateful. "I'll see you around when you're feeling better. Are you sure you're OK?"

She had nodded, swaying, her vision blurring.

"And get some sleep."

She wondered, now, who that was. That decent, half-remembered boy who had shown her that kindness; who had stepped away when it was clear that she was incapable of being amorous. For many wouldn't have and it perturbs her that she doesn't find this shocking; that she takes it as read that she was lucky not to have woken to find her pants shoved aside.

She looks around the room and catches the eye of Rich. Perhaps it was him? There had been one brief, furtive snog in freshers' week. The wrong type: a biochemist from a Kent grammar school; bright not sporty, she had known instinctively that there was too much that was different—though there had been that flinty spark of sexual chemistry. Perhaps that wasn't such a bad start, she thinks now. He had been funny and good looking, too. What *was* she thinking? A different version of her life shimmers—a mirage, elusive, intangible, yet glimpsed, there on the horizon. She had thought herself so clever in choosing James. She'd been so *smug*, but there were other men she could have chosen. And none of them would have stood trial at the Old Bailey; none would have lied on oath then privately admitted to being a rapist; and placed the burden of that knowledge on her.

She takes a heavy sip of port, feels the heat warm her throat, picks up a marzipan fruit and nibbles at its sweetness, trying to focus on the moment and to push such thoughts away.

"Would you mind passing the port?" a voice to her left asks.

"Sorry—sorry." She is briefly befuddled then fills Alex's glass, to her right, and passes the heavy decanter to her left.

The owner of the voice is Rob Phillips—dark, chiseled, good-humored, an old boyfriend of Alex's, now a lawyer; someone she last saw at one of those turn-of-the-millennium weddings. Not married, she sees now from the dent on his ringless left hand; but not, as she recalls, gay.

"So, how are you holding up?" he asks, turning towards her, his voice filled with an intimate warmth as if he is asking because he is interested and not merely being kind.

"Oh, fine. Great. Lovely to be here—even if the Beef Wellington isn't as good as I remembered."

He chuckles, indulging her disingenuity.

"I'm really glad I returned," she adds. "It *is* lovely to be here."

And she is grateful for this moment in time; this chance to indulge in nostalgia, this possibility of escapism. She looks at the heavy oils gracing the walls, the portraits of Tudor benefactors and illustrious alumni, and at the well-natured, smiling faces of her peers, all doing well or managing to cope with whatever life has thrown at them, and breathes deeply, feeling the skin across her stomach stretch tight. She is full for once and finally beginning to relax.

"I didn't mean how you found the Beef Wellington," says Rob, and she can feel his eyes watching her.

"Oh, I know you didn't." She cannot look at him and so she fiddles with a dessert fork, turning it this way and that as she waits for him to take the hint and look away.

"I'm sorry. I didn't mean to intrude. Let's talk about the weather. Or where you're going on holiday. Are you going on holiday?" he asks.

"To France—and to Devon, to my mother's."

"Ah, wonderful. Whereabouts?" And they shift into a less troublesome conversational vein: the best beaches in the South Hams; the merits of going out of season; the infuriating traffic jams down those steep-banked hedgerowed lanes. She hears her voice revert to being the bright, perky voice of Sophie White-house, used for the few constituency events she attends, and those awful conference drinks and fundraising dinners. A glossy voice filled with privilege that has never known any emotional—let alone financial or physical—trauma; that keeps things light, skating over the difficulties of life. She can chat like this for hours, but just as she begins to hanker for something less superficial, a discussion about politics even—though without mentioning James—he looks at her intently, and says: "You know, if you ever need someone to talk to, I can help."

She stiffens, feels her heart flutter against her ribs, her stomach flip. Is this a proposition?

"I . . . I'm fine, thank you." She recoils, like a Jane Austen spinster, alert to and fearful of intrigue.

He smiles as if he should have anticipated this reaction.

"I didn't mean . . . I just meant—look, this is probably completely uncalled for, and crass of me to mention it, but I know a good divorce lawyer, should you ever think you need one." He smiles and all the artifice of their conversation is stripped away. She looks at him directly, detects in those dark eyes both a need for practicality and a frank awareness that fairy-tale marriages are anything but. That until death us do part need no longer bind.

"Are you a divorce lawyer?"

"No. I'm not hustling for work. Jo and I got divorced two years ago and I used a colleague. She was very good, made things easier than they might have been. Look—here's my card." He fumbles in his wallet, and hands her a crisp, thick rectangle. "Sorry. Not my place. Just—you know. I've been there. The endless compromises you make in a marriage. The attempts to fix something that perhaps can't be fixed." He grimaces, his move-

ments exaggerated now and comic: the self-deprecating Englishman taken to extremes. It is effective and endearing and she can't
help softening.

"Thank you, but I don't anticipate calling," she manages, and
is surprised that her voice is firm and clear.

He shrugs as if to say there are no hard feelings and returns
to his wineglass, swilling the dregs. After a short interval, she
switches to Alex—a successful management consultant and new
mother now, who is showing off pictures of her one-year-old
twins, born through IVF.

"Oh, they are *adorable*, Alex."

Her friend beams with pride, embarks on a lengthy anec-
dote about their precocious speech—tedious and yet the glow
on Alex's face makes it bearable—and she tries to ignore Rob's
suggestion which prods like an insistent toddler. *Divorce. The endless compromises made in a marriage. A lawyer who made things easier
than they might have been.*

Beside her, Rob starts a conversation with Andrea, a woman
she barely recognizes, who is sitting opposite. Their voices swell
and rise and she sips her red wine, feeling the room grow warmer
and still more intimate; leaning against Alex—now talking about
her babies' sophisticated palates—feeling the warmth of her
friend's arm against hers, recalling a friendship that might be rekindled after all these years.

At one point, she senses that someone is looking at her. She
looks up and diagonally across two tables sees a woman's face:
dark eyes, blonde hair in an ill-kempt bob, an unsmiling mouth

that fails to twitch in recognition or display any warmth when Sophie smiles. Odd. Her smile falters as the woman turns away.

Alex is still talking and so she slips back into listening, offering approval when required, umming and ahhing, while marveling at the happiness her friend accepts unthinkingly. She felt like that when Emily was born and James was smitten with his first experience of fatherhood. Then again, more acutely, after Finn's birth. Such brief, precious slivers of time.

Her mind rambles, fretting about that woman—her head now hidden behind a thick bank of dinner jackets—and about Rob who has unleashed a perturbing train of thought with his intervention. Divorce. The endless compromise.

It is only when she is sure that he is not looking that she takes the card and slips it into her purse.

———————

Later, much later, they spill out into the quad. It is past midnight and many of them are making for bed, a couple, she notes with amusement, with one another—a second-year romance rekindled, if only for one night.

Rob waves a cheery farewell. "Sorry if I overstepped the mark," he begins but she cuts him short.

"Not at all. No need to apologize." Her tone, polite, detached, is that same she uses with constituents who persist in ringing them at Thurlsdon, desperate for James's attention. Rob half raises his hand, revealing a crumpled dress shirt—it is that time of night—and disappears up a Gothic staircase in the corner of the quad.

"Heading for the bar?" Alex tucks her arm into Sophie's and they make their way around the lawn. The night is warm, the stars as bright as she remembers them on that night when she lay in the dew and watched them spinning; and, as she looks up, she stumbles, the drink telling on her—or perhaps this bout of nostalgia, this sense of other, lost versions of her life.

"You all right?" Alex holds her steady as she puts her shoe back on, squeezing her hand.

"Sorry, yes." The gentleness of her hand-holding, of this easily resumed friendship, stirs her to tears. They haven't talked of James. She imagines chatting into the early hours then realizes that's impossible because how can she risk opening up to anyone about him?

"I'll be with you in a second. I just need a couple of minutes."

"If you're sure? What can I get you? A half a cider for old time's sake? Or a bottle of Bud, wasn't that what you used to drink?"

She hasn't drunk beer for years.

"Actually, please could I have a single malt with ice?"

"Well, if you're sure?"

"Honestly. I promise I'll be down in a couple of minutes. I just need to sit here for a bit to think things over."

Alex's eyes darken. She is no fool, and suddenly Sophie cannot bear her pity.

"Promise?"

"I promise."

"Well, then. I'll see you in a bit." And her old friend slips across the grass.

For a while she just sits on a bench tucked away in the corner of the quad, watching them drift to the bar or off to the JCR. The old cliques have reasserted themselves, the science geeks barely speaking to the arts graduates; the past snobberies still prevalent—though it is the geeks who run the world now, the historians and English graduates all teachers or journalists, unless they have become management consultants and accountants on graduation, their artistic leanings boxed away.

The bench is solid beneath her thighs, and the chill takes the edge off her giddiness as she tries to focus on those who are near her, and to imagine the eighteen-year-olds haunting their middle-aged selves. Some have barely changed, a few are unrecognizable, the bleached hair or the dreadlocks sported until they started attending job interviews now tamed into neat bobs and receding short-back-and-sides.

As the figures ebb away, she becomes conscious of someone sitting down beside her. She glances at this intruder and feels that creep of trepidation. It is the woman who glowered at her at dinner and she still isn't smiling, but gives a long, labored sigh.

"I'm so sorry—I'm afraid I can't remember your name." Sophie tries to assert control of the situation.

"Ali. Ali Jessop. Alison at college. I thought it made me sound more adult." The woman turns to look at her directly, and Sophie sees that she is quite tipsy, her eyes bloodshot and lit with a curious, unnerving fire.

"Don't worry. You didn't know me." Ali seems to read her mind. "I wasn't one of the beautiful ones. I read maths, not your subject."

"Oh." She tries to relax, but there is a layer of resentment anchoring this woman's voice. Did she once slight her or is she one of those women who unaccountably resent those who are more attractive than themselves? Perhaps she feels out of place, bad roots in a mumsy bob, a little overweight? Her thin black tights have a ladder racing up her calf that she doesn't seem to have noticed. Sophie would always notice. She clutches at these possibilities before considering the likelihood that this is the person with which she will have to spar this evening: not a domineering PPE graduate jealous of her husband, but some earnest Labour supporter.

"I'm so sorry I don't remember you," she manages. "I'm hopeless with names. Did we have friends in common?"

"Oh yes." Ali draws the syllables out in a bitter, guttural laugh. "Do you remember Holly? Holly Berry?"

Her scalp tightens with that sense of premonition and the image of a girl half-remembered—and thought of only recently.

"Yes. Yes, of course. In fact I was only thinking of her a few months ago. Someone reminded me of her."

"Your old tutorial partner."

"Yes, briefly. We were quite friendly that first term and then she left, suddenly, at the end of first year. I never knew why." She pauses. "I'm sorry. I hadn't realized you were friends."

"Why would you? You didn't remember me in the least."

"No, well, quite." She is wrong-footed and tries to steer the conversation into less belligerent waters. "Is she well? Are you still in touch with her?"

"I'm still in touch with her, yes."

Ali stares at her for a moment then leans back on the bench and looks straight in front of her at a bedroom high in the middle line of the quad, below the sundial. Sophie waits, puzzled by her behavior, and increasingly apprehensive that this somewhat drunk yet articulate woman is about to hurl an emotional grenade.

"As to whether she's well—well, she's well enough. She's *professionally* successful. Unmarried; no children."

"What does she do?" She clutches at straws.

Ali turns and looks at her directly. "She's a barrister."

And there it is: that frisson of fear, so intense the air around her perceptibly chills and every sensation becomes heightened. Earnest Holly—plump, painfully right-on, almost pretty, rather sweet, somehow unworldly—is a *barrister*. Kate Woodcroft flashes into her mind and she dismisses the image at once. That's not even a possibility. And yet Holly became someone as authoritative—as powerful—as her.

"That was Holly's bedroom." Ali jerks her eyes up. "I found her there afterwards. She'd locked the door and it took twenty minutes for me to persuade her to open it. When I did, she wouldn't let me touch her: arms wrapped tight around herself; swamped in those baggy clothes I'd finally persuaded her not to wear." Her voice catches, a moment of weakness, and she steadies it, still not looking at Sophie; eyes straight ahead, as if she is determined to finally have her say.

"You wonder why she left? What made her give up her Oxford degree when she had fought so hard to get here? What could make a young woman do that?" She turns and looks at her.

"I don't know," Sophie grasps for any wild, possible explanation though her insides are falling away, and she feels as if she is tumbling inside herself. She knows what is coming. "Did she get pregnant?"

"She was raped."

The words are whispered: just three syllables, shots from a gun that reverberate and resonate.

"Your husband has form, Sophie," Ali says. Her voice is low and pragmatic, saddened not malevolent. "I am only telling you this because I'm drunk; I had to get drunk to say it. But that doesn't mean it's not true. He raped her as an eighteen-year-old virgin at the end of our first year. I don't imagine he's ever considered the impact of what he's done; perhaps he didn't even realize—thought it was just another casual sexual encounter. But he did it all the same."

The ugly words swarm around her and she stands, desperate to escape. Her legs feel insubstantial but her heart is racing, blood thudding through her head.

"Don't be absurd." She knows she sounds preposterous, but she has to say something. "You don't know what you're saying. You're *lying*! What a nasty, *vicious* thing to say."

Ali looks up at her from the bench, gives a minimal shrug, just the smallest of movements. "I'm not—and I'm so sorry."

"You little *bitch*." The words take Sophie aback but her self-preservation is stronger than she realized. Whatever the truth, she can't let people think this of James.

She must get away from this woman, and she turns, head held high, kitten heels clicking fast upon the path as she stalks away. Click, click, click. Keep your posture straight; keep walking away from her; don't run; you're nearly there. She tries to cling to something positive. The children! She imagines Finn's arms tight around her, then sees Emily's face, just a little doubtful when told Daddy was in court because a lady was unkind. She twists on a heel, falters, stumbles, then half runs as the truth comes crashing down on her, the facts neatly aligning like a Rubik's Cube slotting into place.

At the library, she starts to slow but Ali's voice follows her as she leaves the quad; a final taunt—low and mocking—that will hound her in the long hours of a sleepless night and continue to nag her over the coming days and weeks.

She tries to pretend it is never said, but the night is still and the quad empty.

"I'm telling the truth—and I think you know it."

# Thirty-two
## Sophie
### 3 October 2017

The drinks reception at the conference hotel is packed. Heaving with delegates exhausted from a long day's lobbying, their smooth faces sheened in sweat and adrenaline and the thrill of being in the same room as so many MPs.

The white wine is medium dry and warm. At the *Spectator* party, they serve Pol Roger champagne; at every other there is only this, concentrated orange juice, or fizzy water. Sophie swigs it anyway, tasting the thinness of the wine and the kick of the afterburn that strips her mouth and should, with any luck, soon numb the rest of her. She is drinking far more these days.

Where *is* her husband? She scans the room, conscious that he is still her focal point and wishing that she could relax and not continually note his absence, check his presence. But then, she is only here for James. It's ridiculous. It's not as if she doesn't think of leaving him. Every morning she wakes and for a split second lies there in calm ignorance: in that semiconscious state in which she is only aware of the warmth of her bed and the crispness of her sheets, for she is fastidious about weekly or twice-weekly sheet changing. In this state, the day still holds the potential for contentment, for it is contentment, rather than anything more ambitious, like happiness, that she craves.

And then, perhaps half a second later, the illusion is broken and she remembers. The memory comes as a physical pain. A corroding of her stomach and an aching of her heart so that she is briefly paralyzed by the weight of her sorrow and the burden of a knowledge that could consume her if she did not swing her legs over the side of the bed and get up, up, up, up for there are children to get to school and the day to get on with and no time for introspection, which must be banished before she obsesses completely and it eats her away.

She tries applying the CBT techniques taught by Peggy— with whom she still cannot be truthful, of course, but who has proved helpful. But most of the time distraction, in the form of exercise and the perpetual, ruthless, unnecessary reorganization of her house, is what works best.

In this way, she manages to box up the thoughts that kalei- doscope in those waking moments, and as she showers, before the welcome interruption of the children. Is James a habitual rapist? Was it just Olivia and Holly—for she has accepted what Ali says, a fact she finds almost unbearably sorrowful—or were there other young women beyond those two—these incidents not blips? Will there be others still? A stream of lovers whose wishes he casually overrides because his need is more important? Just the thought stymies her, in the bathroom; makes her want to stay hidden under the running water forever.

Does he ever think about what he has done? They never discuss it, of course, and he was so steadfast in his opinion—*I told the truth, near enough. Or the truth as I saw it. She wanted sex several times in similar situations*—that she knows his view won't have changed. But if he still has such a flexible approach to consent and to telling the truth, then what does that say about her? The fact that she is still married to him.

When these thoughts press in, she cleans neurotically: drenching the corners of the cupboards with antibacterial spray; culling the children's rooms of toys they have long outgrown, but which they will mourn when they notice; folding underwear according to the strictures of a lifestyle guru, any odd socks or imperfect garments recycled, for her house will be rigorously ordered if nothing else is.

And, eventually, the churning turmoil of her mind begins to fade. Being away from London helps; away from James, with Ginny in Devon; and, incredibly, at the end of August, on a family holiday in France with him. He is charming with the children and loving to her. And though she feels nothing when he touches her, she knows that she needs to appear to thaw for the sake of Emily and Finn. They are—must be—her priority.

It becomes increasingly bearable to put on an act, to talk about new starts, and things getting better, because this is what a large part of her—the part that tries to forget what Ali told her and what James has admitted—so desperately wants to believe. And yet, on the rare occasions when they make love, she imagines organizing her kitchen cupboards, the Kilner jars replaced with

Jamie Oliver ones perhaps—with the duck-egg blue lids. Just as she knows—from knowing James—that it becomes second nature to detach oneself when having an affair, so she annexes her real self. She goes through the motions with her husband, while the real Sophie—the Sophie who was Sophie Greenaway perhaps, the girl who could scull down a river, confident, complete without a charismatic man to cling to—exists elsewhere.

And so she manages, she just about manages. Taking each day at a time; thinking purely of the children; looking on any possible bright side—she lives by these mottos, slipping a smile on her face when required. Look at her here, in this thickly carpeted conference hotel: the one blasted apart by an IRA bomber in the mid-1980s. Five people were killed then. She is conscious of this fact, and it grounds her. However vast her problems, they are nothing compared to the finality of death.

She takes another glass from a waiter and drinks to that thought, aware her face is a mask of contemplation at odds with the frivolity of those around her. "Cheer up. It might never happen!" A red-faced chap, pink shirt tugging at the waist to reveal a sausage-like roll of fat, puts a hand in the small of her back as he sidles past and she recoils from his moist palm, her body tense. "No need to glower, dear!" He holds up his hands in mock surrender, aggression palpable behind his thin veneer of affability. She smiles, her face taut, and turns away.

But someone else catches her eye. A lean man in late middle age who is listening to Malcolm Thwaites, head cocked to one side, dark eyes flickering over his face intently. His navy suit shines—it looks a little threadbare—and dandruff brushes his shoulders, lean fingers toy with a glass of red. She recognizes him from court: Jim Stephens, one of the reporters who filled the press benches, and who shouted at her that terrible morning when James arrived to give evidence. "Does the PM still have full confidence in your husband, Sophie?" A question that still sparks a sting of fear. She remembers how determined he was to provoke a response and how this jarred with his shambolic manner—that shabby raincoat; his breath, as he came too close to them, sharp with coffee and cigarettes.

Her scalp pricks. He doesn't work in the lobby, so why is he here? He must be sniffing for dirt on James. At last year's party conference, her husband was sleeping with his researcher. Who's to say that James isn't such a risk-taker that he's back to his old ways? Or is he probing for a different story? The newspapers are still obsessed with that photo of the Libs: the one with Tom and James preening on the steps, an indelible, resonant image of their privilege. She thinks of the terrible event at the end of her first year. James's anguish when he told her the next day, eyes red-rimmed and uncomprehending. The only time she has ever seen him cry. Please, God, don't let him have a sniff of that story.

The journalist catches her eye then raises his glass. Heat creeps up her neck and she turns and pushes through the banks of tight-suited activists, determined to put some distance between her and him. She grabs another glass of wine. Anything to distract her. There, that's better. Once you're on to your third, the sweetness becomes less cloying. She drinks steadily and quickly, accepts a top-up, her stomach fizzing with acid and fear.

She must find James, for this is meant to be part of his rehabilitation, this mingling with the party faithful, showing that he is willing to put in the hard graft—the hand-pressing and attentive listening—and that he has learned from his fall from grace. We all love a repentant bad boy and they have lapped him up—listening to his *mea culpa* at a fringe meeting on the importance of family unity; watching in apparent awe as his voice cracked and he bit on his knuckles to stem his tears. They couldn't get enough of him, these couples in their sixties and seventies, who she might have assumed would be judgemental, and the forthright women in their fifties in their bright peacock-blue or magenta jackets. "You have to admire someone who can hold their hands up and say they were wrong but they have learned from it," one opines, and she wants to grab that stupid woman and scream in her face.

But of course she can't. The new, more cynical Sophie—and how she hates that he has made her like this—must stand dutifully while he courts them all, playing the penitent with precision, feigning an interest she knows he cannot feel. She could almost admire his performance were it not that she cannot trust a word he says. *We all adjust the truth from time to time,* he had told her, in such a blasé tone that it almost sounded reasonable. And yet it wasn't. And it isn't. Most people don't do that. It is only now that she is beginning to realize how frequently he plays with the truth, through elisions, omissions, half-truths, and manages to shift it in this way.

Well there is no point staying here. She scours the room one last time and spies someone she wishes she could ignore: Chris Clarke. He catches her eye and she looks away too late, for he is moving towards her, the crush of the crowd parting as he pushes his way seamlessly through.

He places his hand below her elbow and steers her to a quieter spot of the room, beside some doors that can be slid open and a table crammed with empty glasses and bowls greased with the shards of peanuts and crisps. Jim Stephens is on the far side of the room with his back to them and the lobby journalists are still filing copy. The delegates are too far away to hear.

"So, these are better circumstances in which to meet." His tone is consciously upbeat, but his smile doesn't meet his eyes.

"You mean rather than in court?"

He blinks, mole-like.

"I'm sorry," she adds. Anything to make him go away.

"Cheer up. He's doing well." His eyes scan the room. The home secretary is making his way through the throng, a gaggle of prospective MPs doughnuting around him. "He could be back in the Home Office before you know it."

"Come off it." Her tone is dry.

"Undersecretary of state, in charge of drugs policy. Possibly a poisoned chalice, but he's coped with far worse, hasn't he? And of course he still has the confidence of the prime minister. An audacious move but the PM thinks he could manage it."

"For fuck's sake."

He glances at her, startled. She never swears and the words have slipped from her, involuntarily. A bubble of rage swells inside her. Not that post! How could Tom be so *fucking* stupid, so unthinking? She imagines the PM smiling his charming, blameless smile, barely considering the arrogance of that decision—the riskiness of his behavior, and of James's, too. They have got away with everything before now, his logic would run, so what's to stop him making this decision? After all, he's the prime minister. But, oh, the arrogance, the hypocrisy of it all.

She looks at Chris and she is aware that her eyes are burning, the tears inevitable, and that she needs to get away from him quickly before she says something she will regret.

"Is there something I should know?" He looks at her properly now, pale eyes alert, as she scoops up her jacket and handbag, every fiber of her vibrating as she resists the need to flee.

"Is the PM being too kind?"

She almost wonders if he is being disingenuous.

"Do you really have *no* idea?"

He doesn't nod, won't make any concession to his ignorance. She stares down at the carpet, noting the thickness of the tread.

"You might want to ask them about a party post-finals. Several of the Libertines. Tom and James. June 1993."

And with that she leaves the low-ceilinged room, with its oppressive heat and braying noise and awful people who scheme and plot and gossip, and heads for the relative cool of Brighton seafront on a chilly early October night.

# Thirty-three

## James

### 5 June 1993

Alec's third-floor set felt cramped. All the third-year Libertines were there after one last blowout, the relief at having survived finals cloaking faces uncharacteristically dulled to a workhouse grey.

James stretched out in a leather armchair, feeling the effects of the champagne on top of an almost febrile exhaustion. He was dead-tired: the result of too little sleep for too many nights. He had been cramming. There had been much late-night cramming. He would get a first—his confidence was sufficiently robust for him to still think this—but it was only through taking an essay-crisis approach to exams: surviving on Pro Plus, Marlboro Lights, and coffee to push him through those miserable midnight hours, then whisky to nudge him into sleep. Coke seemed superfluous. He took his papers in a state of hypervigilance; the most difficult economics questions braved on four hours' kip.

It wasn't what he had intended. He was disciplined about sport and fitness; disciplined about leavening his academic work with enjoyment. He'd almost taken that to extremes. Still, he thought he'd pulled it off, the Oxford first and the sporting blue—stamps on a passport that would take him to places few knew existed: clubs within clubs; inner circles within those he already circumnavigated with ease.

He shifted, fractious. Too much caffeine and booze running through his veins. He would go for a long run tomorrow morning to the university parks then across to Jericho and up through Port Meadow, following the Thames to Godstow, where the first boat trained. He would skirt over Oxford's green lungs in the clear early light, before the city got going for the day and while life felt fresh and unsullied, and he would feel like his old self once again—fit, virile, able to stretch and run without feeling the insistent pressure of needing to revise; of knowing that twenty-four hours' worth of exams would determine his academic worth. His energy—pent up as he lounged in libraries, long legs knocking under the desk, shoulders striking the bookcases as he rocked back in his chair—finally given an outlet; muscles straining; heart pumping; blood whooshing as his trainers grew moist with dew and he pounded the sun-dappled streets.

He stretched his arms above him, feeling the nerves running up from his shoulders and casually noting his long, well-proportioned fingers. Well, you know what they say about fingers? Now that his head was rapidly emptying of the knowledge crammed in the past four weeks, he found himself thinking incessantly of one thing. The final fortnight of term lay ahead of him—drinking, rowing, punting, and sex. Lots of sex. He would take Soph upstream from the Cherwell Boat House, picnic in one of the university park fields, pluck her—that was a good Shakespearean euphemism—in the long grasses with the sun beating down on them, clouds scudding across a sky of searing blue. Perhaps they'd cycle further afield, to Woodstock and Blenheim, for he had the time now to pay her some attention. She had first-year exams, but they weren't important and it was good that she was busy. The trouble with women, apart from them lacking the courage of their convictions, was that they could be demanding. Soph seemed to realize he couldn't be doing with neediness, but still, he sensed it: a carefully suppressed undertow that would catch him and drag him down if he gave any indication he really cared.

He shrugged the idea away, thought instead of one long hedonistic summer. He wasn't quite sure how she would fit into this. He assumed their relationship would peter out by September, when he started his new life in London, but before that there was plenty of time to meet. He hadn't suggested a holiday; he didn't want her to get too keen, and besides, he was off to Italy for three weeks, where Nick's parents had a villa, then sailing in St. Mawes with the old dears.

But there were weeks while the *parentes* were away and she should come up. An empty house, a sultry summer. He could see her strewn across his bed, a sheet between her legs. A couple of carefree months; the end of a prolonged, indulged adolescence. A final period of no responsibility or expectation—except to enjoy himself. Because in September, he would be working for the leading firm of management consultants. The prospect didn't fill him with massive enthusiasm, to be honest, but if he wanted a career in politics he needed a life before it, and the chance to earn some serious money.

He downed the tumbler of whisky Nick had filled and opened a beer. The casement windows were flung open to the night, and Alec and Tom had clambered out to perch on the stone balcony overlooking the Meadows. The sound of their un-trammelled laughter drifted back into the room, floated down towards the Thames.

From the roof, you could stand on the lead flashings and lean back against the slates so that you looked up at the stars, or climb along the ridge, like Alec. He could hear scampering on the tiles, sensed he was clambering. James had never liked that. Scaling walls was one thing, roofs another. He was keen to move up, not look down. Curious that he might be reckless about some things—women; study; the odd recreational class A drug now that the boat race was long finished—but that, with others, his strong sense of self-preservation kicked in.

He stumbled in the direction of Alec and Tom, keen for fresh air. The night was still, and despite the wide-open windows, the room was thick with smoke and the stale breath of men ham-mered on beer and champagne. George, crouched over a coffee table rammed with glasses and empty beer bottles, was snorting a line of coke. In the bog, Cassius—stomach bulging over his fly—retched. He felt a twinge of disgust. Now that their Oxford lives were all but over, he and Tom should distance themselves from this lot, not just out of self-preservation but self-respect.

He reached the balcony just as the Hon. Alec scrabbled down

from the roof, brandishing a tiny polythene bag of powder. Beside him, Tom—late after a secret-squirrel trip up to London—was trying to laugh but the tightness to his jaw betrayed his anxiety, indicated that he would really rather Alec gave the substance back, immediately. Alec, indulged and irrepressible, was unpredictable when high—capable of scattering the chemical snow down into the quad, his manic laughter a reproof to anyone concerned that it was best not to alert the college authorities to the illegal substances in his set.

He was gibbering now but he didn't seem to want to throw it away.

"Oh man, you genius." He threw an arm around Tom. "C'mon, let's try it." His pupils were large and dulled as sloes. Whatever he'd taken, he'd had too much.

James felt a prick of apprehension, a growing awareness of some new and potentially bad experience. He scrutinized the bag, swinging like a dejected condom, took in that peculiar mix of excitement and wariness glancing across Tom's face.

Alec was jittery, excitement crackling from him. "Oh man. This will be awesome!"

Tom, concentrating, nodded; drew a tube of silver foil from his duffel bag, and a drinking straw. "Got your lighter?"

Alec brandished his grandfather's slightly tarnished silver heirloom and flicked it. A plume of orange burst from its top.

James's spine tightened with a cold prickle of fear.

"Is that what I think it is?"

Tom shrugged.

"It's smack?"

His best friend nodded.

"Don't worry. It's top stuff. The stuff I had last week with Thynne."

"*You'd trust that fuckwit?*"

"Oh, come on, James. He's a mate."

"He's a cokehead." James moved away, biting hard on his rising contempt. Tom had been partying hard with Charlie Thynne since his last exam, a trustafarian who'd graduated the year before and whose name was apposite. Tom had been full of the fact he'd tried smack with him in town last weekend. All James could see was Charlie's nerviness, his restlessness in his own body. He wanted to shake the man, get him running down a towpath, or push him until he was dizzy from the exertion of an ergo. His slight limbs and delicate, pallid face gave James the creeps.

He turned back to the balcony where Tom was placing the smack on a piece of foil as reverently as a vicar officiating at communion.

"For fuck's sake, Tom." He tried to focus. He couldn't let Tom become like that—turning paranoid and pathetic—nor could either of them risk it if they wanted some sort of a political career.

"Ease up, James. One last blowout, innit?" Alec, all mockney insouciance, winked as Tom flicked the lighter beneath the foil and the powder began to melt into a brown liquid.

"Like this?" Alec, ever greedy for new sensations, took the straw and inhaled. "Aaaah . . . maann." He looked almost post-coital. A look of intense relaxation flooded his face.

The sound galvanized Tom, who grabbed the straw and copied his friend. "Aw . . . shiiiiiit!" His voice deepened, his vowels melting to become ever smoother, his limbs softening against the balcony, the edges blurring between flesh and stone.

James was suddenly sober. He wrenched the straw from Tom's hand and raced to the toilet with the screw of polythene. Cassius was coiled round the cistern. His fat body fell against him and James gave him an involuntary kick.

"What the fuck!"

He just resisted giving him a second.

"What the *fuck*, James!"

"Shut up." His voice was savage as he tipped the powder in the pan and pulled the flush. The powder vortexed out of sight, but the screw of polythene bobbed, irrepressible. He shoved a wad of paper on top and jerked the flush, again and again.

"What the fuck, James. *What* the fuck?"

"Shut *up*!" His knuckles gripped the flush, and he felt as if he was holding his breath, unable to move, to risk Cassius seeing what he was doing. "Thank fuck." His breath eased from him. The polythene was swallowed and gobbled away.

Tom. He needed to check on Tom. He ran back to the balcony, past George and Nick, who were lolling on the battered leather sofa, crowned with smoky halos.

"James?" Nick half stirred.

"Have a drink." George held his glass up. "Or some coke. Go on, man." He jumped up, flung a wiry arm around James and clasped him tight, his body damp, his breath hot on his cheek.

"Not now, George." It was no effort to shrug off George, but he did so elegantly, keeping his anger in check.

"James!" George was affronted, but James pushed on. He didn't need these losers. All that mattered was Tom, his best friend for nearly ten years, now smiling beatifically at him.

"Tom—come here, mate. Come here." He had to stop himself from grabbing his shoulders and shaking him as he slumped. He put his arms around him. "Tom—time to go, mate. You don't need this. You don't need fucking *heroin*." His voice dropped to a hiss. He grabbed Tom's cheeks and tried to cut through the blurriness of his gaze, fought to keep his voice calm though his whole being was convulsed with rage and an eviscerating sorrow that bubbled out and exploded in a coldly vicious whisper. "It's in a different league to coke, you *tit*."

"Whaaat." Tom's face was soft and flushed. "I love you."

"Yeah. Let's just get out of here. Now, yeah?" He used his anger to half pull, half lift Tom and hold his twelve-stone frame against him. "You don't want to be like him." He glanced at the Hon. Alec, crumpled against the balcony. "Has he had too much of it?"

"Whaaaa?"

"Perhaps we should take that. Don't want him to do any more, just in any case." James scrumpled the scorched foil and thrust it deep in his pocket, his fingers smarting at the residual heat. Even touching it made him feel dirty. "Come on then. Come *on*." He flung Tom's arm over his shoulders, began to half drag, half move him.

"No . . . stay here." Tom's legs seemed unable to work.

"No!" He was taut with anger. "I am not leaving you here. You are not a *fucking junkie!*"

And he saw a flicker of something like recognition in Tom's eyes, then.

"'K."

"Let's just get the fuck out of here." He couldn't say why he felt this chilling urge to flee. Just that it was strong and immediate, as intense a shot of adrenaline as any he'd experienced at the start of a race. His closest friend couldn't slip from him like this, drift into something that would haunt or destroy him. The drug was an uncontrollable, unknown darkness—something he sensed could overwhelm Tom quickly or would be a dirty secret that could fester and taint.

He half carried him across the room, whispering reassurance, taking heart that Tom, despite the comfort of the drug, was letting himself be guided, his body heavy and slumped against his.

"We'll just go now. Alec won't say a thing and I doubt the others will have noticed."

"Dizzy."

"Yeah. Right. Well, that's what happens." He frog-marched him past the others, conscious of the ball of foil nestled against his leg.

"Heading off," James called back into the paneled rooms where Nick and George were snorting fresh lines of coke. "Off to wake Soph. Tom's coming."

They were greeted by raucous brays. "Lucky girl." "Can she cope with you both?" "Does she want a third?"—the last from George.

"Very good." James refused to be riled, almost pushed Tom back through the door and down the staircase, the oak door creaking like a sigh of relief.

And they were off, James manhandling Tom down the three flights of stairs, supporting him when he stopped on the worn steps, ambushed by dizziness. When they reached the quad, Tom leaned behind a hedge and was violently sick.

"Better now?"

"Hot." He looked flushed. "Dizzy."

"Well let's get the fuck out of here."

They stumbled around the quad to the back gate, James still half supporting him, trying to make him walk faster. It was so late they saw no one. Once they were out of the college, they paused and looked back up at Alec's room. The windows were still flung open, and a figure was standing on the balcony, face turned up to the moon, his expression, above the cream silk blouse, and his unbuttoned waistcoat, one of intense bliss.

"What a tosser. Probably thinks he can fly." James shook his head and turned away, started to stride across the sandy gravel, his arm still around Tom's waist, half tugging, half coercing. It was only as they reached the edge of the Meadows that the thought—the terrible thought—began to sink in.

And then they heard the cry. The most awful sound—mad, mirth-filled, and quickly mirthless—and the heavy thud of a young man's body smacking onto gravel, followed by the slithering of slates.

"Fuck. *Run!*" The instinct was immediate. His insides turned to ice and he started to sprint.

"But what about Alec?" Tom dithered, waking from a stupor.

"Run, you fucker." He grabbed his wrist, gripping it firmly, his fingers digging in.

"But Alec . . ."

"Fucking run." He half dragged him and they were off through the gates and up towards the high street, feet pounding over the dusty ground, adrenaline turning them cold sober, years of cross-country running powering them as they sped away.

"But Alec? We need to call an ambulance." Tom's voice was a bleat.

"You can't do that. You gave him the smack, you idiot."

"Fuck." The enormity of what had happened seemed to hit Tom, and his mouth twisted as if there was too much emotion to contain.

"Shit. I've still got the foil." James gestured at his pocket. "Fuck."

"Gotta get rid of it." Tom's face hardened, self-preservation pushing away compassion. "Top of Brasenose Lane."

He hung a left and they ran through the streets to the public litter bin, pressed the foil down below the empty McDonald's cartons and chocolate wrappers, the cans of Special Brew, and the banana peels.

They were crossing a Rubicon, but Tom—with a ruthlessness James would see when he leapfrogged over others to secure a safe seat and maneuvered to become party leader—had shrugged off his scruples and was racing towards his college. James chased him, heart pulsing, blackness fizzing at the edge of his brain.

At the door to his room, Tom doubled over.

"What about an ambulance?" He panted heavily.

"The others will have done that. Or the porter's lodge."

"You're sure?" Tom's breath caught in fat sobs. He was close to tears.

"To be frank, he's not going to have survived that."

"Fuck." Tom's whole face folded in on itself. "Fuck, fuck, fuck," he said.

"Look. Go to bed. Try to get some sleep. I'll come by first thing in the morning." James's whole body was shaking, pure, distilled fear pulsing. They hugged briefly, James slapping Tom between his shoulder blades, clasping him to him.

"I owe you."

"Not in the least. We weren't there; we didn't see it happen."

"We weren't. We didn't," Tom repeated. If they said it convincingly enough, perhaps they would be believed.

"I'll be round first thing."

Tom hung his head. "Omerta of the Libertines," he muttered.

James grimaced. They would have to fucking hope so.

"Not a word from me."

———————

He was safe in Shrewsbury College, lying tight in Sophie's arms, by the time the police caught up with him the next morning. They'd left the ill-fated party when it became so raucous, he told the officers. He had a beautiful girlfriend, and well, he'd rather be with her, if they caught his drift? As for drugs, they'd seen no evidence of that, though they had left early. Heroin? Christ, no. Alec, though dissolute, was no junkie. Totally out of character. A one-off. No, of course they didn't know of a supplier. James, tempted to bark in incredulity, spoke quietly, somberly; conscious that he was using what, years later, he would think of as his compassionate Conservatism face.

The college authorities backed up their alibis, offered good character references. James was a rower, about as clean-cut as you could get. A member of the dining club, yes, but you couldn't really drink and be a blue. He had huge self-discipline. Besides, he'd talked of going into politics; was hardly likely to be embroiled in drugs, if that was the case. And Tom? Academically brilliant, on course for a top first—his results would bear this out. Two young men with the brightest of futures ahead of them, a credit to their school, and it had been thought, to the university.

They had gotten away with it. They waited for someone to mention that Tom had supplied the smack, but either the Omerta of the Libs held, or the rest of them had been too out of it to notice. It had all been so brief, out there on the balcony, and James had quickly whisked the smack away.

The officers—who would later charge George Fortescue with possession of cocaine—gained nothing with which to implicate them, and couldn't help but be convinced by these well-spoken students—both courteous; both clearly traumatized by the tragedy; one singled out as a future politician. You could sense he would lead.

They thanked them for their time and focused on those who were present when the Hon. Alec Fisher—well-liked geography student on course for a gentleman's third; cricketer; violinist; beloved son and brother—tragically lost his life.

# THIRTY-FOUR
## SOPHIE
### 3 OCTOBER 2017

The charcoal waves suck up the shingle and spit it out again as they pound relentlessly on the Sussex shore.

Sophie watches, transfixed, lulled by the regular rhythmic motion; imagining them washing over her; bombarded by thoughts that make her heart ache, her mind churn.

This being Brighton, she has struggled to be alone. The promenade is thronged with delegates and lovers, and she has to walk to Hove to find a bench where she can sit by herself and think. She keeps her tears in check, alert to passersby who give her more than a cursory glance, their attention piqued by a somber woman who stares out to sea or, avoiding eye contact, looks down at her feet.

Sitting there, she thinks of Alec. Not just some rich cokehead, but someone's son, someone's brother, and whatever the Libs might have claimed afterwards, their friend. She remembers the photographs of his funeral, covered in all the papers—his father stooped under the burden of his grief, his mother prematurely aged, her grey eyes pools of pain shining from a mask of a face.

She remembers James the morning after Alec's death—his rabbit-red eyes, his sense of crisis, his vulnerability. She hadn't known the dead boy, and so the bulk of her anguish had been for James. She had been so terrified he would be arrested and had managed to convince herself he was loving, loyal, almost noble in throwing away the smack to stop his friends from taking it, and in getting Tom away. She didn't learn that they had seen Alec's fall for many years—still doubted she knew the full story—but she knew enough to understand quite what Tom owed him. She didn't think James so noble after hearing that final, chilling fact. And, if there had been an intense—if misplaced—loyalty then she knew his strong self-preservation, his ruthlessness about shaping the truth to suit him, was also at play.

She thinks, sitting here by the shore. Really thinks. Lets the thoughts keep on coming. Wonders why she pointed Chris in the direction of this secret: a secret he will keep while he works for Tom, at least, but which now gives him excessive power. Was it just the presence of that journalist that jittered her up? Or was it a dog-weary exhaustion with Tom and James's belief that they were somehow untouchable? They said Blair was Teflon-like, but these two believe they are in a different league now.

She remains dry-eyed as she makes her way back to the conference hotel. It is a quarter to nine. The point at which drinks receptions are petering out or segueing into drinks in the bar for those without a prearranged dinner. But the reception for LGBT Tories is still in full swing. The air is rank with the sweet vinegary scent of crisps and too much alcohol and her instinct is to leave and call James from their room. But then she catches sight of him and feels that instinctive leap she imagines she will always feel, though the feeling is one of sharp recognition rather than anything warmer. He doesn't see her. Well, of course he doesn't. He is too busy working the room.

And he does it so well, head inclined as he talks to a young woman as if she is the only person who matters: eyes focused, one hand lightly touching her arm. And there is something perturbing in his smile and the flush on the face of the prospective parliamentary candidate for Sutton North who is allowing her professional guard to slip just a little, and who, despite knowing about his reputation—about his court case, for goodness' sake—is letting herself act just like any normal young woman flattered by the attention of a good-looking man.

She watches, transfixed, as her husband double-clamps his hands over this woman's petite hand and looks at her warmly. She knows what it feels like to bask in that smile. To give oneself up to this gaze that says frankly, unashamedly: *Hey, you're rather lovely*. That says, in a different situation, sex would be more than a possibility, and it would be rather good.

And she knows then, with that glance, with that tiniest of betrayals, that she can never trust him again properly, and that her well of wifely goodwill and loyalty, which has overflowed for so many years, has been drained quite dry. That she will never feel that love for him ever again. It is over. Quite emphatically. She has reached her tipping point.

The knowledge comes to her starkly. She feels no rage—or

not at this moment—just a calm numbness. This is just how it is. If it involves women, or telling the truth, or facing up to the past, if it involves showing any real integrity, then James will never change.

She has always believed in redemption, and she has tried so hard to think the best of him. Their marriage has continued, her hoping that he might have some sort of Damascene conversion, might see that his is not the true version of events. But, though she's an optimist, she is no fool. She glances at him again, watches the warmth play across his face, so that he could be in his midthirties. And then she sees it: a quick glance sideways to check there is no one more interesting before he focuses on the young woman again.

She leaves the reception, abandoning him to the crush and to the general adulation, to an evening during which he will try to call her—but not more than once for he will be confident hers is the body he can curl up to late that night, after a little light extramarital flirtation, his calm port in any storm. Her anger is growing now, welling in her throat as if it would choke her. A physical thing: this rage. *Breathe deeply*, she tells herself, *calm yourself. Think properly and clearly. Do nothing impetuous.*

She will leave him. That much is clear. In their room, in the conference hotel, she brings out the thick card that has been hidden away in her purse, behind the John Lewis card and the black Coutts card; the business card given to her by Rob Phillips—reassuringly authoritative and expensive-looking, the card of someone who is able to help. She runs her finger over the watermarked creaminess, reading the raised font like a line of braille that will provide all answers in her state of current blindness. Though she is clear-sighted about her husband and his inability to ever change, she does not know how to navigate the future; cannot see all her options; knows she must just take tiny steps now, one at a time.

An image of Emily hugging James as tight as can be, as if trying to keep hold of her daddy with the force of her passion, crosses her mind, then one of Finn—a mini James, physically, but unlike him in character, more unquestionably *her* child. She imagines hugging him now; the curve of his cheek against hers, the memory of babyhood a ghostlike whisper still, and she feels a sharp twist of guilt at the pain she knows she will inflict on them once she calls this number; once she sets in train the process of separating from their father. And then she thinks of her current half-life, her continual emotional pain.

She lies down on the bed, with its heavy cover that slips and slithers and gives the temporary illusion of opulence; feels the reassuring heft of the Egyptian cotton pillowcase beneath her head. From this angle, things seem a little more clear. Her marriage is over, and though she doubts this will be a calm process of conscious uncoupling, she knows James will do the right thing by the children. He is not a mean man.

Oh, but he is flawed. She thinks of his casual acceptance of his perjury and his assumption that she will keep his secret. She thinks of his arrogance—those words that spool through her mind in the middle of the night.

"I told the truth, near enough. Or the truth as I saw it," he said.

"You committed perjury." She can taste her horror.

She remembers his shrug, and his taunt. "And what are you going to do about it?"

And what *is* she going to do? She remembers the female detective outside the court: conscientious looking, midthirties. DC Rydon, the name James mentioned. Blood whooshes through her. How would she react if Sophie gave her a call?

But she knows she couldn't face another case. Wouldn't her motive be questioned? An archetypal woman scorned. Besides, she couldn't do that to her children, however morally right it might be; however much it is what Olivia—poor disbelieved Olivia—deserves.

And then she thinks of Chris Clarke. She could call him and furnish him with further details that would ensure James's political hopes were not just scuppered but buried so deep that they could never resurface; that he would forever languish as a backbencher, perhaps rising to be the chair of a select committee, but not one with any real power? And it is not that she's vindictive; it's that the thought of him and Tom riding roughshod over the truth like this more than perturbs her. Gilded youths whose gilt has worn thin. Is really rather tarnished now.

Her breath quickens at the riskiness of it all. She could call Jim Stephens, or perhaps James's contemporary at college, now on the *Times*, Mark Fitzwilliam? And though she knows she will do none of these things immediately, perhaps not for years, still the possibility strengthens her, makes her feel less impotent, less alone.

"The trouble with women is they lack the courage of their convictions," James would say, of female colleagues or of her, when she was torn by indecision. And she knew he was only half-joking. His certainty has always been stronger than hers.

But then she thinks of the women who have shown courage and strength. Olivia, standing in court, her most traumatic experience scrutinized and questioned; who risked James's lies proving more persuasive than her truth. Kitty, steadfast, supportive, doing the right thing, though it must have been difficult. Even Ali Jessop showing such fierce loyalty to Holly, a tigerish protectiveness, as she revealed her best friend's secret. And perhaps, in some drunken, cack-handed way, she had wanted to help Sophie, too.

She curls up, watching the motes of dust that dance in the beam of her light, and makes herself think of Holly—studious, unworldly; somehow soft around the edges; and just before she vanished, so painfully withdrawn she was almost a recluse. A barrister now, Ali said. The very definition of an assertive woman. Her mind drifts to Kate Woodcroft as she bore down on James, provoking that telling flash of anger. No lack of conviction there.

She toys with a chain around her neck, touching the bones of her clavicle, at the top of her ribs, feeling her frailty and then imagining the layers of muscle that could grow firmer and stronger, binding her body in a tight embrace. She is sculling on the Thames—the power surging through her feet, legs, glutes, back, and arms; her body poised, connected, *invincible*; happiness surging as she cuts through the water and she watches it dripping from her blades.

"The trouble with women is they don't know what they want," she once heard James expand to Tom, and the two of them had laughed like schoolboys. But she is inching her way to a better understanding of what she wants, at least.

She swings her legs to the side of the bed and sits up straight, knees primly together, phone in her lap. A stance that suggests she is concentrating, that she means business. And with one slim finger, she touches the screen.

# Thirty-five

## Kate

### 7 December 2018

My wig slumps on the desk where I've tossed it. My heels scissor where I've kicked them. The start of December: the end of a very long week.

Outside my office, the sky explodes with color: powder blue; burnished orange; a near-fluorescent pink. The air is crisp with the promise of frost. It will be cold tonight for anyone bedding down in a nest of cardboard. I think of the girl who disappeared last winter; hope, against all expectation, that she is somehow managing a better life.

A clatter of steps on the staircase—a rush for drinks before the first of the Christmas parties. Perhaps I should join my junior colleagues, for it's been a good week. Things are going well in my people-trafficking case. I'm prosecuting, of course. Sixty Afghan immigrants, ages two to sixty-eight, packed into a shipping container and smuggled into Tilbury docks. Each of the five defendants has their own counsel and there are various claims and counterclaims that have made the process cumbersome and sometimes tedious. But it's been refreshing to work on a case about power and exploitation that doesn't involve sex.

We'll have final speeches next week. I look down at my closing speech, written when I first received the trial documents; rewritten this week to include the critical points winkled out in cross-examination. I have polished it until not one word is superfluous; have rehearsed it until it is pitch perfect. I don't need to practice it again.

Besides, it's a Friday night. There are other things I could do. I have a "date" tomorrow. The thought makes me cringe. Ali set it up. Rob Phillips, a lawyer from college, whom she met at that gaudy last year. Divorced. Two kids. My instinct was to turn it down very firmly. I want no reminders of that place, and besides, he has too much baggage. But then, we all have baggage. I'm finally trying to shed mine. Since the trial, I've sought help and talking has improved things: reduced the flashbacks; countered the self-loathing. It's still not something I find easy, though, in any way.

Still, a lot has changed since the acquittal. I've rowed back from prosecuting sexual offenses and turned to more generalized crime, though it's serious stuff and still high profile. There's this trafficking case, and coming up, the trial of a gang who stole art to order forty million pounds worth of Chinese jade and porcelain filched from provincial museums. The demand for sexual offense work is still there, and the flood of historic sexual abuse grows ever wider and faster flowing, spilling from entertainment into football now and no doubt other sports. Occasionally, I'm tempted to venture back, particularly when I think of adult victims being ripped apart and disbelieved for a second time. But then my sense of self-preservation kicks in. I'm sure I will return, but I can't stomach the daily diet of it any longer. Not at the moment. Not for a while.

I lean back in my chair, focusing on stretching the length of me, enjoying the sensation of my nerves firing from toes to fingertips. It's been two years since Brian handed me that billet doux of documents and reopened the wounds I'd told myself had long healed over. More than nineteen months since James Whitehouse stood up in the dock at the Old Bailey and was cleared.

Time to move on—for others have, not least Sophie who was granted a quickie divorce in March on the grounds of his unreasonable behavior. The news allowed the papers to rehash the case and hint at the Libertines' antics, and yet it doesn't seem to have done him any harm. He's back in government: junior minister in the Department for Transport with responsibility for rail security and building development. A deeply dull, if worthy, post that doesn't appear to be a reward, but that will earn him some brownie points and let him hustle his way back. I bet a hundred quid he'll be promoted in the next ministerial reshuffle. The thought leaves a bitter taste, as does a recent photograph of him with the PM, apparently sharing a private joke, for he has clearly been rehabilitated; his career resurrected and that friendship rekindled—if it was ever allowed to die down.

He has a new girlfriend, too, far younger than his ex-wife—a corporate lawyer in her late twenties. A photo of her at the time of the divorce showed her striding along Threadneedle Street, head down, face obscured behind a sheet of dark, ironed hair. I had expected someone less intelligent and wondered why such a bright woman would be involved with someone once accused of rape. But, of course, his charm is indelible, and he was acquitted. No smoke without fire? Not, it seems, where James Whitehouse is concerned.

My stomach grumbles and I take a sip of Diet Coke. That's another change: I've stopped drinking spirits, and these days, my fridge is stocked with food. White wine plays a part, but I eat now. I'm no longer scrawny, but lean.

My life's a little more balanced, too, and if I still seem obsessed with James Whitehouse then, believe me, I'm not. I can go days, weeks even, without thinking of him. Yet the fact he was acquitted still rankles, an irritant that seems to mock me. And, despite his job apparently being low profile, I still catch glimpses of him in the papers; am constantly reminded of him—and of my professional failure—whenever I appear at the Bailey. It's a footnote to my teenage obsession, or perhaps a minor counterpoint—dog-whistle quiet but just within earshot. If his name's mentioned, if there's the slightest whiff of a connection, it's something I can't help but hear.

I'm thinking about all this as Brian knocks on the door. A brisk rat-a-tat-tat, distinct to him, that means business.

"Come in." I smile as he enters, relieved to be distracted. "Have you got something juicy?"

The tops of his ears are tinged pink and he is smirking as if trying to suppress a secret. There's no sheaf of documents, no billet doux, in his hands, though, only the *Chronicle*, London's daily paper.

"What is it?" There's a sparkle in his eyes, and I'm impatient to know the reason. He glances down, enjoying his momentary power.

"Old Jim Stephens has been busy." He whistles through thinned lips.

I'd forgotten he knew the journalist—a contact from years back when Fleet Street meant Fleet Street; newspaper offices crammed into the stretch of London running down to the Royal Courts of Justice; news reporters working within spitting distance of where we are now and the other Inns of Court.

"Quite a splash he's got . . ."

"Oh, give it here." I reach across, impatient with his teasing. He dances backwards two steps, a little jig, then relinquishes it with a grin he can only get away with because we've worked together for twenty years.

"Interesting, eh?"

I'm dimly aware of him looking at me, hoping for a reaction, but I can't glance at him. I'm too preoccupied by the words on the page. The air seems to still into one of those pin-sharp moments—like the moment I got my Oxford letter; like that moment in the cloisters, the rasp of stone on my back, his voice in my ear.

PM QUIZZED OVER OXFORD DEATH reads the headline in bold capitals across the front of the paper above a photo of the prime minister, looking simultaneously grim-faced and shifty.

"Thames Valley Police reopen investigation into pal's drug death in 1993," the first of two bullet points adds. I read the second bullet point, and my heart begins to thud. "Minister James White-house also to be questioned over upper-class death." And the blood is galloping through my head, now, a great surging whoosh as I drink in the details, key words springing from the text: death . . . drugs . . . exclusive drinking club . . . debauchery . . . the Libertines . . . and a date in early June 1993.

And it is the same date when he raped me: June 5. This death—of the Hon. Alec Fisher—happened the same early summer's night when he ran into me in the cloisters. I remember the Libertine outfit I'd secretly thought rather dashing: cream silk shirt with cravat, fitted waistcoat, the trousers he'd zipped himself into, hiding the evidence of what happened away. I remember the fact he seemed to have come from a party—his breath sweet with whisky and a hint of Marlboro Lights. And above all, I remember his intense nerviness. Eyes dilated not with coke, but with the adrenaline that had sent him powering around the quad and an energy, a recklessness, a compulsion for physical release that perhaps wasn't just about wanting sex and not giving a damn how he got it—who he had to overpower to get it—but was a reaction to a sensation just as powerful. Was a response to his intense fear.

Death. Sex. Power. They were all at play that night. I make a curious sound, halfway between a gulp and a catch at the back of my throat, and pretend to turn it into a cough, hoping it escapes Brian's attention. I swig at the Diet Coke, furiously thinking as I tip my head backwards and hide my pricking eyes.

But, "You all right, miss?" My clerk crouches down by me;

concerned, paternal, peering into my face; spotting, I know, the tears that turn my gaze glassy. How well does he know me? How much does he really guess? He has seen me grow from pupil to junior to QC; has watched me mature, as a barrister and woman, and has caught me crying—most recently, not that long ago, one evening when I thought everyone had left the office, just after James Whitehouse was acquitted.

"I'm fine," I say briskly, in a tone that is fooling no one. "What incredible news, as you say." I clear my throat. "He must be pretty sure of his sources."

"Can't run something like this without knowing it's true."

"What's the BBC saying?" I reach for my laptop, eager to deflect his attention, searching for the latest news, and all the time wondering if this is it: the point at which James Whitehouse's boundless, unfathomable luck runs out.

"Oh, they're running the story," Brian says, and I'm not sure if I can deal with this: any further, terrible, daily reminders of what James and his Oxford cronies got up to and yet, a bubble of hope floats up inside me; a delicate feeling that builds because I know, with a flinty certainty, that *of course* I can deal with it; I can cope with whatever sordid details emerge. Because Jim Stephens and his colleagues will be digging for the truth and I am on the side of the truth, rather than merely on the side of the winners, and if some darker truth comes out; and if James Whitehouse falls from grace at last, then somehow I will feel exonerated, and irrational though I know this is, I will no longer be to blame for what happened in any way at all.

Brian is talking as this conviction grows inside me; and the tone of his voice, soft yet gravelly with its Cockney twang, has shifted, I realize, no longer conversational or gossipy but so un-expectedly tender that I stop scrolling through the *BBC News* home page and listen to what he has to say.

He is watching me, closely, and it's as if he knows exactly what I need to hear. And, though I know the law does not always punish the guilty—that a skilled barrister can win even if the evi-dence is stacked against her client; that advocacy is about being more persuasive than your opponent—I also know that, in the court of public opinion, things are rather different and more than one morally questionable act seems more than a coincidence; can—if uttered sufficiently often and loudly—completely ruin a man.

I think all this as Brian talks and his words encapsulate this conviction so that it is wrapped tight and presented to me as a finished package; a fact far sweeter than any billet doux.

"Don't you worry," he says, and his smile mirrors mine—the merest ghost of a smile, it is so tentative, but a smile, nonetheless. "He's not going to get away with it this time."

# Author's Note

*Anatomy of a Scandal* owes much to my experience as a news reporter, political correspondent, and student reading English at Oxford in the nineties. But it is clearly a work of fiction, set in a world without reference to Brexit or the US election and offering an alternative prime minister and politicians.

The Oxford I describe is also fictionalized. There are no Shrewsbury or Walsingham colleges, although the former may bear some geographical resemblance to my old college. If Holly resembles the unsophisticated, provincial student I once was, though, her story, thankfully, is not mine.

# ACKNOWLEDGMENTS

Sometimes, when researching a novel, you have a massive stroke of luck. Mine was watching Eloise Marshall prosecuting at the Old Bailey and subsequently shadowing her in a rape trial at another Crown Court. She then read chunks of my copy and dealt with numerous queries. I could not be more grateful.

A second was reading *The Devil's Advocate: A Spry Polemic on How to Be Seriously Good in Court* by Iain Morley, QC, formerly of Eloise's chambers, 23 Essex Street. One line—"Truth is a tricky area. Rightly or wrongly, adversarial advocacy is not an inquiry into the truth"—preoccupied me so much I tweaked and borrowed it. I am indebted to him for this; to Hannah Evans, of 23 Essex Street, for recommending it; to the Bar Council press office; and to Simon Christie, in the early stages of research.

Huge thanks are due to my incomparable agent, Lizzy Kremer, who was the most passionate advocate of this novel from the start; and to the rights team at David Higham Associates— Alice Howe, Emma Jamison, Emily Randle, Camilla Dubini and Margaux Vialleron—whose enthusiasm and energy has meant *Anatomy of a Scandal* will be translated into fifteen languages.

My editors, Jo Dickinson at Simon & Schuster UK and Emily Bestler at Emily Bestler Books, were a delight to work with. I am grateful for their clear-sighted, collaborative approach, their thoughtful ideas and their light touch. Ian Austin was a sharp and sensible copy editor; and Martin Soames, for Simons, Muirhead & Burton LLP, assuaged much of my anxiety. I could not have had a better editorial experience.

I am lucky to be part of the Prime Writers, a group of writers who were all published for the first time over the age of forty (I was forty-one). Whether it was through word races, or reminiscences of student experiences, they have helped more than they can know. Special thanks goes to Terry Stiastny, who not only discussed plot issues but also, in summarizing it for a contact, provided the title. Karin Salvaggio, Sarah Louise Jasmon, Claire Fuller and Peggy Riley chivvied me in word races; and Dominic Utton, Rachael Lucas, James Hannah, and Jon Teckman checked terminology or provided details of research.

Before writing novels, I was a political correspondent on the *Guardian*. A conversation with my former boss and political editor, Mike White, proved invaluable in sparking ideas at the start; my former colleague Andy Sparrow was assiduous and generous in fact checking, as was the BBC's Ben Wright.

Thanks are also due to Shelley Spratt, of Cambridgeshire police press office, and the press office at Addaction. As with all the experts who helped, if errors have crept in they are entirely mine. On two occasions I have used artistic license to maintain pace.

Finally, I am so grateful to my family. As an English graduate,

I briefly flirted with the idea of following in my father's footsteps and entering the law. I would have been a disaster but Chris Hall's enthusiasm for his subject pricked my interest, and whet my appetite for the drama of the court.

My mother, Bobby Hall, and my sister, Laura Tennant, continue to offer boundless support. But the trio to whom I am most grateful are my husband, Phil, and children, Jack and Ella. *Anatomy of a Scandal* involved venturing into dark places most of us would prefer not to think about. Family life—with all its love, noise, and energy—was a welcome antidote to that.

# ANATOMY OF A SCANDAL
## SARAH VAUGHAN

### READING GROUP GUIDE

This reading group guide for *Anatomy of a Scandal* includes discussion questions and ideas for enhancing your book club. The suggested questions are intended to help your reading group find new and interesting angles and topics for your discussion. We hope that these ideas will enrich your conversation and increase your enjoyment of the book.

### TOPICS & QUESTIONS FOR DISCUSSION

1. One of the themes of *Anatomy of a Scandal* is what is seen versus what is hidden or secret. From the simplest element of Kate putting on her robe and wig versus wearing her "civilian" clothes, to the upright, clean-cut facade of James's public persona versus his carefully concealed past, the major characters in the novel have secret sides of themselves. In what other ways does Sarah Vaughan emphasize the dual natures of characters and situations?

2. While at Oxford University, the characters live with many traditions and within ancient buildings full of history. How is the past interwoven into the characters' lives? How do the settings add to the atmosphere and reflect the themes of the novel?

3. On page 112, Sophie thinks to herself, "she imagined a veneer of serenity encasing her, a hard impenetrable polish." What does this tell you about Sophie as a character? When and how do you see this hard shell protecting her during the novel? Do you think it also harms her?

4. What does Holly's physical transformation communicate about her emotions and internal life? What physical elements of Holly remain in her new identity as Kate?

5. When Kate sees Olivia testifying for the first time, she thinks, "She is about to reveal herself as emphatically as if she were cut to the bone" (p. 123). How does the trial reveal character traits?

What subtle traits does Sarah imply through the characters' testimonies and actions in court rather than tell us in the more explicit narration?

6. Each woman in the novel is confronted with a series of choices. Which choices do the women feel they must make? Do you think they had other options than the ones they went with?

7. When Sophie confronts James after the court has found him not guilty of raping Olivia, saying she knows that he didn't tell the whole truth to the jury, he responds, "I told the truth, near enough. Or the truth as I saw it. . . . We all adjust the truth from time to time" (p. 312). As a group, discuss the small and large ways in which the various characters adjust the truth throughout the novel.

8. What was the impact on you as readers of realizing Kate wasn't a reliable narrator? Did it lessen your sympathy toward her?

9. At the end of the novel, Brian tells Kate not to worry, that James won't "get away with it this time" (p. 388). What do you think will happen to James? Will he be held accountable?

10. If there were one more chapter in *Anatomy of a Scandal*, what do you imagine would happen in it?

## ENHANCE YOUR BOOK CLUB

1. There are many portrayals of political scandals in the media. As a group, watch an episode of a television show such as *The Good Wife*, *Scandal*, or *House of Cards* and compare it to *Anatomy of a Scandal*. Are there similar techniques that the scriptwriters and Sarah Vaughan use to build suspense? What literary and visual symbols are employed to enhance the novel's and shows' themes?

2. If your book club has not already read Hilary Mantel's *Bring Up the Bodies*, choose it for your next read and discuss the similarities in political scandals across the eras.

3. To learn more about Sarah Vaughan, read more about her other writings, and connect with her online, visit her official website at sarahvaughanauthor.com.